For Good Men To Do Nothing

by Roland Ladley

The fourth of the Sam Green novels

GW00761558

First edition prepared for publication with CreateSpace July 2018

For Claire, who has put up with me through thick and thin.
And for Rosemary – an eye for detail and an injection of enthusiasm when I needed it most.

The world will not be destroyed by those who do evil, but by those who watch them without doing anything.

Albert Einstein

Prologue

6°11'58.7"N 49°25'10.8"E, off the Somali coast

Victoria Mitchell's head hurt. Too much red wine, exacerbated by the pitch and yaw of the yacht and the melodic *slap* of the sea against the hull. The blistering sun didn't help, even though she was partially shaded by the open cockpit's canopy. She glanced at the instrument panel. They were making a couple of knots. Which was nowhere near fast enough for her. Thankfully the wind was behind them - but the western Indian Ocean's 'Great Whirl' current spun clockwise, northward along the Somali coast. As a result, heading south they were pushing against three or four knots. At least with both the mainsail and spinnaker up they were making some headway.

But a couple of knots was nowhere near fast enough.

They'd left Suez what seemed like an epoch ago. The canal had been exotic and the real start of their circumnavigation of Africa. They'd jostled between supertankers, huge container ships and the odd traditional Egyptian fishing boat with its sail hung at a jaunty angle from a central mast.

Their 43-foot Sega, *Money for Nothing II* - her husband Paul's pride and joy - motored nearly all of the 120 miles of the canal under steam. Out in the Red Sea they'd found space and wind to make headway under sail. They'd berthed for a couple of days at Port Jeddah in Saudi to take on fuel, water and provisions - which had been an experience all of its own. A third-world port in a super-rich, second-world country. They'd overnighted again at Djibouti. They next intended to make landfall at Mombasa, Kenya.

She knew that the 1,800 mile stretch from Djibouti to Mombasa, about 15 days at 5 knots, was the most dangerous leg of the journey. Piracy was rife; from big ships to small sailing boats - no one was safe. They'd been advised to remain at least 50 miles off the coast and Paul had plotted that for them. But with the convex shape of the coastline, the further from land the longer it would take. It was a balancing act. Currently they were about 30 miles offshore and, apart from a far-distant tanker, they'd seen nothing for two days.

To be accurate, and something she reminded her husband of every couple of days, they'd been *strongly* advised not to travel this coastline. But Paul was nothing if not pig-headed. And since he'd sold the business, planned and then embarked on this journey, Victoria had experienced a single-mindedness in her husband that she'd not witnessed before. They were going. Nothing would stop them.

They were both competent sailors and they'd made some pretty significant trips before. They'd completed 'The Azores and Back' race in 2011. Other than both of them falling asleep at the helm at points, they had coped remarkably well in difficult seas. So when Paul had suggested the round-Africa trip a year ago, it wasn't the sailing that bothered her. No, they could do that. It was the piracy - particularly along the Somali coast - that frightened her.

'I'll go without you, if necessary.' She remembered Paul telling her as she hummed and hawed.

'Why not sail the Atlantic?' Had been her response.

'No. It's Africa, or nothing.'

That had been the end of the conversation.

And here they were, just over a year later. Sailing a 40-odd-foot bucket of fibreglass through some of the most dangerous waters in the world. Unprotected.

Victoria yawned. She shook her head feebly, trying to force the cotton wool that fogged her mind to exit: stage left. She half stood, checking the horizon, placed her finger on the autopilot to make sure the reading was right, and then reached into her blouse pocket for her packet of Embassy Number 1s.

She lit and dragged.

God, that's good.

She'd smoked all her life. She knew that it would kill her. Eventually. But, along with red wine, it was what kept her going.

No. That was a crass statement.

They had £20 million in the bank and, both in their fifties, had no need to work again. *Money for Nothing II* may have been over 20 years old, but she was still an expensive yacht in immaculate condition - and worth £100,000 of anyone's money. Victoria remained married to her first husband. And they were on a journey of a lifetime.

She shouldn't need anything to keep her going?

Maybe. Maybe not.

There were no kids, even though she'd longed for them. And whilst Paul was a brilliant technophile and very capable entrepreneur, he was an inattentive husband.

Money wasn't everything.

If I had my time again?

She'd met Paul Mitchell at Cambridge. They were both reading computer science, or a subset of that. He was a good coder - she was better. But he had an eye for opportunity that eluded her. Together they made a great business team. Less so as lovers. Success followed, but there was no time for a family. As he ploughed his furrow, making them millions, she became distracted and took to wine to complement the fags. He didn't seem to notice. He was too busy on the next project. And, wow, in the end, what a project.

There was noise below.

'What time is it?' Paul, grumpy after a short sleep. During long legs neither of them took more than four hours before coming on deck to relieve the other.

She checked her watch.

'Ten-fifteen. You've got another 45 minutes yet.'

There was more clattering down below. He was probably trying to make himself a coffee. He wouldn't ask her if she wanted one. It wasn't that he was naturally selfish, his mind was always on other things.

She looked from the entrance of the cabin where Paul would emerge sometime soon and glanced up to the horizon. Just a dark blue slab of water, above which was a translucent, light blue sky. A single cloud bobbed along like a lone sheep on blue-painted downs.

More noise downstairs. Paul swore.

For no reason she checked behind her.

And double-took.

Shit.

She reached for their stabilised binos. She focused them, calculating angles.

About four miles out was a small boat. It got lost as the sea gently rose and fell. But it was definitely a boat - the light blue sky was tinged with black; probably unburnt diesel.

Twenty-five degrees from their rear starboard side.

She reached for the chart. It was like a normal map, but all blues, yellows and whites. She could have used the yacht's GPS digital screen, but the map had a better scale and, at a glance, showed up to 50 miles. They were travelling south-south-west: 207 degrees. That would make the bearing to the boat about due north. She looked at the map following due north from where she thought they were: *Dinowda*. A small Somali fishing village about 35 miles away.

Bandit country.

'Paul!' Her voice higher pitched than normal.

'What?' More clattering from downstairs.

'Come up here now. We've got company.'

There was too long a pause. He was faffing about.

'Paul!' More nervous now.

She checked over her shoulder. The boat was gaining. It was probably doing ten or 12 knots. If it kept its current course it would be with them in half-an-hour. Maybe sooner.

She stood up and, briefly catching a handrail against an unexpected swell, looked at the radar. The oncoming boat didn't bleep. It was out of range. She twiddled a knob and the scale on the radar grew. It bleeped now.

'What is it?'

Paul was at the cabin door, lower than her, his head at knee height.

'Look.' She pointed behind them. 'There's a boat. About 4 miles away.'

An odd expression, which she couldn't compute, flashed in her husband's eyes. *Excitement?*

He was out of the cabin and roughly took the binos from her. As she checked the radar, he looked.

'Well?' She wanted answers.

'It's too early to say, but it's probably just a fishing boat, you know, fishing?'

She didn't buy that.

'Give me the binos.' Any red-wine induced fog was gone. She was alert as a sniper.

'Hang on.' Exasperation now tinged his voice. He looked through the binos again.

'It's not coming for us. It's heading more easterly.'

Victoria squinted, trying to focus on something which wasn't staying still for long enough. No, it wasn't heading east, it was coming for them.

She knew it.

'Give me the damn binos!'

He did as instructed.

She looked again.

It was a RIB. A big one. And it was doing more than ten knots.

'It's coming for us!' She was almost screaming.

Get a grip woman ...

He didn't seem bothered. Was he still hung over? He looked at the boat that was definitely heading their way, and then back to her. His face was scrunched up - his expression was consternation - when what she really wanted to see was clarity. Action, maybe. He was lifeless. Stuck to the spot.

'I'm calling "mayday" - all stations.' Victoria reached for the radio's handset.

'Hang on, hang on.' He grabbed her wrist.

'What the hell do you want us to wait for? Until we see the whites of their eyes? They're coming for us!' She shook her wrist and he let go. She picked up the handset, checked the frequency on the radio set, took one last look at the speck-turned-RIB that was bearing down on them, and pressed the pressel on the handset.

'Mayday, mayday. Hello all-stations, this is British yacht *Money For Nothing II*, mayday, mayday. We are at ...', she looked across at the GPS numbers and read them out, '...6 degrees 11 minutes 58.7 seconds north, and 49 degrees 25 minutes 10.8 seconds east, heading south-southeast at two knots.' She took a breath. 'We are being pursued by a RIB-type boat. Possible pirates. Over.'

Paul was looking in the direction of the RIB. He had one hand on a rail and the other was on his hip. She caught a glimpse of his face. *What was that look?*

There was no radio reply, just the *slap, slap, slap* of water on hull.

Victoria was about to retransmit the message when the airways burst into life. After a static *squelch*, the reply was crackly - but decipherable.

'Hello, *Money For Nothing II*, this is *USS Hurricane*. Confirm, 6 degrees 11 minutes 58.7 seconds north, and 49 degrees 25 minutes 10.8 seconds east. Over.'

Paul turned and glared at the loudspeaker that was mounted forward of main instrument panel, then he looked at her. His face was unreadable.

What is up with him?

The question was countered as relief flooded through Victoria's veins.

She hadn't picked up the detail of the response from the US ship, so she transmitted their position again.

'We are at 6 degrees 11 minutes 58.7 seconds north, and 49 degrees 25 minutes 10.8 seconds east. Over.'

Another look in the direction of the RIB. She didn't need any binoculars now. It was approaching fast.

Squelch. 'We have that. Can you confirm that the incoming vessel is hostile? Over.'

'Paul? Surely? They're pirates?'

He was mute. It was though some sort of paralysing disease had overcome him. She got nothing in response.

She raised the binos to her eyes. It was a 30-foot RIB; it was on the plane. Maybe two big outboards. Doing 20 knots? Possibly four or five men. *Was that a weapon?*

'It's a large RIB. Pushing out 20 knots and closing fast. Four or five men. I can't see any more than that. Over.'

The reply was instant.

'OK, *Money For Nothing.* We are about 150 nautical miles south of you. We'll have a chopper in the air in 15 minutes, it'll be with you in an hour. My advice is ...'

An hour? We'll be dead in 20 minutes.

'... do whatever the hostiles ask of you. Do not fight. Do not argue. We'll be with you as soon as we can. In the meantime keep this channel open. Over.'

Victoria pulled the handset from her face and looked at it as though it were infected.

'They'll be here in ten minutes, Vicky.'

It was the first sign of recognition from Paul since she'd spotted the RIB. She was at a loss as to what to do, or say. Did he expect a response? Should she respond to the US ship? She was losing her grip. They were being pursued by pirates. And help was an hour away.

It was all going to end horribly. She just knew it.

Fear

Chapter 1

Present Day

Hotel Post, Alpbach. Austria

Sam woke with a start. Instantly she had complete clarity. It was the way her brain was wired. She didn't need an alarm clock - she woke when she had to. And, unlike most people, she didn't require that additional five minutes to clear the night's sleep from her mind. Awake; alive. It wasn't a trait she necessarily complemented herself on. She wished she could wake, turn over and then sleep all day. Sadly that never happened. There was a bit of her old military training mixed in there somewhere. But mostly it was her unnecessarily overactive brain.

With one eye open she was looking across at the hotel's radio alarm: a neon red 7.25 am. She sensed an empty bed. She didn't move her torso, but lifted her right arm and prodded behind her. Nothing. A vacancy. *Zimmer frei*. Her German was picking up.

Last night's affair hadn't lasted beyond the entangling of limbs, lubricated by the sweat of exertion. Was it something she had said? She knew she was often poor company, uncomfortable with small talk and pleasantries. After some mild flirting across the bar, they'd spoken about camper vans and skiing, and sturdy footwear (in that order) - they were her chosen topics. She sensed a polite lack of interest, but the fact that they were both on their own and both in good shape, stimulated a physical draw. A sexual magnetism of sorts. But, as was always the case with her, it hadn't lasted.

She sat up, blinked and looked around the small, feather duvet-filled room. Nothing. Not a single sign that she'd had company. Naked, she hopped out of bed and checked her wallet. It was a bottle of Riesling lighter than when she had last looked, but it hadn't been touched by her company. She opened the top drawer of the pine chest. Her passport was there. She absently flicked through it. It still had its Russian work visa, and two West African stamps: Liberia and Sierra Leone.

Sam put her wallet and passport in her bumbag and took a quick peek out of the window to check that the ski lifts were working. They were. Disappointed but not surprised that she'd be skiing alone, she headed for the shower.

At the ornate pine reception desk Sam paid the very jolly Austrian concierge with cash. She then booked the same room for tonight. This was day five, so the concierge wasn't surprised by her actions. For her it was force of habit. Always be prepared for quick escape. Never stay in the same place two nights in a row. Pay by cash and take all your important documents with you.

Her SIS 'case officer' and her Army analyst's training had drummed into her a number of standard operating procedures. As a civvy for the past 12 months they were mostly pointless, it was habit. Well, habit and her OCD. *Get real – definitely more OCD than habit.* It meant that whilst she was ready for anything, nothing actually happened. And she was constantly worn out. Check this; twice. *What's that?* Why is that there? Why isn't that there? What's that number plate? Her photographic memory constantly filling up with, now, worthless trivia.

Since she left SIS, she'd done some internet research into PTSD - it still plagued her from Afghanistan - and OCD. She hoped that the reports would say that time was a good healer. That, at some point, her memory would be so full it couldn't remember anything else. Perhaps soon she'd be able to see a face and not have its features indelibly inked onto her consciousness.

Maybe then she'd be able to turn over and sleep all day?

The reports were inconclusive. Trauma did funny things to the brain. And, if you were on the autistic spectrum to begin with, the results could be significant and long-lasting.

Outside, having collected her skis and poles from the hotel's cellar, she made her way to the ski-bus. She really hoped she didn't bump into last night's excursion. She wouldn't know what to say. She'd probably blurt out something like, 'Did you check the footy? Good result for The Canaries?' There'd be an awkward silence and she'd mumble and leave - taking her embarrassment with her.

Alpbach, a very British resort in the middle of the Austrian Tyrol, was half-crowded. Mid-January was neither here nor there when it came to the ski season, but she travelled now because she knew she was pretty certain to get some half-decent snow. And the kids would be at school. During her time in the Army she'd trained here with the Military Intelligence ski team. It was just a season, but it was enough for her to get a bronze at the Army downhills a couple of weeks later. It was a charming, chocolate box resort, even if the skiing was hardly expansive.

Whoa!

Sam stopped in her tracks, her boots sliding on the icy pavement. She used her poles to steady herself.

Across the street at the entrance to the more modern and upmarket Böglerhof Hotel, she spotted a face - more accurately a pair of eyes - that threw up a red flag.

The eyes belonged to a late middle-aged man, maybe 55; medium height and build, wearing an expensive, black Spyder ski jacket. Someone else was carrying his skis and poles. The eyes wore a blue bobble hat, low down on the head, and a red and black, wool checked scarf covered the mouth. It was as though the eyes' owner was hoping to be incognito.

But Sam recognised the eyes; she knew she did. Even if the rest of the face was doing its best to go unnoticed. She'd seen the eyes in the newspapers some years back. Initially it was a big splash on a broadsheet. Probably *The Times*. The article ran for several days and it made the telly and the other papers.

She recognised the eyes for sure.

Their stares met just as Sam silently mouthed his name. There was a spark. Only briefly. The eyes knew that she was looking at them.

They turned away from her gaze, the rest of the head following. The head said something over its shoulder to the stockier man who was carrying his skis. Sam was too far away to pick up what was said. The other man (younger, bigger and less expensively dressed - black ski trousers, red jacket with distinctive blue flashes and a white ski helmet she'd easily pick out in a crowd) shot Sam a long look. She blinked, as if to capture the complete image; and was immediately embarrassed for staring.

No, I'm not embarrassed. Suspicious? Yes, more like it.

Sam shook her head as if to reset it, had a quick glance at the frozen pavement that was her route and, as only anyone can in ski boots, waddled onwards towards the ski-bus stop.

Creech US Air Force Base, Las Vegas, US

Master Sergeant Rick Rodgers tweaked the joystick that, via multiple satellites, instructed the ailerons on the wings of his MQ-9 'Reaper' to alter its course. He glanced at the airspeed indicator: 143 knots. That would do for now. And the bearing? 169 degrees, magnetic. That was also OK.

He had four LCD screens in front of him: two 24-inchers, one on top of each other, and two smaller screens side by side lower down. The lower 24-incher displayed the pilot's view. He could alter the picture electronically as if he were strapped to the front of the drone. Just now he was looking straight ahead, and down about 45 degrees.

And all he could see was dark jungle. Miles and miles of it.

He pushed back in the brown leather chair. It rocked slightly. He stretched his neck from side to side, trying to banish the stiffness from the basketball he had played last night with his buddies. He was in good shape. He knew that. But at 36 he wasn't getting any younger. His recent pilot-training at Pueblo had mostly been about learning to fly the drone. But the instructors also pushed the would-be pilots physically. He was one of four enlists to be given the chance to compete for their drone wings, along with 20 officers. It was the first time the Air Force had allowed enlisted men to train as pilots. He had made it, close to top of the cohort. He was good behind the stick - he'd proved that. But he was also always in the top five of any of the physical assessments. Not bad for an old man.

But, boy, recovery was so much more difficult nowadays.

He shot a glance sideways. 'You got anything, Lance?'

Captain Lance Travis was his sidekick. He was sitting in the seat next to him. Their 'cockpit' was at the end of a small beige, windowless shipping container. The pair of them with their instruments were crammed against the back wall. They shared a central LED which could display any one of their own screens, and Lance had another four of his own. His job was surveillance. And death.

Their $17 million Reaper was fitted with extra fuel on the internal pylons and four Hellfire IIs, surface-to-ground missiles, further along the wings. Lance's job was to find the target, designate it and, once Rick had launched - missile launch was always the pilot's call - check the Hellfire's trajectory as it found its own way to the target. Subsequently Lance, using the variety of sensors aboard the 3,800-pound unmanned aerial vehicle

(UAV), established mission success and checked for collateral.

'Nothing. It's all dark green, getting darker. And it's all clear. I'll be switching to infrared in 30 minutes.'

The Reaper was flying at 32,000 feet, and yet Lance could easily pick out single human targets. And if they were interested, between them they could get close enough and zoom hard enough to read the label on a pair of jeans - in daylight. At night they could establish the make of a truck from its engine's hotspot and the size of its warm tyres. They lost some resolution at night, but onboard millimetric radar and some state-of-the-art thermal imaging sensors meant that there weren't many places a hostile could hide - at any time.

With up to 30 hours' endurance it wasn't beyond a Reaper to start its mission circling over Damascus and finish with plenty of AVTUR to spare in Baghdad.

But Damascus wasn't their mission. Nor was Baghdad.

Today, more accurately this evening, they were flying along the Venezuelan/Colombian border. They'd flown the Reaper out of Creech, wheels up at 5.30 pm, and would land back at base in seven hours' time. They were the only operational crew not piloting drones out of al-Udeid in Qatar, or from Bagram in Afghanistan.

Rick wasn't sure how he felt about that.

There were 212 Reapers in service with the Air Force; training told him that about 120 of those were operational at any one point. With average mission lengths of around six to eight hours (beyond that even the sharpest pilots lost their edge), maybe 40 were in the air at any one point. Speaking to buddies and fellow pilots at Creech, most were used for search-and-destroy in Afghanistan, Syria, Iraq and lately in Yemen. They were all piloted from Creech, with just groundcrew forward to patch, make up, refuel and rearm the UAVs in theatre. Reapers were remotely-piloted vehicles. At over 6,000 miles from Las Vegas to mid-Asia, Rick thought they were stretching the definition of 'remote'.

For the Reapers flying out of Qatar and Afghanistan, he guessed that scores of terrorists were taken out each week, with some crews at Creech notching up over 1,000 confirmed kills in a tour. Afghanistan and certain parts of the Middle East were target-rich environments.

Yet here, now, he and Lance were loitering above the South American jungle looking for who knows what? Not a badass in sight.

No, he wasn't sure how he felt about his assignment.

He'd been posted to Creech just three months ago. He was delighted to have been selected to fly directly out of training and equally happy to have been posted to 432nd Operations

Group, a 25-minute drive from Las Vegas. As an Army brat he had lived all over the world; Vegas was just another notch on his belt. His pop, a tanky, had mostly been based in Hohenfels, Germany. But the family had spent time at Fort Lewis in Washington State among a couple of others. Pop had finished up as a command sergeant major at Camp Blanding, Florida, where he'd finally bought a boat and retired. Rick hadn't suffered the fate of other army kids, and had managed to restrict himself to only six schools before he'd been old enough to apply for the Air Force. And whilst his pop was initially unhappy about his choice of service ('Everyone hates the Air Force, son.'), he had beamed a big smile a couple of months ago when Rick had been presented with his wings.

Not only was he only one of two enlisted men to have passed the course. He was also the only black man. Yup, sure. His pop was pleased about that.

A couple of weeks later, having moved into the mess at Creech, they were given their aircraft and mission areas. Rick was caught off guard.

'Master Sergeant Rodgers!', the colonel had called out.

'Yessir!'

'You're joining Captain Travis. It's a new mission of which you'll be briefed later.'

'Yessir!'

The colonel had continued down the assignment list, with the remaining pilots flying Afghanistan or the mid-east.

And that was that. He'd hung around after the briefing and tracked down Captain Lance Travis. He was as bemused as Rick. At 31 Lance was an experienced UAV Sensor Operator with 650 confirmed kills, nearly all of them in Afghanistan and Pakistan. He'd been taken off routine search-and-destroy missions that morning, which were his bread and butter. He was none the wiser as to their 'new mission'.

They'd made their way to the canteen where, once they'd got their coffee and sat down, a young-looking major had found them and accompanied them to the colonel's office.

'Bring your coffee. The boss is very chilled.'

The briefing was just them, the colonel, the major and a middle-aged man wearing a suit, who looked stern and business-like. Rick thought he was possibly State Department or from General Atomics who manufactured the Reaper (maybe they were going to test-fly a new UAV?). Or he could be CIA or Homeland Security. He quickly dismissed the latter; both organisations had their own Reapers.

Whatever, he stood at the back of the room and wasn't introduced.

'Gentlemen, you're going to fly a Reaper from Creech. South. Across the Gulf of Mexico and into Venezuela.' The colonel smiled a knowing smile, as if he were sharing the biggest ever secret. 'All of the work we do here at Creech is secret. But this is especially so. You've been chosen, not only because you are good at what you do, but because we need to rely completely on your integrity. Do we understand each other?'

Rick wasn't sure what to think. Lance may be an old hand, but he was hardly an experienced pilot. Maybe there was something about his background; the fact that he was a recently commissioned enlist making him seem more trustworthy?

Less inclined to ask questions?

He wasn't sure.

'Yessir!', rang out in unison.

The colonel had walked around the room, staring out of the window as if gathering his thoughts. He turned to them.

'You'll be given a mission summary before each flight. Flight paths will be tight, and you'll have little discretion with route planning. I will personally check all of the details before you fly and either I, or the major here, will always be on base should there be issues or questions mid-mission. Is that clear?'

We're going to fly a Reaper into Venezuela, a country on the edge of civil war, and one we have subjected to black ops for half a century? Are you sure?

'Yessir!', from Lance. Rick had been deep in thought and blurted out, 'Yessir!' a little too late to appear completely compliant.

The colonel paused, shooting Rick a quizzical look.

'Good. Good. Details of your first mission will be emailed to you within two hours. You're flying tonight.'

That had been it. Rick had glanced at the civvy on the way out of the office, but hadn't caught his eye.

Four hours later he was staring at jungle.

And this was their seventeenth mission. Seventeen dreary flights scouring the western jungles of Venezuela looking for 'new activity'.

'New activity' was defined in the mission statement as: recent clearings, new or resurfaced roads, new or refurbished buildings, and any changes to water courses. After the first flight he and Lance had spent the following morning redefining 'new activity' to see if they could expand the list - if nothing else to make their job slightly more interesting. The first mission had been very dull. Their path had covered about 850 square miles of jungle, using a zig-zag pattern, south to north. They'd entered Venezuelan airspace at 36,000 feet, dropping to 32,000 once they were away from habitation. They'd left Venezuelan airspace two-and-a-half hours later. None the wiser.

On mission 15 late into the evening, Lance had found a new road branching from some old blacktop. It led to a clearing in the jungle that could have been big enough for a short airstrip. Or a decent-sized poppy plantation. Lance had picked it up using the drone's thermal imager, the strip darker where the surrounding jungle had kept its heat for longer. Rick had put the Reaper into 'loiter' whilst Lance checked the most recent mapping and satellite photographs. After a second run Lance confirmed what he had seen and that he had taken plenty of footage.

As Rick flew the Reaper back over the Gulf of Mexico, Lance top-and-tailed the imagery and emailed it to the colonel. They'd had nothing back from him.

Tonight they were running close to the Colombian border. The mission was an hour longer than usual as the flight path had to take in the contorted line of the border. The colonel was clear: under no circumstances were they to stray into Colombian airspace. That made flying slightly more fun. But, he felt for Lance. Almost 100 hours in the air and only an airstrip to report.

No badasses. The Hellfires went out with them. And they came back again.

Shit!?

A red light flashed on his console. The Reaper, currently on autopilot, veered left, the pilot's LED struggling to keep up with the speed of turn - a blur of greens and blacks. Rick's balance went as his brain struggled to rationalise the sudden movement on the screen. He obviously felt no g-force, but like a video roller-coaster it didn't stop your brain being fooled by the imagery.

'What the fuck are you doing, Rick?' Lance's screens were also awash with moving pictures as the sensors followed the airframe.

Rick switched off autopilot and regained control. He checked bearing, altitude and pitch. All was calm, except a red light flashed continuously on one of the lower monitors. He pressed a button and checked the error code: navigation sync error.

'Wait ...' He put his hand up to stop further questions from Lance.

He racked his brain.

Navigation sync error. A disparity between GPS readings and the inboard gyroscopes. The latter was a fall-back navigational system if the GPS went down. It used their wheels-up coordinates and a series of sophisticated gyroscopes to track and report current location. It wasn't as accurate as GPS and became less so the further away they got from their start location. Pilots could reset the gyroscopes' start point in flight if they were confident with the GPS readings.

He pressed a couple of other buttons on a keypad.

Error: 23.57 miles.

What the hell is happening?

The autopilot had started to correct the error. It used the GPS as the primary source of navigational information, unless the pilot told it otherwise. It thought they were off course. And had started to sort it out.

Why was the GPS reading over 20 miles out? All of a sudden?

'I've got a GPS error.'

'I can see that. Do you know why?' Lance was leaning across the central console.

'No. It happened suddenly, as if the bird had been flying using gyroscopes, and then it suddenly picked up a GPS signal. Doesn't make sense?'

'Where are we headed?'

'Shit!'

Rick knew then that the Reaper was no longer in Venezuelan airspace. They had been running very close to the border when the navigational system had gone haywire. The Reaper's autocorrect had sent them west. They were now in Colombian airspace. In the minute or so of confusion he'd taken his eye off the ball.

At 160 miles-an-hour they might have strayed maybe ten or 15 miles across the border. But Rick knew that that was ten or 15 miles too far.

He threw the joystick hard left, checked the bearing was due east and upped the airspeed.

Inneralpbach, Austria

Sam twisted both heels, pushing her weight down through her knees. Her skis cut into the top layer of freshly-pisted snow, forcing out a spray of white powder. She skidded for about a metre and came to a halt. She leant forward on her poles and took in the view to the village of Inneralpbach a mile or so below. It was perfect skiing weather. Cold and crisp - the early morning sun glancing through the trees, picking out the water crystals that were frozen in the air - like suspended silver slivers in a recently-shaken snow dome.

She was a third of the way down the Red 8, resting on a thin shelf, ready to launch herself down the next slope which lay beckoning downwards between dark green pines. It was a good morning. One of the best.

The deep cutting sound of approaching snowboarders caught her attention. She turned to look back through the gap in the trees from where she had just come. Two young lads, *no a boy and a girl*, expertly carved their way onto the shelf and, without a pause, jumped off the lip and, with a holler, sped down the next part of the run. Even though Sam was a good skier, there was no way she could have kept up with the momentum of a pair of deft snowboarders who had age on their side.

Another *swoosh* and an older female skier stopped a few metres from her on the ledge. She was dressed fabulously in black trousers and a cream-white top with fake fur around the hood. She looked at Sam and smiled. And then, with the grace of a local who had skied all her life, dropped over the ledge and carved her way fabulously down the slope.

For no other reason than infatuation, Sam followed the woman, matching her turns as best she could.

Swish, swoosh. Swish, swoosh.

The woman with the cream parka made it look easier than it was, and it wasn't long before Sam missed a turn and she had to push a bit harder to keep up. But it was fun - mesmerisingly so.

She was so entranced chasing her quarry that she failed to hear the skier behind her who was moving quicker than her, in a straight line - without slowing turns. A blunt object on a collision course.

Smack!

Ouch!

Oi!

As she tumbled she sensed the other skier was a man. Possibly 30 kilos heavier than her? Out of control? Shit happens.

Her own speed and the gradient of the slope translated into a bundle of movement - arms, legs (her skis still attached; she had her bindings set for racing), snow and then more arms and legs. And more snow. The wind was taken from her, and her right shoulder which, since the episode on the

Russian oligarch's superyacht tended to 'pop-out', did just that - but thankfully only long enough for it to quickly find its way back into its proper place.

Shit! That hurt.

Friction and impact slowed Sam's decent and, in a defensive manoeuvre when she felt she was coming out of the next tumble, she dug her heels into the ground. Her momentum swung her body upright, at which point she twisted her feet so her skis pointed downhill. And then she was off - upright and unbalanced, covered in snow, but back on two legs.

Shaken, not stirred.

She skid-stopped as soon as she was ready - and just before the slope ran out and turned right into the trees.

She was panting - and waiting. She needed a second to stop her brain from spinning and get her world back into focus. *Check.* Her shoulder hurt, but not overly so. All limbs intact. All OK.

Concussion?

I don't think so.

Eyesight? Yes, that works ... where's the idiot?

There he was. The skier who had knocked her down. Twenty metres from her, up the slope. The skier with the unmistakable red jacket with distinctive blue flashes. With a white helmet she could easily pick out in a crowd.

Except there wasn't a crowd. They were among the first on the slopes heading to Inneralpbach, which was at the far end of the resort. Only the most committed got this far, this early.

She looked beyond the man, further up the slope. A couple of lads were on their way down. Competent skiers, but not experts. She looked again at the man. He was staring directly at her whilst unzipping his jacket - halfway to his waist, leaving a single pole planted in the snow.

What?!

What was he reaching for?

The two skiers didn't stop. They shot past Sam at a reasonable pace just as she saw the man's hand hesitate inside his jacket. Keeping something hidden. But not that well-hidden. She could see enough.

He was holding the stock of a handgun.

She had a split second.

She didn't waste it.

She was off.

Sam didn't give the man with the red ski jacket a second glance. Like a langlaufer, she ran her skis down a short, low-gradient schuss that cut a track between tight pines. Soon she was right behind the lads - two had become three. As they shot out of the trees and made the last major turn into the long run home, she was skiing beside them; among them. Egging them on, blurting out,

'*Wollen-Sie ein Rennen?*' She got ahead, racing hard and then letting them catch her.

They were up for it. Loving it.

All the time Sam glanced behind, keeping an eye on the man with the red ski jacket. He was a competent skier, but no Franz Klammer. Soon laddish youth and some decent Army ski-training had stolen them 20 metres. Then 40.

They were close to the end of the slope; the village, all cuckoo clock and snowy roofs. And the lift, a big steel and wooden building spewing cables, came into focus. Sam needed a plan. She had two choices: catch the bubble back up the mountain and out-ski her pursuer; or dash into the village and lose herself in the crowd.

The man with the red ski jacket wouldn't shoot her in the village. *Would he?*

But she had no transport in Inneralpbach. She'd need to catch a ski bus. Which meant hanging around at a bus stop. Possibly forever ... that's what it would feel like.

That's not going to do. She needed to break clean from the man with the red ski jacket with blue flashes. In retrospect the sort of fashion sense she'd expect from a likely killer.

The two lads skid-stopped and yelled something with the word '*Fräulein*' in it. Sam ignored them and kept her skis parallel, nipping and turning past skiers and walkers milling around at the bottom of the bubble.

Her momentum kept her going until she hit the ice and gravel of the lift's car park. She skidded to a halt, unclipped her right ski off with her left (a trick an Army instructor had taught her - it always looked *so* cool) and, still in one movement, used her right boot to release her left ski. They were in her arms, and she was waddling/striding to the metal stairs that led to the bubble lift in a couple of seconds. She didn't look behind.

Sam took the stairs two at a time (*I must get lighter ski boots!*), flashed her forearm at the ticket machine which registered the pass in her jacket, and pushed the rotating bar with her thigh which gave way, affording access to the bubble lift.

The 'bubble cars' arrived about every ten seconds. There were nearly always three cars on the platform at any one point. One just about to leave, one accepting passengers, and one just arriving. Designed to carry no more than eight skiers, they were all suspended from an oval-shaped chain and wire contraption inside the terminal - and all of them moved at a very sedentary pace. If red-jacket-with-blue-flashes man was on her heels he could well join her in the same car. Which would make for an uncomfortable ride.

Sam didn't lose momentum. The car that was just about to leave the farther side of the oval as it prepared to be whipped up the mountain by a second, faster-moving wire.

She waddled quickly after it. She slipped past a red-and-white chain which was meant to stop skiers getting onto the car as its doors closed and it was transferred to the speeding wire back up the mountain.

Sam squeezed between the closing doors, one boot caught between the rubber that provided the seal. If she didn't get it inside the car, she might lose it.

She heard the shout, '*Was zur hölle machst du?!*', from the lift operator as she forced the doors open far enough to retrieve her errant boot. Thankfully he didn't stop the car.

She had made it and she still hadn't looked behind.

Phew.

Breathe.

All skis, poles and covered in snow from her earlier fall, she realised that she was not alone in the bubble. The elegant woman with the cream parka was squatting on the plastic bum rail. Skis in one hand, poles in another.

She was beautiful. Her sharp, regal features framed poetically by the ruff of the white fur. A touch of red lipstick, and enough rouge to highlight her Aryan cheekbones.

She smiled disarmingly at Sam.

'*Grüß Gott.*'

Sam checked herself. She knew she looked a sight. She knew that she was red-faced and sweaty.

That her auburn curls escaping the side of her helmet would be frosted with snow, collected on the fall. She held her skis and poles in a muddle, like a teenage beginner after a hard day in ski school.

Elegance versus catastrophe.

Oh well.

'*Grüß Gott,*' she replied sheepishly.

The bubble launched. Sam rearranged her skis and poles, placing the ends on the floor. She wiped the condensation from the window and peered at the bubble behind her. She couldn't make out anything in the second car, there was too much condensation on the windows. A quick glance downwards picked out the car park and the metal stairs rising to the lift's entrance. There, at the bottom of the stairs, was red-jacket-with-blue-flashes man. He was breathing hard and on his mobile.

She had lost him.

For now?

Chapter 2

Punat Bay, Krk, Croatia

Jakov Vuković pulled hard on the oars of his single scull. The boat shot forward then lost some momentum as the cold, salty water of the bay dragged against the shiny hull. With his feet strapped onto the end of the rails, he used his legs to pull his backside towards his feet as the heads of the oars flew backward, parallel with the surface of the water ready to be planted again. In. Drive. Draw. Recover.

In. Drive. Draw. Recover. Work hard!

He reckoned he was close to 22 strokes per -minute. Once he was completely warm he'd up that stroke-rate to 26 and try and hold it for 125 strokes. At that rate he would cover about 800 metres. Then he'd warm down for a further 25 strokes towards the end of the bay - where the Krk peninsula closes in on the Punat coastline. There the water would become choppy as it opened onto the Adriatic; it wasn't the safest place to row. So, he'd slowly manoeuvre the boat around until it was facing back into the bay.

Then he'd start again. Do another run.

And then another.

It was hard but necessary winter training. He had his first race in two months and the nationals a month after that. He'd be ready. This year he'd definitely be ready.

Getting warm on the water was tricky this early in the season. It wasn't like being a runner - although he did plenty of training runs on the track. Warming up as a runner was a matter of wearing the right clothing and working your muscles hard. Good clothing retained the heat your muscles produced. Here, on the water, he was constantly being soaked with something that felt close to ice melt. The wind generated by his own speed cooled the dampness further. As his body delivered heat, the conditions sapped it away. The cold was distracting. And working cool muscles wasn't the best form of training. But needs must.

As he turned at the end of the bay the light from the rising sun, which was still behind the mountains in the east, bounced off the clouds and presented him with the early stages of dawn. *Fabulous*. He started again.

In. Drive. Draw. Recover. *In. Drive. Draw. Recover.*

Soon he'd be opposite Samostan Island and its monastery, about halfway along his training run. He didn't like to hang about at that point. The place - the island - was spooky. Sitting in the middle of the bay it was and always had been a subject of rumour, speculation and mystery.

It lived up to its reputation even today. No one was allowed onto the island. Its shore was cordoned off with swimming buoys, about 50 metres out. There was a sign on every other buoy explicitly forbidding landing. On shore there was an intact, if ancient, stone wall about a metre and a half high. Behind the wall a thick mass of Mediterranean pines; slightly bent, addled trunks supporting a low, splodge of thick, dark spiky green foliage. All you could see of the monastery was a limestone-white, square bell tower topped with a low-pitched red roof poking above the pines. The bell only rang on Sundays - a distant, haunting sound.

The village was rife with rumour as to what the monks did in the monastery. Every bar had a different story. 'The cellars are full of missing children, chained to the floor and fed on cockroaches.' 'The monks are all over a hundred years old; the island's well holds magical water that keeps them alive.' And, his favourite: 'The monastery is a cover for an international organisation of lizard-like people who run the world.'

What was for sure was that no one he'd met had ever set foot on the island. A couple of mute monks rowed over twice a week to collect food, and there was talk of a small pleasure craft coming round from Krk in the night to drop off and collect visitors. But he'd never seen it. Punat was a very catholic village and everyone knew to give the monks their space. That rule had been passed down through the generations. Tourists were kept away by the signs on the buoys, and when a stray pedalo had beached a couple of years ago, a monk had very quickly shooed the tourists away.

But that didn't stop the rumours.

As his arms and legs screamed out for mercy, he glanced to his right. Yes, there it was. The small, but very mysterious island of Samostan.

As he sculled, his progress back up the bay was slowed as a sudden gust of the Bora wind blew down from the mountains. The wind cut right through him as the originally pond-like water spawned white horses atop six-inch waves. If it carried on like this he'd have to paddle in.

Fuck!

He caught a crab - that is, his right oar hit the water a split second early and immediately its and his body's position were all at odds with each other. The oar, which was connected to the boat by a metal ring, reared up, catching Jakov under the arm with such force that it ripped the ligaments below his shoulder.

No!

The end of the right oar continued its flight upwards, lifting and skewing him out of the boat - but his feet were strapped onto the rail and they wouldn't allow the oar to finish its job. The right oar snapped out from under his arm the moment his left oar dug deep into the sea. It sprang aggressively under the boat, twisting the hull, lifting it out of the water. One oar had propelled him in one direction and now the other, the boat and his strapped feet wanted him to go the other way.

The next thing he knew he was in the sea, the boat on its side and still toppling, his body floundering with his feet tied onto the rail. The icy cold of the water jolted him; it dimmed any pain he felt in his right arm and the other bits of his body which had suffered the force of the pivoting oars. But it didn't dim the fear of what would happen next.

I have to get my feet free.

Twisting his body, he lifted his head above the surface of the water and took a breath. Then, with both eyes open he ducked under the surface of the water and reached for the straps that held his feet in place.

One ... make it! Two ...

He was free.

And then the pain hit him, so much so he almost passed out. His right arm was useless and his left hurt like hell.

His head was just above water and he took a breath - but he hadn't quite calculated where his mouth was with reference to the choppy surface. His lungs took in, what seemed to him, a couple of litres of icy salt water.

Jakov coughed and spluttered, the violent movement sending pulses of pain down his arm.

41

Calm down! He coughed some more, and more pain came. Once he was breathing again, he trod water for a second. And then his primeval instincts kicked in.

Swim - you fool, swim!

And that's what he did. With one working arm.

He reached the island's white swimming buoys in a couple of minutes and took a short rest clinging onto the air-filled plastic ball. By now he was shivering uncontrollably. He had to keep moving.

It took him another three or so minutes to make it to the rocky shore of the island. He hit his knee badly on an underwater craggy outcrop and, what with everything else, he couldn't stop himself from sobbing. Sobbing in pain, but also in relief that he had made it ashore. He was safe.

At least from drowning. As he crawled awkwardly off the rocks, the wind continued to leach any temperature his body's shivering was generating.

He was getting colder and colder.

On hands and knees he picked his way off the shoreline and into some bushes.

Next was the rock wall. It looked bigger close up than from the shore. With monumental effort he stood, using a couple of protruding rocks to steady himself. Once upright, he had a quick look behind him to see if there was any movement on the water. Maybe someone had spotted him going over and taken a boat out to rescue him?

No. The village, which was in the westerly lee of the mountains, was still cloaked in early morning darkness. There were a few lights on the harbourside, but no sign of movement.

He faced the wall.

This is going to be tricky.

He put his hands on the top layer of stones, and found a foothold. He tried to lift his torso onto the top of the wall, but his wet foot slipped - and he fell.

Fuck!

Fuck. That hurt.

And still the shivering continued.

He took a deep breath and literally gritted his chattering teeth. His next attempt was successful and, leaving his right arm to dangle, he managed to get both legs on top of and then over the wall, the sharp, jagged limestone rocks digging into his stomach.

He fell on the other side of the wall, *clump*, and was surprised that his landing wasn't accompanied by any new pain. He looked around him. It was dark. Almost like night. He was on a tarmac path? A newly laid path? He touched it with a flat hand to check that he was right. Yes, it was tarmac. It seemed to run parallel with the wall.

Jakov stood up gingerly, holding his right arm with his left - it hurt so much more if it were left to hang free. He looked further inland: pine trees, the gnarled-bark trunks leaving the earth at different angles. None of them was straight.

At man-height it was all impenetrably black.

No, hang on.

He squinted in the darkness.

In the trees, maybe five metres, was a fence. A tall green wire fence, possibly two metres high. It looked new and sturdy, topped with very efficient barbed wire. Definitely designed to keep people out. He was stuck. The sea and a nasty rock wall on one side; an impenetrable fence on the other.

And his body was a useless, shivering wreck.

What's that noise?

It was then that he realised he was in real trouble.

It started as a far-off yelp. Which soon became a series of angry barks. No, not angry: vicious. He would have been comfortable if the terrifying noise was coming from the woods. He would have felt protected by the fence. But it wasn't. It was coming from behind him. Along the tarmac path. Just around the corner. And the barks were getting louder.

He turned away from the noise to run. But his legs wouldn't carry him. He was exhausted. He took a few, pathetic shuffling steps. And then the Doberman was on him, launching open-mouthed at his flaccid arm.

Jakov went down with the dog at his side, its teeth closing on his lower arm. He really wanted to care, to fight. But his brain made the decision that the best thing to do now was to shut down.

Just before it did, a question flashed into his dimming consciousness: *do monks have attack dogs?*

His brain didn't wait for an answer.

Englischer Garten, Munich, Germany

The taxi dropped Sam off at the end of Gellertstraße. She was effectively working blind. She was looking for a huge pad somewhere near Munich's main park, Englischer Garten. And that's all the instructions she'd been able to give the taxi driver: '*Großes Haus, Englischer Garten. Bitte.*' The taxi driver, in a typically efficient German way, had replied '*Ja!*', smiled at the mad Englishwoman and pulled the mustard yellow Mercedes into the heavy city traffic.

She wasn't happy. Not at all. It had been a rubbish day, made more rubbish by the fact that she had absolutely no idea what was going on. She was tense. Irritable. And now she was looking for a house among thousands with her search engine working with limited info.

She was trying to find an old friend, colleague - almost lover? - of hers: Wolfgang. Sorry,

Count Wolfgang Neuenburg II. Wolfgang's now-deceased parents - his father had died before Sam had met Wolfgang, and his mother was shot dead in front of both of them in a disused warehouse in Berlin - owned much of the bottom right chunk of Germany. She'd spent an evening at his schloß in the Bayerischer Wald a few years ago. At some point during their liaison he'd mentioned that his mother lived in a big house near Englischer Garten in Munich. And, as Munich was commuting distance from Wörgl, which is where she'd caught the train earlier today, it was an obvious starting point.

With few options she had to go somewhere; staying in Alpbach after her brush with red-ski-jacket man wasn't one of them. And Wolfgang had talents. Talents that she could use right about now.

She'd skied straight off the mountain, waddled into the first clothing shop she could find and, for the exorbitant price of €749, had bought herself a pair of heavy cotton trousers, a dark grey multi-purpose jacket, a decent pair of walking shoes, some black gloves and an oversized black beanie. She'd left her skis, poles and boots outside a ski-hire shop, and ditched her ski trousers and jacket in the nearest bin. She was hardly incognito, but at least she wasn't wearing what she'd had on first thing.

Sam had made the decision not to return to the hotel. And, whilst it broke a piece of her heart, she decided to leave Bertie, her bright yellow VW T5 camper van, in the hotel's car park. She hoped one day - once she had got to the bottom of what the hell was happening - to return and pick him up. She certainly couldn't afford to buy another one.

Now changed, but without a toothbrush to her name, she had to find an escape route. But which one?

Chance was on her side. As she approached Alpbach's small coach station a local bus was in the process of pulling away from its stop. As Alpbach was at the end of a valley, it could only go one way. So, she jumped aboard. At the bottom of the mountain she got off at Wörgl, where she knew there was a train station on the mainline between Innsbruck and Munich. Both had airports - and she chose the latter.

Throughout her 6-hour journey to Munich she'd employed the evasion techniques she'd learnt as an SIS case officer. It was simple stuff you could pick up from the *Ladybird Book of Spying:* doubling back; making late turns; altering your pace. However, the key ingredient to not being tailed, or successfully losing a tail, was to surprise yourself with your own decisions. If you were caught off guard by your own route choices, you could bet that any tail would be just as flummoxed.

Leaving Bertie behind and a chance climb-aboard a random departing bus - without any clear plan as to what to do next - was exactly what would have got her full marks at the SIS training base at Fort Monckton. She knew she hadn't been followed.

Airports were out. As was hiring a car. And using her phone - which she'd turned off in the bubble as the cable car projected her to the top of the mountain. In Russia, just over a year ago, every security agency and their wives had managed to track her across the Urals because she'd had to pay for flights using a credit card with her name on it; and had used her phone to gather necessary data.

Now it was cash only and 'call no one'. That must be her mantra. She had no real idea how sophisticated her latest enemy was, but 'the eyes' from this morning had told her a bit of the story. She knew of the man. She knew what he did, or had done, for a living. If he wanted to find her, he almost certainly could. Without SIS credentials and associated multiple aliases, Sam was just plain Sam Green. She was on her own. So, it was cash - and call no one. That was it.

All that led to her current half-baked plan. She couldn't fly but could bus and train it round most of Europe. She couldn't cross a non-Schengen border as that would mean showing her passport, but she did have most of the continent at her disposal. So, where should she go? Who did she know who might be able to help her unpick what was behind the latest debacle that was her life?

Count Wolfgang Neuenburg II.

She and Wolfgang had been thrown together by a series of unfortunate events three years ago. It was all to do with planes crashing, an ultra-orthodox Christian sect, and two rogue ex-CIA agents - one of whom was now (thankfully) dead. The live one, Ralph Bell, cropped up in Sam's dreams more often than she would have wanted. Even awake she saw him at least once a week. In a crowd. On a bus. On TV. None of them was Bell. She knew straight away that it was her imagination playing tricks on her - she had a thing with faces. But that didn't stop facsimiles of him popping up time and again in some unexpected place. She shivered at the thought.

She'd only spoken to Wolfgang briefly after the events of three years ago. They'd lived in each other's pockets for a week as the conspiracy unfolded - it was fair to say that they'd 'got close'. But the death of his mother, some pretty serious injuries, and their abominable two-day internment in a shipping container, had put paid to any feelings they might have had for each other.

But, he lived in southern Germany - which was as close as you could get to the Austrian Tyrol. And he was an expert computer hacker and programmer. And that's the skill she needed right now.

First, though, she had to find him. Then hope that he was home. And then hope he would see her. None of those three was a dead cert.

It was getting dark. Huge houses rimmed Englischer Garten. They were all set back from reasonably narrow roads. Cars parked on both sides constricted the roads further. Some of the frontages were fenced; the remainder used bushes and trees to create a barrier. One or two of the mansions had been split into flats, which meant Sam could strike them off immediately. The Neuenburgs would own the whole shebang. The other good news was that most of the houses had postboxes fixed to their gates - another German trait. Slim, coloured, metalled boxes with a slot for mail, under which was the emblematic post horn of the Deutsche Bundespost. Nearly all of the ones she'd seen so far displayed a name tag.

Sam checked her watch. It was 4.35 pm. She was hungry, which was making her more irritable. She'd give herself an hour and a half of looking. Then she'd go and find something to eat. She decided not to plan beyond that.

There it was. She was 80 minutes into the 90 minutes she'd assigned for her wandering and she was just about to give up and feed her hunger. The house was easily the biggest on Flemingstraße. Its ornate gardens, lit by Narnia-style street lamps, were a beautiful combination of manicured lawns and under-control rhododendrons.

The plaque above the slit on the postbox told her all she needed to know: Neuenburg. And there were some lights on.

Success.

There was an intercom beside the gate. Sam rang it. A pause. She rang again, a little too soon after the first press. The connecting speaker in the house was probably six miles away from an able-bodied human, down endless corridors. But irritation, fuelled by a nagging hunger, had turned to impatience.

Feed me. Soon.

There was a *click*.

'*Guten Abend – Wer is da, bitte*', the box crackled.

A young woman's voice?

Sam put her mouth close to the speaker. She decided on English.

'Good evening. I am here to see Wolfgang. Is he in?'

There was a moment of silence.

'Who is this?'

'Sam Green. I'm an old friend of Wolfgang's.'

The intercom went silent. There was a metallic *clunk* as a bolt withdrew somewhere and then the large, ornate, metal gates started to move sideward, into a concrete recess which Sam hadn't noticed before.

That's clever. Where am I - Tracy Island?

Sam shrugged her shoulders and set off down the drive.

The house was on four floors. But, like nearly all German dwellings, there was almost certainly a cellar. It was white-rendered, the bottom floor had tall bay windows and the entrance was defined by a large, raised porch with a white, triangular balustrade supported by four Roman columns. Either side of the over-sized, double, wooden front doors was a topiary tree. The trees were lit up by very tasteful white lights. The place was majestic, but somehow understated.

Sam took the four steps up the porch two at a time. She then strode across the marbled floor to an inset, brown welcome mat. As she did, the left-hand door, with its huge brass hexagonal handle, opened.

She could now put a face to the voice on the intercom.

The apparition at the door was something off the front page of *Stern* magazine. Sam first thought it might be Claudia Schiffer's daughter, all blonde flowing locks with a face to rival Aubrey Hepburn's - and a figure made from the best bits in the body-parts cupboard. The apparition was dressed very casually: dark blue leggings and an all-white button-up collared shirt with tails that hung down to her thighs.

Was the shirt one of Wolfgang's?

Sam aged the apparition in her late 20s. And for a reason she couldn't put her finger on, she was immediately more irritated than she had been a few moments previously. It may have been because Sam was dressed all chunky greys and blacks, with cloddy walking shoes topped with a beanie cum tea cosy. Maybe ...

Give it up, girl. What is wrong with you?

She metaphorically shook herself. Then she looked round the apparition, to the lobby beyond.

'Hi, I guess you speak English?', Sam asked.

It smiled.

God, that's beautiful.

'Of course. Wolfgang is on his way. Would you come in, please?'

Wolfgang had attended some snooty boarding school in England and then went on to study the violin at The Royal College of Music in London - as a result, his English was impeccable and unaffected by accent. The apparition's had a German twang: Wolfgang pronounced 'Volfgang'. That was annoyingly attractive as well.

The apparition stood to one side and, with her hand, showed Sam into the lobby. She accepted. It was all deeply varnished pine, off-white walls and thick pile, cream carpets. A double staircase rose in front of her, and oil paintings of Wolfgang's ancestors adorned the walls. To her left was a corridor. A door opened at the end of it and out hobbled Wolfgang.

In many ways he was exactly as she remembered him. He was wearing 'hunting, shooting, fishing' cords, a white viyella checked shirt, brown brogues and, what she thought was, a red cashmere cardigan. He was something straight out of a Savile Row catalogue.

He was still tall, still off-blond and still rakishly attractive. But two things had changed. First, as he got closer and the light of the lobby allowed for more definition, he looked older. A lot older. His complexion was pallid. He had bags under his eyes and he was thinner on top. Second, and more striking, he was using a wooden walking stick. In typical Wolfgang style it was beautifully carved with an ebony handle and gold banding. But, by the way he was half-dragging his right leg, he needed it.

He stopped a few feet from her. Cocked his head to one side. And smiled - the same smile that had disarmed her time and again during that turbulent week three years ago.

'Hello, Sam. I was just about to call you. It seems that serendipity has beaten me to it. Nice hat ...'

What? I was just about to call you?

He was waiting for a reply. She was waiting for her brain to catch up.

'Hello, Wolfgang ...', she nodded to his leg. 'Are you OK?'

He smiled again. The apparition moved slowly round, closer to him. The three of them were now in a loose triangle.

'You always did look after me, Sam,' He let out a small laugh. 'It's nothing. My doctor tells me it's arthritis, caused by the wound, compounded a little by the shock of mother.' His expression soured, ever so slightly. The smile was lost. 'I get by.'

'Anyway!' He was smiling again now. 'You've met Ingeborg?' He lifted his stick and playfully pointed at the apparition.

Ingeborg? No, I could never get used to that ...

'Uh, no.' Sam held out her hand. Ingeborg took it tenderly and shook it. 'I'm Sam. Wolfgang and I ...'

Ingeborg stopped her with a flashing smile and a nod of recognition.

'I know all about you, Sam. Wolfgang has told me everything. At least three times.'

Sam sensed the last sentence was meant as a compliment, so she too forced a smile.

'Oh dear. I'll have to tell you the truth if we can find the time.' It was the best she could do.

Wolfgang continued. 'Are you staying? We have supper in 30 minutes - pork of course! You must stay, Sam. We have a lot to discuss.' Wolfgang was animated now.

Sam hesitated. She had no idea why. She had nowhere else to go. She was as hungry as a waking bear, and now, in the safety of a huge house in Munich, she was tired. And, back on mission, she needed Wolfgang's advice - and maybe support. A delicious supper, wine that she knew she wouldn't be able to find in Tesco, and a good night's sleep under a duvet the size of Wiltshire was exactly what she needed.

'Yes, please, Wolfgang. That would be ideal.'

Sam put the last spoonful of kirsch cherries and chocolate ice cream into her mouth. It was, like the rest of the meal, delicious. If she'd been at home, she'd have picked up the bowl and licked it clean. But it was probably not the best choice of manners, what with half of Wolfgang's family staring down at her from the walls of the large dining room. She placed the silver spoon back on the ornately decorated bowl (her mum, bless her soul, would have picked it up and looked for the manufacturer's mark), took the damask napkin from her lap and placed it on the table. That was something else she'd learnt by watching Wolfgang - whose manners were impeccable.

The three of them had been served without ceremony by a matronly woman called Elisabeth, whom Wolfgang thanked and complimented continuously.

'Elisabeth is the best cook in Bavaria. Isn't that so Elisabeth?'

Sam sensed that Elisabeth's English was patchy and admonished Wolfgang playfully under her breath, *'Du würdest kein gutes Schweinefleisch wissen, wenn du dich in der Rückseite bissest.'*

Wolfgang started to translate, but Sam stopped him.

'My German's picking up. Personally, I don't wholly agree with Elisabeth. You probably would know decent pork if it bit you on the backside.'

They all laughed.

It had been a very convivial supper. Just the three of them: Wolfgang, herself, and now the more-easily-named 'Inge'. Sam could cope with Inge. It still didn't do the woman justice. She would have preferred Sophia or Alexia.

Inge didn't say much. To be fair, she didn't get much chance. Sam and Wolfgang rambled on about their past, how he was coping with the estate, whether or not he'd got his father's Audi Quattro fixed, having smashed it about when they had last been together. She led the conversation, avoiding any gruesome bits, and Wolfgang seemed fine about filling in the details. She was so happy that he was at least some way back to being the man she remembered before his mother had been murdered.

Inge sat politely and smiled a lot. Sam didn't get the sense that she was a dumb blonde; far from it. She just seemed incredibly well brought up and knew when two old pals wanted to reminisce. What Sam didn't know was how she fitted into everything. But that would come.

Wolfgang put his spoon down and lifted his napkin to the table. He took a breath.

'Well, Sam. How are you coping now that you're not working?'

What? I haven't told him I'm not working.

'Uh, fine Wolfgang. Thanks. I'm sort of between jobs.'

'You don't miss Secret Intelligence Service, then?'

Sam was struggling. Where this was going? *How did he know?* Working with SIS was a secret. She'd never told anyone outside of the organisation. Maybe she'd had too much of the red wine - wine that was so thick she could have skated on it.

'No. No, I don't. Thanks ...'

Wolfgang continued, 'And what about your dealings with the erstwhile oligarch Sokolov? I guess that they've left some lasting impressions on you?'

What? *What?!*

That was too much. How did he know about her dealings with the Russian oligarch-in-chief? She was working for SIS at the time. Everything she did was classified. Nothing made the news, not even her part in preventing the dirty bomb from exploding in Rome.

She didn't say anything. She looked across at Inge, who had sensed the uncomfortableness of the conversation and was fiddling with her napkin.

Sam looked back at Wolfgang. His expression was gentle, kind. But he was clearly expecting an answer.

She spoke softly.

'How do you know about Sokolov, Wolfgang?'

He reached behind him and took hold of his walking stick. He pushed his chair back as he stood.

'Come with me Sam Green. I've got something to show you.' He turned to Inge and touched her arm gently. 'Would you give Sam and me some time? And maybe ask Elisabeth to bring some coffee to the cellar?'

Inge beamed a smile at Wolfgang, placing her hand on top of his.

'Of course. Of course.'

Wolfgang led Sam through a maze of corridors until they reached a metal door. He took out a key from a pocket in his cords and opened it. A light went on, illuminating a small room, no bigger than a hotel lift. There was another metal door in front of them.

'Please come in, Sam, and close the door.'

Sam was in a trance. She trusted Wolfgang. But, even so, this was all well off the weird scale.

And Sokolov? What had Wolfgang been up to? She couldn't shake that thought.

She pulled the door to. Wolfgang took out a second key and opened the new door. Immediately Sam sensed a change of pressure, as though they were leaving an airlock. The new air smelt fresh - and it was cooler.

Wolfgang led them down a set of concrete steps. The walls were clinically white. Everywhere was clean. Fifteen steps later she knew why.

The space at the bottom of the stairs was about the size of a large conference room. There were no windows. On one of the long sides of room were banks and banks of, what Sam assumed were, computers, hard-drives and other technical equipment. The end wall held six large computer screens. One was showing a muted CNN, the other five were awash with charts and information that Sam couldn't make out.

The second, long wall to her left was what interested her most.

Top to tail it was a transparent display board. It must have been five metres long and two high; it filled the whole wall. Cleverly, the board displayed computer-generated photographs and information, although how the images were projected onto or from behind the wall was a mystery to her.

Wolfgang was watching her intently.

'It's non-opaque liquid crystal. Embedded in glass. If you look very closely you can see the individual cells and the micron-thick wires that turn them on, change their colour and turn them off. It's fun, isn't it?'

But Sam wasn't listening. She'd got past the sexy *Minority Report* screen and how clever it was. She was much more interested in what it was displaying. She'd made it to the centre of the room. She faced the LCD-painted wall, her mouth slightly ajar.

Top-middle of the massive display board was the crest of The Church of the White Cross: a black background with a white crucifix that appeared to be being strangled by white thorns. The next level down, in a horizontal line, were the flags of eleven countries: the US, the UK, Germany, Spain, Italy, Croatia, Russia, Sweden, Venezuela, Mexico and Austria. Under these flags appeared to be spaces for five portrait photos - mug shots. Two, above two, above one. Only about a third of the spaces were filled with a photo. Under each photo there was space for a name. About half were filled. A couple of the spaces had names, but no image.

Sam scanned it all quickly. She stopped, hovering on a face she recognised, holding her breath. She flicked her eyes from that photo and scanned until she recognised another. And then three more.

This is madness.

Underneath the country mugshots, along the bottom of the display board was a space for other photos. There were six faces, but there was space for more. She immediately recognised two of them. One in particular jolted her as if she had stepped on a landmine. She held her breath.

What the ...

Sam was silent. But at least now she was breathing. Shallowly. Wolfgang was also quiet. He was letting her grasp the enormity of what she was looking at. The sound of computer fans filled the room - a quiet, but ever-present hum. She scanned the images again. There were 37.

She had seen the images and the names. She remembered them. She could now pick out any of the faces in a police line-up. That's the way it worked.

'What is this, Wolfgang?' Her hands spread apart, encompassing the whole board.

He stepped forward so that he was a few inches from the screen. He touched one of the images with a finger and a mass of information appeared next to the mugshot. It looked like a Wikipedia entry.

He stared intently at the board, his face reflected in the glass.

'I haven't left the house in two and a half years. I spend nearly every moment of every day down here. I have built this ...', it was his turn to demonstrate everything in the room, '... with my bare hands. And this ...', he now pointed at the screen, '... is the sum of its labour.'

He removed his finger and the detail disappeared. He tenderly touched another. More detail appeared.

'OK, Wolfgang. I get that. But *what* is it?'

Sam knew what it was, but she wanted Wolfgang to explain it. It was his take on the hierarchy of The Church of the White Cross, the organisation the CIA had taken down just under three years ago in Abilene, Texas. The Church was an ultra-orthodox Christian sect that had orchestrated a number of anti-Islamic attacks across North America and Europe. Bizarrely, but cleverly, they had funded and supported Islamic terror plots so as to inflame Western sensitivity against Muslims. *Fuelling the fire* of a smouldering religious war.

As an SIS case officer in Moscow, she had access to nearly all of SIS's files. In her few spare moments, she had kept a check on The Church and what her pals in the UK - and their counterparts in the CIA - were doing about it. From what she could glean, the US had done a pretty good job of pulling the organisation apart, both in the States and with help from the likes of Europol, in Europe. As far as she knew, it was defunct. Toothless.

Wolfgang obviously didn't agree with that prognosis.

He turned to Sam, his face now etched with passion.

'This is them, Sam. It's the bastards who killed my mother and almost killed us. Unlike her, they remain a living being. A functioning organisation. They have tentacles all over the world, they continue to promote and enact their own form of terrorism and, who knows what they are planning next? They almost killed the German chancellor. You prevented that! What will these people do next?'

Sam didn't say anything. She went up to a mugshot she recognised. It was under the Russian flag. She gently put her finger on the man who had dominated her life twelve months ago. A drop-down list appeared.

The title was: Nikolay Sokolov. She would never forget his face. She blinked at the blurb and recognised every word. At the bottom, in red letters, were the words: DECEASED.

Sokolov? The Church of the White Cross?
No?

She moved to a second photo. It was at the bottom of the screen, and not associated with a country. The face was that of the black man, Ralph Bell. The face that pervaded her consciousness, night and day. He was ex-CIA and involved with both the Ebola terror incident and the British Special Reconnaissance Regiment abductions and murders. Their paths had crossed too many times for comfort. He was a monster of the first order. She was sure that Wolfgang harboured the same feelings. She touched his face - information appeared. Some of it she recognised. Other stuff was new. She memorised it.

The third, also at the bottom, was the biggest surprise to her. The photo was of Paul Mitchell. He was the founder of the hugely successful electronic currency: *e-dollar*, a rival to *Bitcoin*. He was assumed dead. He had been kidnapped from his yacht by Somali pirates in 2013 - and then murdered. She touched his face. She scanned the words and remembered them - there was no DECEASED on the bottom of the factsheet. That was correct. She knew he was alive.

Because his were the eyes she'd seen in Alpbach this morning.

She touched the two final photos of the faces she recognised, and read the blurbs. A very senior UK politician. An Italian monsignor, very high up in the Vatican. The rest would have to wait.

'Sokolov was a member of The Church?'

Wolfgang nodded.

'And, are you sure about Mitchell?'

'Yes.' He said quietly, his chin resting on his hand. 'I believe he's the equivalent of me - does The Church's programming and hacking.'

'And you've got all of this ...', she pointed at the screen, '... from all of this.' She pointed at the computers.

He nodded.

'How confident are you? I mean, the UK politician? Really?'

Wolfgang moved quickly over to one of the consoles under the four screens on the side wall. He made a few keystrokes on a pad and the whole large screen changed. All the country flags were gone, as were all the mugshots. In their place were about 100 new photos of, nearly all, men. They weren't all head shots. Some were fuzzy pictures, taken from a distance. Some looked to be glossy shots from a magazine. Some might have been captured from a news clip.

'These are the ones I'm not sure about.' He was excited now. 'Each country - and currently I only have eleven confirmed, but there could be more - has five major players. One in politics. One in the military. One is a policeman. One's a spy. And one's in religion. It's cellular. Each one of these may control many more within their organisations - hence this set of photos.' He was pointing at the board. 'I am pretty confident The Church works on controlling or influencing a country using the five strands.' He held up a hand: four fingers and a thumb. He moved each as he spoke. 'Politics, military, police, intelligence and church. Five - nearly exclusively - men. High up in those organisations in each country. If you own those, you have control and reach.'

Sam couldn't compute the photos in front of her. There were too many. So, she didn't try. Her mind was reeling with the enormity of it all. That Sokolov was a member of The Church. *Did that really make sense?* That the man she'd crossed this morning would pop up on an e-display in a Munich cellar this evening. It was too bizarre for words.

But ...

Was this just fanaticism? Had Wolfgang suffered too much? Was he clutching at straws? Seeing things that weren't actually there? None of SIS's weekly bulletins had mentioned The Church of the White Cross. And, if he had this, surely SIS would have it too?

'Did you get this from any country's intelligence services? How did you know what I was up to? How did you find out about Sokolov? Have you been spying on me?'

So many questions.

Wolfgang deflected. 'I am a hacker; a programmer. Albeit a passive one. You know me Sam, you know what I can do? I have some access to the BND, the German Secret Service, network. And, yes, I have been able to look at some of the stuff the SIS in Vauxhall have been up to.'

Sam was about to say something, but Wolfgang was on a roll.

'I think I know more than anyone. Your ex-people may have some more depth here and there, but I'm guessing that nobody is looking at The

Church of the White Cross as I am; worldwide. It's alive Sam. And working in at least eleven countries that I'm aware of.'

He'd moved to the centre of the main screen and faced her. He took her hand in his. They were a few inches apart. Sam looked into his eyes. Behind the tiredness and the worn expression, she could see a fire burning brightly.

'Why were you going to phone me?'

He smiled a half-smile.

'Because ... because, I need your help. There's only so much I can do here, in this cellar. I need someone on the ground. Someone out there.' He shot a glance skyward. 'And you're very good at that.'

Sam looked back at the screen. Glanced at Sokolov, then Mitchell and finally to Bell.

'I've seen this and read some of the detail, Wolfgang. You know I won't forget any of it. As a result, I'm going to have to share this with my old friends. You understand that?'

Wolfgang contorted his face and then let out a sigh. He rocked his head from side-to-side.

'I know. I know. But, please, please, do not mention where you have got this from. I am safe here. I feel safe. The techniques I use are so technically arcane, no one can find me. And Inge. I love her Sam. I couldn't bear to lose her. You understand that.' He released Sam's hand.

A bell rang.

'That'll be Elisabeth.' His tone had changed. It was lighter - frivolous. He started hobbling off toward the stairs.

'I'll go, Wolfgang.' Sam's voice followed him.

Still walking, he turned his head.

'You can't. You won't be able to get out.' He had the keys out of his pocket and jangled them.

She let him go, turned back to the board for a second and then wandered around the room. Whilst touching the computer towers she looked back at the screen. She took none of it in - her brain was still in a tizz.

Wolfgang was a genius behind the keyboard. Her SIS colleagues had been in awe of his abilities. But he was also broken. Maybe irrecoverably. Someone upstairs had played him; messed badly with his life. And she knew what that could do to a person. She had been there; lost loved ones. Faced death; sometimes longed for it. She had muddled through by throwing caution out of the window and then slamming it shut. And, so far, she had only just survived.

But he was significantly brighter than she was, and who knows how major trauma might affect such a brilliant mind.

Was this all the work of an unhinged person? Was he desperate to find things that weren't actually there?

Sam wasn't sure. But, the events of today were in his favour. She'd recognised Paul Mitchell this morning. She was convinced of it. A man presumed dead. *A man who didn't want to be found?* And, minutes later, someone seemed intent on doing her harm. Now, she was staring at his photograph under the banner of an organisation she knew were ruthless beyond compare. It was as good an explanation of her rubbish day as any other she could think of.

Maybe he was right?

He came back down the stairs balancing a cafetière of coffee and two porcelain mugs. All on a silver salver.

'OK, Wolfgang. What now?'

Chapter 3

Creech US Air Force Base, Las Vegas

Rick glanced up from his secure laptop and stared absently out of the window. Clear blue skies. It must be close to 70 degrees outside. And it was only January. That was fine for everyone else, but for him the gloss of a Las Vegas posting had very quickly proven to be veneer-thick. The draw of the sunshine and The Strip had lost its magnetism. He had no appetite for a trip into town. None at all. More important, he had no time. He needed to fathom out what went wrong with his Reaper the night before last.

He stood and stretched, checking his watch as he did. It was 6.23 pm. He'd been at this, in his mess room, all day and most of last night. Poring over the computer logs from his Reaper's mission. Looking time and again at the sync between the GPS signal and the on-board gyroscopic nav system. He wasn't getting anywhere. Whichever way he looked at it, the data told the same unfathomable story.

He walked over to the small kitchen: a half-refrigerator, a single electric stove and a sink. He put the kettle on. He needed more coffee. Although, as his stomach reminded him, he should probably eat something. He would. Soon. He'd spend another hour looking at everything he had. Then he'd leave his room, go to the canteen and get something to fill his stomach.

It had been a torrid 48 hours. The colonel had called him and Lance in at 8.30 yesterday morning. The major was there, as was the man in the suit. He standing at the back as before. The boss sat 'all official', behind his desk.

The colonel had started by saying they'd had a complaint from the Colombian government about an airframe incursion into their territory the previous evening. The details the colonel gave were surprisingly accurate considering the Reaper is just a drone and has a minimal radar signature.

'What went wrong, Master Sergeant Rodgers?' The colonel's tone was sharp; uncompromising. He added, 'This'd better be good.'

Rick explained what had happened. It was a mirror of what he had published in his post-flight report. The colonel already had it warts 'n all. The drone had jumped mid-mission, veered off one course onto another; almost as if a new GPS signal had come on line. Rick had taken control within, maybe, ten seconds. But as they were so close to the border it had been impossible to alter the course quickly enough to prevent an incursion. Reapers weren't F16s; they don't turn on a pin. It takes time to spin them around.

The colonel listened impassively. His face displaying annoyance.

When Rick finished, the colonel waited. He'd picked up a pen and was jabbing the nib onto a pad. He was staring at Rick, who was sure he saw the colonel's nostrils billowing.

'Well, we're doing our best to sort this out at governmental level. What is uncomfortable for us is whether or not this leaks to the Venezuelans. I assumed you guessed that what we were doing was without their consent?

The colonel didn't have a chance to hang a question mark on the end of his sentence. The response from behind Rick was sharp.

'That's enough Colonel McIntyre. I don't think these men need to know any more.'

Rick turned and caught the expression on the suit's face. It was daggers. The colonel had just crossed a line of his own.

You and I both, boss.

The colonel coughed. And then went on the attack.

'Rodgers - you're grounded.'

What?

'I need you to look over your Reaper's readouts and establish what happened last night. However, you are to do this on your own. Under no circumstances are you to engage with any other member of the base. This mission remains top-secret - only the five of us.' The colonel used a finger to quickly point around the room. 'Because of that, I have removed all of your security permissions, except those pertaining to your bird and its peripherals.'

With that bombshell he stood up, walked round his desk and placed an arm on Rick's shoulder.

Bad cop had just turned not so bad cop.

'You're a good pilot Rick. And we need good pilots. This may have been an avionics anomaly - and there is nothing in your report that isn't corroborated in Captain Travis's.' He nodded to Lance who was standing to attention beside Rick. 'But, in the end you were the pilot. It was your mission. You have to sort this out.'

He removed his hand from Rick's shoulder and walked back round the desk.

'You have three days. If you can't establish a viable rationale for what went wrong in that time, then we're going to have to rethink the whole mission strategy.' He paused. Rick realised soon enough that it was for effect. 'And then we'll have to reconsider your position as a pilot here with the 432nd. So, find out what happened. And, can I remind you that you are on your own - we cannot afford to widen this investigation to include any other members of the base. Is that understood?'

At that point Rick wanted to ask, 'And, if I can't work out why my Reaper decided to have a fit, then where will you send me?' But decided against it.

'Yessir.'

The colonel pointed to Lance.

'Captain Travis, you're assigned back to al-Udeid. Report to the ops room once this meeting is over. They are expecting you. Not a word about this mission. Understood?'

'Yessir!'

Rick got the impression that Lance was very pleased with the last order.

'That's all, gentlemen.'

The meeting was over.

Since then Rick had revisited the avionics data what seemed like a thousand times. And he was always presented with the same result. At 23.37.20 local the GPS positional data jumped. At one moment it read 4°51'20.1" north and 67°46'40.8" west. The next: 4°53'42.9"; 67°52'26.9".

He remembered checking synchronisation about 20 minutes before the jump. At that point the on-board gyroscopes matched the original GPS signal to within a few seconds - maybe 40 feet. Then, without warning, they were 13 miles out of sync. It was that significant.

At 23.37.21 the autopilot dramatically changed the course of the Reaper. In its mind it had about 13 miles to make up, and it wasn't hanging about to cover that distance. Before Rick knew it, they were in Colombia. That is, if you believed the UAV's gyroscopes. If, on the other hand, you believed the GPS, they had remained in Venezuela throughout. It was doing his head in.

He couldn't reconcile the diversion. No matter which way he looked at it. He was screwed.

At the time of the incident Rick decided not to believe either of the readings and made a gross error correction. He brought the Reaper well within Venezuelan airspace, took her up to 42,000 feet, the UAV's maximum altitude, turned her about and put her on a trajectory for home.

He was then faced with a bigger problem. Landing with a conflicting navigational system.

First up he had to find Creech. Which of his navigational aids should he trust? GPS or gyroscopes? Ideally neither. If he were in a single-seat Cessna, he'd fly 'old-school': pick up a known landmark and use bearing and speed to get the bird home. But there were very few, if any, landmarks on the preferred route back to Creech. And it was dark. Their flight plan was designed to be as incognito as possible. It avoided all major hubs. And with thickening cloud cover over the southern US east of The Rockies, picking out decent known points was going to be tricky, even if he aimed for them.

Within a couple of minutes the Reaper's GPS receiver answered the question for him. As the drone hit the Venezuelan coast, it jumped again.

This time correcting its original movement. Rick checked both readings. The GPS and gyroscopic displays were within a tenth of a second of each other.

How does that happen?

He and Lance had a brief conversation about it. Lance had been scouring all of the base's navigational literature for possible beacons. He was looking for anything that could help them get the Reaper safely back to Creech. The latest jump confused the hell out of him too.

At least now, Rick had two navigational aids whose readings were on the same map.

'I'm going to run with GPS. When we get her home we'll carry out a fly-past of Runway II first off. And if that all looks good, I'll bring her round to land.'

And that's what he'd done. The GPS signal was definitely back. Accurate to within 2 metres. Good enough to land a Boeing 777 at Bullhead International in thick fog.

So why the jump?

Why?

He needed to find out. Soon.

Rick put some creamer in his coffee. Brought the mug to his nose and smelt it.

I need this ...

He had tonight, tomorrow and all of the next night to solve this. If he didn't, then he guessed he'd be back at the 737th in Lackland, training recruits.

He sat back behind his desk. Took a sip of his coffee. Scratched his chin.

What now?

What he hadn't done was look over any of the imagery. That was Lance's arena. At Pueblo the trainee pilots spent just a couple of weeks having a poke around the sensor suite on the Reaper, whilst having the technology explained to them in the classroom. They then had a further two weeks studying the output. It was cursory. Enough to understand the Sensor Operator's role, but not much more.

It was complex stuff, and Rick wasn't sure he understood all of it. Reapers were fitted with Raytheon's MTS-B sensor suite. This included an infrared (IR) camera, colour daytime TV, and an image intensifier (II) for very low-light operations. The most expensive bit of kit was a multi-mode radar, which produced high-resolution photo-quality images in all weather. It did two things extremely well. First, the two-strip synthetic aperture radar (SAR) used clever algorithms to detect man-made objects. Second, the moving target indicator (MTI) radar could pick out a non-stationary human at anything from as slow as one mile-an-hour. A trundling tank, for which it had been originally designed to find, was a turkey shoot for Raytheon's MTI.

Feeling that he was wasting his time, but with little else to occupy himself, Rick opened the imagery file. He discounted the more pedestrian sensor equipment: the IR and II cameras, and the daytime TV. Instead, he went straight for one of the big-boys and clicked on the 'SAR' file. After a couple of minutes he had the time-appropriate SAR imaging on his laptop - that taken either side of the jump. The resolution was fabulous; sort of sideward looking and monochrome, giving the images a 3-D effect. But his screen was too small, and it wasn't touch-sensitive. Zooming in and out had to be done using his mouse. It was tiresome.

He looked at his watch. It was 7.46 pm.

Is this a waste of time?

He'd give it an hour - as planned. Then he'd have some food. Then he'd go back to the navigational outputs again and see if he had missed anything.

Rick's stomach shouted at him, telling him to check his watch. It was 10.37 pm. He was still studying the imagery, and he still hadn't eaten. And there was a good reason for that.

He'd now had a good look over all of the imagery. The TV pictures were hopeless; they had shown what he, the pilot, had been looking at - lots of night-time jungle. The II, which amplifies ambient light and delivers imagery in shades of green, was a sea of dark green. There was a partial moon during the flight which had given very little light for the II to work with; the canopy reflected nothing of consequence. The IR was also fruitless. The jungle's temperature differentials were small. The imagery was a sea of dark orange.

The SAR imagery was equally as dull. The stills afforded much more resolution of the ground beneath the canopy, but the results were uncluttered and uninteresting.

On his first look-see, the moving MTI imagery taken either side of the jump displayed no movement. There was nothing in the radar's field of vision. Rick had half-expected to pick up something below, or in a gap in the jungle's canopy. The place must have been alive with all manner of creatures moving about. But the video showed zip.

He had taken a second look and was about to give up when he spotted something: a fleeting image in the top-left corner of screen - within the blurring of the radar's maximum range. A small rectangular object moving at about three miles-an-hour. Difficult to see; easy to miss. Then, as the drone flew on, it was gone. It was in shot for about a second, maybe two.

As far as he knew God had yet to make anything rectangular. What he had seen, or thought he had seen, was man-made.

He took a screenshot of the image, noted the date/time stamp and went back to the navigational data. He needed to check that the object was in

Venezuela. *Was it before the jump?* After a couple of minutes he had an answer: it was. It didn't matter whether he believed the GPS (which he didn't), or the gyroscopes. They both gave the same answer: the slow-moving rectangle was in Venezuela on the original flight path.

That would definitely make it 'new activity', a big tick against the mission's objectives. The boss needed to know this.

He went back to the MTI shots.

The problem Rick had was that he wasn't an image analyst. As a result, it was tricky to work out what the object might be. As it was at the edge of the radar's range, it would be distorted - by how much he didn't know. Somehow, he needed to take account of that. He couldn't establish its size nor, from what he could see, make a reasoned judgement as to what it might be.

So, he took a guess.

His untrained eye said: *truck*.

His stomach churned. He had to eat something before his belly took out a chunk of its own lining.

First, one more look at the static, SAR imaging.

Rick reopened the appropriate folder and scrolled the images forward until he had a set of photos two seconds either side of the MTI's shot of the truck.

He played with the pictures, zooming in and zooming out.

Nothing.

Hang on ...

There it was - top right. Was it?

No ... Yes ... No ...

There was definitely something box-like among the trees, the SAR making its best attempt to look beneath the canopy. But at this range it was very fuzzy. It could be the truck?

Rick moved the image so its top-right was centre screen. He enlarged what was in front of him. It pixelated.

He stared at it.

That's odd.

He was too close. He was seeing too many pixels. He needed to make sense of the blur. He stood up and walked away from the screen.

Rick stared back at the laptop from a couple of metres - at the SAR image taken at the same time the MTI had spotted a truck.

There it was. Well, there *something* was.

There was a box (could be the truck?). And ... his mind paused. He squinted his eyes, desperately trying to find some focus.

Ahead of it is a building?

Maybe two buildings? A truck and two buildings.

Wait ...

On top of one of the buildings was an oval shape - more accurately, one side of an oval shape. Like half an egg; side on.

Rick titled his head to one side. And then the other.

Untrained eye.

His *very* untrained eye was looking at a truck heading towards two buildings. And on top of one of the buildings was a big satellite dish.

He rushed to sit down. He screen-captured what he had, then he minimised the sensor tabs he had opened and maximised the navigational ones. He reached for a pad and a pencil and made a few calculations.

Shit.

He was in a rush. He needed to check the Reaper's flight path using the computer's navigational planning tool. And he needed to do that right now.

If his broad-order calculations were right, what he'd almost missed from the imagery would have been directly under their original flight path on the next pass. If the autopilot hadn't veered them off into another country, Lance would have had a ringside seat at what was, as far as Rick was now concerned, the greatest show on earth. Certainly the greatest show in Venezuela seen from a drone.

But they didn't get a chance to overfly what his untrained eye had assumed was a truck, two buildings and a big satellite dish

Because someone had messed with their GPS. Someone, who didn't want them to fly over their, whatever it was - with its two buildings and a satellite dish, had messed with their GPS.

How does that happen?

Samostan Monastery, Punat Bay, Krk, Croatia

Jakov felt himself coming to. Before he opened his eyes he sensed an ache in his right arm - all over. But his brain was full of cotton wool. He couldn't hold his consciousness and drifted back to sleep.

He woke again. This time his eyes opened and the light - all bright white and shiny silver - was too much for his mind to cope with. He shut his eyes, tried to banish the fog and focused on what might be happening to him.

What's going on? Where am I?

It came back to him in a shot: he'd caught a crab; arms hurt like nothing else; out of the boat; swam to shore; freezing cold; climbed the wall ... got chased down by an attack dog!

What?!

That made him open his eyes. And he forced them to stay open. The bright white and the silver coalesced into recognisable shapes. Walls and cupboards. Bed posts and technical machines. He was in what he assumed was a hospital ward. Or a single room in a hospital.

Relief.

Jakov was lying on his back, surrounded by medical instruments. He had two drips in his left forearm and there were bandages up his right. The room was clinical - no windows, but it had a door with some glass in it. Everything was immaculate and, surprising for his country, it all looked new and ordered.

And there was someone else in the room with him.

The 'someone else' was a man. He was sitting on a tall stool by the door. Clean jeans, a light-blue open-necked collared shirt. Fair-skinned, but dark hair, cut short. Late-30s. He didn't look like a doctor - more like an IT professional, straight from Google. He was sipping a drink from a Styrofoam cup.

'Hi ...' Jakov tried to raise his left hand to accompany his salutation, but realised that it was tied to the bed. With leather straps.

'What the fuck?' The expletive left his lips before he had time to check himself. He stared at the man, and then at his restraints. He tried to move again but the leather straps and a shot of pain, which overrode the dull ache, put paid to that.

'What's going on? Where am I?' Any relief he might have felt a couple of seconds ago was now gone. It had been replaced by fear.

The man stood, placed the cup on a surface - it immediately looked incongruous against the shiny, silver medical equipment, and walked to Jakov's bedside. He stood still and then smiled. It was the smile of a man in charge. Confident and calm.

The man spoke; slowly - in English. Each word pronounced very clearly. As he spoke he used a finger to trace Jakov's body. From his knee to his forehead.

'What - are - we - going - to - do - with - you - Jakov - Vuković?' The man tapped Jakov's forehead in time to his name.

Jakov felt the question was rhetorical, but it was definitely for his benefit. He was struggling to compute everything that had and was happening to him. The man spoke in English - authoritatively. Jakov spoke good English. It was his foreign language of choice at school, and international rowing events were all conducted in English. He had to be good. He had improved his schoolboy English by continuing his language studies at Zagreb University. He was pretty fluent.

But, how did the IT consultant know that? How did he know that he would understand every word?

And, where was he? Why was he strapped onto the bed? What was happening? *And how did the man know my name?* So many frustrating questions.

There was an impasse. Jakov didn't reply, and the man just stood there - his expression turning from impassive calmness to one of concern. He tilted his head to one side. His look of concern deepened and he pulled up one side of his mouth.

Jakov decided to speak.

'Where am I? How come you know my name?'

The man now had a bored look on his face.

How many emotions has the IT consultant got left?

The man looked at the machines that Jakov was plugged into. He placed a hand gently on the metal box which Jakov assumed was reading his pulse. It displayed a big '58'. The man then raised his hand and touched the drips. Almost caressing them.

He spoke, the same slow, well-enunciated tone; complete control.

'I'm not a doctor, you understand. But I do know what these things do.' He was looking at Jakov now, whilst resting a finger on the larger of the two bags of fluid that hung close to Jakov's bed.

'This one is saline, to rehydrate you. Which seems odd to me as you didn't lose a lot of blood, and you spent most of the time in the water. But, as I said, I am not a doctor. They know best.' He then took a finger and pointed to the smaller drip. 'This. Now, this is much more interesting.' The man was smiling now. There was something odd about the smile. Sardonic? Was the man playing with him?

'This contains morphine. It's the drug that has been keeping you calm and pain free for about ...', he put a finger to his lips as if in thought, '... let me see. That's it: about four hours.' He eyes shot across to the red butterfly clip at the bottom of the drip. 'If I turn this lever here ...', he paused, '... I can increase the morphine levels. If I open it fully, you'd be out cold in a couple of minutes.' And then he added whimsically. 'Dead in ten.'

Jakov was speechless. His mouth opened to say something, but nothing came out. He was scared. More scared than he had ever been in his life. He'd been launched from his scull, smashing his shoulder to bits. He'd then been mauled by an attack dog. Now, this man, with the flick of a switch, could end his life. All of this coming from an early-morning training session.

'Please don't.' Jakov found some words. Pleading ones. He hated them as soon as they left his lips.

The man pulled his hand away from the switch, as if it were red hot. 'Oops! Mustn't touch that!' He smiled again. Jakov thought it was the smile of a deranged man.

'Now, we do need to work out what to do with you.' The man walked back to his stool picking up his coffee cup as he did. He sat down, his shoulders relaxing. He seemed bored again, staring around the room. All of a sudden Jakov felt less threatened.

'Let's sort something out, Jakov. Are you listening?'

Jakov nodded. He had no idea where this was going.

'If we decide to keep you, the authorities will find a body in a week or so's time - easily mistakable as yours. It'll be a hobo - we'll find one from somewhere. Anyway, the body will be unrecognisable. The damage of salt water can be perishing. We will bribe the mortician to say the dental records are yours. There will be a funeral, and you will be remembered for being the only son of Mr and Mrs Vuković, Punat's most successful rower. Fluent in English with a first in economics. One of Croatia's brightest and best ... who died tragically whilst training in the bay.' He emphasised 'tragically' by putting on a sad face. 'There will be some tears and a brief period of mourning. But, soon enough, everybody will move on. Blah-di-blah.'

The man was using his hands to help tell the story. And he was enjoying himself. Jakov, on the other hand, wasn't enjoying it at all.

If we decide to keep you? There is another option?

'If, on the other hand, you become problematic. Or we quickly realise that you are of no further use – although I grant you that a first in economics has its draw - they will find the real body of Jakov Vuković.' He pointed at Jakov accusingly. 'Yours. The one you're wearing now.' He put one hand round his neck, and the other above his head, signifying a noose - his eyes out on stalks. He swung his shoulder as if he were hanging.

'It's - mostly - up - to - you.' The words staccato as if the man were trying to communicate whilst dangling from the rafters, his legs free to float about.

The man dropped his hands and smiled again. He then stood quickly.

'I'm going to leave you now. For a while. When I'm gone I want you to think over our little chat. And when I come back, we're going to have another discussion. And you're going to help me make the decision. Do I play with the red switch? Or don't I?'

With that the man put a hand on a metal pad by the door; it opened automatically. Once he'd left, the door shut of its own accord - clinically, as if with an airtight seal. At that point Jakov realised that there was no handle.

Headquarters SIS, Vauxhall, London

Jane Baker reached for some files that were on the corner of her desk. She then picked up her iPad and, struggling to manage everything she was already carrying, she reached for a notepad and a pen. She was heading off to a cabal with her team. The meeting was titled: 'Qatar - next steps?'

Qatar, currently under the cosh of a number of Arab states but still doing plenty of business with the US military and some trade with the Brits, was a conundrum for SIS. In Doha, the country's capital, Jane oversaw a small team: two case officers and a couple of admin staff. They worked out of the basement of the British Embassy. Their reach was good but, with the current fragility of world politics, they probably needed to widen their intelligence network in this strategically-placed Gulf state.

The indigenous Qataris, just one eighth of the total population of their small but immensely rich sovereign state (the rest were expats), had a pragmatic and business-like approach with most countries. The problem was, they also had the same pragmatic and business-like approach with a number of terrorist organisations and terrorist-sponsoring regimes. Having the third largest natural gas reserves in the world, and run by an efficient if authoritarian monarchy, they played politics with everyone. The US was top of the list -

money buying the Qataris a lot of space and, most of the time, a good number of friends. Their current relationship with the US was complex. On one hand, the US was pushing its Arab allies to sanction Qatar so that it played less politics with, say, Iran and Hamas. On the other, US's largest military operating-base in the Gulf, al-Udeid air base, was on Qatari real estate. And the US had just sold $21 billion's worth of military equipment to the Qataris, including $12 billion of F-15 fighter jets. Jane wasn't sure if the Americans saw the conflict of interests.

It was this sort of unfathomable *realpolitik* that meant Jane felt uncomfortable with the level of SIS presence in Qatar. With the organisation's numbers now heading north to 3,000, the chief, C, had agreed that they should look at posting a further case officer to the Embassy. Last night, after a short meeting, they had both agreed that any detailed analysis work would remain here at Babylon - using the 11-man team she had on the floor. But, for intelligence gathering and running of agents, you couldn't beat a competent case officer in country.

Boots on the ground, as her army pals would say.

As she stood to leave for the meeting, she caught a glimpse of herself in the three-quarter length mirror that hung on the wall beside her desk. She sighed. She was getting older. No doubt about that. She kept herself in good shape, using the basement gym three or four times a week, and she was big into yoga. But long days and short weekends had taken their toll. She put the files, the iPad and her notebook down, and stared straight at the reflection of Jane Baker: 42; unmarried; no long-term boyfriend; five feet eight in her tights; dressed like she was heading off to the country for the weekend - brown wool skirt, a cream blouse and a green woollen cardy. She used a single finger to place a strand of stray, curly blonde hair behind her right ear. She tilted her head to one side and then straightened it again.

Mmm. I'm looking a bit saggy.

Using her two index fingers she placed them on their respective cheeks and raised the skin towards her ears. *That's better*. The laughter lines had gone. That simple movement had taken years off her.

Jane dropped her fingers and smiled at the ridiculousness of it all. Here she was, two promotions from the top job and she was thinking about what she looked like? As if anyone she dealt with was interested. They wanted her because she had the organisational aptitude of a barrel-load of monkeys. And she had some decent leadership skills. She had been a case officer, serving in China and Iraq, had run a couple of teams here at Vauxhall, and was now responsible for the whole of the Middle East and north Africa: 87 case officers and 50 other assorted staff, based in 17 embassies and high commissions. She also directed a further 11 dedicated analysts and intelligence officers here at Babylon. And, not forgetting, she had a call on the pool of 'ready-to-move' case officers and analysts who were stood by when needed.

And she mustn't forget Claire. Her fabulous PA.

Who had just walked in.

'Frank wants to come and see you at five. He's been looking over some of the traffic concerning the latest collision between the US frigate and the Greek container ship in Manila Bay. He reckons he might have something that no one else has picked up.'

Jane, feeling a little conspicuous that Claire might have caught her demonstrating her own facelift, nodded.

'That's fine, Claire, thanks.'

'Shall I bring you a coffee to the meeting?'

Jane stopped herself from picking up the files. She smiled at Claire.

'That would be great Claire, thanks.'

As she walked out, Claire turned her head to one side. 'Remember you have the Joint Intelligence Committee (JIC) at 8.30 tomorrow morning - over the river. Keep Frank's meeting short and then go home and get some rest.'

It was an order. And Claire didn't wait for an answer. A second later she was gone.

Jane reached for her iPad just as her mobile pinged.

She picked it up and looked at the screen. It was an SMS from Sam Green. A little shiver shot down her spine. She'd not spoken to Sam for over six months; not since Sam had agreed to take the redundancy package from SIS.

Jane checked her watch. She was close to being late. They'd have to wait. She opened the text. It read:

> *Jane. Call me on +49 7795 314423. Thanks. Sam. xxx*

The +49 was a German mobile; not Sam's usual one she had just used to SMS Jane. *Where was she?* What was she up to? Why go for a change of number?

Jane highlighted the new number, the action throwing up a screen asking if she wanted it dialled. She accepted the instruction.

The phone rang with a long, single, repeating dial tone. A German phone. Operating in Germany,

'Hello. Jane?'

It was Sam. It was good to hear her voice. Really good.

She missed her. Missed her idiosyncratic ways. Missed the way she was blunt, to the point, but without meaning to be. Missed her analyst's mind. Not only did Sam have a photographic memory, but a touch of autism (they joked about that) seemed to bring everything she studied into sharp focus. Sam had a knack for picking out what others didn't. Her OCD (they joked about that as well) then ensured that Sam interrogated whatever she was looking at to an inch of its life. Her Army and SIS training had brought all those skills into a single package. Nobody in the building doubted that she was the best analyst SIS had ever employed.

And Jane missed Sam's integrity - her ability to always do the right thing, no matter what the consequences were to herself. Even if the right thing was sometimes, well, the wrong thing.

That was the problem. That's why they, SIS and Sam, had parted company. After Russia and Rome.

Shades of grey. Sam didn't have any. It made her an outstanding SIS case officer whilst, at the same time, presenting dilemmas and dangers to herself and to the organisation. Nuance wasn't Sam's middle name. If she had one, which she didn't, it would probably be 'blatant'.

'Hello, Sam. How are you?' Jane knew it was a superfluous question. Sam would ignore it.

'Fine. Look, I need to meet up with you. In a professional capacity, if that's OK? I'll be back in the UK tomorrow. Can you find me half an hour?'

The words came out in a splurge, with little punctuation. Jane missed that as well.

'Why did we need to swap phones, Sam?'

There was a pause.

'Because I'm being pursued, followed. I'm not sure what to call it. But I'm pretty certain my number will be compromised by now.' Sam was agitated. Jane could hear it in her voice.

'Tell me more, Sam.' Jane trusted Sam completely. But, before she took a sledgehammer to tomorrow's programme, she needed more. Something tangible.

There was silence.

Then. 'Do you remember the businessman who was taken hostage off a yacht in 2013 - east coast of Africa? Don't mention his name!'

What?

'No, sorry. Go on, Sam. Tell me his name. Give me something.'

'No!' The reply was rasping; exasperated. 'If they're using speech-recognition, they'll pick up this conversation. You must remember. 2013. June. A high-profile British businessman, taken from a yacht. Off East Africa.'

Sam was being clever; she always was. She was telling the story without using easily recognisable words like 'Somalia'. Or the man's name. A decent adversary with GCHQ-level equipment would have speech-recognition software available. Such systems could randomly search 10,000 mobile calls - simultaneously. The processing used algorithms that could pick out single-trigger words. Once detected, the machines locked onto the conversation and everything was recorded.

Sam continued, frustration ever present. 'You must know who I mean?'

Jane knew it would always be a surprise to Sam that not everyone had the capacity to remember everything they had ever seen - and access it at a moment's notice. In this case, though, Jane could picture Paul Mitchell's face. The founder of *e-dollar*. And now six feet under.

'Yes. Go on.'

There was another pause.

'He's not dead. I've seen him. In an Austrian resort. A couple of days ago.'

Jane tried to say something, but Sam was on a roll.

'They tried to take me out. After I recognised him. I saw a handgun. On the slopes. They were going to "deal with the problem". And I was that problem. I'm sure of it.'

Jane was going to disappoint Sam. Mitchell was dead. As a dead as ... a dead person.

'Sam.' Jane let her old friend's name hang, stopping Sam in her tracks. 'It's not possible. The man is dead. Definitely. Dead.'

Jane could sense the exasperation levels rising on the other end of the line.

'No, Jane. He's not. I saw him! And, and this is why I want to meet with you, I have seen other intelligence that paints a picture that he is alive and well.'

It was Jane's turn to be blunt.

'It's not possible Sam. I'm sorry. I know how good you are with faces, but it's four years later - and I know the man is dead.'

'How come?' The reply shot back across the ether.

Jane paused. She couldn't tell Sam that one of SIS's case officers had seen Paul Mitchell's body in Mogadishu. The estate had failed to pay the ransom. Neither they, nor the SAS, had been able to reach the man. About a week later, on a tip-off from a local informant, one of their men from the Embassy had been allowed to see the body before it had been burnt by the local militia. Paul Mitchell was dead. No matter what Sam Green said.

'I know Sam. I just know. It's safe to say that we have irrefutable proof that the man is dead.' She let that hang. 'Can you give me something else?'

There was silence. Jane could picture Sam. Incensed. Angry. Not getting her way.

'You're wrong Jane. I don't know what proof you have, but I know he's alive. I have seen him. And I believe he's involved with the organisation that you and I dealt with in Germany four years ago. Along with 36 others. I have seen their faces. Been given access to some of the intelligence. Don't ask me where I've got this information from, Jane. I can't divulge that. But I do want to share what I have with you. Face-to-face.'

The Church of the White Cross? Surely not?

Jane was semi-interested now. But only semi. They and the CIA had kept tracks on The Church of the White Cross. After the CIA and FBI had dismantled it, it had remained a defunct organisation. Although, and this was a concern, both the FBI and IRS had not been able to retrieve somewhere in the region of $2 billion from The Church's accounts; probably in The Bahamas.

'Give me another name, Sam.'

There was a pause.

'Min AF.'

The Minister of the Armed Forces?

'No, Sam. What, a Church member?'

'Yes, Jane. I believe so.'

'And you have this intelligence from where?'

'I can't tell you.'

Jane was losing it. She glanced up at the clock on the wall. She was ten-minutes late for her meeting. She was never late for a meeting. This bizarre conversation needed to end. Min AF was not a member of The Church of the White Cross. What Sam didn't know was that MI5 had a file on the man. And Jane had seen it. Recently. He was not whiter than white. But his issue was an over-reliance on alcohol; not a religious fanaticism that compelled him to bomb mosques and murder left-wing and centrist politicians.

No. Not Min AF.

'Look, Sam. I'm late for a meeting. Min AF shouldn't be on any list you may, or may not have seen. He shouldn't. Can I call you later? And maybe then we can arrange to meet, maybe the day after tomorrow?'

There was no reply from Sam Green. Just the constant hum of a line disconnected.

Frankfurt Tankstelle, A2 Autobahn, Germany

Sam hung up the phone. She'd had enough. Jane had trumped both her king of hearts and ace of diamonds. And she was furious. Mostly with herself.

What was she up to? More critically, what was Wolfgang up to? He was not himself. He was all mad-scientist like, spending days and days in a hermetically-sealed dungeon - wishing his life away. Chasing shadows. Seeing and believing what he wanted to see and hoped to believe.

Over the past 24 hours, she and Wolfgang had been through nearly all of the 'intelligence' that he had uncovered. Without detailed interrogation, it all seemed so plausible. It made sense. And yet, Wolfgang was just a singleton. A man working on his own, without the resources or the horsepower of SIS - or the CIA. And he wanted, no *needed*, to vent his anger on something. He had to have a cause.

And Jane had just proved that. Hadn't she? That Wolfgang was a loner, building a house of cards?

Jane was sure Paul Mitchell was dead. She had 'irrefutable proof' that that was the case. Sam translated this statement in her head. Someone must have seen the body. Someone Jane trusted. SAS or Special Reconnaissance Regiment? Or one of her team?

And Nicholas Stone? Min AF? He was a beacon on Wolfgang's wall, shining so brightly Sam couldn't miss him. Sam knew the man. She had met him in Helmand all those years ago. From her five-minute conversation with him as she explained how she developed the current IED threat, she hadn't taken to him. His breath had a lingering smell of peppermint. Which, ever the cynic, Sam had put down to 'one too many' the night before. Whilst everyone else in theatre was dry.

Jane had said 'Min AF shouldn't be on any list you may, or may not, have seen. He shouldn't.'

SIS staff were trained to be exact. To use one word, not two. To elaborate wasn't something spies and analysts did. They only stated what they knew. What they had seen. Not what they thought they had seen. If Jane said Min AF shouldn't be on the list, then that meant she'd seen his file. Something else was there. And, as very few people have two major flags on their file - and still get to remain in a key post, that something wasn't belonging to an ultra-orthodox Christian sect.

So, Wolfgang was wrong about Nicholas Stone? And she, Sam Green - was she wrong about Paul Mitchell? Were her analyst skills fading?

Sam stared at her phone. One of three Wolfgang had given her, along with five SIMs, so that she wasn't restricted to a single number. She put the phone down by the gearstick of the new Golf GTi he had lent her 'indefinitely'; one of seven cars in his Munich house's garage. Along with the car, she had reluctantly agreed to take one of his credit cards - she was brassic. She had agreed to do some digging for him. Some leg work. And he had insisted that he finance the operation. Money to him wasn't the object. He had bank-loads of it.

The object was to bring down The Church of the White Cross. Once and for all.

If it exists.

Sam stared out of the windscreen. Sleet lashed against the glass. Germany was miserable when it was like this. Dark. Grey. Forbidding.

She felt sick. Bewildered. Lost.

Friendless.

The closest person she could consider as a good pal was Jane. Her old boss. And just now, Jane had gone to a meeting rather than talk to her.

It was the story of her recent life. Short bursts of close companionship, followed by deserts of loneliness. A week of chaos, and then months of inactivity. And through all of this rubbish she didn't anyone with whom to share it. No shoulder to cry on. No ear to berate.

Sam was shocked, but not surprised, to feel wetness on her cheek. It was just tears of frustration. It was the fact that she'd made a fool out of herself, to someone she trusted. Would it be too strong to say to someone she loved, like a sister? Sam was an ex-military intelligence sergeant. She was an SIS-trained analyst and had passed SIS's case officer course - an 18-week test designed to graduate only the country's brightest and best. That's what they had told her.

Now she was darting across Europe, trying to put together a jigsaw the pieces of which probably weren't meant to link together. Working with a man who was likely a bunch of grapes short of a cheese board. She felt like an idiot.

What am I playing at?

A tear dropped onto her cotton slacks. It left a dark stain against the dreadfully beige material. She couldn't even get her fashion sense right. No wonder her lovers were always gone by the morning.

And yet ... and yet, she still believed in herself. She did. Resolutely so. Her mind didn't play tricks on her. It didn't. Her eyes saw things;

and they read things. Her brain stored them. Compartmentalised them for easy access. That's how it worked. And it hadn't been broken yet.

She had seen Paul Mitchell's eyes outside the Böglerhof yesterday. And, if she needed corroboration, Wolfgang had his mugshot plastered on his cellar wall. In both cases he was alive and well. What had been Wolfgang's corroboration? 'I have seen code on the Dark Web, which had been written by Mitchell - on a recently defunct website. It was no more than six months old, used fleetingly by The Church. Expert programmers are like old masters. They have an unmistakable coding style. I recognised Mitchell's style immediately.'

Could they both be wrong?

She wiped her tears away with the cuff of her fleece. The cogs had stopped whirring. She had calmed down. She was still feeling sorry for herself, but, you know, *sod them*. Being down had never stopped her before.

She turned the Golf over. Its 227 bhp engine (she'd read it somewhere) burst into life. Sam had already driven about 200 kilometres in the new car. And was loving it. Shame it was bright red. Hardly a car for the incognito.

She stuck the Golf in gear, pulled out of its parking space and sped off onto the autobahn.

Sam had a plan. Well - it was a next step.
Hardly a plan.

She'd catch the ferry. Hook of Holland to Harwich - not an obvious choice if you were looking for a bright red Golf GTi. She'd go and see Mrs Mitchell. Give her the good news. Tell her that her husband was alive. Alive and well. And skiing in the Austrian Alps

And then she'd see what the woman's reaction was.

Chapter 4

Samostan Monastery, Punat Bay, Krk, Croatia

Jakov was wide awake. He was sitting up with one of those full-width bed trays providing a shelf for a fulsome lunch that had been brought in by a monk. A monk. At least he knew he was still on the island; in the monastery. He tried to engage the monk, who was dressed traditionally in a brown wool habit, but got nothing back in return. Just a lunch of meat, cheese and bread - and a mug of decent coffee.

The monk freed Jakov's left arm to allow him to eat. He was hungry. He didn't know whether to scoff first or ask a belly-full of questions.

He tried to do both.

Between mouthfuls.

'Why am I being kept here against my will?'

Nothing. He chomped some food.

'My name is Jakov Vuković. Could you please let the authorities know where I am?'

Still nothing. He had a swig of coffee and changed tack.

'What's your name?'

The monk was sitting on the same stool the deranged man had sat on earlier that morning. He still didn't reply; he didn't even look Jakov in the eye.

Jakov tried six or seven other questions as he finished his lunch. There was no reply to any of them. Once the plate and mug were empty the monk re-strapped his arm, picked up the tray, and left.

That was about an hour ago. And now he needed to go to the toilet. Pretty badly.

'Hey! Anyone there?' Nothing. 'I need to go to the toilet!' He shouted.

Nothing.

He looked around him. On one side of the bed were the drips. On the other a metal rack with three machines, one of which displayed his pulse. The other two were all knobs and switches, and some other displays showing stuff he didn't comprehend.

Ahh!

On top of the rack, next to a box which dispensed surgical gloves, was a small, white plastic box with a red push-button on top.

But he couldn't reach it. His arms were strapped to the bed. He farcically attempted to reach the button with his nose, by stretching his torso and extending his neck. It wasn't going to happen.

Shit!

He was frustrated as hell; he felt tears rising.

There was movement at the door's window. It opened and a monk came in.

Are they telepathic?

The monk turned immediately right and stood by the door, holding it open. In walked the deranged man. In three strides he was next to the morphine drip; he reached for the red butterfly switch.

Jakov felt his bowels move.

'Wait! Stop!'

The deranged man paused. Theatrically - both hands no more than a centimetre from the drip. He looked down at Jakov. His face impassive.

'What? You have decided to be good and do as we wish?'

Jakov was both scared stiff and now very uncomfortable. He felt a wet warmth between his buttocks and the sheet. Soon there would be a smell.

'Yes, of course! What is it that you want?' High pitched and pleading. Not a great sound.

The deranged man visibly sniffed. He wafted one hand in front of his nose. He shook his head.

'Oh dear.' The deranged man moved away from the bed and stood by the monk. It was all play-acting. If Jakov wasn't tied to the bed and being threatened with his life - and if he hadn't just crapped himself - he would have loved to have leapt up and punched the man in the face.

'Look, Jakov Vuković, it's very simple. My friend here,' he gestured to the monk who was looking straight ahead - no expression, 'will sort this mess out,' he waved at the bed, 'and look after you whilst you are fixed. And then we will set you to work.'

The deranged man was nodding quickly, small darting movements, like it was a question.

Jakov nodded back.

'There will be rules and restrictions. And some pretty unpleasant consequences if you don't do exactly, and I mean *exactly*, what we say.' He nodded vigorously again. Jakov did the same.

The deranged man's face lightened.

'So, we have an agreement. Good!' He clapped his hands. 'I'm so pleased. Whilst I am a lover of the red switch, I *do* like it when we take on a new member of the team. Think of it as helping with Croatia's burgeoning unemployment.'

He looked at his watch.

'Now, if you don't mind, I have more important things to do. My friend here will attend to you.'

As he turned to leave, Jakov shouted after him, 'What do I call you?'

The deranged man stopped dead in his tracks, his back to Jakov. It was another theatrical move. He turned his head slowly, looking down over his shoulder. At that point Jakov noticed his thick, dark eyebrows. They defined his face and cast a shadow over his menacing eyes.

'You don't call me anything. You don't speak to me unless I ask you a question. And, my friend here,' he gestured to the monk, 'and his very nice pals, have sworn an oath of silence. So, you won't get much from them either.'

He strode out of the room shouting behind him, 'If I were you I'd get used to my own company ....' The words trailing as he walked away down whatever corridor he was in.

Headquarters SIS, Vauxhall, London

Jane gathered her things into a reasonably neat pile on the conference table in front of her. Her team were leaving - the only action fell to one of her senior staff: select the best case officer currently completing their Arabic language training and dispatch them to Qatar - asap. If that meant cutting their language course short, then so be it. They could find fluency on the job.

She'd asked Frank to stay behind. He loitered beside her as the remaining members of the team left the glass-walled room.

'You wanted to see me, Frank? Something about the USS Beaverbrook? It's hardly our area?'

She offered Frank a chair next to her. He sat.

Frank was her best analyst. He'd been in the team for eight years, at first alongside Sam and, when she left to become a case officer, he took the mantle of lead analyst. He was very good and thankfully lacked ambition to move on. Mid-height, scruffy dark hair, jeans and a Status Quo t-shirt and, now with an analyst's paunch, he was as much a part of Babylon's furniture as she was.

'Thanks Jane. I was pondering over the weekend, you see. And I've been in touch with a pal of mine at Langley. We're both thinking along the same lines. I know it's not ...'

Jane smiled and held up a hand. Frank was gabbling.

'Slow down Frank. I've got a bit of time for this. What's the conspiracy?'

'Do you mind?' He showed Jane his secure SIS Samsung phone, using it to point at the beamer that was on the table in front of them.

'Go ahead.' Jane made herself slightly more comfortable. Frank had a slideshow. This may take a while.

Actually, it didn't. He only had three slides, which he explained with the clarity of a secondary school teacher.

The first slide showed, diagrammatically, the satellite orbits of the 31 US Department of Defense (DoD) GPS satellites. Frank explained that each satellite travelled at 7,000 miles-an-hour, at an altitude of 12,000 miles above the earth. Satellites maintain their very exacting orbit with small thruster rockets; they last around ten years and are constantly being replaced.

'And these birds are the same ones we all use? Satnavs and mobiles?' Jane interrupted.

'Yes. Correct. Except Joe Public's accuracy is limited - they don't have the level of permissions that the DoD have. But we all get our navigational info from the same 31 satellites.'

He swiped on his phone.

Frank described the second slide - how GPS works at the receiver's end. If you can lock onto three satellites you get positional details - in lat and long; to an accuracy of half a metre if you have a military spec receiver. Five metres, for mere commoners. If you lock onto a fourth satellite you can access the third dimension: altitude above sea level. The fourth dimension (Jane's brain was struggling to cope with anything more than three), time, was available by receiving just one satellite signal.

'GPS works in any weather and, as most receivers can normally pick up more than four satellites, GPS is pretty bomb proof.' Frank completed slide two.

Jane thought she now had a bit of an idea of where this was going.

'Who guards the guards?' She asked.

Frank smiled at the ancient Roman reference.

'You mean, who controls the satellites?'

'Yes, of course.'

'You're ahead of me.'

The third slide was a 2-D map of the world. Marked on it were twelve locations.

Frank explained. "The master-control station is located at Schriever Air Force Base in Colorado Springs.' Frank used a laser pointer to mark the spot. 'Originally there were five monitor-stations: Cape Canaveral, Florida; Hawaii; Ascension Island in the Atlantic Ocean; Diego Garcia Atoll in the Indian Ocean; and Kwajalein Island in the South Pacific.' Again, he used his laser pointer to show the locations.

'Six additional monitoring stations were added in 2005: locations in Argentina, Bahrain, the UK, Ecuador, Washington DC, and Australia. Each of the stations checks the exact altitude, position, speed, and overall health of the orbiting satellites.'

Jane put her hand up again. Frank paused. She stood and walked to the green-tinged window that had views over the Thames. She gently placed a hand again the glass.

'Could someone mess with the GPS?' She asked.

'It's possible.' Replied Frank. 'My CIA pal tells me that you could alter the data beamed to a single GPS satellite if you hacked into one of the monitoring stations. It's a big "if". It's been tried before - with no success.'

'Which could then transmit rogue positional data to anyone who was in line of sight to receive it? Altering the course of a US frigate, for example?'

'Yes, but no.'

'What do you mean?' Jane was facing Frank now.

'There are too many safeguards. Even if you could hack into the system and alter the positional data transmitted by a single GPS satellite - which my Langley friend tells me is impossible - as most receivers pick up at least eight GPS signals any rogue data would be dismissed. Out of hand.'

Jane though for a second.

'Like eight separate pieces of advice; say, girlfriends telling you whether to date a guy or not - where seven of them are saying "no" and the eighth saying "yes". You'd disregard the rogue advice?'

Frank seemed confused by the analogy. Relationships weren't his thing.

'Pretty much, I guess. In any case, if that were to happen and the destroyer changed course accordingly, then every other GPS receiver in a 500-mile radius would have gone haywire as well. You'd have had ships, planes and automobiles altering course all over the place. A 747 destined for KL would have landed on a non-existent runway forty miles away. We would have noticed.'

'Then, why do you think the Beaverbrook's crash is linked to the GPS system?' Jane pointed at the slide on the wall.

'Every GPS receiver has its own unique serial number which is embedded in a pretty unsophisticated microchip. What the clever hacker would need to do is speak directly to that receiver. Give it separate instructions. Single it out for special navigational treatment.'

Jane looked at her watch. She was tiring. She needed to heed Claire's advice and head on home. Tomorrow's JIC meeting required her fullest attention.

'But you just told me that your CIA pal reckons that you can't get into the system. So how can you possibly do that?'

Frank breathed out heavily. He looked as tired as Jane felt. His team's plate was full of Syrian and Afghanistani images. They were trying desperately to establish a link between the Syrian regime and the Taliban in southwest Afghanistan. If those two organisations came together it would make a very capable terrorist grouping. It was sapping work, staring at screens all day. No wonder he was excited by something as unlikely as rogue GPS signals.

'The USS Beaverbrook altered course at 3.46 am, two Wednesdays ago. It wasn't a dramatic change - the e-log report shows about four degrees. The course alteration was recommended by the onboard navigational computer and sanctioned by the second XO, sorry executive officer.'

Jane waved her hand dismissively. She knew what XO meant.

'It was a dark but clear night. All of the ship's emergency systems were working. After ten minutes an alarm sounded. The XO spotted the Greek container ship on the radar - they were just three miles apart and closing at fifteen knots. He took immediate action, altered course and informed the captain. As the ship veered away from the collision, the container ship nudged its course towards the destroyer. The XO couldn't avoid a collision. The rest is history.'

'Why did the computer recommend a change of course?' Jane asked.

'The more interesting question is "why did the Greek container ship also alter its course to expedite the crash?"'

'That is a more interesting question. Do we know the answer?'

Frank had a resigned look on his face. He'd obviously only got so far.

'The Greek shipping company are keeping their investigation on close hold. We know two things. First the ship was on autopilot. Second the ship's VDR, sorry Voyage Data Recorder - it's a ship's equivalent of an aircraft's black box - shows a change of course enacted by the autopilot at about the same time the frigate initially altered its course.

They were both following rogue data - data they appeared to have received at the same time. Data that sent them on a collision course.'

Jane's tiredness was gone now. Whilst completely out of her area, this was fascinating stuff.

'And how do you give two ships' GPSs the wrong coordinates?'

Frank played with his phone. The beamer went black. He stood.

'We don't know; yet. But my Langley pal and I think that if you talk to the satellite yourself ...'

'What, like beaming from your own ground-based station?' Jane interrupted.

'Yes.' Frank waved his arms about loosely. 'You know, speak to individual GPS receivers via a satellite and override the incoming GPS data. Navigational microsurgery, if you like. Use the receiver's unique reference number. Tell them they're not where they think they are. The autopilot does the rest. Sounds fanciful?'

Jane recognised that they were at the end of the sum of all knowledge. She gathered her things to leave.

'And your oppo has had this conversation with his boss?'

'He's going to today. He expects to get laughed out of the building. But he's not sure anyone else has a better answer.'

Jane smiled and moved to the door. She opened it and beckoned Frank out.

'Get in touch with the Defence Science and Technology Lab (dstl) and get a boffin on it. Hand it over to them for a couple of days and then crack on with the mid-Asian problem. Come back to me if and when you have something. Clear?'

Frank was out in the main, open-plan office - 40 'hot-desks', nearly all of which were filled with a mix of case officers and analysts.

'Sure thing, Jane.'

Jane touched his arm.

'Well done Frank. Good effort.'

Convention Center Drive, Las Vegas, US

Rick was heading west along Convention Centre Drive. High to his left was The Encore resort. Closer, to his right, was a small shopping mall where 45 minutes previously he had left his car. Having eaten too much food at a small roadside diner on the way in from Creech, he had parked up and gone for a long walk - with no particular ambition. He needed to get away from uniform. Away from the base; the smell of AVTUR and constant melody of groups of airmen jogging round the camp singing out the latest marching song.

And he needed some provisions. Some coffee and some butter. The shopping mall on

Convention Centre Drive was as good a place as any to stock up. He'd do that next.

His pace was brisk, the late winter sunshine hot enough to make him sweat. He'd worn shorts, t-shirt and his new trainers. He could have been any tourist who had roamed away from The Strip. He liked that. Incognito.

Especially now. Now that he'd submitted his report to the colonel, which he'd finished before he'd hit the sack last night. A report that, the more he thought about it, the crazier it seemed. He'd opened it with his conclusion, a paragraph he remembered word for word:

> *Master Sergeant Rodgers' Reaper GPS navigational system threw a 15-mile error at 23.37 on Jan 10. The error forced the autopilot to alter the aircraft's course. Having checked the imagery from the Reaper's file, at the time of the error the aircraft was seconds away from flying over an unmapped, modern facility of at least two buildings and a sizeable satellite dish. It is my belief that the Reaper was fed rogue navigational data to ensure that it didn't discover the unmapped buildings.*

It was madness. The conclusion threw up so many questions that he was unable to answer. How did someone (something?) manage to affect the

Reaper's GPS? Who would do it - and who had the technological knowhow to make that happen? And, what was the building complex they veered away from? There were many more.

He shook his head, banishing the madness. He focused on the traffic, searching for a safe place to cross. It was mid-afternoon. The road was quiet enough, but there were still vehicles to avoid. He checked over his shoulder. A red saloon, followed by a big Mack truck hauling a rusty-brown shipping container. No gap in the traffic yet.

Ahead of him were two cars, one a smart, silver-blue Mustang - the new model; the other a nondescript grey saloon. He couldn't make it out. Behind them was a black GMC Savana. A big van with blacked-out windows. He couldn't shake FBI surveillance from his head. He laughed to himself.

The Mustang and the second car drove past. The Savana slowed, as if it were about to turn across the traffic into the mall.

But it didn't cross the traffic.

And it hadn't slowed to make a turn. Rick was about to find out that the van had slowed for him.

The driver of the Savana pulled up at the exact moment Rick was level with the van's sliding door. It was a neat bit of driving - they were both moving in opposite directions and it would have been easy to overshoot.

Rick was confused; his pace faltered.

Are they stopping for me? To ask me something? Maybe they're lost?

None of those questions was the right one.

It happened in an instant. The sliding-door flew back. Before Rick could react to the man in the back of the Savana who was brandishing a handgun, it was too late.

Bang! Bang!

A double tap. Two shots in very close order. The second shot was higher than the first. Nobody can hold a handgun completely steady after a round has left the barrel. The barrel rises due to the explosive force from bullet's cartridge, the gun pivoting on the firer's wrist.

The first round hit Rick just below the rib cage and tore through his liver and left a six-inch hole in his back. It was a marker for the second round which was meant for the heart. But the shooter had miscalculated the effect that the stopping vehicle would have on his balance; he rocked a fraction. The shot went higher and further right than intended. It still hit Rick in the chest, but missed his heart by a couple of inches. Instead, it smashed through his rib cage, deflecting high right and exited through his shoulder. By then the round was tumbling and taking with it veins, bone, sinew and cartilage. The hole in his shoulder was wider and uglier than that from the first round. Fixing that would take twelve hours of surgery. And that's only if he made it to the hospital before the combination of blood-loss and shock did for him.

The door of the Savana was slammed shut before Rick hit the pavement. The van sped off, quickly mixing into traffic. There were no other pedestrians to check on the van's plate, and the noise of the two shots were similar to a large car backfiring. And this was Vegas. A couple of cars saw Rick fall to the ground, but drove past his body. They saw a scruffy black man who had been shot in broad daylight and made the wrong assumption that this was a gang killing.

Best not to get involved. The police will be here soon enough.

As Rick's heart pumped half-a-pint of blood a minute onto the pavement the police didn't turn up.

But an ambulance did. Within 90 seconds of the shooting. It had just left Sunrise Hospital and was heading for an old-folks' home to taxi a patient for a check-up. As always, they were looking for business.

The driver saw a black man on the pavement in a pool of blood. Picking up a black man was always a risky call. Would he have insurance? The driver slowed the vehicle down to get a better look. *Decent Nike trainers.*

It's worth a punt.

Sam gingerly drove the Golf off the ferry. It wasn't her car, but she'd already grown to love it. She didn't want to dent it, or scrape the undercarriage. She had this thing with possessions. All of her stuff was in good order - for its age. That's because she looked after all of her stuff to within an inch of its life. It wasn't necessarily because they had monetary value, or that they would be difficult to replace. It was mostly because everything she owned had its own personality. They had feelings. They depended on her to be looked after. And, if they were lost, some other lunatic would be responsible for making sure they were OK. And that wouldn't do.

The Golf was in pristine condition. It had fewer than 6,000 kilometres on the clock - hardly run in. The leather seats smelt of recently-dead cow, and the switches clicked like they belonged to a precision instrument. And the engine - wow. She wasn't a great driver. Wolfgang had been behind the wheel of his Dad's Audi Quattro three years ago when they were being chased down by a BMW M3. Four-wheel drive muscle versus two-wheel drive brains. Wolfgang had driven the Quattro brilliantly. And after Sam had put a couple of rounds through the M3's radiator grill, they had made a clean escape.

No, she wasn't as good a driver as Wolfgang. But the Golf's engine was incredibly eager, and very forgiving. So, after a couple of hours behind the wheel, she was beginning to feel like she was.

Sam managed the ferry's ramps carefully, got through UK customs with surprising ease and pulled up on the first layby that presented itself on the A120. It was 2.30 in the morning, and dark. She needed to rest. Since yesterday afternoon's phone call with Jane her mind hadn't stopped whirring. Who was right? Wolfgang? Or the whole of the British intelligence service?

Was Mitchell dead? Was Stone a member of The Church of the White Cross? Or just an alcoholic - who also happened to be responsible for the British military?

Jane versus Wolfgang.

An interesting dilemma.

Wolfgang was a loaner - but a hugely capable one. A man who played the internet as well as he played his Höffner violin. A man on a mission, with the capacity and intellect to unearth and unpick the most well-hidden conspiracies.

Jane was an incredibly competent operator. And nobody second-guessed Her Majesty's Secret Intelligence Service. But, Sam had been in the middle of that organisation. Experienced its flaws. Worked among many brilliant, but one or two fallible, people. And, 12 months ago, she and Jane had fallen out over a matter of principle. Whether or not the lives of thousands of Italians and tourists were more or less important than the status of a British-owned informant in the highest echelon of the Russian government. A man with so much reach, Vauxhall knew what the Russian premier was going to do before he made the decision.

Sam had sided with the thousands. Jane with the oligarch.

Whom should Sam trust now?

She picked up one of the mobiles that Wolfgang had given to her. She dialled his number.

It rang. And rang.

A muffled, 'What? Who is this? Do you know what time it is?'

It was Wolfgang. She, not surprisingly for the time of day, had woken him.

For some reason Sam spoke quietly, as if not to wake Wolfgang further.

'It's me.' Sam didn't say anymore. She knew Wolfgang had a voice-recognition App on his phone which, in addition to the displayed number, allowed the receiver to verify the caller.

'Hi. I was asleep.'

They had agreed not to use names. And speak in loose code where they could.

'I know. Sorry. I have a dilemma.'

'At this time of the morning. Surely, the answer is "sleep", regardless of the other choices.'

Sam smiled to herself. Who said the Germans were humourless?

'I spoke with my ex-boss. She reckons that the guy I saw in Austria is no longer with us. Confirmed. And that there's no way the British military "higher-up" could be "with The Church".'

There was silence for a couple of seconds. Sam couldn't lose the image of Wolfgang probably snuggled up under a feather duvet with the apparition that was Inge. It made her stomach churn. She had no idea why.

Wolfgang was brighter now. 'She's wrong. You've seen the man - physically. And I've seen his electronic fingerprints. As for the other guy, I showed you some of the proof. I have some more. I'll need to dig it out, but I'm pretty sure I have SMS records between him and a known Church figure in the States. And, also, I have his bank details - I think there are four accounts. One, which is well hidden and based in The Bahamas, has multiple high-figure transactions from many countries. Including, if I remember, Croatia.'

Wolfgang paused for a second. In the background Sam heard a female voice.

'Wer ist es?'

'Es ist Sam, geh schlafen.'

There was a feminine grunt, and then Wolfgang repeated himself.

'She's wrong. We're right.'

Sam pulled the phone from her ear and studied it. She was at a loss. She needed to do something, even if it were just to occupy her time.

If she switched off now, she knew she'd spiral downhill. Depression, a major part of the PTSD for her, had never been far away since she'd been badly injured in Afghanistan all those years ago. She was best kept busy. Employed. Without a focus her brain turned against itself and picked a helluva fight; from which there were no winners.

She put the phone back to her ear.

'Get me the man's wife's home address. All of them, if she has more than one.'

'The supposedly-dead man's wife or the military's one?' Wolfgang's tone had changed. He moved up a couple of gears from sleepy, through mildly awake, to alert.

'The possibly-dead one. I'm going to pay her a visit. And if I get nothing from that, I'll go and see the other chap. Confront him. Set some hares running.'

Sam had no plan. So, she would do what she did best. Blunder about, press some buttons and hope that none of them was the ejector seat.

'OK. I'll have that with you in a couple of hours.' Wolfgang paused. 'And, in the meantime, get some sleep? Please?'

'Sure, sure.'

The car rocked as an articulated lorry sped past a little too close for comfort.

'Give my love to Inge?'

Sam wasn't sure if it were a statement or a question. She still had no idea how she felt about the Wolfgang/Inge relationship. It was a stupid, irrational feeling and she hated herself for having it.

   Stupid, stupid.

Chapter 5

Brandon Parva, Norfolk, United Kingdom

Sam pulled the Golf onto the grass verge of the single-track road. She was careful to make sure there was room for another car to pass, not that she'd seen one during the last half an hour. She was in deepest Norfolk, a county renowned for being at the end of nowhere; farming communities that hadn't changed hands for centuries. Everyone married to everyone else's cousin.

Google Maps told her that she was just short of Welborne Manor which, according to Wolfgang, was the last known address of Victoria Mitchell. He'd texted it through first thing this morning. The *ping* from Sam's phone had woken her from a deep, cold and restless sleep - the clothes she had bought in Alpbach may have been good quality, but there were hardly enough layers for a roadside January night in southeast England. For her, though, being awake and cold was better than where she had been before the *ping*. Her dream had taken her back to Afghanistan - the whine of the mortar round as it fell to the ground. The deafening explosion, the blast, the pain. And the sight of the love of her life lying dead in the sand; her own insides hanging from a hole that shouldn't have been there. Then she was drowning in a sea of blood, guts and camouflage netting. And still the mortar rounds fell ...

Being awake, more often than not, was better than being asleep.

The drive to Brandon Parva, a small, dispersed village randomly arranged around an ancient church, had been painless enough and taken two hours. Sam had stopped for breakfast at a roadside caravan. She was dead against eating processed food, but the smell of the bacon sizzling on the industrial griddle was too much for her aching stomach. When she asked for the rind to be removed from the bacon, the man cooking had looked at her as if she had two heads.

'There's no discount for that, love.' The words rising and falling lyrically in a rich Norfolk accent.

Sam wasn't sure if his comment were a joke. So, she didn't reply, but gave him her best, humouring smile.

That was an hour ago. She was still hungry.

She got out of the car, stretched and walked down the road. After a few yards, in the middle distance, she spotted a two-floor, red-brick Edwardian house with a red-tile roof and white-painted windows. It was set back from the road, but hardly hidden. She took a quick glance back at the Golf (Did she lock it? Should she check?), dismissed her OCD thought process and walked on.

An engraved metal sign announced her arrival at Welborne Manor. The house had an 'in and out' gravel drive, the garden was mostly laid to lawn and what looked like an old stable off to one side had been converted into a double garage. The manor's boundaries appeared to be defined by a mixture of hedgerows and small copses. Sam thought she spotted an irrigation channel running down one side of the front lawn. Norfolk was as flat as a loose guitar string, and most of the county was either at or slightly below sea level.

Sam stood and waited where the 'out' bit of the gravel drive met the road's tarmac. She studied the house further. Parked to one side of the central front door was a car: a black Toyota Prius c - she couldn't stop herself; when in focus, she'd pick out and remember the licence plate. Access to the front door was afforded by a semicircular set of low brick stairs. The third of the four downstairs windows was open, which seemed strange to Sam as it was cold - the frost still lingering on the grass. But at least it meant someone was at home. Hopefully that someone was Victoria Mitchell.

Sam had no particular plan. Victoria Mitchell wasn't expecting her. Sam's arrival would be a surprise and she was sure to get a further shock when Sam asked the only question she wanted an answer to: do you think your husband is still alive?

She was sure that the answer would be, 'No!'. But the woman's reaction would throw up some clues. Sam had a thing with faces. She could spot a lie from 1,000 paces. Decode an expression like a safebreaker.

Also, seeing the inside of the house would help to unpick any story. She had to - *had to* - get into the house. She'd break in if necessary. She was a trained analyst. She was good at looking. She knew what to spot. Signs of a man. Or, just as significant, an overwhelming sense that the house no longer had a man in it.

Look for what should be there, but isn't. Not necessarily, *what shouldn't be there, but is.* It was the key to unlocking any scene - any image.

If Victoria Mitchell were hiding her husband, she'd go out of the way to remove any current traces of him in the house. Make the place overtly feminine. Work too hard. If she wasn't hiding him, there would be the odd bit of him here and there.

Sam would sense if Victoria Mitchell knew her husband were alive by her reaction, not necessarily her answers, to Sam's questions. The way she laid her house out would seal any suspicion.

She checked her watch. It was 10.37 am.
Let's do this.

It took Sam half a minute to reach the brick stairs, which she climbed in a single stride. To the left of the door was a brass bell-pull. She gave it a tug. In the distance she heard a *clang*.

A few seconds later the door opened and a late-middle-aged woman, probably in her early sixties, mid-height, slim, off-blonde and dressed for the country, came to the door.

The woman had sparkling eyes, sunk into a face that had been through a number of seasons - wrinkles cut deep into her skin; crow's feet drawn from the corners of her eyes. In her right hand she held a lit cigarette. Sam couldn't make out the brand.

The woman smiled, but confusion was the underlying expression. She took a drag of her cigarette.

'Hello. Can I help you?' The accent was very English, almost aristocratic.

'Victoria Mitchell?' Sam asked.

'Yes. Who are you?'

Sam had thought through a number of options in response to that question. First was the truth. She was ex-SIS, she'd spotted Paul Mitchell in a skiing village in Austria and was wondering what Mrs Mitchell thought about that?

That was Plan A.

Not sensing open hostility, she opted for Plan B.

'I'm Sam Green.' Sam offered her right hand. Rather inelegantly Victoria Mitchell put the cigarette in her mouth, allowing her to shake Sam's hand.

The woman took a second drag, released Sam's hand and retrieved the cigarette from her mouth. She tilted her head to one side and blew the smoke away from Sam's face.

Embassy Number 1s. Sam had the make.

'And?' Victoria Mitchell's smile had vanished.

'I work for the Foreign Office.' Sam waited for a split second to see if the woman picked up on the disguise often used by SIS employees when talking about where they worked. Nothing. 'And I'm here to ask you a few questions about you and your late husband's ill-fated sailing trip to the Indian Ocean. If you don't mind?'

Sam had Victoria Mitchell's face framed against the winter gloom of the interior of the house. She could make out every change of expression.

But there was nothing. Just confusion. No sense that Sam had touched a nerve; that the woman might be about to be asked some questions she'd have difficulty fielding.

'What questions? Why now?'

Sam was no closer to getting inside the house. This would need to be good.

'I'm following up on some of the route choices made by you and your husband. One of my responsibilities is the FCO's travel advice website. Its style hasn't been revamped since your trip. Clearly our advice wasn't anywhere near direct enough when you were planning your route. I'd like to work on that - and I'm visiting a number of people who, and I don't mean to underplay the horrors you experienced, had trouble on overseas trips because we, well, hadn't given clear enough advice.'

Still no apprehension from Victoria Mitchell. Sam thought she sensed an overwhelming sadness, but no guilt. She took another drag of her cigarette.

'I don't think the advice we got was anything other than exemplary. It was my husband who was dogmatic. Pig-headed more like.' She paused, as if she were recounting a memory. Sam couldn't tell if the woman's tone were chastising or one of affection. Perhaps a bit of both?

'But I'm happy to take any questions. Would you like a cup of tea?' She pulled the door fully ajar. The defences were down.

'Would you like to see my ID?' Sam hoped she didn't. She had illegally kept her 'protocol officer' card from Moscow. It was clearly a Foreign Office ID, but the Moscow Embassy top line would need a little explanation.

Victoria Mitchell smiled as she directed Sam inside.

'No, that won't be necessary. You look trustworthy enough. And who else would think up such a bizarre story?'

'Indeed.' Sam replied, following the woman through the large, wood-panelled lobby into the Laura Ashley-patterned sitting room.

Sam found the next 30 minutes unremarkable. Victoria Mitchell gave no sign that she thought her husband was anything other than dead. And the sitting room (and a corridor and one of the downstairs loos - Sam had asked to go) looked as Sam expected it to look if it were the case. The rooms were feminine with no distinguishable male touches. But, in one corner of the sitting room was a baby grand piano whose top acted as a photograph depository. Among 20 or so silver-framed photos were a couple showing Victoria and Paul Mitchell. One was a wedding photo; she was dressed beautifully in a plain, long ivory-white, silk and tulle dress - and he was wearing tails. A second was a holiday photo of the pair of them on a motor yacht off the coast of, what was probably, Italy. The third was Paul Mitchell on his own, holding a trophy. On inspection Sam saw that it was The Queen's Award for Enterprise. The date on the trophy was 2012, a year before his kidnap.

Whilst Sam looked over the photos, Victoria Mitchell had recounted the story of her husband's abduction. She chain-smoked as she spoke.

'It was bizarre. He was out of it, submissive almost - from the moment I spotted the pirate boat hunting us down. There was no way we could outrun them. And the American Navy, who answered my distress call, didn't arrive until over an hour later. Paul was quickly tied up and taken on board their RIB. He made no attempt to fight, or to argue. He just let it happen.'

'I kicked and screamed and, as a result, got a rifle butt in the face - it knocked me out cold and left a scar on my forehead.' She pointed to a Harry Potter-like mark just below her hairline. Her makeup hid the nasty scar well.

'When I woke, my head spinning like a top, he was gone. And there was blood everywhere. At first I thought that maybe they'd killed him, but then I realised that the blood was coming from my head. I was just about to wash it down when I heard a helicopter half-a-mile to starboard. It took them a while to get the winch down, but about ten minutes later I was in the arms of a hunk of a Navy Seal. And I was in the surgery of the American ship 40 minutes later, accompanied by a blinding headache.'

Sam had stopped looking at the photos. She studied Victoria Mitchell, who had taken another drag of her cigarette. She seemed vacant - disinterested. The end of the story possibly signalling the end of her life - certainly a major chapter in it.

Their eyes met. The woman fidgeted.
Do you want to tell me something?
Victoria Mitchell took another drag.

'The rest is history, I suppose? They didn't pursue the pirates' RIB because I had to be seen by a doctor. They took the safe choice even though, over the drone of the helicopter blades, I shouted at them to forget about me and to find Paul.' She was back in the room now. Any hint of being distracted was lost.

'It must have been very hard on you?' Sam asked kindly.

Victoria Mitchell turned away from Sam and stared out of the window, across the lawn in the direction of the Golf.

'You could say that.' She paused and gave a short, feminine laugh. 'Money's not an issue, you know? Paul made a lot of it when he sold the business before the trip. And we were advised by your people not to pay a ransom, although finding $5 million was going to be tough against the timeframe they had given us. So there was, sorry, is, plenty of cash hanging about.' She paused again. Sam moved a couple of strides towards the woman, but checked herself.

'But ...'

Sam couldn't see her face; the woman was still facing the window. Again, she sensed a wistfulness. Which was odd because Victoria Mitchell didn't seem like a woman who was either vague or distracted.

'... I do miss him.' She turned now, and their eyes met. Sam thought she saw dampness in the corner of her eyes. That was to be expected?

'Anyway. Look, I have someone coming here for a meeting in ...', she looked at the tall grandfather clock that had been chiming every 15 minutes since Sam had been close enough to hear, 'about 20 minutes. Do you have enough?'

Sam tapped on her phone theatrically. She had been using it to take notes - like any conscientious FCO staff officer. She had also been using it to take the odd discreet photo.

'No, that's, err, perfect. Thank you. You have been most generous with your time. It will help with the website redesign. And thank you for revisiting what must still be a very harrowing affair.'

They talked about nothing as Victoria Mitchell led Sam to the door of the sitting room. She paused. Sam thought the woman was about to add something of consequence. They both stopped and looked at each other. Sam wanted to shout, 'Come on, ... let it out!'. But thought better of it.

Nothing. Just a weak smile.

But there was something there?

'Can I text you my number? In case there's something else you think of. Something that you might want to tell me.'

Confusion again from Victoria Mitchell. Why would she want this stranger's number? Sam studied her face closely.

She dithered. And then said, 'Yes, of course. Why not. If I think of anything I'll give you a call.'

She then read out her number - Sam tapped it onto her phone. Five seconds later she had pressed 'Send'. Her SMS read:

if you want to tell me something, this is my number. Sam Green

They shook hands again and said their goodbyes. As Sam jumped down the steps she heard the door close behind her.

She walked slowly back down the gravel path, more slowly than she ordinarily would have. It crossed her mind to turn around, to go back and ask some more penetrating questions. To allow the woman to release what Sam thought she was hiding. But she didn't.

Just before she reached the end of the drive Sam did turn her head for one last look at the manor. And that's when the enigmatic Mrs Victoria Mitchell got just slightly more interesting.

Sam could see her at the open window. Not looking Sam's way, but silhouetted against the interior's lighter background. She was on the phone. Sam was too far away to hear any of the conversation, but it was clear that Victoria Mitchell was having a very heated discussion with someone. Her free hand was emphatically slicing the air.

And then the silhouette turned, and all motion stopped.

She's looking at me?

At which point Victoria Mitchell closed the open window and pulled across the curtain.

Flemingstraße, Munich, Germany

Wolfgang paced up and down the small space in the cellar between the stairs and his terminals. He had been speaking to Sam and he needed inspiration. She'd just finished with Paul Mitchell's wife, Victoria. Sam was convinced there was something more to Victoria than just bereft widow. Something that Sam couldn't put her finger on.

'When we chatted she was the perfect rich man's ex-wife. But, once or twice, I really felt she wanted to tell me something. But didn't. Or couldn't. And then when I left she was straight on the phone to someone.' Sam had said. 'Can you access her calls?'

'Not without her phone number. Any chance?

'No, not her landline, but I do have her mobile.' Sam had gone quiet and then Wolfgang noticed an alert on one of his screens. He had the number.

'She smokes Embassy Number 1s, if that adds anything to anything.' Sam had come back with eventually.

If it were a joke, he had no witty comeback. He was in the cellar. There was no humour here.

'I'm tired Wolfgang. And hungry. I'm going to eat something more substantial than a thin slice of pork between two bits of white bread. And then I'm going to use your generous expense account to buy myself some clothes. I then need a plan. You think about it. I'll think about it. And let's talk later.'

They'd said their goodbyes and hung up.

She needed him to spark - he knew that. And he needed inspiration.

Which frustrated him, as he knew he was close to his limitations. He had pushed the boundaries of his hacking - mostly using the Dark Web. If he pushed any harder he'd have to cut corners and that would leave him exposed. He'd set up a number of peer-to-peer encrypted links on the Dark Web, with other 'unknown' hackers who seemed to hack for the sake of it. A couple of them appeared to enjoy tracking The Church's *e-dollar* transactions. Having sifted through pages and pages of their data and days and days of his own work, he had been able to piece together the outline infrastructure of The Church of the White Cross. He'd paid for their services, but it had been worth it and saved him a lot of time.

The Church had a number of ever-changing, ever-moving exclusive websites. The layered encryption and the number of intermediate server-jumps made it almost impossible for him to access a single site without being asked to join - ordinarily you could only get onto a site having been given a username and password. This was the usual Dark Web process. When, eventually, he'd been able to access a site using very complex hacking algorithms, it had closed before he was able to interrogate it in detail. In a very brief window what he did get was the usernames of a number of visitors to the site - which he'd then tracked via other routes. He came across a second Church site by accident. Here he was able to download some generic information about the organisation's vision and further add to its top-level structure.

What was interesting, but maybe not surprising, was that he'd uncovered more about individual Church members using Clearnet (the Dark Web's term for the World Wide Web), email and social media interactions, than through his Dark Web hacking. That was because some people were lazy - or just arrogant; they obviously thought that they could get away without the secrecy afforded by the cryptography employed on the Dark Web.

Whatever, he was at an impasse. He had done as much as he could. Three years of work had built a structure; defined an organisation. It had delivered intel on 30 or so members of The Church. What he was waiting for now was for one of them to make an electronic mistake. To slip up. For a website to remain open long enough for him to interrogate it in detail. But even then, the output would be two-dimensional. Electronic. Ones-and-noughts. Sought and captured from a distance.

What he *really* needed was that third dimension. He needed for the amorphous to come into sharp relief. Flesh on the bones.

And for that he needed Sam Green.

Computers didn't do inflection; not really. That's why business people still liked to meet face-to-face. Computers, and the images they generated, didn't have a pulse. They didn't sweat. He'd been on the ground with Sam when they had blundered into The Church of the White Cross in Berlin. Smacked headlong into it. His mother had been a victim of their unspeakable cruelty. Sam and he were to be next. Somehow, they had made it out alive. Much of that was due to Sam's tenacity, combined with the timely intervention of the German *polizei*. He'd been close to death at that point. A minute later and she would have been shot dead. And he would have succumbed to loss of blood and raging hypothermia.

But, even though he had been at death's door, he'd felt more alive then than he did now.

The sun. Rain. Wind. Flesh. Bullets. Blood. Pain.

Fear.

They were real. You could feel those. Sense them. *Smell them.*

That's how you get to know what's really going down.

He knew he couldn't be exposed to them again. He was too frail. Too ... weak.

But Sam could.

She was out there now. Blundering around. What was it she used to say? *Pressing buttons.* Sensing. Feeling. Breathing.

But now she needed direction. And he needed to help her find it. He had to be her wingman. Help her get ahead of those who were already chasing her.

He stopped pacing and moved quickly back to his chair. He pulled the keyboard towards him and got typing. In a search box he had designed for working deep in the Dark Web he typed: *Paul Mitchell - e-dollar.*

The off-white box, filled with the black text he had just written, stood out against the charcoal-grey screen.

He pressed return; his state-of-the-art computers flashed up a page of search results. Biting on the forefinger of his left knuckle, he scrolled down the list using his right hand. There were 26,543 entries. He flicked them down a page at a time.

Ten minutes later. Nothing.

Another ten - the list was getting more and more obscure and less and less relevant.

He flicked the screen again and then, abruptly, stopped himself. He slowly scrolled up again.

There was an indecipherable entry which looked interesting:

1oshge_pmitchell/hja67>Hyg4fg/account /k/walteringrisbank/ghed7&/

From that search line three key words struck a chord: *pmitchell; account; walteringrisbank.*

He knew he wouldn't be able to follow the link from the current page - that would require a much more detailed workout with the Dark Web. Instead, he opened a Clearnet Google tab, one that any mortal would recognise.

He typed in: *walter ingris bank.* And pressed return.

And there it was. The first entry in Google:

Walter Ingris Bank | Investment Bank, Nassau, The Bahamas.

Wolfgang sat back in his chair. He had 15 other tenuous links from Church individuals with 'finance transactions' in The Bahamas. The results had been account numbers, but no names - and he had failed to find details of a bank that might be being used for The Church's financial dealings. He had tried numerous times to complete the chain. Searching the net was like that. Just now if he had typed: *Paul Mitchell banking details*, which he knew he had done before, the search criteria would have delivered a completely different set of results. That was the way it worked.

It didn't matter. He had a potential bank now.

He checked his watch. It was 5.15 pm. An hour before Elisabeth would call him and Inge for supper. He focused back on the screen, his hands hovering over the keyboard, imaginarily typing.

And then he got to it.

Headquarters SIS, Vauxhall, London

Jane stared at the screen. She had a couple of secure tabs open.

One was the Paul Mitchell file, which had been closed in early 2014 and, as far as she could tell, hadn't been revisited since. Piracy and kidnapping weren't her bailiwick, so this was the first time she had looked at the file in any detail. In the case of Mitchell's kidnap it seemed to Jane that SIS's role had been as an observer whilst the FCO and the family, actually just Victoria Mitchell, dealt with the ransom demand - which was a hefty $5 million. The FCO desk officer in London liaised with the skeleton-manned Embassy in Mogadishu, whilst keeping the SIS desk officer at Babylon informed. In return, SIS had used their single case officer in Mogadishu to monitor signals traffic and work his agents. He ran an informant who was embedded in another pirate grouping. The pair of them had tried to piece together what the Mitchell kidnap team looked like.

For operations such as these, SIS brought together a bespoke multi-agency team. In the Mitchell case staff were co-opted from Defence Intelligence, GCHQ (the UK's signals/wire intercept organisation), the Met Police (with links to Interpol and Europol), Special Forces (to effect a rescue op should it be on the cards), and one of the embedded CIA staff on exchange from Langley. There were 25 pages of case notes in the file. The team, based in Babylon, had worked relentlessly.

Sadly, however, they hadn't been able to prevent Mitchell's murder.

Jane scribbled down on a pad the post-operation report's headlines:

- *the family dithered over the ransom payment;*
- *the in-country FCO liaison stalled the pirates for three days;*
- *the pirates cut all communications on the fourth day;*

- *day five, SIS's Mogadishu case officer, Steven Field, learnt from his local informant that Mitchell had been killed;*
- *Field was taken to see the body three days later (day eight), after which he confirmed that Mitchell was dead;*
- *the pirates subsequently burned the body; no repatriation was possible.*

Field attributed a 95% level of certainty that the body was that of Paul Mitchell. In SIS speak that was irrefutable evidence. It wouldn't have been from checking dental records, the sure-fire way of confirming a body, as SIS staff weren't trained to carry out such a postmortem. In Mitchell's case, Jane reckoned that Field would have seen the corpse, probably by then in some state of decay due to the heat. And he was able to attach that level of certainty having seen associated documentation - Mitchell's driving licence, or maybe a passport. If she had been responsible for the operation, that would have been good enough for her.

Jane remembered the case's outcome from a weekly sitrep that all SIS staff were sent (and were obliged to read). Outcome: Mitchell had been murdered by his captors. His body had been confirmed by an SIS case officer. Operation failed because the family didn't pay the ransom in time and/or his captors believed they were close to being compromised.

Jane's notetaking was interrupted. Her door opened and Claire popped in.

'I've got what I can on Victoria Mitchell. Do you want me to leave it on the cloud, or email it to you?'

Jane looked up from her pad and smiled. She had asked Claire to do a Level 2 search on Victoria Mitchell: background history from late teens until the present day; intelligence services, police and Interpol records; and police records on the subject's parents.

'Thanks Claire. Leave it on the cloud. What are the headlines?'

Claire was now fully in the room, standing directly in front of Jane's desk.

'How are you doing today?' Claire's tone was motherly.

Jane couldn't stifle a yawn. She put her hand in front of her open mouth a little too late to be wholly polite.

'Sorry. I'm fine. It's just, well, my conversation with Sam yesterday. She, you know ... gets to me. I always feel that she's one step ahead.' Jane waved her hands about absently. 'She's never been wrong about anything ...', after which she quickly added, '... but, she doesn't always make the right judgement call with the facts that she has. She's ..?'

She searched for an appropriate word.

'Maverick?' Claire finished Jane's sentence for her.

'Yes, possibly.'

Jane stood and stretched her back.

'To be fair, her judgement is excellent. It's just ... it's not always in tune with the best interests of SIS. And, as a result, the government.'

Claire didn't say anything. It was clear that she was letting Jane get this out of her system.

After a short pause Jane nodded to Claire, as if to say, 'give me all you've got.'

'Victoria Mitchell has no intelligence, nor police record. Nothing - it's completely clean. Not even a speeding ticket. Her parents were both pillars of a small Oxford village; they're both now deceased. One was an ex-GP, the other an ex-magistrate. They're clean.'

'Anything else of interest in her background, other than being married to the erstwhile owner of the highly successful *e-dollar* business venture?' Jane asked.

'No. not really. A first from Cambridge in computer science. Thirty percent owner of *e-dollar* at the point of sale. An MBA from Aston University. She's a keen sailor and now runs a successful web-based horticultural business in mid-Norfolk.' Claire paused. It was a playful pause; her accompanying smile was tight lipped.

Jane sensed there was something more.

'And?'

'Her sister is Judy Strand, the Shakespearean cum EastEnders actress.'

'No! Really? Well I never.'

'And, probably not relevant, but interesting, Victoria almost followed her sister onto the stage. She was in the thick of the Footlights crew during her time at Cambridge. She was given a lead role in their Edinburgh Festival show in the early 80s.'

'But she stuck to the more profitable computer programming route?' Jane added, not expecting an answer.

'Or, Plan C, which is more like a "B plus": she married a man who went on to become a multimillionaire entrepreneur.' Claire smiled again.

'Indeed. Thanks, Claire.' Jane went to sit down.

As she did, Claire asked, 'Tea?'

'No thanks.' She motioned to a mug on her desk. 'It's lukewarm. I promise to finish it.'

Claire raised both hands, smiled again and left.

By the time the door closed Jane was already typing into the 'search' box on SIS's secure database.

Steven Field.

She pressed 'return' and almost immediately a drop-down box offered her options, one of which was, 'Personnel File'.

She clicked on it.

What was presented made her push back in her chair and breathe out heavily.

Steven Field. Dishonourably discharged. 17 July 2015.

Jane was a good skim-reader. She could work a page of A4 about every 15 seconds and rarely missed much. This, however, needed her fullest attention. Almost childlike she read the second paragraph out loud:

> *Case officer Steven Field, at the time 'N12' in the Nairobi Embassy, was found guilty of severe lack of discipline and integrity by SIS's ethics committee on 7 July 2015. At the time of the hearing he had been suspended on full pay and had returned to the UK. The committee's findings are detailed in paragraph 7 of this report. By way of summary, Case officer Field was caught and pleaded guilty to various counts of receiving illicit payments (to the tune of £425,000) from Kenyan government officials. The same officials were under SIS scrutiny for election-rigging, drug-running and embezzlement. As a result, the ethics committee had no alternative than to discharge Steven Field*

from Secret Intelligence Service without further pay. His rights to an SIS pension have also been waived.

'Well, I'll be damned.' Jane whispered.

She hollered at the door, 'Claire!'

A second later the door opened and Claire appeared.

'The intercom was still working last time I looked.'

'Sure.' Jane smile was brief and workmanlike.

'Can you check my phone records from yesterday. Pick out the number that Sam called me on, please. And can you arrange a meeting with her as soon as practical?'

Claire sensed the urgency and dropped any further attempt at humour.

'Sure.' And then she was out of the office.

Chapter 6

Sunrise Hospital, Las Vegas, US

Retired Command Sergeant Major Austin Rodgers was as composed as any father could be just before they were allowed to see their badly wounded son. His own military training had been severe and exacting. In his last role as a senior trainer he had demanded that his soldiers face adversity head on. 'What doesn't kill you, makes you stronger.' Whilst he was serving that had been his personal motto. He couldn't remember a single day when he didn't bark that particular edict. In his final role at Camp Blanding he knew his nickname was 'makes you stronger'. At his retirement party, as well as a very smart TAG Heuer watch which he was wearing today, the unit presented him with a baseball hat emblazoned with the same words.

He wasn't sure if he believed in them right now. When the state trooper's car had pulled up outside their whitewashed, clapboard house which nestled idyllically in among the pines and the dunes southwest of St Augustine Beach, his and Martha's world had been smashed to smithereens.

At first he'd assumed the worst. He had been the bearer of the worst possible news three times before. Twice during an Iraq tour and once due to a training accident, where a young lad had been run over by an Abrams tank - as he slept. Night manoeuvres were dangerous, especially in training. He'd taken a pastor with him on all three occasions, both of them in dress uniform. The two Iraq widows and the mother of the third knew what was coming as soon as they had opened the door. For him, the experience was a more frightening and more horrible experience than any enemy he had faced.

When he spotted the trooper's car pull up on their drive and the policeman, having got out, check that he was smart by using the Dodge Charger's wing mirror, he knew this wasn't a routine call.

'Martha. Sit Down. We've got company. And it don't look good.'

Within a few minutes Austin had booked a flight from Jacksonville to Las Vegas. Martha didn't fly - unless she had a huge pile of pills from the doctor, a procedure that they'd got used to when he was based in Germany. But there wasn't time for any of that - one of them needed to be at Rick's bedside as soon as possible. The trooper's notes gave Rick a 50% chance of making it through the next 24 hours. He'd go. Martha would hold the fort.

And now here he was. Sunrise hospital. As good as any. With, according to the nurse at reception, one of the best surgeons in Nevada.

Good. Rick didn't deserve to die. He was a good boy. Hard-working and bright. The apple of his pop's eye.

A nurse had led him to a half-opaque glass and wood door. There was a sign at hip height. It read: *Intensive Treatment Unit*. Underneath was a white plastic board on which was scrawled: *Rodgers. Post-op. Hemingway.*

The nurse blocked the door with her arm. It was a gentle, not a malicious act.

'Doctor Hemingway is in the room with your son at the moment. The anaesthetist finished an hour ago. There was some discussion, I believe, as to whether he should be kept in an induced coma, but I think the doctor decided against that.'

Austin hovered a bit too close to the door than was necessary. He wanted to go in. To ask the doctor a hundred questions. But the nurse held him steady and he worked hard to control his frustration. He wasn't used to not getting his own way. He was a command sergeant major - with that rank came power and respect, not that he ever misused it.

'Thank you. Can I see him now?'

The nurse smiled. It was the first time that Austin had noticed how pretty she was. She was short, Hispanic and had a smile that would stop a 30-ton Bradley fighting-vehicle at 100 feet.

'Let me go in and see the doctor. I'll be right out.'

Austin bit his lip. He wanted to see his son *now*.

The nurse took a couple of minutes, coming back out of the room with another tank-stopping smile.

'Please go in. The doctor will see you.'

'Thank you.' He had to stop himself from barging past her.

Austin didn't make out the doctor's, 'Hello Mr Rodgers, I'm Doctor Hemingway'. Nor did he see the man's outstretched hand. He was too overcome by the mummy-like state of his son. There were wires and drips everywhere. And more machines than in the cockpit of the space shuttle he'd looked over at the Kennedy Space Centre a couple of months ago. And there was more bandage than flesh.

'Is he going to be all right?' Austin's voice crackled.

The doctor, who was standing at the end of the bed and still had his hand out, extended it further and placed it on Austin's forearm.

Austin shot him a glance. He knew he must look like a coyote in the headlights.

'It's going to be touch and go, sir. Your son, I'm assuming he's your son?'

Austin nodded, his head flitting between the doctor and Rick.

'He's suffered two major traumas. His liver was badly perforated as was one of his lungs.

Thankfully no major arteries were severed, but he lost a lot of blood. Surgery took almost 12 hours. I have removed half a lung and a chunk of liver. Fixed a lot of other stuff inside and sewn him up. He's in good shape, which is going to help. But the body doesn't like being torn apart and then having bits of itself removed. The next 12 hours will be crucial.'

'Thanks. Can I?' Austin pointed to Rick's bedside.

The doctor nodded with a half-smile.

'I'd like you to put on a mask please.' He was pointing to a box on a shelf to the right of the bed.

'Sure.' Austin picked up a mask and, not taking his eyes off his son, he moved to his bedside. A few seconds later he looked for a chair, found one a few feet away, pulled it up and sat down.

Without looking away from Rick, he pleaded, 'Will he wake up?'

The doctor hadn't moved from the end of the bed.

'He will be coming round from the operation in a couple of hours. He's heavily sedated. I'd like to have a chat with him when he comes to. When I'm happy, the police have asked that I give them a call - they'd like to talk to him as well. But that's not going to be until at least ...'

Austin didn't allow the doctor to finish his sentence.

'Does anyone know what happened?'

'No, sorry. The ambulance found him by chance - within probably a minute of the shooting. Any longer and he wouldn't have made it. He was downtown. He still had his wallet on him, so it wasn't a mugging. Probably drive-by.' There was a pause and then, 'Was he into gangs? Drugs?'

What?

'What are you saying?' Austin had to stop himself from shouting at the man.

The doctor wasn't fazed.

'Sorry, it just seems such an odd thing to have happened in broad daylight in that particular part of the town. I saw his military ID. Maybe it was terrorist-related?'

Austin was confused. He was getting on for mid-sixties but he had all his faculties. Terrorism? *In Vegas?*

Maybe it wasn't so off-the-scale? His son was a Reaper pilot. Killing the enemy from afar. Easier to kill a drone pilot in downtown Vegas than an armed soldier in Kabul.

Was he a prime target?

'I don't know. Has anyone told his base? Creech?'

'I'm not sure. We'd need to talk to reception. The police obviously found you. So, I guess they've be in touch with the CO there?'

Austin shook his head. Not in dismay, just in bewilderment. It was all mad. His son shot in the street. Possibly terrorist-related? What was the world coming to?

The doctor had allowed him to stay at Rick's bedside. He checked his watch. It was 8.17 pm. He'd been in the hospital for over three hours. And hadn't moved from his chair.

Austin wasn't a demonstrative man. It was a military thing. Touching and telling people what you thought about them - unless it was a chastisement - wasn't his way. But he had held Rick's hand since the doctor had left the room. He had spoken to his son, things he had never said to him before. Stuff from his heart. Things he should have said a long time ago.

He prayed as well, which was a long time coming. He hadn't prayed since Baghdad. Since that fateful November day when he'd been in the forward command post. Mike-Three-Zero-Charlie. A small brick-and-mud house, six of them, a couple of radios and a map. Controlling reconnaissance teams on the ground.

The flash, the noise - and then the gunfire. Smoke and cordite. He'd struggled to reach his helmet, which he'd taken off to get some fresh air to his head. He'd been hit in the leg by a piece of shrapnel, the Russian RGP rocket-launched grenade smashing the glass in the window and exploding against the back wall killing his friend,

Luke, in an instant. The firefight that followed lasted an hour.

An hour.

An hour before backup came. One radio had been destroyed in the initial blast. The second took a bullet ten minutes later. He had just managed to make a call to the Forward Operating Base (FOB). But the attack had been part of a simultaneous assault by local militia. Everyone was penned in.

'Do you want air support?', was the return call from HQ, the radio operator's voice difficult to hear above the sound of gunfire at their location.

He didn't have time to reply before the radio took a round, the green metal box flung across the room, the handset ripped from his grasp as its wire obediently followed its master.

If he had been a few seconds quicker they could have had an Apache overhead - maybe in a couple of minutes. But, and he'd asked himself this question a thousand times since, would it have made a difference? The area was heavily built-up. There was mayhem all around them. A pilot wouldn't have been able to make out red from blue. His five other teammates would have just as likely been ripped to pieces by the chopper's M230 chain gun as by the continuous fusillade of enemy rounds that eventually had turned their two-storey building into a one-storey pile of rubble.

An hour in hell. With, by the end, five dead teammates.

No. he hadn't been able to pray since that November day.

But he had prayed today. Offered his own life for his son's. Told The Lord to take anything he wanted. But Rick.

He closed his eyes.

And prayed some more.

'I didn't think you prayed?' The voice was weak and stuttery.

With his eyes closed and his mind in a dark place, he thought maybe God was admonishing him.

But it wasn't God.

He opened his eyes and found Rick looking back at him.

'Rick!'

The darkness evaporated. He had his boy back.

Rick coughed, a shallow cough which was immediately accompanied by a yelp of pain. The coughing seemed to bring on more coughing. His chest rose and fell, and his shoulders shuddered. More cries. And then blood rose from his chest with the coughing, splattering the pristine sheets and running down the side of his mouth. It was something from a horror movie.

The machines made noises that indicated alarm and, before Austin had a chance to shout 'nurse', one he hadn't seen before ran into the room.

The next five minutes were crazy. His son coughed. More blood came. The nurse ordered Austin away from the bed; he moved to the only window, its blind shut since he'd come into the room. The nurse took Rick by the shoulders and pushed him against the bed whilst issuing calm words. She played with the machines and fiddled with the drips. She offered some more calming words, wiping the blood from his chin with a cloth. Eventually the chaos was subsumed in calm.

Rick looked out of it, but the machines made reassuring pings, and green LED screens seemed to show signs of life.

'I've increased your sedative slightly.' The nurse was talking to Rick. 'Everything will be fine now. Try and suppress any cough you may have.'

Rick breathed shallowly, his eyes glazed but open.

The nurse turned to Austin.

'I think he needs to rest now, probably on his own. The coughing is a natural reaction to the surgery. It will pass. The blood was left over from the surgery. I don't think there is any new injury. The increased sedative will allow him to sleep for a bit longer.'

'Can I have a few words with him before I have to leave?'

The nurse looked at her watch.

'Two minutes. No more.'

'Thanks.'

As the nurse left Austin pulled up his chair and sat down. He took Rick's hand in his.

'Your mom is at home, son. She sends her love. You're going to be OK. You just need some time.'

Rick turned his head slightly so that he was facing Austin. His eyes were damp with tears.

'In my jacket pocket ...' Rick's words were hardly audible.

Austin was confused. Was his son delirious?

'What son? What's in your jacket pocket?'

Rick closed his eyes and just before he fell off to sleep he uttered, 'Report.' And then he was out of it.

Austin squeezed his son's hand tight and couldn't stop his own tears from forming. It was the first time he'd cried since his childhood.

Will he make it?

The nurse came back into the room and walked to the end of the bed. She put both hands on the bedstead.

'The doctor will be doing his rounds first thing tomorrow. I suggest you go and get yourself a cup of coffee from the canteen and maybe wait for his report? He should have something concrete to tell you at, say, 7 am?'

Austin didn't want to go, but he was trained to follow orders. He took one last look at his son, squeezed his hand tight and stood. He was about to leave the room when he remembered what Rick had said.

He stopped just before the door.

'May I have a look at my son's jacket? He said there was something in his pocket that I might be interested in.'

'Sure. His clothes are hung up in the wardrobe over there. Please remember that his jacket has bullet holes in it. I wouldn't want you to be distressed.'

'Sure.' Austin nodded a patronising nod. He had seen enough bullet holes in his time.

He opened the wardrobe door and pulled out his son's jacket. He put his hand in each of the pockets in turn, but couldn't find anything. He was about to put the jacket back, when something made him look again. *Ahh, there it was.* He'd missed a memory stick in the top left-hand pocket. A small, lime-green flash drive with no markings.

He studied it for a second and then put it in his trouser pocket.

He had no idea what his son was talking about. Maybe in a couple of hours he'd be able to speak to him some more and get to the bottom of this 'report'.

Jane stood at Frank's desk. She thought he hadn't noticed. He was intensely manipulating an image of an Arab-dressed man on his main screen - the background was a wood-panelled office. On a second screen was another photo, this time of a group on the open-back of a Toyota Hilux. Jane counted five men squeezed together. All of them were carrying rifles, probably AKs, the barrels pointing skyward.

'This is Ahmad Malouf.' He had noticed her.

He was pointing at the main screen. 'This photo was taken in Damascus earlier this year. Ahmad Malouf is a sidekick of the current Syrian Minister of Defence. He's a "senior civil servant",' Frank used his fingers to denote speech marks, 'without portfolio, as far as our team there can ascertain.'

He now pointed at the second screen and using a single finger, he drew an e-box to highlight the face of one of the men on the back of the Hilux. He spread two fingers across the screen and the image enlarged and pixelated. Cynthia, SIS's mainframe, used its very powerful image-enhancing software to bring the face in the box back into focus.

'This could also be him.' He turned back to his first screen and opened a new tab - throwing up a map of Iran and Afghanistan. He zoomed in on a border-crossing point in the east of Iran.

'Interestingly the photo of the Hilux was taken crossing the Iranian/Afghan border here, at Zaranj. The DTG is here ...' He pointed at the date/time/group at the bottom of the photo. It read: 071430ZJan17. Jane's brain decoded it with ease.

'That's a week ago? Who took it?'

'It's a US photo. Taken by a CIA informant working with the Iranian border security team. We had the one taken in the Ministry; they had the one at the border. If this is Malouf,' he was pointing back at the second screen, 'then we have irrefutable proof linking the Syrian regime in Damascus to some, as yet unknown, cell in Afghanistan.'

Jane scratched her chin.

'It's a helluva trick getting from Syria to the Iranian/Afghan border. If they drove they'd have had to make it through Turkey or Iraq and then through the whole of Iran?'

'Unless they flew and picked up a ride in country?'

'Then why not fly straight into Afghanistan?'

'Stingers?'

Frank's comment was overstating the deployment of the US hand-held anti-aircraft (AA) Stinger missile system, both in capability and deployment. Jane was unsure that the US had

169

troops in the southwest of Afghanistan, and she didn't think the ANA (Afghan National Army) had been issued with Stingers.

'Maybe. Maybe not.'

She bent forward and looked at both the images of the man. They did look very similar. Cynthia's face recognition programme would be able to give them a degree of certainty once Frank had run it.

'Great work.' She then changed tack. 'Anything from Sam?'

Frank looked up and over his shoulder to Jane.

'No, sorry. The number she phoned you on is dead, or off. Her original number is the same story. I've looked through her closed file and there are no other numbers. Do you want me to spread the net wider?'

Jane thought for a second. Sam was probably covering her back and switching phones.

'Yes, please. Put an alert out through Border Force and stick her details on a countrywide alert. All bases: phone, credit card, hotels. I need to track her down.'

Frank had already opened a new tab, the title displaying 'Border Force Personnel Security Alert'.

'Thanks.' Jane turned to leave, but then added, 'Anything from your CIA pal on the "who messed with my GPS?" conspiracy?'

Frank titled his head to one side. He stared through Jane and seemed to be focusing on the ceiling.

'No, it's funny. His desk has gone silent. There's an automated "out-of-office" response on his email and he's not answering his phone. I suppose he could be on holiday, or there's been some other catastrophe with which he has had to deal. But I've got to know him quite well. I would have thought he might have said something to me before he disappeared?'

Jane studied Frank's face. He was a darling. Hard-working, excellent with images and video. And a heart of gold. She thought she registered 'concern' on his face.

'Check it out Frank. And if you don't get a sensible reply, come back to me and I'll go up the chain.'

'Sure, Jane, sure.'

Terminal 5, London's Heathrow Airport

Sam stared absently at the departures board. She was looking for a flight to Nassau - The Bahamas.

There it was: BA253. Departing at 9.40am, gate number B36. The clock on the display said it was 7.25am. She had plenty of time.

It had been a bit of a whirl since she'd spoken to Wolfgang yesterday afternoon. She'd done exactly as she'd said she would after she'd phoned him from Victoria Mitchell's place. She'd driven to Norwich, found TK Maxx and then spent £180 on a range of winter clothes that suited her off-the-shelf, 'trekking' vogue. *Shabby safari*. As she absently shopped, always looking at the price before she held the selected garment up against her appropriate body part(s), she asked herself, 'what should I do next?'

The resounding answer was: not sure.

A year ago she would have had access to the best intelligence depository in the world. She would have used Cynthia's vast search capacity to unpick and then piece together the question: 'who is Victoria Mitchell?'. At the same time she would have liaised with GCHQ and, having gained appropriate authority, asked them to tap Mitchell's phone and review her call history. It may have taken a couple of hours, but soon enough she'd have been much closer to working out what was going on with Mr and Mrs Mitchell. And she could have photofit of the red-ski-jacket-man from Alpbach - and discovered who he was.

Instead she was at a loss.

That was until Wolfgang called.

As a precaution Sam had removed the two SIMs she'd used so far from her phone. She'd loaded a third into the unlocked Motorola Wolfgang had given her and, just as she was paying the nice lady behind the TK Maxx counter, it rang.

'Sorry.' She said to the woman. She pressed the green connect button, turned away from the counter and put the phone to her ear.

'Yes?'

'It's me. I have your next mission, should you choose to accept it.'

Very droll.

'Give me a second.'

Sam paid the woman, took hold of the red-and-white logo'd plastic bag and started to make her way to the exit. On the way out she spotted a pair of Salomon walking trousers which she had missed earlier. They looked to be her size. *Bugger.* She may come back for them once she'd taken the call.

'How can I help you?' Sam was outside now.

'Have you been shopping?'

Sam dropped the bag on the floor, reached into the pocket of her jacket and pulled out her black beanie. The wind was whistling in from The Steppes having just crossed the North Sea - its first stop was Norwich High Street. She deftly pulled the sides of the hat down over her ears with her free hand.

'Yes. Thank you. You'll be pleased to hear that I didn't spend a great deal.'

'Ahh. Good. You might want to take it all back. I fancy that you have paid for the wrong wardrobe.'

What?

'What?'

'I have bought a ticket for you out of Heathrow tomorrow morning, leaving between 9 and 10 am. I have taken the liberty of booking you into the Sofitel, which is a half-mile walk from the Terminal. The reviews on TripAdvisor are very good. They particularly rate the breakfasts.'

Sam had turned her back on the wind. It was perishing.

'What? What are you playing at?' In the mayhem Sam almost finished the sentence with Wolfgang's name. But checked herself.

'I was able to turn over a few more stones yesterday. When you get to the hotel we'll set you up with a password to securely access the hard drives here. You can look through the intelligence I've found - and check your flight details. I don't want to mention them now. In short, and to whet your appetite, I've established a positive link between the husband of your woman, and an offshore bank account. And, with no other assistance than Lady Luck, I think I have an "in". That is, *you* have an "in". We should talk more using the secure interface when you get to the hotel.'

Sam was confused, but now interested. She knew better than to ask for any more details.

'What should my wardrobe look like?'

'I'd buy a bikini.'

That's a great help.

'And some flipflops?'

'Those too.'

'And how did you manage to do all of this without my passport?'

'Come on …', Wolfgang almost fell into the same trap that Sam had avoided and mentioned her by name, 'I am a hacker. This is what I do.'

That was yesterday afternoon. Now well-rested and particularly well fed, she had a medium-sized rucksack full of hot-weather gear and was heading for The Bahamas.

Sam approached the British Airways Clubworld (a nice, but unnecessary touch from Wolfgang) check-in. Behind the desk was a slightly overweight, middle-aged woman with a forced smile and too much make-up. She looked Sam up and down as though she was definitely at the wrong check-in. Sam wondered if it were her empire-building shorts, her Jesus sandals, or her light-blue baseball cap with its palm tree emblem - or maybe all three - that was putting the woman off.

'Passport and e-ticket, please.' That fake smile again. It was beginning to irritate Sam.

She handed over her passport and showed the e-ticket details from her phone. The woman smiled again. Sam was sure she saw her make-up cracking.

The next five minutes were unsettling, and it wasn't miss smiley-pants that was the cause.

As the woman logged her in, Sam noticed the expression on her face change as she worked the keyboard and monitor (which Sam couldn't see). The woman glanced up at Sam, and then back down at the monitor. Twice. She smiled again, this time with a touch of nervousness, her head tilted patronisingly to one side. And then she typed some more - more than Sam remembered being necessary from the last time she flew.

Another smile.

Was that a touch of sweat on her forehead? Sam wanted to reach out and mop it up with The Simpsons-motif hanky she had in her pocket (which she'd found in the 'reduced' red-label section of TK Maxx - *bargain*).

'Is that your only bag?' The woman pointed to her rucksack.

Sam didn't take her eyes off smiley-pants. She gave her her best terrorist look. At which point she thought that the woman had squeezed her knees together.

'Yes.' Without looking at her bag.

''Good. On the conveyor please.'

Sam did as she was asked.

And then, with renewed efficiency, her bag was labelled and dispatched down the chute. In a rush the woman handed back Sam's passport and boarding pass.

'Flight's in two hours. Gate B36. You'll have time for a coffee.' More smiles.

Ugh!

Sam warily took her passport back and nodded - slowly.

'Thank you.' She let her stare linger. For effect.

'You're welcome.' That smile again, but it could have been a grimace. Was it tinged with relief?

As Sam walked towards the departure gate, she turned to look back at the desk. The woman was gone. She'd left in a rush.

She revisited the last ten minutes.

Am I tagged? Is there a flag against my name? If I were a threat I'd have been immediately surrounded by men with guns, shown to a small room without any windows and had parts of me searched that usually didn't see the light of day. So, I'm not a threat - per se. But someone wants to know where I'm going?

When she was an SIS case officer she'd had three aliases, and could fly around the globe pretty much unnoticed. Those days were gone. Today she was just Sam Green. Wolfgang had had no other alternative than to book her on a flight using her own credentials. If someone wanted to find her, or follow her, they'd just need access to the Border Force's secure travel inventory. Any half-decent hacker could do that.

I'm tagged? Probably.

Alarm bells rang in the back of her head. She involuntarily hunched her shoulders. And pouted.

But Sam had no option other than to run with the plan. She was off to The Bahamas to meet a friend of Wolfgang's deceased father: a Lukas Müller. He was the 2IC of Walter Ingris Bank. Walter Ingris was a respectable offshore set-up which, among other attributes, laundered and hid money for people who didn't want it to be found. Sure, the bank probably had plenty of clients who operated within the boundaries of the law. But this type of bank doesn't ask many questions. They just take your money.

And, and this was key, Wolfgang had established a clear linkage between Paul Mitchell, his current business dealings and Walter Ingris. He reckoned that, with numerous accounts linked to The Bahamas, it was likely that the bank was The Church's main financial hub. Sam had seen the evidence last night. It looked pretty conclusive.

Wolfgang had assured Sam that he could arrange a meeting between her and Herr Müller, and that she would know what questions to ask. Especially as Müller was an old family friend who, on checking his BND (*Bundesnachrichtendienst* - the German Federal Intelligence Organisation) records, had a penchant for young boys.

'You will know how to handle him, I'm sure. I'll set up a meeting once you've acclimatised. Leave it with me.'

So, Sam now had at least two sets of unpleasant people who might be interested in her itinerary: Mitchell and The Church of the White Cross; and Walter Ingris Bank. Both would be able to follow her around the globe. She was sure of that.

She'd definitely needed to be on her guard.

Sunrise Hospital, Las Vegas

Austin woke with a start. He'd been sleeping on a soft chair in the hospital cafe. His back ached and his left arm had pins and needles. As he rubbed his eyes he glanced at his watch. It was 7.25am. Hopefully the doctor would have seen Rick by now.

He stood and stretched. The cafe was empty, save for an elderly woman in hospital robes nursing a cup of coffee. She smiled at him. He managed a smile back.

Rick's room was in a separate block and three floors higher. Austin walked quickly but it still took him over five minutes to cover the distance. He didn't take the lift but, as was his way, he took the stairs two at a time. When he opened the stairwell door he was breathing hard. It felt good.

Unfortunately, that feeling didn't last. As he turned into the corridor off which his son's room was located, he was met by third-degree chaos.

There were cops everywhere. The route past reception was cordoned with black and yellow 'Police Do Not Cross' tape. A young cop had his notepad out and was interviewing a nurse. Next to him was a man in a white SOCO (Scenes Of Crime Officer) suit. His hood was off his head and he was inspecting an evidence bag. Austin couldn't see what was in it.

As he stepped down the corridor he was immediately met by another cop, who firmly stopped him in his tracks.

'Sorry, sir. There's been an incident. I'm afraid I'm going to have to ask you to leave.'

'But, my son. Lieutenant Rick Rodgers. He's in a room down the corridor.' Austin pointed down towards Rick's room. He spotted it immediately. There was another cop standing outside the door.

'Are you Lieutenant Rodger's father?' The cop had a concerned look on his face.

Austin was losing it now. He felt dizzy. The exertion of bounding up the stairs, combined with knowing what was probably coming next, was taking its toll.

'Yes. That's me.' His reply was weak. The dizziness was getting worse. Nausea was now its companion.

'I'd like you to come with me, sir. I'm afraid we have some bad news.'

As the policeman led Austin away, down the corridor in the opposite direction to Rick's room, he unconsciously reached for the pocket in his shirt. As soon as he felt the pen drive safe in his pocket, his legs gave way.

Chapter 7

The cell's door opened - Jakov couldn't think of a better word to describe the locked bed/sink/toilet/desk/chair space in which he'd slept. It was a monk. The same monk who had taken him from his hospital bed the night before and showed him to the room. Jakov had no idea what his name was. He knew better than to ask.

He'd slept fitfully. His right arm was sore as hell, even with the painkillers they had given him. He had tossed and turned all night. The dog-bite wound was seeping something horrible and, having checked first thing, he noticed a red track coming out from the top of the bandages heading to his shoulder. That didn't look right.

The monk was carrying a small first-aid satchel. He motioned for Jakov to sit on the only chair in the room - and then he proceeded to remove the olive drab t-shirt Jakov was wearing. The t-shirt, along with a pair of dark green pyjama trousers complete with tie-up cord and some black Crocs, would appear to be his issued garb. He had no idea where they had come from.

The monk deftly removed the bandages and looked over the wound. Jakov's shoulder was still two sizes bigger than it should be, the result, he assumed, of the dislocation. He had two dog bites on his forearm. The first was a long laceration which had been expertly stitched - the dog's first attempt to bring him down. Whilst red and enlarged, it looked like it was on the mend. The second gash was where the dog's teeth had embedded themselves in his arm and held on - it was further up towards his elbow. It was this wound that was not happy. There were six butterfly stitches, two of which were seeping pus and seemed to be the source of the infection tracking up his arm.

The monk opened his satchel and took out a hypodermic needle and a small vial of something (the writing was too small for Jakov to make it out). He filled the needle, cleared the air from the syringe and, without warning, stuck the tip into Jakov's forearm, just above the highest wound. It was too close to the gash to be anywhere near comfortable. Jakov let out a low-pitched cry and his eyes watered.

'Yow! What the ...?'

The monk ignored him. He then removed a toothpaste tubed-shape of what Jakov assumed was antiseptic cream and, very gently, smoothed it over the wound. That didn't hurt. Next was a new set of bandages which the monk secured firmly - but not so tight that it was painful.

Finally, he showed Jakov a bottle of pills - the label read: *Cefalexin*. The monk signalled for

Jakov's open hand and shook two-light-and-dark-green capsules into his palm. He walked to the sink and came back with a mug of water. He then made a swallowing gesture and, as if to show the dosage, stuck two fingers up in a victory salute, dropped them, made the salute again, and then did the same thing a third time.

Who needs speech?

'Antibiotics? Two tablets, three times a day?'

The monk nodded.

He then helped Jakov put his t-shirt back on and provided a green fleece which he'd brought with him. He packed up his satchel and led him from the room, locking the door behind them with a key.

The corridor was as Jakov remembered: white walls and recessed steel doors on both sides. His room was halfway down the hall. It had a single window which was barred - the glass opaque. There were no windows in the corridor. The light was artificial, glaring from neon tubes overhead. It was like he imagined the inside of a barrack block.

This time, rather than turning right to the surgery a few doors down from his cell, they turned left, then right, and then right again, walking out through a set of half-glass double doors into a courtyard. They were met by a ten-degree drop in temperature.

Jakov took it all in. The monastery was a two-storey, hollow square - the outside copying the inside in appearance: a barrack block. All the windows were small; white-framed against the cream render of the walls. The red-tiled roof was high-pitched. At one corner there was the bell tower - it rose a storey higher than the main building. In the middle of one of the four sides of the sizeable quadrangle was a large arch which housed a full-height studded metal door. In the middle of the three remaining sides were sets of double doors, like the one from which they had just exited.

In the centre of the courtyard was an ornate pond embellished with a small fountain. The courtyard was cobbled and around its outside, against the building's walls, were numerous benches. Jakov counted three monks sitting on the benches. One was reading a book and two more were on laptops. They were all wearing habits, they all had their heads shaved, and Jakov thought it unlikely that he would be able to tell any of them apart.

Overall Jakov got a sense of peace and order, but in a modern way. The place was pristine. There was no grass growing between the cobbles. The wooden benches were all freshly-oiled. And the white windows were double-glazed replacements. There were discreet but state-of-the-art cameras under the eaves of the roof. Someone had a very tidy - and suspicious - mind. And he guessed that money wasn't a problem either.

He realised his monk was letting him take it all in. The monk smiled, took hold of his left forearm and led Jakov around the square.

They passed two monks sitting on a bench who both looked up and nodded to Jakov in a kindly way. Jakov's monk nodded politely in return.

They stopped by the main arch with the metal doors. Whilst looking Jakov straight in the eye, his monk pointed to the doors and wagged his finger slowly.

Going out through those is not allowed.

Got it.

They finally finished their circuit at the third set of double doors. His monk led him through the doors into a hall about the size of a half tennis court. It was the canteen. There were eight tables and probably 25 chairs. There were a few monks sitting here and there, mostly in pairs, eating their breakfast. It was unearthly quiet. Above the silence he heard the gentle 'clank' of metal against china.

And then he spotted him. In one corner, sitting on his own: the deranged man.

Who had just spotted Jakov.

'Ahh, Jakov Vuković! Come and have some breakfast.' He waved his arm theatrically. The words were no louder than normal speaking volume, but in the quiet of the monastery they bellowed across the room. None of the monks took any notice.

He glanced at his minder, who nodded deferentially and used a hand to show Jakov the way.

Jakov, who suddenly realised he was holding his arm like an old war wound, picked his way through the tables towards his captor.

'Sit, sit!' Still too loud for the surroundings. He was offering the seat opposite.

Jakov gingerly sat down, wincing as the motion caused his shoulder to protest.

'How's the injury?'

Jakov didn't enjoy the feigned interest, but knew he had no choice but to reply.

'Fine, thanks.' After his previous pathetic behaviour in front of the deranged man, he thought he'd try to show some strength. 'It would have been better if you hadn't set your dogs on me.'

'Ahh. The hounds!' The deranged man made a scary face and put his hands up in mock horror.

He immediately dropped the acting.

'Should have read the notices on the buoys. Hey?'

Jakov nodded. 'Sure.'

They were interrupted by his monk. He had brought a tray of scrambled eggs served on a bagel, and a cup of coffee. Next to the cup was a small jug of milk and some sugar. He was beginning to like his monk. He'd have to think of an appropriate name for the man.

'Eat. Eat! You have a busy day ahead of you.' The deranged man (he'd have to think of an appropriate name for him as well; Hannibal was looking like a good choice) thrust his empty mug towards the monk.

'Coffee!' It was an order. There was no politeness.

His monk (*Karlo?*) took the cup without any protest; he nodded again and left the table.

'Think of today as a sort of induction. Your friend will show you round, you'll have your hair cut - very short. It's our anti-lice programme ...', his words were quick-fire, the 'anti-lice' statement accompanied by a clown-like facial expression of disgust, '... no, no. Not really.' A giggle. 'Just easier to look after.' He put his finger to his mouth in mock thought. 'And then you'll be taken to your place of work. Initially you'll be in the gardens - we like to be self-sufficient here. Well, actually ...', more theatrics, 'I'm partial to steak and champagne, so we have that shipped in. But, for the rest of you it's a healthy diet - nearly all of it home-grown. You'll like it, I'm sure.'

Jakov couldn't stop staring at the man's mouth - his expressions. It was like watching a highly-charged comic actor who was working overtime during an audition.

Ahh. No, he had it. Jim Carrey and *The Mask*. Only more sinister and more off his head. As Jakov took a mouthful of eggs the deranged man stopped. His head pushed back. He looked confused.

'Sorry. Is anything wrong? Have I got something between my teeth?' He opened his lips with his teeth together, like a Cheshire cat. 'Anything?', the word lost between clenched teeth,

'No, I thought not. Well, you've found your room? Your friend will show you where you can go, and where you can't. And take you to meals. Think of it like boarding school.'

The monk had returned with the deranged man's coffee. He took a swig and placed it back on the table.

'Mmm. Well, I must be off. Time's money, etc, etc.'

He stood quickly and walked round so that he was at Jakov's right hand side.

Jakov looked up nervously. The deranged man looked down, meeting his stare. A power play. He now had a sinister grin on his face.

Oh God, what now?

'Hannibal' gently placed his hand on Jakov's right shoulder. The smallest of touches sent an imaginary streak of pain through his body. He prepared himself for the worst.

'We have an agreement, yes?'

Jakov nodded.

189

'I have complete control here, yes?'

Jakov nodded some more.

'The work we are doing is *very* important and one day, once you and I have built up a level of trust, I might share some of it with you.'

He very gently put some pressure on Jakov's shoulder. Jakov stared at his half-eaten plate of eggs. He felt the pain rising, and tears forming. He closed his eyes. He thought he might throw up.

'Now, be good. Promise?'

He squeezed some more. Jakov couldn't prevent a 'yelp' rising from his throat. He nodded, acknowledging the Hannibal's comment.

'Excellent, excellent.' He released his hand and turned to the monk.

'Get him to work. And keep a close eye on him.' He scowled, all hint of theatre had vanished.

The monk bowed his head.

Jakov opened his eyes. He glanced round the room. None of the monks had batted an eyelid. They were going about their business as though the induction and gentle torture of a local boy was second nature to them.

What have I got myself involved with?

Frank was puzzled. He'd had a 'ping' from Border Force. It was an automated notification email. It showed that a 'Sam Green', with Sam's passport number, had boarded a plane from Heathrow to Nassau. BA253. It was now mid-flight with an arrival time of 14.20 local. Frank checked time zones. The Bahamas were 5 hours behind the UK. And there was a star against the booking. Frank opened a separate tab. It read:

> *Ticket not booked by passenger. Booker unknown. Booking reference BA235$/dghry/23356.*

Booker unknown? Someone, not Sam, or not one of Sam's known accounts, had booked her on a flight to The Bahamas. Not only that, but the person booking the flight has used arcane processes so that they could not be easily traced.

The Bahamas?

What was Sam up to? Why was someone else booking her flight for her? And in such a way that the security services wouldn't know who it was? And why did Jane want to talk to Sam?

Frank looked across at the glass-walled cabin that was Jane's room. She wasn't in - but Claire was.

He opened up SIS's secure chat.

To Claire: *Where's Jane?*

He pressed return and then looked across the floor to where Claire was, just 20 feet away. She popped her head up from behind her screen. And then dropped down again.

Claire is typing ... *you have got legs.*
To Claire: *yeah, but where's Jane?*
Claire is typing ... *with the boss. Will be out of it for an hour at least. You should try walking. It's underrated.*
To Claire: *yeah, should do. Don't want to scuff my new trainers.*
Claire is typing ... *you can't take them with you when you die (of inertia).*

Frank smiled to himself. And suddenly felt mischievous.

With some effort he clambered onto his chair; it swivelled a bit as he got up and he almost lost his balance. Then, with dexterity he didn't realise he had, he placed one foot on top of his main screen and pointed to a new grey-and-peach Adidas trainer.

Claire looked up over her screen and gave Frank a withering look.

Frank got down. As he did he had a quick glance round the office. One or two people were giving him odd looks, and there was a smile here and there. But this was Babylon. The organisation was full to the brim with highly-strung misfits and oddballs - pranks were commonplace, almost encouraged. What they did from day to day was crucial to the safety and security of the country's interests overseas; they all needed to let off steam every so often.

Back to work.

He'd brief Jane later. He needed to look after Sam.

Although he'd not seen or been in touch with Sam for almost a year - other than the odd postcard, he considered her to be a very good friend. They had worked side by side as analysts in the early days. She had brought her Military Intelligence experience with her and, after a few weeks driving the desk, she was quickly as good as any other analyst in the building. As well as a photographic memory she had an uncanny knack for detail. She saw things - found things - in images, and on paper, that others didn't. She blamed her OCD and other ailments. He put it down to bags of tenacity. She was a machine; one without a rheostat. She worked until she dropped. He'd never come across anyone like her. Whichever the reason, the outcome in terms of the delivery of intelligence was often spectacular.

They had worked through the German affair together - he acted as her sidekick as she charged around Europe with the German count (*what was his name?*) helping to uncover the ultra-right Christian sect, The Church of the White Cross. And then, when she had been posted to Moscow, he had again supported her as she and the American intern had chased and prevented the terror attack in Rome. They had almost lost her three times - and on all three occasions he had felt sick to his core. He didn't mind admitting that he had a huge soft spot for Sam Green.

Though, women weren't his thing. He wasn't gay, it was just that at five-foot-five, now with a tummy and dressed like a 70s-rock groupie, he was hardly God's gift. So, he never really got close enough to find out what women were like. He'd like to. He would. He'd also like to fly to New Zealand and do *The Lord of the Rings* tour on motorbike. There were lots of things he'd *like* to do.

But, work was where he was at his most comfortable.

And, just now, he needed to find out what Sam Green was up to. She might need his help.

Frank opened his email and typed a GCHQ address into the 'To' box. He filled in the title: *Sam Green - SIS retiree - update.*

The email was to the pal of his at Cheltenham who was already looking over Sam's phone numbers. It read:

Hi Beth,

A couple of things. I guess there's nothing from either of the numbers I gave you ref Sam Green? Second, I'm going to forward you a Border Force alert concerning Sam. She appears to be on a plane to Nassau (lucky her). What is interesting is that she didn't book the flight herself. It was done by a third party and, I guess via multiple ISPs, the party's details are hidden. I'm going to try the SFO (Serious Fraud Office) *and see if they can help. In the meantime can you do your best?*

Use the same case number for the work.

Thanks. Give us a call if you get anything.

Frank xx

He read the mail then pressed 'Send'. He'd brief Jane as soon as she was back in the office.

Lynden Pindling International, Nassau, The Bahamas

Sam got a sniff of the heat at the front exit of the 777. The gap between the aircraft's door and the

195

bridge ramp was large enough to remind unwary passengers that it was hot out there - 82 degrees according to the pilot. The ramp wasn't air conditioned, but the terminal was, so the blast of heat was short-lived. It didn't matter. Sam knew that soon enough she'd have to get used to the heat. That wouldn't be a problem - military training in Jordan and Belize, operations in Afghanistan and three weeks of nonsense in West Africa had taught her how to cope.

It wasn't the heat she was concerned about. It was the fact that she was, more likely than not, being monitored. Maybe followed. This was something else she had experienced before and it wasn't a great feeling. Thankfully her SIS training had taught her how to lose a tail, and she was good at it.

She'd checked the plane. The 777 carried anywhere between 314 and 396 passengers. Sam reckoned BA253 was carrying 267 passengers. She had walked the length of the aircraft - twice. She counted as she walked (she didn't need to, she just couldn't stop herself) like a school teacher checking kids on a bus. As she walked she looked for a tail. Statistics taught her that 76% of professional tails were male. It wasn't that women didn't make great spies - 40% of Mossad were women and SIS were close to a 50/50 balance - it's just that tailing more naturally fell to men because they were less conspicuous than their female equivalent. Women didn't tend to hang about on street corners. And the ones who did, more often than not attracted a lot of unnecessary attention.

She had focused on the men.

Two were possibles, giving away their intent by trying very hard not to look at her as she had drifted past. 'Trying not to look' was an obvious tail's trait (there was little about surveillance and informant-running that wasn't common sense), and could be a giveaway. However, on Sam's second pass both men were flat out; one looked like he had drunk his fill from the complimentary bar and the other was zedding to the world. So, no tails on the aircraft as far as she could tell. She would do a final check in the baggage hall.

Getting through immigration control was straightforward - the local behind the desk showed no particular interest in Sam. And, in the small but roomy baggage reclaim hall, Sam made a final once over. Nothing.

Job one - tick. She'd have to start again in the arrivals lounge.

Lynden Pindling International Airport, named after Sir Lynden Pindling, the 'Father of the Bahamian Nation' - Sam had asked a stewardess, was more a small regional airport than international hub. There were 6 commercial aircraft on the apron and a scattering of lesser prop-planes. The arrivals hall had an interestingly-curved concrete ceiling and there were a few places to buy something to eat, a couple of shops, two car rental desks and signs to various other modes of transport.

Wolfgang had booked Sam a hire car with Avis. She made her way towards their desk, stopping short to look like she was tying her shoelace. With her back to the car-rental desk, she knelt on one knee scanning the hall for a local tail.

Looking left. Nothing.

Right. Nothing.

Hang on.

There was a local on the rail opposite the customs exit doors - the ones she'd just come through. He was holding an A4-sized card, on which was written 'Mr Jones'.

Mr Jones? Really?

And he was standing at an odd angle, half-facing the arrivees and half-looking around the hall. He shot Sam a quick glance, noticed her stare and immediately turned to face the exit doors.

An airport 'pick up'. Good choice of cover. You have to look for someone, but you're not an obvious tail. But this guy wasn't very subtle.

And Mr Jones - poor choice of name.

Sam studied the man's back. He was tall, six-two, well-built and wore 'professional' clothing - smart black slacks and an open-necked red shirt. He had a mobile telephone pouch hung from a snakeskin belt, and Sam caught the hint of a heavy gold chain around his neck.

She stood, moving away from the Avis desk towards the main exit, and then darted into a shop selling cards, trinkets and other tourist tat. Sam positioned herself between a carousel of baseball caps and the shop window, with semi-clear views of her potential tail.

She took off her cap with the palm motif and tried on a red one (not her colour, all that auburn hair) with 'The Bahamas' announcing themselves in yellow letters just above the peak. She feigned fitting it as she studied the man with the snakeskin belt. After a few seconds he wildly turned his head (*really not subtle at all - needs more training*), but this time he couldn't see Sam. His whole body turned. He was now facing away from the arrival doors. She thought she spotted a hint of alarm as the man took a couple of steps towards the Avis desk. He then glanced left and right.

Panic mode now?

Whilst wholly frustrated that she had picked up a tail, Sam congratulated herself on being reasonably well-hidden. To reduce the chance of being discovered she dropped on her haunches and waited to see what would happen next.

The man took a few steps to the left, and then to the right. *Real panic now.* Sam was beginning to enjoy this. He then walked quickly to the woman behind the Avis counter. Sam couldn't hear what was being said, but it was pretty obvious that he was enquiring about her. The woman pointed towards the shop. Sam dropped even further, curling into a ball.

But it was no good. Either the Avis woman was particularly adept at noticing people, or the pair of them were in cahoots and she had been observing Sam from the get-go.

How does that work? Who are these people?

With the red mist beginning to descend - *can't I go anywhere without some fucker chasing me?* - and with no time to think through her options, she made a play.

She took her new favourite baseball cap to the counter and casually offered to pay for it. With a lethargy that she recognised from West Africa, the smart-looking female cashier took her time to take Sam's money, fiddle at the till and then give her her change.

Sam stared at her open hand.

What?

There were now two conflicting issues that were pissing her off: her tail and her change. The price on the baseball cap was $15 - not a sum she would normally part with for any head gear, but needs must. She'd handed over a $20 bill and counted $3.95 in the palm of her hand. There'd been a mistake.

For an instant she'd forgotten about the man with the snakeskin belt who was now almost certainly in the shop with her. She fought it, but her OCD wouldn't allow her to be short-changed.

'The cap was $15.' Sam stated, trying to hide her frustration.

The woman looked through her.

'Tax.'

'Tax?' Sam was losing it now. This was a tax-free country. That's why terrorist organisations like The Church of The White Cross launder their money here. There's no government asking questions - looking for capital gains tax, or any other tax you can think of.

'VAT. Standard.' The woman's single-word answers made the ends of Sam's fingers itch. She so wanted to hand the cap back and recover her cash.

Or do some other damage.

When, what she really needed to do was to take back control. To forget about the taxes in a tax haven. And get on with her play.

Sam breathed deeply. Three times. *Calm.*

'Thanks.'

The woman smiled a rubbish, fleeting smile she probably used for all tourists.

Sam picked up her rucksack and bought herself some time by putting the new cap in the top compartment. As she did so she caught sight of her tail. He was by the door. *Looking at the baseball caps?* She sighed an inner sigh. When this was over she was going to set up business in The Bahamas running a security firm. And make a fortune.

The play.

Sam took a couple of strides forward trying to look as uncoordinated as she could. She held her bag in an odd way, not slinging it. She stopped mid-shop and played with a zip.

And then she absently bumped into her tail.

She got a good look at him. He was ugly-looking, mid-30s with a chipped front tooth. She'd recognise him again - anywhere. If she had access to SIS's mainframe, Cynthia, she'd be able to use the photofit software and, if the man had a record anywhere, she'd have his name within the hour.

She didn't have access to SIS's mainframe.

But she did have her tail's mobile, which she slipped into her pocket.

Next stop Avis, behind which was a beautiful black woman whose lipstick was as red as the Avis skirt she was wearing.

'Hello. How can I help?'

Well, first, if you don't mind, I'd like to dive over the desk and throttle you to an inch of your life. Then I'm going to ask you who you are working for? And when we're done with that I'm going to stick you in the boot of an SUV and drive to a secluded beach ...

Get a grip.

'You have a car for me? Sam Green.'

Getting the car took another 20 minutes. Sam really didn't want to take a car. She would be using her name when she didn't need to, the car would be tagged and wherever she went on the small island (Sam reckoned New Providence was half the size of the Isle of Man) they, whoever 'they' were, would be able to track her.

A random taxi would be the textbook choice.

But her tail had changed all that. She would lose control in a taxi. Assuming her tail thought she was just some blundering fool, incapable of walking in a straight line, then she'd be better in a car. More control.

She'd take a car.

'Not that one.' Sam said when the woman handed the keys over. Sam checked over her shoulder. Her tail, the man with the snakeskin belt, was 20 metres away trying to look nonchalant.

'Sorry?'

'I don't want that car, I'd like another?' Sam was at least trying to add some randomness to her decision making.

'I'm sorry, I don't understand.'

Sam looked at the key fob. It read '251336', which Sam assumed was the car's number plate.

'I don't like the number. Bad Juju.' Sam had no idea if Bahamians had a thing with witchcraft, but it was the first thought that came into her head.

'I'm a tarot card reader.' She added.

The woman took the key and looked at the fob. She scrunched up her face. And then, holding the keys at arm's length as if they were diseased, deposited them in a tray to one side.

'OK. OK.' The woman nodding nervously as she spoke.

It took another ten minutes to sort a different car. The woman showed Sam the plate details on a piece of paper before finishing the transaction.

'That's fine, thanks. Good Juju.' *Oh dear.*

And that was that.

Sam had a non-bad Juju car; certainly one which hadn't been prearranged with her name plastered all over it.

Next, she had to lose her tail. Then find a new hotel. Wolfgang had booked her into a suite at *Atlantis* - Sam had seen the price; it had made her eyes water. And it also had her name on it. She needed somewhere fresh.

From there she could check out her tail's mobile (probably with Wolfgang's help). And then meet up with the paedophile banker.

Getting off this island, if she ever got that far, was going to be an altogether more interesting proposition.

Against the boredom of her life that was everything before she had bumped into Paul Mitchell on the ski-slopes of Austria, things had ratcheted up a notch or two.

That wasn't such a bad thing. Was it?

The white Suzuki Swift didn't have a satnav. There was a fold-up map on the passenger seat. But Sam didn't need either. In the Sofitel at Heathrow she had looked over the island using Google Maps, zooming in on the capital Nassau to pick up some of the minor streets. There was a road around the island's coast, two east to west through the middle, and seven more north to south. There were plenty more smaller roads, with Nassau being particularly busy. She'd spent ten minutes looking at the detail and had seen enough; like a camera, she remembered what she had seen. As for navigation, as with a number of things that went on upstairs which she couldn't control, it came naturally to her.

Sam found the car easily, threw her rucksack on the back seat and headed east towards Nassau. She hadn't looked for her tail - she assumed he would follow her in a vehicle, and that she'd be able to spot him more discreetly from behind the wheel rather than trying to pick him up in the car park.

The first four miles were dual carriageway: JFK Drive. She'd then have a couple of choices as to how to get into Nassau. And if she then wanted to go onto Paradise Island, the major resort where Wolfgang had booked her hotel, she'd need to cross the only bridge between the capital and the tiny island. Sam wasn't keen on that idea, no matter how glamorous the suite that Wolfgang had booked. It was bad enough being stuck on a small island, without exacerbating the whole shebang by driving onto an even smaller one. No, she'd find a hotel in Nassau - not on Paradise Island.

The other advice she'd picked up from various internet travel sources was 'to stick to the main carriageways and avoid minor roads, especially in the middle of the island'. Gang crime was rife. In 2015, out of an island population of 250,000 people, there had been 150 murders. Most were gun and knife killings - and nearly all of the dead were local men with links to other crime.

That was sound advice.

But, she had a tail to lose. And it was daylight.

She'd be OK. She would.

After less than a mile Sam had picked up her tail. He was driving a blush metallic-pink Nissan Cube, a ridiculous looking car which, after just ten minutes on The Bahamian roads, seemed ubiquitous. It was probably Japan getting rid of the vehicles that no one in their right mind would have bought in the first place. Looking like it sounded - a box on four wheels - she'd easily be able to find it in a crowd, especially as there was a distinctive crack in its front bumper. That was another rule that her new friend had broken. Make sure your vehicle is unmarked. The other two were: always drive black or silver, and never adorn a tailing car with accessories. In short: don't tail in a car that shouts. Snakeskin-belt man had failed on every count.

She'd be awash with work when she came out here to set up her new business.

Losing a vehicle tail wasn't like it was in the movies. Unless you were driving across The States, with endless flat roads (and no state troopers), you could never guarantee to outrun a tail and it was foolish to think you could. Driving down the pavement or jumping a gap of a rising bridge, the must-dos in any action movie, weren't included in the SIS evasive-driving course.

And there was the more difficult ask when losing a tail without being compromised. In her case she wanted snakeskin-belt man *to lose her* - and think that it was his fault.

SIS's breaking-clean mantra in a car was: *brake - turn - accelerate; brake - turn - accelerate.* That is, make a very late decision say, turn left, accelerate from the turn and follow up with another snap turn. Repeat if necessary.

It helped that Sam had a good idea of the road layout.

JFK - straight over a roundabout onto Thompson Boulevard.

She reckoned there were three left turns off Thompson Boulevard that could be immediately followed by another sharp left. Left hand turns were good - they drove on the left over here.

207

Making one quickly would be easier than cutting across traffic.

Her plan was: make a quick left, then, looking like an incompetent, turn left again. If she'd not lost the Cube by then, she'd hang another left back onto the main drag. A woman driver who had just got lost and, by chance, found herself again.

She'd try that before a set of traffic lights in half a mile. If it didn't work, she'd have to think of Plan B.

The roads were adequately maintained - the odd dinner-plate-sized pothole asking a lot of the Swift's suspension. But the traffic was nuts. Sam was almost taken out at a roundabout by a truck the size of a house. *How many lanes do you want?* There was no road discipline and even less road sense. Cars pulled out just before you got to their junction, they tailgated, and stopped and turned without warning. Only one car in five looked roadworthy. Having working indicators was clearly not a prerequisite to passing the local MoT. Using them was clearly against the law.

And horns. They were as much a part of The Bahamian driving psyche as was texting whilst you drove.

All of these things were to Sam's advantage.

First, though, she needed to put a couple of cars between her and the Cube.

She accelerated to pass a 1980s gold Dodge Diplomat - the driver was the coolest dude on the road. Getting past was a tight fit on, what was now, a single-tracked road. As a result her manoeuvre was accompanied by horns, shaking fists and looks of dismay from the drivers of the cars that had to swerve.

Calm down everyone.

She had one car between her and the Cube. Tick.

Left hand turn one - in 200 metres. Keep your eyes peeled.

There was a rusty-red Chevy van in front of her. She accelerated again.

More horns. A near miss with an old, white Ford pickup with four locals sitting on the side of the open boot. She picked out 'Oi, white girl! Wassupppp?', before she shot past.

Concentrate.

There it was. The left hand turn. On its corner was a street vendor selling a few green oranges off a rickety old table.

She slammed on her brakes. The Chevy didn't spot her deceleration and loomed large in her rear-view mirror - she turned and accelerated just before the Chevy's grille joined her rucksack in the back seat. More horns.

The nearly-new Swift, which was nimble, spun on a pin, its rear left wheel lifting as the front right squealed in protest.

As the car regained its composure she floored the accelerator. Fifteen then 20 miles an hour.

Brake! Now turn! Just the other side of that wooden shack-cum-bungalow.

The Swift obliged.

Floor it! It reacted again.

The road ahead bore gently right - both sides of the road were peppered with shacks and yards, broken fences and clapped-out motors. Sam checked her rear-view mirror. Nothing.

Shit!

There was a kid on the street. She swerved to miss him.

She looked behind again. *Fuck.* There it was: the Cube. Fifty metres. Her tail may be rubbish on foot, but he was OK behind the wheel. He was accelerating fast. And she had lost the surprise.

And he knew that she knew ...

Bugger.

She would have failed her SIS evasive-driving course.

And she couldn't drive too quickly down these streets - she'd already swerved to avoid one kid, and now there were a couple of women on the side of the street.

She had about ten seconds on the Cube.

Plan B.

Turn!

Sam spun the Swift right, into a yard, between a rusty fence and a palm tree. To her right was a pastel-blue wooden shack with a veranda that needed more than just a coat of paint. To the left of the shack was a drive that led to a shed at the rear. There was a car-width gap between an industrial-sized gas bottle and a wreck of another car - which Sam didn't recognise because it was missing most of its front.

A Toyota Corolla?

She sped into the gap and then mercilessly twisted the car right behind the house and threw on the brakes. There were four old fridges to her front and another dismantled car to her left - the rest of the yard was overgrown with head-high shrubs; the odd tyre here and there adding to the obstacle course.

Sam reached for her rucksack and was out of the car in no time. It took her less than a second to make one of three choices: back fence (*looks too high for a clean jump*); side fence (*too much undergrowth?*); the back door of the shack which was ajar (*who knows what's inside?*).

In security terms what people fail to realise is that you can, pretty much, do anything once - providing you do it with confidence and/or speed. It's when you set a pattern that you open yourself up for discovery - and likely attack.

She was about to put that theory to the test.

Sam rushed the back door, closing it behind her. Inside she found a kitchen which matched the state of the shack; but it was tidy. On the only chair, seated at a wooden table, was an old man with an open bottle of rum and a half-filled glass in his hand. If he were surprised that a younger white woman had barged into his kitchen, he didn't show it.

He mumbled some words which were drowned out by a mechanical screech and the sound of metal hitting metal that she assumed was her tail's Cube discovering the Swift.

Get a move on.

Sam had fished out her wallet from her waist belt. She took out a $50 note.

'Hi.' She placed the note on the table as close to the man's free hand as she could reach.

'I wasn't here.' She raised a straight finger to her lips. And, using the universal signal of quiet, she blew a 'shhh'.

She gave the man a split second to register what she was asking. He shrugged his shoulders, picked up the note, looked at it and raised his glass to his mouth.

Then she was gone. Out the other side of the house, into the front yard and left, back the way she had come.

She sprinted, keeping low for the first 30 yards in case snakeskin-belt man was looking her way from the backyard. All pretence of 'dumb female' was gone. She was a fugitive on a small island, tracked down by people she didn't know or understand.

As she ran, sweat came like a shower. She had kept herself in shape and the rucksack was no issue. But the heat was impenetrable. She was soaked from head to foot.

Within a minute and a half she was back in the road she had come from. She dropped the sprint to a jog, turning left - north, towards Nassau centre. She took the next right at a corner signalled by a huge cotton tree, its roots starting well before the trunk hit the ground, spreading out but still married to the tree by thin webs of bark.

She was jogging and looking. She needed to regroup.

A bar. Well, a ramshackle green, red and yellow wooden building with a sign proclaiming it was 'Mike's Club'. There were a couple of locals sitting at an outside table. More rum. Behind them was a door leading to the bar's innards.

Sam slipped inside, trying to control her breathing. There was a single window at the back and two Formica-covered tables and associated chairs. Behind a makeshift counter was a middle-aged local - and a refrigerator. He looked at Sam as though she were something that had crawled out from under a piece of furniture.

'What do you want, white girl?' His accent straight from the Bronx - all muscle and pride.

'Erm.' What Sam wanted was a shower and time to rethink her strategy. This place was the next best thing.

'Fanta?' She asked with her strongest possible voice.

You can do anything once.

The man nodded suspiciously.

'Sure. Why not?'

He reached for the fridge's handle.

Chapter 8

Austin stared at the screen. He was numb; bereft. Lost. After he'd given a statement to the cops in a room a short stroll from his son's private bed, he'd been asked to leave the hospital. The cop (Austin couldn't remember his name) had taken his cell number and asked that he stay in Vegas for the meantime. They would get in touch with him; at some point he'd be called to formally identify Rick's body. When he asked if he could see his son now, the cop had said 'no'. Apparently forensics were all over the room like spilt paint. He'd have a chance to see him at the identification procedure at the morgue.

Identification procedure.

Morgue.

He'd left the hospital in a daze and checked into the nearest hotel.

Austin felt his shirt pocket to make sure he had the cop's card. He did.

The call to his wife was the worst experience of his life. She was crying even before he completed his first sentence. It must have been the tone of his voice. She knew straight away, and she was inconsolable. She didn't scream or shout out, like the mother he'd been to see to tell her of her son's death in training. His wife just sobbed and sobbed.

And he wasn't there to console her. So, he just let her cry. And cry. It broke his heart.

He'd decided not to mention that Rick's death was suspicious. That there were more cops in the building than patients and staff. And that, before he had died, Rick had led him to a flash drive in his jacket pocket, having muttered a single word: 'report'.

His son's last word.

Report.

What could it mean? Why was it so important to him?

He took his eyes off the screen and looked at the lime-green flash drive that was beside the keyboard. He picked it up. Examined it as if it were a piece of fine jewellery or an expensive watch.

What are you?

He closed his eyes and took a deep breath. And then placed the drive in a USB slot on the front of the computer tower.

An inset popped up.

Installing new hardware.

Then a separate box.

Removable Disk (H:)

It disappeared. Austin clicked on 'Computer', then 'Removable Disk' and a new box appeared with an icon showing the flash drive. He double-clicked on the icon. A vertical list of files, photos and documents appeared. It was alphabetical - it filled the page and there was clearly more. Austin wasn't a digital native, but had enough nous to know what to do to find the report.

He found the icon that sorted the files by date and pressed it.

There it was. At the top of the list.

Report   1487...01/11/2017...Word Document...1.2MB

His index finger hovered over the left mouse button. It wavered as if it were practising how to click.

Click.

Austin stared at the screen. The title of the report was on two lines:

<u>Reaper 1487 Mission Stray Report 1-11-17</u>
<u>Significant Findings Within Imagery</u>
<u>Catalogue</u>

Austin's eyes shot to the very top of the screen. In the document's header were the words: USAF SECRET - NOT TO BE DIVULGED.

That rocked him. He quickly looked behind to see if someone was looking in his direction. No one at the moment. His hands became clammy.

He scrolled through the document. It was 14 pages long and contained eight images and two tables. At the end was a signature block:

Rick Rodgers
Lieutenant USAF
432d Operations Group
USAF Creech

Austin scrunched his eyes together and opened them again, hoping that he wasn't looking at a top secret document on an unclassified pen drive that his son had taken off base. Austin was cleared to SECRET and had dealt with a good number of documents and images at that level of classification. He knew that it was a courts martial offence to take classified documentation off base; even worse: off a secure computer system and store it on an unclassified memory stick. What his son had done was illegal. He would have signed the DSA (Defence Secrets Act). He would have been trained and briefed accordingly.

What Austin had in front of him transgressed boundaries that he would never have crossed. What was Rick onto? Why had he knowingly taken an e-copy of a top secret document off base? A document written by him?

Austin was already breaking numerous laws by looking at the document on an unclassified machine. It would leave an imprint on the computer. Somebody could find it.

What is in this report?

Then he thought of his son; lying rigged up to various machines he didn't understand. Torn to pieces by two bullets. His last few words. His hopes. His passion. His love of life. All of which were now gone.

Austin took another glance behind him and then closed the report - and closed down the machine. He removed the pen drive and stared at it for a second.

What are you?

He stood and looked around the suite. In one corner was a vacant machine where the screen was less visible to passers-by.

He picked up his stuff, walked across to the small buffet and poured himself a coffee, adding a touch of sugar. No cream. He was on autopilot. On another mission. He may never had made the rarefied ranks of the officer corps, but he had led soldiers into battle. He'd lost a couple but brought many, many more home. He'd done everything to the best of his ability. He'd worked tirelessly and, he thought, intelligently.

What doesn't kill you, makes you stronger.

He strode purposefully to the oblique screen.

Thirty minutes later Austin had read the report three times. It had taken him a while to decipher some of the technology, and a couple of the USAF acronyms. But he had it now. And he thought he had grasped the significance of what his son had written. Rick, and his Sensor Operator, a Captain Lance Travis, had flown a Reaper over the Venezuelan jungle searching for 'new activity'. The definition of 'new activity' was: roads, buildings, infrastructure - anything that hadn't been previously mapped.

Last week, on their 17th mission, their bird had self-corrected by some 13 miles mid-flight, caused by its GPS signal going out of sync with the internal gyroscopes. That jump took the aircraft into Colombian airspace, an action from which the USAF received a formal rebuke from the Colombian government. It was not clear if the Venezuelan government were aware of the infringement into their neighbour's airspace - or that they knew they had a Reaper flying over their jungle. Venezuela was a country in meltdown; on the brink of civil war. Its government and civil-service were hardly operational.

As the pilot, Rick had been blamed for the mistake and was given two and a half days to the find the cause.

The report, with the aid of images and tables, went on to describe how the Reaper was just about to fly over a new site, deep in the jungle and very close to the Colombian border. The pictures were grainy, but Rick seemed confident that they showed two buildings, a big satellite dish and a vehicle moving towards the site along an unmapped road. There were no detailed pictures because, and this was the crux of Rick's report, the Reaper veered away from the complex just before it was in a position to take decent imagery. And, as a result, had strayed into Colombian airspace.

Rick's supposition, which Austin sensed required a leap of faith, was that the Reaper's GPS signal had been tampered with - thus veering the aircraft off course, and away from the new site. His son had described it as if there were a 'GPS forcefield' around the complex.

The report had not elaborated on how the Reaper's GPS system may have been tampered with. Or who the tamperers might have been.

Austin scrolled back up to the top of the report. It wasn't clear who the report may have been sent to - if indeed it had been sent anywhere. He guessed it would have been an attachment to a secure email, probably to someone in the senior hierarchy at Creech.

Before he closed the report he congratulated Rick posthumously on a good piece of work. It was well-written, logical and covered the bases. Key to a good military report was that a layman could understand it. Austin gave him a big tick for that.

He closed the report and disconnected the flash drive. As he studied the lime-green casing one more time he caught sight of his own reflection in the computer screen. His wife said he looked like Morgan Freeman, his face potted with acne marks from when he was teenager. He had a short, grey beard and 'crew cut' curly hair, which was also tinged grey around his ears. He thought that if there were any resemblance to Morgan Freeman, it was that they were both old and getting jowly.

Austin put the pen drive back in a side pocket of his beige cotton trousers. This time he'd chosen a pocket with a zip - he couldn't afford to lose it.

Where had the report been sent?

Had it been sent? Who had read it? Were the contents so explosive that they had forced someone to attempt to murder his son in the street - and then finish him off in his hospital bed?

He closed his eyes again, rubbing them with a hand. He fought back tears.

Now what? He had to do something. He had to keep himself busy. Should he hand the report to the police? The military could hardly courts martial his dead son, although he wouldn't put it past them giving it a shot. Should he speak to the base? Dig a little? Act stupid - and see whether anyone slips on a skin? What other options did he have? He had an ex-Bureau fishing buddy who might be interested in the story. He trusted him?

Think.

He'd phone the base.

Austin typed 4...3...2...n...d into the search box and the Google people at Santa Clara County did the rest, offering him Creech Air Force base's website. He clicked on the phone directory and found the command post number.

He checked his watch. It was 3.30 pm. He dug out his phone and dialled; it rang three times.

'Creech Air Force Base, how may I help you?' It was a woman's voice.

Austin stammered. He had not thought through what he was going to say.

Fool.

'Can I speak to the commander's office of the 432nd, please?'

'Who am I talking to?'

Shit. He hadn't thought that through either.

'It's Command Sergeant Austin Rodgers. I'm from Camp Blanding.'

There was a pause.

'But you are phoning from a cell, sir.'

'That's right - who am I talking to.' He was going to ignore the woman's obvious security concern and take the initiative.

'It's Airman First Class Bell, sir.'

'Nice to talk to you Airman Bell. Is there someone in the commander's outer office that I can talk to. Maybe a junior commissioned officer?'

'Let me look, sir.' There was a further pause. 'May I ask what it is you are calling about?'

Austin swallowed.

'It's about my son; he is, sorry, was, a Reaper pilot. Master Sergeant Rick Rodgers.'

If the name rang a bell with the airman, she didn't acknowledge it.

'One second, sir.'

It was longer than a second. After about 20 seconds there was a different voice on the phone: male; east coast.

'Command Sergeant Rodgers, this is Major Frank Digby II. I'm glad you phoned, sir. I'm so sorry to hear about your son.'

Austin pulled the phone away from his face and stared at the phone.

They know.

He brought the phone back to his ear.

'Thank you, major. Is it possible to meet with the commander?'

It was now the major's turn to pause.

'I'm sorry, sir, that won't be possible.'

A hint of irritation rose in Austin's throat.

'Why's that, major? Surely my son and I deserve at least that amount of respect?'

'That's not the issue, sir. It's just ... the commander's not in the office.'

This is tough.

'When will he be back, major?'

'He won't be, sir. He's been relieved of command as of yesterday. I'm afraid seeing him is out of the question.'

Headquarters SIS, Vauxhall, London

It was a Saturday. That was four out of the last five Saturdays Jane had been in the office. The place was quiet. A couple of her staff were in, including Frank. None of them was expected to be in unless she called a lockdown. Technically they were all working overtime, but there was no overtime. There was just time. And not enough of it. She had a pile of work to do - including a key brief for C on Yemen which needed to be on his desk for first thing Monday. It was completely natural to anyone in Babylon that the boss signed letters and emails with the single letter 'C'. But she guessed it would be a bit *Ian Fleming* to anyone who came across it for the first time.

Seeing Frank reminded her that he'd sent her a secure chat message late yesterday which she'd not got round to reading.

She opened it.

Sam in The Bahamas. Air ticket booked via unknown third party. Am on it. F

What? The Bahamas?

That was *so* Sam Green.

Using a ticket booked by someone else - what was she up to? Chasing The Church of the White Cross? In The Bahamas?

What was the latest Jane had seen - was it as far back as September? A CIA report that they reckoned The Church had up to $2 billion still unaccounted for. And that money was probably in offshore accounts. Likely to be The Bahamas.

She stood, reaching for a notebook and a propelling pencil. She was halfway to her door when she spotted Frank getting up from his chair; he was heading in her direction.

She opened the door theatrically. In waltzed Frank. Same jeans, a different t-shirt. It was a blue and white 'ape-to-human' evolution t-shirt, starting with a chimp and ending up with a jumping rock-star with a guitar in his hands.

'I didn't realise you played the guitar?' She asked.

'Air guitar. I'm very good.'

Jane smiled. How very Frank.

They both remained standing. Jane spun her pencil between her fingers.

'Sorry, just read your message about Sam. What do you have?'

'Two things. First, GCHQ cannot identify the "unknown" who paid for Sam's ticket. They came across an ISP block on the Dark Web.'

'Dark Web?' Jane gently shook her head. 'And, second?'

'With nothing else to go on, just now I did an all-government sources search for "Sam Green" and came across a seemingly trivial wire from our Consulate in Nassau. A British tourist is presumed missing after an Avis hire car was found abandoned in downtown Nassau.'

'Sam?'

'Yes. The car was hired to a Sam Green, arriving on BA253 yesterday lunchtime.' Frank's tone was business-like.

Jane thought for a moment.

'Sit down, Frank,' Jane pointed to comfy chair in the corner of her office. She took the one next to it.

'There's more, Frank. Sam's call the other day was from a German mobile, as you know. In essence she had come across new evidence of the re-emergence of The Church of the White Cross.'

Frank interrupted.

'You mean Bischoff, the very dead Manning, Ralph Bell - and the wackos from Germany and Texas?'

'Correct. She gave me two new names out of some intelligence to which she'd been privy - she said she'd seen a good number more. The names were: Paul Mitchell and Nicholas Stone.'

Frank thought for a second.

'Mitchell was the businessman abducted and then murdered off the East African coast a few years ago?'

'Correct.'

'And, for the second, she doesn't mean Min AF?'

Jane nodded.

'She does. I've seen his file, Frank. There is no hint of anything other than alcohol dependency.'

Frank scratched his chin.

'And now she's chasing around the Caribbean, using the Dark Web to buy her tickets, and then abandoning her hire car on the same day she collects it from the airport.'

'Or ...', Jane paused, 'She's been abducted?'

They both let that thought hang.

'OK.' Jane broke the silence. 'Let me check something.'

Jane was on her feet, moving quickly round to her desk. Within a second she had the SIS deployment matrix open.

'Let's see. Nassau. Bradley Stokes. He's our man in The Bahamas. Do you know him?' Jane opened a new tab and searched for Bradley Stokes' p-file. *Here it is.* He was, not surprisingly, an older operative: 54. Probably enjoying semi-retirement, keeping an eye on the banks and similar. His history looked sensible and unblemished.

'No, sorry.' Frank replied.

'Me neither. Have I told you that the SIS case officer who confirmed Paul Mitchell's body in Mogadishu was sacked the following year from Kenya for taking bribes?' Jane looked up over her screen.

'No ... so, Paul Mitchell could be alive? His murder was staged? And then his death faked by a bent agent?' Frank had added two and two and got considerably more.

Jane was looking back at her screen. She absently confirmed Frank's suspicion with a, 'mmm'.

'Right.' Jane had a plan. 'I'll get hold of Bradley Stokes. You put a 443 out for Sam.'

Frank looked confused.

'But that's a "case officer missing" alert. Sam no longer works for us.'

'She might as well be now.'

Curry's Motel, Boyd Road, Nassau, The Bahamas

Sam finished the last spoonful of oats and yoghurt and reached for her coffee. The breakfast was perfectly adequate - as was the motel, a two-up, two-down in mid-town Nassau. She had come across it yesterday afternoon by complete chance, wandering north from where she'd deserted the hire car.

En route she'd practised her SIS evasive-tailing routine. It hadn't taken her long to be comfortable that she was clear of snakeskin-belt man. But she was already getting that Nassau was a small and compact city - especially near its centre. A handful of (mostly) criss-crossing single-track roads, lined with two-storey, pastel-washed buildings - nearly all of them in need of repair and those in better shape were lacking a good coat of paint. Whilst it would be easy to lose yourself, the place wasn't big enough to be lost in for long.

For a 'tax haven', Sam couldn't begin to reconcile some of the poverty she had witnessed. OK, so it wasn't Freetown or Monrovia, two capitals she'd visited five years ago where the streets were full of unemployed, disheartened men - and women - eking out a living from near-empty table-top sales of fruit, veg, cigarettes and candy. But the centre was run down. Every third building was a wooden shack - or an ex-house - poorly boarded up, even though most still showed signs of habitation.

The streets also lacked the vibrancy and noise of their West African counterparts. There was no loud music, no women screaming at their men - no hustle; no 'in-your-face'. The place was all pastel as opposed to primary colours. Sam sensed that The Bahamas was laid back; well-off vertical. That may be OK for now, but she reckoned the country was only a couple of bad governments between where it was currently and third-world status. Which would be a shame because, nearly exclusively, the people she had met were lovely. Even the dreadlock-adorned, slightly menacing-looking men, were congenial.

The motel (more guest house than anything else) suited her down to the ground. The room was perfectly comfortable, with air conditioning, a basin and an overhead fan. It had competent Wi-Fi and they took cash - no passport required. She booked in as Elena Kuznetsov, an office worker from St Petersburg. Elena was an old alias of hers from when she'd worked in Moscow. Sam was very fond of Elena. The woman had helped her out of a number of tight spots.

She'd booked in speaking Russian, having done her best to change her appearance in the backyard of Mike's cafe. Her t-shirt for a white blouse, and her baseball cap with a paisley bandana, made from a cotton scarf she had in her rucksack. After an opening salvo in Russian, she wasn't surprised that the young woman behind reception hadn't understood a word. Two years of immersion language-training prior to her SIS posting to Moscow had enabled her to become fluent. She hadn't spoken a word in Russian for over a year. As with most things in her head, accessing the right words in the right order had come naturally.

She then painstakingly asked for a room in a very broken English accent - with a thick Russian clip. That had done the trick. The woman, who smiled and introduced herself as Candy, had booked her in for one night. Sam had paid up front - in cash.

After a shower, she had texted Wolfgang using her fourth SIM. He'd come back to her immediately and, as he'd done in the Sofitel, had remotely accessed her phone and established a secure voice link via a VPN (virtual private network) that he had set up on the Dark Web. The mechanics of it all went over Sam's head. All she knew was that three minutes later they were having a secure conversation, even if there was a slight delay between what one of them said and what the other heard.

Sam explained where she was and why she'd ended up there.

'Do you think it's Victoria Mitchell?' Wolfgang asked.

Sam waited for the delay.

'I can't think of a better reason. I used my real name in Norfolk. And you booked me on a flight as Sam Green. I suppose it's possible that someone in Austria could have tracked down my hotel room. Or your Müller bloke has given the game away? Whatever, it all comes back to the people on that sexy board of yours in the cellar.'

Pause.

'Can't be Müller. I've not given him your details, just your description. What about the conversation with your old boss, Jane? Could it be SIS keeping an eye?'

Sam had considered that option and dismissed it. Snakeskin-belt man was too hopeless to be an SIS employee.

'No. I really don't think so. Anyway, moving on. I have a meeting with Lukas Müller tomorrow ...?' She let the question hang.

'Yes, that's done. Eleven-fifteen tomorrow morning at *The One and Only Ocean Club*, on Paradise Island.'

Sam let her brain work through the ramifications of Wolfgang's statement.

'Does it have to be on Paradise Island? There are two bridges, an "on" and an "off". I will be channelled. Easy meat for a pick-up.'

'Sorry. It was his suggestion. Apparently it's the only place to be seen at on the island - and it's where he does all his business. Other than in the office which, in this case, is no-go. Meeting anywhere else would be unusual for him and attract attention all of its own. He clearly doesn't want that. He's going to meet you under the pretence of a job interview. He's been looking for a new housekeeper ...'

The pause allowed Sam's temper to spike.

'You're enjoying this, aren't you!'

Her response was met with a German chortle.

'Anyway,' more laughter, '... as a family we stayed at *The One and Only* in The Maldives just before my father died. They are *very* special. The coffee and pastries will be good.'

Sam had calmed down.

'If there is more than one *One and Only*, shouldn't they be called The One of Many Ocean Clubs?'

Pause.

'That's a good point. Make that recommendation in the comments book when you are there.' More chuckles.

They spent the next ten minutes discussing the strategy Sam would use in her meeting with Herr Müller. As they did, Sam scrolled down a fact file that Wolfgang had put together on the man. It was particularly unpleasant reading.

Then they discussed the mobile that Sam had stolen from snakeskin-belt man.

'Is it locked?' Wolfgang had asked,

'Yes. I turned it off by taking the back off and removing the battery - I assumed that they, whoever they are, would be able to follow it if data was turned on.'

'Any idea of what the number is?'

'No, sorry.'

'Android or iPhone?'

'Android.'

Wolfgang had gone quiet.

'When you're away from the hotel put the phone on and see if there are any messages or missed calls - Android allows you to see the numbers and some text without the phone being unlocked. If you get anything, SMS the details to me. I can't break into the phone remotely, but I may be able to do something with it here. When you get a break we should think of FedEx-ing the phone to me.'

'Away from the hotel - just in case someone triangulates the phone?'

Sam knew the chances of discovering a person's location by their phone. There were two methods. First, any decent security service can get access to your phone company's towers. They ping your phone, even if you're not using it, and your phone pings the towers back. Three towers would give an accuracy of around 20 square metres. Second, is when you use it. This gives any ordinary hackers a greater degree of freedom to find your phone - and where you are. Accuracy is about 100 square metres. If, however, you're using your phone and have your GPS activated, a sophisticated hacker can see the whites of your eyes.

'Yes, but you're a spy. You know that.'

'Ex-spy. But you're right.'

Sam changed the subject.

'Assuming that I'm not rushed by a team of The Church's spetsnaz, how do you suggest I get off the island? I'd be an idiot to use the airport.' Sam asked.

'I've given that some thought. I've found one or two nefarious options. One works out of Potters Cay, just under the bridge on the Nassau side of the sound that separates Paradise Island from the mainland.'

Sam's brain displayed the map of Nassau that she'd rehearsed in the Sofitel. *Got that.* She'd have another more detailed look on Google Maps once Wolfgang had got off the phone.

'And?'

Pause.

'He runs a powerboat business with extra tanks. He's into "logistics"' Sam imagined Wolfgang using his hands to demonstrate speech marks.

'Drugs?'

'I didn't say that. Nor did he. But he will take any cargo, anywhere. Especially Florida. That route is via Andros - the large Bahamian island west of New Providence. For a price. It's about a ten-hour journey and not without risk. Particularly from the US Border Patrol which has a heavy presence along the southern US coast.'

Sam knew of the US Border Patrol. She remembered the figure of 21,000 agents - they monitored the US's borders by vehicle, boat, aircraft and even horse and UAVs. The current President had recently beefed up their capabilities. It would be a helluva journey.

'Better in the hands of US officials than in a cellar of The Church of the White Cross?' It was a rhetorical question which Wolfgang didn't need to, but answered anyway.

'It might be difficult to tell them apart. We don't know The Church's reach?'

How true.

With that they'd finished the meat of their conversation.

'Be careful, Sam.'

She intended to be.

'Sure, Wolfgang. Thanks. When will you let me know about your man with a boat?'

Pause.

'I'll text your fifth SIM when I have some more detail.'

And that was that.

Back in the restaurant Sam took a final swig of her coffee. She checked her phone. It was 8.45 am. She had plenty of time. She'd get over the bridge - on foot was her first thought - as soon as she could. Then she'd check for a tail before making her way to *The One and Only*.

The One and Only Ocean Club, Paradise Island,
New Providence, The Bahamas

Sam was half an hour early. That suited her. She was standing on the grass verge of a very picturesque and quiet dual carriageway that cut Paradise Island in two. The island was no bigger than a couple of golf courses and most of it was subsumed by the coral pink, high-rise Atlantis resort. The monstrosity dominated both Paradise Island and the capital Nassau. It was something out of Las Vegas - huge, tall, with a covered balcony connecting the main two skyscrapers at goodness knows what floor. Sam had read that it had two aquariums (fish should swim in the sea, not a tank, was her view), a waterpark, scores of pools and ponds, a casino and, she guessed, plenty of well heeled but poorly dressed American tourists.

The last comment was unfair. She was hardly a fashionista barometer.

Whatever.

Herr Müller's meeting was between a rich German banker and his would-be housekeeper. She was wearing a blue cotton skirt, a white blouse and her Jesus sandals - there was little else to choose from. Better dressed than when she'd arrived, for sure. But hardly a beacon of good taste.

She took a minute to turn on snakeskin-belt man's phone. Sure enough the phone's locked screen held a clue. There was a text message from

'Ops', the top line of which read: *need to talk about equipment.* She took a picture of the screen with her own phone and SMS'd the image to Wolfgang.

She then turned off both phones.

The entrance to *The One and Only* was through a grand-looking gap in a tall and thick evergreen hedge. The hotel's sign was understated - but classy. And the road leading up to the resort was well maintained but, surprisingly, had dark-grey kerbstones. Sam didn't get that.

It took her five minutes to saunter up to the main entrance. As she walked she tried very hard to make her rucksack look as small as possible. It was hardly in keeping. A circular drive cut through immaculate lawns and met a smallish, two-storey colonial mansion, painted light blue with white gloss accoutrements. There was a very welcoming, building-height Palladian porch, suspended by white Roman columns - which framed double doors; double doors that were manned by double staff. One door - one flunkey. She was already feeling way out of her depth, and hating the opulence. Give her her trusty yellow VW camper, a loch-side pitch and a mug of tea and she was happy as Larry.

The doors opened. The two local men were wearing appropriate livery. They smiled and, in unison, said, 'Good morning, ma'am. Welcome to *The One and Only Ocean Club.*' It was silky smooth and surprisingly not over the top. Sam was already beginning to feel at home - and hating herself for it.

'Good morning. I'm here for a business meeting. In the beach cafe?'

The left-hand servant - *what do you call them?* - said, 'Straight through, ma'am.' He pointed beyond a vast entrance hall to a lounge and another set of double doors. In the distance Sam picked out a white, medium-size pavilion, and a hint of dark blue ocean beyond it.

'And the lavatories?' Sam needed to freshen up.

'The restrooms are over there, ma'am.'

Sam saw the sign on the door. She nodded and said, 'Thank you.' And left the two doormen - *that's what you call them* - to effuse over their next guest.

Five minutes later she'd sorted out her life, made her way across the lawn, which framed a fabulous infinity pool, and walked into the pavilion. Once there she found a two-seat table by an open window. She sat with her back to a corner, leaving a single seat for her guest.

The beach cafe was so much more than its name suggested. High up on a sand cliff with a white, curving beach below, it was a square, white wood and glass pavilion - the centre of which was all bar. There were elegant stools nestled under the bar, and tables between it and the three-quarter length windows. Out of three sides all you could see was sand, surf, ocean and, in the distance, a thin green sliver of a far-off cay. It was perfect. Made more so by the fact that she was currently the only customer. For a second she forgot herself.

Mmm.

Her wistfulness was interrupted when she spotted Lukas Müller crossing the lawn by the pool. He was as described in the photos Wolfgang had shared with her. In his 60s, mid-height, mid-weight, with a marked, white, flabby face. He wore a beige cotton short-sleeve shirt, blue chinos and a Panama. Straight out of a Graham Greene novel. And he walked with a slight limp.

So, this was a man who put the 'haven' into tax haven - and who, very discreetly and extremely secretively, managed the accounts of The Church of the White Cross. *Probably.* He was a servant of the über-rich who, through shell companies and non-trading firms, held and hid their assets; and through electronic and accounting sleight of hand, disguised and distributed massive wealth, keeping all that worth away from the tax-grabbing hands of governments and their financial agencies. The Panama Papers and LuxLeaks had exposed and embarrassed individuals and corporations, and forced many of them to come clean about how they avoided tax - and how they kept their money as *their money*. But it hadn't stopped the process - it had just slowed it, and made those who wanted their assets hidden, dig a deeper hole.

People like Lukas Müller made it possible. If Sam hadn't despised him for jerking off over images of small boys, she would have hated him for being instrumental in making rich people richer.

For today, though, she'd try very hard to be all smiles.

Müller entered the pavilion. He looked in Sam's direction. She raised a hand. He did the same. He limped over to Sam's table. Before he sat he asked her, his German accent strong, 'What would you like to drink?'

Sam gave him a half-smile.

'Decaf please. Black, no sugar.'

He turned to the barman.

'Jason. Two black French presses; one decaf. And some cashews.'

He knows the barman. Well done him.

Müller sat opposite Sam. He didn't say anything for a while, he just looked out of the window, across the ocean to the horizon.

'This is the very best view in The Bahamas. No?'

Sam had been studying his face. He lacked a tan, but he had four or five sizeable and pronounced moles. And an alcoholic's nose - overlarge and blue-veiny.

'I'll take your word for it. This is only my second day on the island. I spent most of yesterday being chased by a man in a car. He met me at the airport. It wasn't a very encouraging welcome.'

He was still staring at the view.

'That's a shame. I didn't know.'

He turned to her.

'What do you people want from me?'

Sam spoke softly.

'As my friend has told you Herr Müller, I work for the British government. We are close to dismantling The Church of the White Cross. We need a list of names - a hierarchy if you like.'

Müller snorted and shook his head. Smiling he returned to staring out of the window. He didn't say anything for about half a minute. Sam played with a very weighty silver spoon.

Still staring at the view his eventual reply was quiet, but firm.

'So, that's what this is about. What if I said that I have no idea what you're talking about?'

Sam and Wolfgang had war-gamed that question. Wolfgang was confident that Walter Ingris was The Church of the White Cross's main offshore financial hub. Müller was the bank's second-in-command. And he had a very unattractive police record. Chances were he was The Church's man in Nassau. They'd agreed on that.

'Then I'd call you a liar.'

Müller snorted again, but he didn't take his eyes off the view.

'You don't know what you are doing. You have no idea who you are dealing with.'

Sam thought he was remarkably calm. It was though The Church was so powerful that nothing he could tell her would make a blind bit of difference. Or there was something else that was flattening his emotions.

Jason came back with the coffee - two posh cafetières and china cups - and a silver tray brimming with cashews. As he left, Müller slipped him a $50 note. She hated him even more now.

'I think, Herr Müller, you underestimate the security services - yours, as well as mine.' Sam said.

Müller scoffed, his hand now raised to his chin.

His eyes turned to face Sam, his face following momentarily afterwards. His stare was distant. Weak.

'You know, these marks on my face?' He pointed at a mole. 'They're melanomas. And they are killing me, Miss Green ...'

Sam was taken aback that he knew her name. Wolfgang had only told Müller that he was meeting a female colleague of his.

'... yes, they know who you are.' He dismissed the comment with a brush of a hand on the tablecloth, removing an imaginary speck of dust. 'I am dying; maybe a year? Not much more. Who knows? But once they find out I've met with you, I am as good as dead - now.' He paused. 'And so are you.'

There was dampness in his eyes. Sam tried to find some sympathy, but couldn't.

'Why meet with me then?'

He didn't answer the question directly. 'I am not a good man. I have done many bad things - and many things that I regret. You know of some of them, I'm sure. If I could have my time again ...'

Get to the point, Herr Müller.

He stopped and took a long swig of coffee.

'... I might do things differently.'

Then he reached into his shirt pocket and took out a small silver box, about the size of a matchbox. He put it on the table, opened it, and took out a yellow capsule. It reminded Sam of the disgusting cod liver oil tablets her mother used to feed her.

Müller looked at the tablet. He turned it between finger and thumb. His face was sad, his bottom lip protruding a touch.

Sam watched in slow motion as Müller put the capsule into his mouth and bit it. He smiled, a tight-lipped smile. Then, he took a swig of coffee and turned to look out of the window again.

'The best view in The Bahamas.'

And?

His eyes flickered. His mouth opened slightly; he coughed. The gap between his lips let out a dribble and his tongue made an appearance.

And then he was gone.

Fuck - why me?!

Sam caught his head before it hit the table. She looked around. Jason was busy with a customer on the other side of the bar.

The red mist was down. It had descended as quickly as if someone had punched her. She was livid. Furious at the coward of a man. Her life was complicated enough without the added diversion of having a corpse at her coffee table - his head suspended inches from a bowl of roasted cashews. And with her having nothing to show from it.

You yellow-livered bastard!

Think ... girl, think.

It took her a couple of attempts to get Müller's head balanced on a straight forearm. She then stood - her instincts were to flee. Her training, however, told her to watch the man for a few seconds - to check that his head didn't topple.

She glanced to the bar. Jason looked over. Sam smiled and waved. He returned the compliment. She didn't have long. If Jason didn't spot the lack of movement from Herr Müller soon enough, he'd pick up a whiff of the urine. The banker had wet himself.

As gently as she could she checked his pockets. She found a wallet, a mobile and a set of keys - the fob declared the associated car a Lexus. *Of course.*

And then she was off. Müller's wallet held over $500 dollars in various bills. She thrust another $50 bill in Jason's hand - he was having a helluva day. Without waiting for a response she walked quickly back across the lawn, through the lounge and past the doormen.

The car park was a two minute jog away on the other side of a hedge; the running helped eased her tension. It was full of classy cars. She walked the length of the first row.

Jag.

Honda.

Honda.

Lexus.

She tried the key fob. Nothing.

Cadillac.

Volvo.

Lexus - beep, beep!

A black metallic Lexus NX 450 hybrid, SUV. Perfect. *For now.*

Sam opened the driver's door, the fob's proximity key bringing the inside of the vehicle to life. Her left hand found the red 'Start' button whilst her right played with the electric seats - she was struggling to reach the pedals.

The Lexus's engine burst into life and, having started to overheat on her trot from the Club, she was greeted almost immediately by a wash of cold, air conditioned air.

Where now?

Off Paradise Island - for sure. She'd plan her options beyond that as she drove.

Futility

Chapter 9

Paradise Island, The Bahamas

The Lexus was an effortless drive; tiptronic and breathlessly smooth through its automatic gearbox. Sam was at the entrance to the 'off' crossing in no time at all. The bridges were beautiful concrete affairs, rising in a huge, thin arch, before descending to the opposite bank. The sight of them for the second time today dropped her blood pressure by a couple of notches ...

... only for it to spike again when she spotted a dude in the front seat of a white Nissan Navara twin cab. It was parked on the pavement just short of the entrance to the 'off' bridge. Sam was doing 30 miles-an-hour at that point, so he went past in a whizz, but he was definitely holding a camera - and her Lexus was in his viewfinder.

Bugger.

She didn't get much of the man - which further annoyed her. He was white, late middle-aged, sunglasses and a turquoise Miami Dolphins' baseball cap. Nothing else. She slowed down to 15 miles-an-hour and checked her rear-view mirror. She couldn't be certain through her rear and his front windscreen, but she thought she saw the lens of a camera tracking her. More photos.

It was a crude snatch - but effective. There was only one way off the island. She had to cross the bridge at some point. *Tick*. She was tagged.

What now?

On her mind map of Nassau, Sam had logged a shopping mall in the centre of town. *Lots of cars - lots of people.* She'd make her way there.

The Lexus slid through the traffic. Sam steadied the pace and kept an eye out for more interference. By the time she got to the mall, she was pretty sure she wasn't being followed. She parked up, tail in, with a quick escape back onto to the main road. She left the engine running. Still uneasy, she got out and walked round the Lexus. The mall was unremarkable. Pink, one storey and much smaller than you'd get in the UK. A car park for about a hundred cars. It was good enough camouflage.

She jumped back in the Lexus, took out Müller's wallet and studied the dual-tone leather outer. Smooth and expensive.

She reflected on the meeting - and on Müller's suicide. After the initial bristle of anger she was surprised how dispassionate she felt.

Why do people think it's acceptable to top themselves in my presence?

It was the second time it had happened. Last time, in Moscow, it had been an almighty shock - she'd thrown up in her kitchen sink. Müller's, whilst frustrating, hadn't fazed her, but it was pretty unfathomable. Why then? Why her? They'd spent less than ten minutes in each other's company. Early on Sam knew something wasn't right. It was as if their liaison was veering off - heading down a dark passage from which there was no return. In the end maybe it was a fitting finale to a deplorable man's life? He'd sort of said 'sorry'. Wasn't that what he'd done? Attempted to apologise to her for his failures?

And then killed himself.

Wasn't that what had just happened?

Whatever. That was half an hour ago. This was now - and all she had from a key meeting was his phone and a wallet.

Wallet first.

There was the expected array of credit cards and a driver's licence. There was the cash, which was $50 lighter than before she'd stolen it. There was an elaborate ID card titled 'Walter Ingris Bank'. It had an inlaid microchip which probably opened numerous doors at the bank. That could be useful. And a final, less sophisticated card. It was dark blue with a single, pale yellow title along its middle: *Miami Vice*. The embossed name across the bottom of the card read: R Wilder.

R Wilder? An alias? For the exclusive and probably very seedy *Miami Vice* club.

There was nothing else. It was remarkably uninteresting.

Next the mobile. It was an expensive Samsung - the one with the screen that wrapped around the edge of the phone (*why?*). Front, top right was a green flashing light. She touched the screen. It lit up. There were two alerts. One was a missed call from a 'Freddie', with an associated overseas number that she didn't recognise.

And there was an unread SMS:

Where are you now?

And the sender was 'RB'. There was no number.

It took a second for a penny to drop.

Fuck ... no!

RB.

Ralph Bell.

Could it be?

She felt sick. *No!*

She retched, but somehow held the mess below her oesophagus.

Ralph Bell.

The ex-CIA hood and Church member. He'd been central to a failed biological-agent terror attack on the London underground five years ago. They'd come across each other in Liberia and then Sierra Leone. Somehow she'd survived the experience.

He'd also had his filthy hands all over the deaths of three British Special Reconnaissance

252

Regiment soldiers in the Yemen a couple of years ago. His, also ex-CIA, colleague Kurt Manning had been killed by German police after the warehouse incident in Berlin. Unfortunately, Bell hadn't been there at the time, so he hadn't taken a bullet in the head.

Which was a shame.

Sam held the phone directly in front of her - she stared at it like a hypnotist's watch. Her hand was shaking.

Ralph Bell. *Always in my dreams.*

It probably wasn't him. But it could be.

She closed her eyes and dropped the phone on the passenger seat.

And waited. She breathed deeply.

Calm.

No - she couldn't do it. She couldn't get a grip. Müller and now Bell. The anger - and the fear. A heady mixture. She was sweating even though the inside of the Lexus was registering 18 degrees. She was losing it.

'Fuck!'

Still with her eyes shut, she smacked both hands on the rim of the steering wheel.

It wasn't enough.

She wanted to hurt herself. To take back some control. To feel pain - administered by her. Not by someone else. She'd been hurt too many times by foreign hands. The loss of her first love, Chris, in the mortar attack in Afghanistan. Her

Mum and Dad both young to their graves. Uncle Pete, murdered by The Church in a plane crash in the Alps. The burning hell that was the hostel in Kenema. Seeing Wolfgang's mother cold-bloodedly killed in the Berlin warehouse. Sokolov - the despicable oligarch of oligarchs. His brother a deranged serial abuser - she'd seen him raping an innocent girl; and then he was on top of her. Sweat. Blood. And more blood. Vlad, oh, Vlad. Her Russian aid and friend - chasing across his huge country, tracking down the radioactive bomb. Shot, then left to die in a burning shack.

'Fuck!' Louder this time.

She smacked her hands on the rim again.

Shit that hurt.

Her eyes opened. They darted about. She was looking for something sharp. Something that could do some damage. The keys? *Shit.* There weren't any. That's the problem with a modern Lexus.

Breathe.

Her pulse was racing.

Come on.

Phone Wolfgang.

She breathed. Ralph Bell. She could be wrong. But the likelihood was ...

Ralph Bell had phoned Müller. Hadn't he? Was he on the island? He could have phoned from anywhere. Phone contacts' list just showed a name? It didn't mean he was on The Bahamas?

Breathe.

Was he?

Sam snorted. This time, instead of hitting the rim, she gripped it as tightly as she could. She twisted her hands, the leather cover gave, just a touch. She scrunched up her face. And twisted some more.

Breathe.

Come on.

Sam let out a lungful of air through closed lips. It was a feminine, elongated raspberry.

Phone. Wolfgang. An order. To herself.

She took her own phone from her pocket and turned it on.

Breathe.

She dialled Wolfgang.

It rang twice. He picked it up. She started.

'It's me.'

'I know.'

Breathe.

'I've just left our man.'

'Did you get anything?'

That's better. Calm. Do this.

'No.'

Come on.

'That's a shame.'

'He ...', she was struggling to think of the appropriate words, '... he's no longer with us. He did it himself; in front of me. At the club.'

Silence.

'How?'

'A pill. I think he was trying to say sorry. And, I guess, he needed someone to say sorry to. That lucky person was me.'

More silence.

'Sorry.'

'Don't you start. It's not been the best hour of my life. Anyway I have his wallet and mobile.'

Good. Control. Focus.

Sam rattled off the account numbers and other details on Müller's bank cards - she just remembered them; there had been no need to write them down. She put the phone on 'speaker', opened the wallet and took a photo of the Walter Ingris Bank ID card, and then SMS'd it to Wolfgang's number. With the phone on her lap she then described the *Miami Vice* card.

'You should visit that place. When you get there.'

'Lucky me.' Sam swallowed.

'Anything else?'

'He had a missed call on his phone. From a "Freddie".' Sam rattled off the long number.

'Good. And anything else?'

Sam paused, struggling to start her next sentence.

'And ... there was a text.' She stalled.

'Who from?

Sam was just about to say RB when a blue car (she wasn't paying anywhere near enough attention to see what it was) pulled up sharply across the front of the Lexus. That got her attention. She was all eyes and ears now. The frustration and pity were gone. Now she had complete clarity.

She did a sharp 360 visual: *car parked to my immediate left (blue, Mazda 6); none to my immediate right, but there is a black Cube one bay down; one car directly behind (silver Nissan Micra).*

The passenger door of the blue car opened (she'd got it now - a Chevrolet Impala). The vehicle was so close the tall man in the front struggled to get out. He was white, 40-ish, shades, short brown hair and dressed in black - slacks and shirt.

Sam had to make a split-second choice: get out and run or, however ridiculous it sounded, drive? The passenger of the Impala made the choice for her. The tall man was in the process of pulling a handgun from his belt. He wasn't raising it to fire - yet, but the intent was there. The driver, on the far side of the car, was also out on the tarmac.

It was snakeskin-belt man.

Go!

She rammed the Lexus into drive and floored the accelerator.

The man with the gun didn't have a chance to get out of the way. The Lexus hit his door which pinned him against the Impala. Sam caught his face. Surprise. Terror. Pain.

The Lexus didn't have anywhere near enough momentum to force a side-parked Impala out of its way. But it was heavy enough to do for the driver of the Impala.

On the other hand the Micra behind her, with its wheels in the Lexus's direction of travel - *that's possible*?

'Sam?' It was Wolfgang. A squeaky voice from her groin above the sound of a thrashing engine and metal against metal (and bone).

Sam found reverse. And floored it.

Smack!

She kept the revs high, looking over her shoulder for an opportunity to disengage from the Micra. It was moving - they both were. But not very quickly. She glanced forward. The driver was in a heap. He was out of it, his handgun on the floor. But snakeskin-belt man was alive and well, and coming round the front of the Impala.

And he also had a gun.

Shit.

Sam threw the Lexus into drive. There were now a couple of metres between her and the Impala, and a half a metre between the front of the Impala and the next along car - the Cube.

The 430 badge on the back of the Lexus meant 4.3 litres. That's four times larger than the Swift she'd abandoned yesterday. Add in two metres of tarmac, and that was enough to turn the SUV into a battering ram - and for snakeskin-belt man, a potentially lethal weapon. Sam wellied the accelerator at the same time as she turned the steering wheel hard right.

Snakeskin-belt man made the right choice. He was raising the gun to take aim at Sam, but that would have meant standing still long enough to fire off a shot. Which would have put him in the way of 2.3 tonnes of accelerating SUV.

As he launched himself over the bonnet of the Impala, the Lexus smashed an SUV-sized hole between it and the Cube. The grating sound of metal against metal hurt Sam's ears. But she'd cope. The shot that snakeskin-belt man fired off a second later was ear-shattering as it smashed the Lexus's rear glass and ... Sam wasn't sure where it went after that. But all of her limbs were working well enough. She checked.

'Sam!' A squeal.

It was still Wolfgang. Still at groin level.

'I'm busy! Give me a minute!'

But a minute wasn't long enough. She may have smashed the Impala, but she hadn't lost a tail. As soon as she was on the main drag she spotted an old, white Nissan 720 pickup - driven by a local - right behind her. She turned down a side street. It followed. She accelerated. It did the same.

'Shit!'

'Sam!'

The Nissan was no match for the Lexus in a drag race. But this wasn't a drag race. It was a busy city with pedestrians and plenty of cars.

'Wolfgang.'

'Yes. Are you OK?'

'Maybe. Look, what time is the ...', she hunted for the right word, '... passage booked for?' She had no idea why she was trying to disguise her speech. They were on her tail.

'He's on call. Why, are you in a rush?'

'I've had some local trouble and I need to leave as soon as possible. The problem is I still have a tail.'

'I'll get him ready now. Give me five minutes. You're after Potters Cay, under the bridge. Look for a boat called *The Price of Freedom*.'

Sam had taken a couple of turns and the Nissan had stayed with her. Heavy traffic prevented her from pushing hard.

'You're joking? *The Price of Freedom*?'

'No. Sorry.'

'OK. Look, before I go. Müller's phone ...'

'Yes?'

'It had a missed call.' The bile rose in her throat. 'From an RB.'

Sam took another right. She was trying to stay in traffic - in the middle of the city. Where she had lots of company. It took a few seconds for Wolfgang to respond.

'OK. Got it. Stay calm and focused. Let's get you off the island. I'll tell my man to expect you at any time.'

'Thanks.'

As the phone disconnected Sam noticed that the temperature gauge on the Lexus was registering that it wasn't happy - a flashing-red LED-lit radiator sign. She'd probably put a hole in it barging between the cars.

Shit.

How long did she have before the Lexus's vehicle management system shut the car down? What then?

Think.

She had to lose her tail. And then get to Potters Cay. If she headed east she'd hit the far end of the island in about ten minutes. Then, a left turn on East Coast road and follow it north, then west along the seafront back into the city centre. There must be some decent straight bits of road in that seven miles or so - where she could lose the Nissan?

If the Lexus keeps going for that long.

Sam was right. There were a couple of long, straight tracks of road where the Lexus easily outgunned the Nissan. Before long she was a couple of hundred metres ahead of her pursuer. At the end of the island she had to wait a few seconds to turn left onto East Coast Road - as a result she was sure that the Nissan saw the direction she took.

But, after a couple of dodgy overtaking manoeuvres on the coast road, she was well ahead of her tail.

And enjoying herself. The coast road was beautiful. Calm, azure blue seas with the hint of an atoll in the distance. Huge, wealthy estates with names such as Brigadoon, Spanish Landing and Dreamy Skies. And, with the increase in speed of the Lexus, its temperature gauge had dropped out of the red warning zone. Two miles or so to the cay. She might just make it.

Her optimism lasted less than a minute. A flash of blue pulled onto the road behind her. A few seconds later the severely dented wing of the blue Impala was on her tail. There was just the driver - snakeskin-belt man. But she'd already learnt that he could drive.

She pressed the Lexus as hard as she could, always aware that she'd rather leave herself to the mercy of the thug who was following her, than knock over a pedestrian. As a result, the Impala didn't budge. And snakeskin-belt man looked really pissed; his handgun laying blatantly on the dash of the Impala.

Traffic.

Sam reckoned they were no more than a mile from the cay. The tall, pink towers of Atlantis rising incongruously above the two-storey, townhouses. She spotted the bridges - and then the road split, with her lane bearing left onto a single-direction, urban dual carriageway. She pushed the

Lexus through the meandering traffic, as its temperature gauge rose again. She needed to turn right. Soon.

She put a bus between her and the Impala. Then a car.

Now!

She braked hard and turned right. Cutting down a single-track road between more poorly maintained houses. She'd made some ground. The Impala was 40 metres behind her. Ahead was the second urban dual carriageway, moving in the opposite direction. She didn't stop - she squinted and braced her arms against the wheel - and pulled out, hard right, into moving traffic. There was a screech of tyres - and horns. And more horns. But no sound of metal on metal. No *smash*. She checked her rear-view mirror. The gap between her and the Impala was now 50 metres.

Just ahead of her were the concrete arched bridges leading onto Paradise Island. She'd need to take a left between the two. Down onto Potters Cay. To the wharf. And then find *The Price of Freedom*.

She pushed on, slipping the Lexus between two cars. More horns. *Sod them*. She looked at her dash. The temperature gauge now well in the red.

There it is

Sam sped to the junction, braked sharply and then pulled down hard left on the steering wheel. The Lexus's front tyres protested as its back end struggled to keep up.

She accelerated again - she could see the end of the road about 400 metres ahead, a small marina of boats on the quayside directly in front of her.

Sam checked her mirror. *Nothing.* No, *shit*, not nothing. There was the Impala. What should she do? She was caught. Driving down a dead end. Looking for a boat which could be anywhere.

She was 200 metres from the quayside. To her left was a row of dilapidated wooden shacks masquerading as chandlers, fish cafes and bars - immediately beyond was the sea. To her right was a tall, rusty metal fence running along the complete length of road. Behind it was a worn-out parking lot and one of the sets of stanchions for the 'off' bridge. The lot was empty apart from a couple of shells of cars.

The whole place looked ominous. Seedy. Dangerous.

Just when she needed complete control the Lexus took it from her.

The SUV's engine management system had decided that enough was enough. If the woman persisted on driving the car in these conditions she would do permanent damage to the engine. And it wasn't having that. It cut off all the power and, as the car was automatic, almost instantaneously the engine drag slowed the Lexus down to a crawl. And then it stopped.

Fuck!

Sam knew it was lost. The Impala was gaining. There was a madman at the wheel. And he had a gun. She had an unscalable fence to her right. And, to her left, was the sea. Ahead of her, somewhere, was a boat to freedom.

She had to do something.

Try something.

She grabbed her rucksack from the back seat and launched herself out of the Lexus. The Impala was 100 metres away. But it was faced with a road block. Snakeskin-belt man might struggle to squeeze his car between the Lexus and the fence to the right, and the SUV was too close to the shacks on the left for a car to pass. But with both cars clearly expendable - he'd make room?

She ran. As fast as she could. She'd be at the quay in under a minute. Then she'd need to find *The Price of Freedom*.

Crunch. Metal on metal. She felt the fence to her right vibrate - and then bend away from her. The Impala was forcing itself through. The fence was giving way. Of course it would. It would be free in no time. And then it would be over.

Fifty metres. The boats came into focus – the quay stretching to the right.

Three yachts. *No.* An old fishing boat. *No.* A couple of small speed boats. *No.*

The fence gave its final wave, and she heard the revs of the Impala pick up. It was hopeless.

Even if she made the boat, snakeskin-belt man would be climbing aboard with her.

And then a new noise. The *nee-naw* of police sirens. She couldn't stop herself from taking a glance behind. The Impala was free of the fence and gaining. She might make it to the corner - start looking at the other boats before it reached the quayside.

Maybe.

The fence started shimmering again. *More traffic?* The *nee-naws* were getting louder. She turned the corner as the Impala screeched to a halt. It was left hand drive - the car's body was between her and snakeskin-belt man.

She had seconds.

She sprinted harder. Looking left at row upon row of boats.

And there it was, a huge powerboat. At the end of the next boardwalk. Pointy - long - and with four engines on the back. There was a local with dreadlocks looking her way. He had a single, nonchalant hand in the air.

Clump!

Shit! A shot. From a hand gun. Probably 9 mm. A miss. She recognised the sound.

Nee-naw, nee-naw.

'Police! Put down your weapon.' A shout from the corner.

Clump! A thump in her back, lurching her forward - she almost toppled over.

Shit! Was she hit?

Am I hit? Keep going!

She turned left onto the boardwalk. She heard the *thud-thud-thud* of marine outboards burst into life. The smell of petrol a new sensation.

Clump! Clump!

Not at her this time, unless snakeskin-belt man had forgotten how to aim. More distant. *Nee-naw, nee-naw.* Shouting.

The man with the dreadlocks was holding out his hand. As she took it, she spotted the name - *The Price of Freedom* - in exaggerated italics across the back of the white fibreglass hull. He launched her into the boat - she stumbled, falling unceremoniously in a heap on the floor. Then a flash of dreadlocks as he moved quickly to the controls.

More shouting - still at a distance, but closer now. *Nee-naw, nee-naw.* She composed herself. Sat up. Got orientated.

The front of the boat lifted. The back dropped. It accelerated with a turn of speed that threw Sam backwards. She was, literally and metaphorically, all at sea. She glanced up. There was someone on the quayside at the end of the boardwalk. She recognised him.

White, late middle-aged, sunglasses and a turquoise Miami Dolphins' baseball cap.

The man from the bridge. With the camera.

He was staring at her. And then he did something that surprised the hell out of her. He put his thumb up and smiled.

Another harbour-side boat obscured her view. And then they were in the channel, travelling faster than she thought was possible without being airborne.

Samostan Monastery, Punat Bay, Krk, Croatia

Jakov was already at his wit's end. Two days in the garden outside the monastery building, but still contained within an unscalable brick wall. Two days of endless toil. Dig here, sweep there, plant that stuff - no, not like that, like this. 'Karlo', his name for his monk minder, was at his side most of the day. He was kind and forgiving - as, Jakov guessed, any monk would be. They had fed him well, and the antibiotics had started to do their trick. The tracking up to his shoulder looked much less angry and he was beginning to feel better. Even though his shoulder still hurt like hell.

But he hated it. He hated that he was trapped and forced to work on menial tasks. He hated that his parents almost certainly thought he was dead; that he wouldn't get to see his brother, Miklos, or any of his relatives again. He hated that he wasn't able to scull - he had such a good season planned. And he hated that nobody said a word.

Nothing, apart from 'Hannibal', the deranged man who he hadn't seen for two days. It was all torture beyond torture.

He'd rather be dead. Or die trying to get off the island.

The problem was, he wasn't a particularly brave man. He was big and strong - 1.90 metres in his rowing shoes and hovering on 110 kg, nearly all of it muscle. But physical courage wasn't his strong suit. He'd shied away from fights at school. Much too young to have been forced to serve in the Balkan war like most older Croat men, when some of his friends had queued up to join today's Army he'd stayed in the village and worked in his father's shop. He was artistic - and sporty. He found more than enough guts and determination to become a very good rower, but he avoided confrontation.

This, he knew, provided him with a dilemma. He couldn't stay here, no matter how benign his environment. He couldn't. But did he have the courage to try and escape? To face the dogs? Was it possible to get off the island? Was his shoulder strong enough to allow him to swim? Wasn't the water far too cold? Was there a boat?

It was getting dark. Karlo had collected all of the tools and had returned them to a shed which was at the bottom of the walled garden. Jakov checked his watch. It was 5.17 pm. It would be suppertime soon.

The food was good.

But he couldn't stay here.

Karlo took him gently by the forearm and led him through two sets of locked double doors. The monk opened them as he always did via, what Jakov thought was, iris recognition. Now in the quadrangle, his monk pointed at his own watch. It read 5.20. He then flicked up both hands - signifying 20 minutes. He then pointed at the ground.

Here in 20 minutes.

'Am I free to make my own way to my room?'

The monk nodded.

Brilliant.

Jakov grabbed the monk's hand and shook it. Other than sleeping, this would be his first 20 minutes of freedom.

'Thanks. Thanks very much.'

The monk smiled and nodded some more. He mouthed, 'twenty minutes', and then made his way across the courtyard.

Jakov paused. He looked for the closest bench and made a beeline for it. He sat. And thought.

I could be here forever. I'm 23. Time is on my side. I should get to know every nook and cranny of this place. Fit in. Earn some trust. Work out patterns. And then, like some Second World War escape movie, I should make my move. That's what I'll do.

He looked around the quad. He counted the windows. Tried to second-guess what was happening behind each one. If the top floor matched the bottom, there would be a corridor running along the inside with rooms on both sides. He spotted the grainy image of a monk moving left to right on the top floor, window to window of the wing in front of him.

Monk in window. Wall. Monk in window. Wall. No monk.

Logic dictated that the monk was in a room that was at least two windows long. Bigger than his room. He kept looking to see if the monk silhouette returned to the window he had just transited.

Nothing.

He had started. He'd need to write all this down somewhere.

His stare was interrupted by a low-volume siren. He'd heard it before, but had never managed to understand what it was associated with. Now he knew.

The main entrance arch and the associated metal doors were in the wall off to his right. A yellow flashing light above the arch (which he'd not noticed before) accompanied the siren. Both were signalling that the doors were opening. He counted in his head: *one - two - three*. The doors were now fully opened. Another fact; he'd need to write that down.

Then a shiver of fear spasmed down his spine.

Into the courtyard walked 'Hannibal'. He was accompanied by a medium-build black man, who was smartly but casually dressed. He was holding a silver drinks-can in his hand. They were in animated conversation.

'What do you mean, she got away?' Hannibal was angry - incensed. His voice raised.

'There was a fracas at the docks. Our man was shot dead; a second was badly wounded somewhere inland. We can only assume that she escaped on a boat - headed for Florida.' The black man replied. He seemed casual; unworried by Hannibal's histrionics.

'Incompetence! And Müller is dead also?' Hannibal's voice boomed across the quad. There were a couple of monks walking along one side of the square. They carried on, heads bowed, outwardly unaware of the exchange.

'Correct. Suicide.'

Hannibal raised his hands in mock indignation.

'Do we have any idea if he gave anything away?'

Both men had stopped in the middle of the quad by the fountain. The black man had another sip from his can.

'Possibly, possibly not. He had restricted access. We're working on changing account numbers and some other necessary alterations. It should be done in the next couple of hours. I'm not worried.'

'What sort of cake and arse party are you Americans running?'

The black man didn't flinch. He seemed impervious to Hannibal's tirade.

'I think we need to remember where the money's coming from, Freddie.'

Hannibal, now renamed 'Freddie', turned to one side and kicked a stone with his foot.

'What can you tell me about Miss "slippery" Green?'

The black man ran a hand through his short hair.

'Ex-SIS/MI6. We've come across her before. I've met her. She's tenacious, but not indestructible. I've got someone in Miami keeping an eye out for her. We'll track her down in a matter of days.'

'How come I don't know of her?'

'In the scheme of things, she's been a small cog. As they all are. She's a nuisance - no more. Throughout you've had bigger fish to fry. Getting the network in place. Planning the event. You've done a great job. The US are really pleased.'

Freddie grunted. The black man's platitudes seemed to have calmed things down a bit.

He turned again, catching Jakov staring at them. Jakov was sure he saw him say, 'What the fuck ...', under his breath. Then he was all smiles.

A moment of silence and then, 'Jakov, come here.'

Jakov was immediately unsure.

'Come. Come.' Freddie was beckoning with his hand.

Jakov stood and wearily walked towards the two men. Freddie welcomed him with an arm around his shoulder - which must have looked odd; Jakov was fifteen centimetres taller than he was. Freddie squeezed his dislocated shoulder. A spike of pain shot down his arm. His knees almost crumpled.

'Did you hear all of that Jakov? Were you listening?' Both of the sentences came through gritted teeth.

'No ... I.'

Jakov didn't have time to finish his reply. Freddie removed his arm and, in an instance, faced Jakov - now with both hands on Jakov's shoulders. Their height difference was stark.

'Don't ... listen ... to ... other ... people's ... conversations! Didn't your mother teach you anything?'

Jakov was forming an appropriately weak reply when Freddie raised himself on tiptoes and smacked his forehead against Jakov's nose.

The pain was overwhelming. His legs gave way as his hands instinctively reached for his face. He was sure he let out a yelp, but it didn't register because, as he dropped to his knees, Freddie's fist smashed against the side of his head.

Then blackness.

Headquarters SIS, Vauxhall, London

Jane closed her computer. It had been another very long day. In at 7 am. Lunch on the hoof. A trip over the Thames for a meeting at the FCO. Back again. An impromptu cabal with the chief and all of his senior team to discuss the evolving Korean crisis - two leaders screaming at each other from across the playground. SIS didn't have boots in North Korea, but GCHQ were central to gathering SIGINT (signals intelligence) from a variety of sources on the peninsula. And their rep from Langley had some useful input.

She'd not made the gym as she had planned. *Never mind.* She'd knock up something from her fridge when she got home and whilst it was on the hob, she'd do some yoga. It was hardly cardiovascular - but it would do.

She stood and gathered her things. Through the glass wall she counted five of her staff still in the office. She would have a chat to all of them individually as she left - encourage them to go home.

One of them was Frank; he was on the phone. The only analyst, she guessed, who was still in the building. *Bless him.*

She put her empty lunch box in the top of her daysack and reached for her scarf and heavy woollen coat. *Home.* A 20-minute tube journey followed by a five-minute walk.

There was a rattle on the door. It opened. Frank's head appeared.

'Got five minutes? I think you'll want to hear this.'

Jane swung her head from side to side, releasing her shoulder-length hair from the neck of her coat. She flicked the bottom of her hair with the flat tops of her hands to make sure it was all free.

'Sure, Frank. What have you got?'

'I've just got off the phone from The Bahamas.'

'Bradley Stokes?'

'Yeah. Do you know the geography of the islands?'

'Uh, not really. Archipelago, off the east coast of Florida. Capital is Nassau. Ex-Brit colony. Tax haven?' It wasn't a bad summary, but her expertise was the Middle East, North Africa, mid-Asia and all of Europe.

'Seven hundred islands at an average of 200 miles southeast of the southern tip of Florida.

You're right about the tax haven. It's also a big 007 theme park. A number of scenes from a couple of Bond films have been shot there.' Frank added.

'And your point is?'

'Sorry. Bradley spotted Sam driving a very smart Lexus off Paradise Island ....'. Jane had lost the detailed geography; Frank noticed. 'Sorry, let me explain. I've been studying this.'

Jane let him have his moment.

'Nassau is on the island of New Providence, pretty much in the middle of The Bahamas. New Providence is a tiny island - think Isle of White, but a bit smaller and without any white cliffs.' Frank took a breath. 'Paradise Island is a tiny, *weenie* island blistered onto the northern coast of New Providence. It's where most of the hotel action is. It seems that Sam was on the island - Bradley doesn't know why. He snapped her coming off the only bridge.'

'Driving a smart Lexus?'

'Correct. A 430 NX. Black metallic. About £75k's worth.'

'That's good. We know she's alive.'

Frank put up his hand, gently stopping Jane mid-track.

'There's more. After tagging Sam, and via the local police radio, Bradley got wind of a shooting incident involving a black Lexus in a local mall. By the time he got there it was all over, other than some frightened and confused locals - and a couple of police cars. Then there was another radio report of a chase on the east of the island involving ...'

'A black Lexus.'

'Yeah, that's right. The police headed east. Bradley headed north to the centre of town. He told me he was trying to get into Sam's head. After what we'd told him, the airport was out - so it was a boat or nothing. By chance he arrived at the docks at the same time as Sam, the Lexus and a chase-car.'

By now Jane had plumped her bottom on the corner of her desk and got comfortable. She felt as if she was hearing the first draft of a movie script.

'Bradley has police sirens fitted to his pickup. And, and he knows this is not usual SIS protocol, he was armed. A 9mm Sig Sauer P226. His own - not from SIS's armoury. It's the island mentality. All those pirates.' Frank grinned.

Does SIS's one-man office in Nassau have an armoury?

If she wasn't fascinated by the story, Jane's eyes would have rolled in their sockets. An elderly case officer running around a former British colony with a non-issue pistol under the seat of his car, and police sirens in the grille. Whatever next? A magnetic, flashing blue light which he throws on the roof?

'Anyway,' Frank was excited - there was obviously more and it seemed very unlikely the bad guys were going to come out on top. 'He puts the blue light on his roof, throws on the siren and chases the Lexus and the Impala down the docks.'

'Impala? That's a deer, isn't it?'

'Yeah - yeah. It's also a US car; a Chevrolet, I think. I didn't ask as I didn't want to appear thick. Anyway.' Frank was in full swing. 'As Bradley turns into the docks he sees Sam's Lexus abandoned and the Impala squeezing past it - knocking over a fence. Sam's car seems to have come to a halt halfway down the docks. So, quick thinking, Bradley follows the Impala through the gap and, as the driver gets out at the quay and takes a shot at Sam, Bradley does the whole, "Stop, Police or I'll shoot!", routine. The guy takes a second shot at Sam - he thinks the shooter might have winged her, so he slots the bad guy. A double-tap. And he's down.'

'*Slots* the bad guy?'

'Yeah, you know. Slots.' Frank raised his right hand and took a couple of imaginary shots.

'And Sam?'

'Oh. Yeah. He runs to catch her up, but he's too late. She's on a massive powerboat with four engines as big as your head. Off it goes, down the sound and into the bay.'

'Sam made it off the island?'

'Appears so, yeah.'

'And did Bradley give any indication on how Sam was? Had she been shot?'

'He didn't know. He just said that she had sat up and looked at him. So, he thought that she was probably OK.'

Frank was very pleased with himself.

Jane blew out through an open mouth. Doubtless the British Consulate and The Bahamian government would knock up some appropriate cover story. And, regardless of how gung-ho Case Officer Stokes appears to have been, he probably just saved Sam Green's life. She'd have a chat with the Consulate General tomorrow about some form of commendation. And then get him marched back in for a reprimand. SIS couldn't be doing with maverick case officers gunning people down in the street.

'Thanks Frank. A lot. And where do we think Sam's gone?'

'The States. Bradley reckons it's the only sensible option in a big speed boat - unless the whole boat is full of fuel, which he doubts. I reckon it's a ten-hour journey, assuming they get past the US Border Patrol maritime teams. She'll be there in, say, six hours.'

'OK. Good.' Jane thought for a second. 'Do two things for me. One, tonight. Get in touch with the British Consulate in Miami and tell them what you have. And, tomorrow, try and work out how Sam Green might have arranged to get off the island on a bloody big powerboat. She must be working with someone. Look at all her history.

There was that UN chap in New York. And the congressman's daughter from last year. Oh, and the German count. Wolfgang. That's him. Check him out as well.'

Frank nodded.

'And the Russian FSB guy - Vlad?'

'No. I think FSB involvement is extremely unlikely. But, I will speak to my CIA oppo at Langley now. Let him know where we are with Sam. I'll also ask him to reopen the Greyshoe file - make it live. I think The Church of the White Cross needs much more of our attention than we have been giving it hitherto. Don't you think?'

Chapter 10

Flemingstraße, Munich, Germany

Wolfgang stood, pushing his chair away. What did he have? He walked over to the wall-length glass board and with some sweeping movements of his hand, segments of the screen changed, and two sections were enlarged.

The two enlargements were individually titled with a country's name and next to it, its flag: Croatia and Venezuela. The Croatian box had only one mugshot complete out of the five allocated spaces. The photo was of a man wearing army uniform; his badges displayed the rank of general. Wolfgang had known about the guy for over a year, picking up his details from CCTV footage of a likely Church meeting in Zagreb. The other four boxes were empty. But, after Sam's call yesterday he could now add a new telephone number and an incomplete name. The partial name was 'Freddie'; the number had turned out to be a Croatian landline.

He typed what he had into an empty Croatian mugshot box using the on-display keyboard.

Interrogating the detail yesterday had been tricky and had required him to hack into Hrvatski Telekom's database - the Croatian national telephone company. It was something he'd not done before and it had taken him most of last night to find a usable portal. Once inside, he'd accessed 'Freddie's' account and then followed a number of useful trails.

The first thing he did was to find the missed call. That was straightforward. Freddie had called Müller using a Croatian landline about 20 minutes before the arranged meeting with Sam at *The One and Only*. Müller had obviously not picked it up; his mind on other things - like taking his own life. The landline details were obscure - which surprised him. The country code was a decipherable '+385': Croatia. Next, for mere mortals, there were 21 different area codes. Zagreb, the capital, was a single '1', Istria '52', etc. He got that. Strangely, however, the area code for Freddie's landline was '61' - it didn't match any of the 21 declared Croatian codes.

Back to the drawing board.

Eventually, after some long-screwdriver hacking, Wolfgang had found the reason. Deep within Hrvatski Telekom's filing system was a contract between the company's CEO and the Ministry of Interior. The document was classified 'CONFIDENTIAL'. It was three pages long, but, with help from Google Translate, the outcome was clear. Hrvatski Telekom had been given authority by the Ministry of Interior to set up a new, secure landline code: 61. With it came 40 separate 6-figure numbers.

Wolfgang had spent a further hour trying to establish where or what the area '61' looked like - but had been beaten by the need to sleep. It was 3.30 in the morning and Elisabeth had knocked so loudly on the metal entrance door, he thought she'd burst through and fall down the stairs. He'd accepted her matronly direction - and left the cellar for his bed.

Four hours later, after a scrummy breakfast of boiled eggs and freshly baked *Brötchen* lashed with unsalted butter, he'd come back down to the cellar and worked on Freddie's account - focusing on the arcane landline number. Freddie was sparing with his account. He used the line very infrequently and only to five numbers, one of which was Müller's. Records over the past six months showed him phoning Müller ten times.

The other four numbers were fascinating.

One was to the mobile number of the Croatian army general who was on Wolfgang's database - and whose mugshot he already had. That was a good piece of corroboration.

A second was to a cell phone in the US. This was interesting but not useful. All US cell numbers are assigned randomly by NANPA (North American Numbering Plan Administration), so a US cell has no geographical or other association. There were exceptions. Some companies buy a

1,000 consecutive numbers at a time. He'd need to check later to see if the number was associated with a particular company. Getting into NANPA was like taking a bone from a dachshund. Easy-peasy.

The third number opened a new door for him.

Freddie liked to call Venezuela. Often. The Venezuelan number was a landline with an area code that belonged to Amazonas - deep in the south of the country, a state that bordered Brazil and Colombia. Wolfgang had opened Google Maps to study southern Venezuela. It was barely populated; all jungle and rivers.

His current database included Venezuela as one of his 11 countries - its box was open in front of him. He knew the country was in a bad way. The current socialist government, the United Socialist Party, or Chavistas, had been in power for 27 years. A burgeoning opposition was blaming the Chavistas for running an autocracy, increasing their power base and reneging on social reform. For an oil-rich country, the shortages of basic supplies and foodstuffs were extraordinary and clashes between the government and the opposition were violent; law and order had broken down. Some commentators had declared that Venezuela was in a state of civil war.

Until yesterday Wolfgang had two Venezuelans on his board. One was the leading civil servant in The Ministry of Interior, Justice and

Peace - Diego Rojas. The second was Cardinal Pedro Pérez, a senior figure in the Venezuelan catholic church; Wolfgang had made a side-note on his database that 80% of Venezuelans were practising Catholics. The cardinal had some reach,

Now he reckoned he had a third name for his board - well, almost. He had the landline number that Freddie called in the Amazonas; it was a big state and he couldn't get a clearer picture than that.

The fifth and last on Freddie's call list was a +44 7795 number. He'd checked - it was a Virgin UK Mobile number. Somewhere in the deep folds of his mind it rang a bell, but he couldn't put his finger on it. This was mainly because Venezuela was writ large across his consciousness. Venezuela. Amazonas. *The Church of the White Cross?*

It didn't make much sense.

He'd ignored the fifth number and tried a different tack.

Forty minutes ago he'd blanket-searched his database for any Venezuelan linkages. There were 28. Not surprisingly 27 were associated with the cardinal and the senior civil servant. He dismissed those. The 28th was much, *much* more interesting. It was details of a flight booked from Schiphol, Holland, to Caracas. The flight was three weeks previously. After a short hack into KLM's website he found a mobile number associated with the flight. It was the same +44 7795 UK number -

assigned to Virgin UK. The fifth number Freddie phoned on his landline.

Caracas. And a UK mobile number - which rang a bell somewhere? And Freddie?

Wait. Think!

If only he had Sam's retentive memory. Was it a number that he recognised?

He was convinced it was one of his long-standing loose ends. *Think!* Hadn't a UK mobile cropped up on ten or so other call registers from known (according to him) Church members? He did a quick search of the database.

There it is!

The +44 7795 number - and 12 connections across the whole board. The same Virgin Mobile number that Freddie called from his Croatian landline.

A new connection.

Previously he'd not been able to establish who the number belonged to, or where it was based. He still hadn't. But, with the Freddie linkage he now thought it key to the whole matrix.

Wolfgang looked hard at the Venezuelan and Croatian boxes on the board for a couple of seconds.

He then spoke out loud to himself pointing at the board, following connections as he did.

'Freddie phones on his secretive Croatian landline: Müller; a Croatian general; a, as yet unassigned, US cell; a UK mobile number with multiple Church links and a flight to Caracas; and, a landline in the Amazonas, Venezuela.' He paused and thought. 'Neither of you ...', he was now pointing at photos of Cardinal Pérez and the civil servant Rojas, 'travel outside of Caracas - I'm pretty certain of that. But ...', he touched on a third, empty mugshot box for Venezuela. A form popped up. There were several empty fields, one of which was 'telephone number'.

He typed in the Amazonas landline number. In the title box he typed 'Unknown'.

He then hovered over the fourth mugshot box. He prodded it and an equivalent form appeared. He typed 'Anomaly' on the top line and then added the +44 7795 number.

'You, whoever you are, flew into Caracas three weeks ago. You have multiple links to at least 12 other Church members - and the mysterious Croatian, Freddie. And you spend time in a country that he calls often.'

Who are you?
And who is Freddie?
Are they both key?
And, what's a UK number doing in Caracas?
I don't know.

That was his next job. He'd interrogated Freddie as far as he could at the moment. Now he'd get into Virgin UK and try and find out more about this mysterious number.

And that threw up his now recurring problem. Every time he opened a new lead, such as Freddie and this Virgin UK Number, it spawned 30 more. He only had so many hours in the day. He could really do with a team of people working for him - people who were as good at this as he was. Unfortunately he didn't have that luxury.

St Augustine Beach, St Augustine, Florida

Austin and his retired FBI pal, Mike Dawson, struggled with their gear. They both had their set ways when it came to fishing on the beach. And they both had their own fishing 'pack': a box full of bait, spare reels, tackle, knives and other tools. Two long rods each. A chair, a rod holder (Austin's screwed into the sand - his pal's was a tripod affair) and buckets. And, not forgetting, the obligatory food and beer cooler.

It was a 500 yard trek from the car park to the beach. And both men needed a breather by the time they got to the water's edge.

Austin dumped his gear on dry sand. He looked across the ocean to the infinite horizon. It was a perfect day. Thick, light-blue icing on top of a dark blue cake. He was rubbish at metaphors, but that worked for him. The sky was cloudless, the sun was one-tenth of its way from east to west - bright but not blazing, and a whiff of wind caught the top of the water, ripples riding the surface. The fish would be in-shore soon. Searching for warmer water and the food that comes with it. If he and Mike were lucky they may catch a red drum or two.

Not that he was bothered. This short-notice trip wasn't about fishing. It had another purpose.

He'd got back from Las Vegas yesterday lunchtime. Himself, his carry-on case and the lime-green flash drive. First thing yesterday he'd been asked by the cops to formally identify Rick's body. He'd seen more cadavers than he cared to remember, but watching the sheet being lifted to expose his son's white face was more than he could bear. He thought he was going to collapse again - but his stomach took his attention elsewhere. It lurched; a pathetic moment. Humiliating and agonising. He had made it to the bench before his breakfast sullied the metal pan of the mortician's sink.

'Yes. That's him. That's Rick.' He had said, wiping the puke from his chin with the back of his hand whilst leaning over the sink.

The next 12 hours were a blur. He had made a couple of calls, including one to a local undertaker who, having taken his credit card details, had agreed to collect Rick's body after the autopsy and deliver it to Florida. Austin had no idea when that would be - nor had the cops. They reckoned that it would be at least a month before Rick's body would be released.

Once he'd finished at the morgue, Austin couldn't stay in Vegas any longer. Rick was dead. His wife was living. She needed him; Rick would cope.

He was home eight hours later. His wife didn't meet him at the airport; driving wasn't her favourite hobby. He'd got a taxi home and was met by a waterfall of tears. She sobbed and sobbed. He hugged and hugged. It was as gruelling as it was saddening. Rick was their only child - biological events had made a second out of the question. And now he was gone.

He'd made supper - which was a rare occurrence. And stacked the dishwasher. His wife was away with the pixies. She pushed her food about her plate and then went to bed. Later he'd taken her up a mug of hot chocolate when there had been more tears - and more hugs.

By the time he'd finished the chores it was close to 10 pm. He poured himself a bourbon and took his usual chair on the back porch. The sun was down, the air cool and all he could hear was the odd cricket call - and his wife's sobs through the bedroom window.

It was a beautiful view even in the dark. The end of their garden, which was mostly laid to lawn, was 80 feet away. At that point the dunes rose to about 20 feet, peppered with thorny bushes - a haven for critters of all kinds. Above them were the stars, winking at him on a blanket of blue black.

On any other evening it would have been a perfect place to sit. Last night it had helped - it really had. But only a bit. He'd reached into his pocket and picked out the flash drive. He turned it round in his fingers, the light from the back door picking up the lime green - a luminescent stick of radioactive material.

What now?

Tomorrow would normally have been golf day. He was part of a regular foursome. Four retirees of all shapes and sizes. In a moment of lucidity before he left Vegas yesterday, he'd emailed the group and cancelled. He thought he'd said something along the lines of, 'I'm not feeling that good. Maybe next week?'

So, tomorrow was a non-golf day. A different day. Different from every other tomorrow. It was a day without Rick. A day without their murdered son.

Another day more distant from his death.

He could look at that two ways. Either, he could wake up closer to when, in many years' time, he and his wife's life might have returned to something close to normality - whatever that may look like; the pragmatic soldier trained to move on from the last setback.

Or.

He'd find himself a further day removed from the cause of Rick's death. A day lost. A day when he should have been pursuing his son's murderers. A day allowing the evidence to cool.

He took a sip of his drink and pondered that thought.

Damn it.

At that point he'd stood and gone inside, leaving his bourbon on the glass-topped wicker table.

He'd picked up the phone and dialled Mike's number.

'Mike here.'

'Hi, Mike. Fishing tomorrow?'

'What, first thing?' No hesitation.

'Sure. Are you up for that?'

'Yeah. If I'm out of the house before eight, Cynth won't notice. See you then?'

'Sure thing. I'll pick you up.'

Austin had put the phone back on the cradle. Stony faced, he stared into space.

I cannot rest.

That was last night.

And this was now. By the beach. A beautiful day. Fishing. A cooler full of beef jerky and beer. On any other day he'd have been as close to nirvana as was possible.

But the day was neither beautiful, nor was he close to any sort of heaven.

Having fetched Mike from his house, it had taken Austin half an hour to tell him what had happened to his son. Ten minutes of that was on the short drive to the beach. The last 20 sitting in the car. Mike had, as Austin expected, handled the whole thing brilliantly. Like a true pal. Like an FBI agent with 35 years' experience.

In the telling Austin hadn't mentioned the secret report. Not then.

Once they had both set up and cast their lines, Austin pulled out a couple of stubbies, walked the ten yards that separated his rod from Mike's, and offered him a can.

Mike took it with a smile.

'Thanks, Austin. And, look, I'm so sorry about Rick. He was a great guy. The best. I can't begin to imagine.' He pulled the ring and took a swig of his beer.

'If there is anything I can do ...'

Austin nodded and took a couple of gulps of his can. He wasn't a great drinker. He'd seen the impact of alcohol addiction on so many soldiers. Just now, though, he needed something to help overcome a hurdle in his mind.

'Thanks, Mike. Means a lot.' He took another swig. 'Actually there is something you can do for me. If you don't mind.' Austin looked away from Mike - across the vast ocean. Next stop Africa. Part of him wanted to take their 35 foot yacht and sail away. And never come back.

'Sure, Austin. Sure. We're old pals. Help is what friends are for.'

Austin looked back at Mike and smiled. He knew he had tears in his eyes. He knew that what he was going to say now might ruin his son's reputation and could, if someone was feeling vindictive, land his son's father in jail.

'Before Rick died he told me to find a flash drive that was in his jacket pocket ...'

Twenty-five minutes later Austin had told Mike everything. They'd had a five-minute interval when Austin had to run to his rod to haul in, and then throw back, a small red drum. But other than that it was one-way traffic.

Mike was an experienced federal agent - and a very good listener. He'd never shared the details of his career with Austin, other than what job he was doing when he had reached retirement age: Executive Assistant Director. Austin remembered looking it up when he'd got his hands on a computer. It was a senior post.

'That's something else, Austin. Do you mind if I have another beer?'

Austin went back to cool box and fished out two more stubbies.

'Do you know if he passed the report on to anyone? Could it be possible that it was just in draft?'

'I can't say for sure, but I think he sent it to his boss.'

'How do you know?'

'When I tried to get in touch with the commander of the 432nd, he'd been moved on. And this was just two days after Rick was shot. If he'd submitted the report to his boss, who'd then shared it someone else - someone who didn't want anyone to find out about Venezuela - then it makes sense that both Rick and his boss were dangerous - they knew too much?'

Mike put up both hands.

'Whoa. Hang on, Austin. That's one helluva conspiracy theory.'

It was Mike's turn to look out at the ocean.

Don't I know it.

'What do you want me to do, Austin?'

'I want you to take the report and share it with some of your buddies at the Bureau. See if it makes any sense at all. Look ...'

Mike turned back to Austin. His face was open, broad-cheeked. Austin knew he could trust him.

'... Rick wrote a report. A pretty sensational report about a set-up in Venezuela that didn't want to be found. A day after he'd written the report he got gunned down in the street - in daylight. Twenty-four hours after that, someone messes with the machines that were keeping him alive. Someone wanted Rick dead. My son. Just a newly-promoted lieutenant in the Air Force. A nobody.' He knew it sounded like a plea. 'And, to top it all, a day later his boss, to whom the report was almost certainly directed, is removed from post. These events have to be connected?'

Mike chewed on his lip.

'Where's the flash drive now.'

Austin touched his pocket.

'Here.'

'Is it password-protected?'

'No.'

'Give it me, Austin. Please.'

Austin took it out of his pocket and handed it over to his friend.

'What are you going to do with it?

'I know the top man in the Jacksonville office. He's an old pal. I'll speak to him this afternoon - and arrange for a copy of the report to be shared. That may take a little longer. I might have to go there myself.'

Austin smiled. It was the first time he'd managed a smile in four days.

'Thanks Mike. It's great to know that I'm not alone in this.'

Mike nodded.

'You understand that Rick's name might be mud once this gets out. You know, "Lieutenant takes secret documents off base."'.

It was Austin's turn to nod.

Mike continued. 'And you too. Possession of classified documents is a federal offence?'

He nodded again. He knew the gravity of the situation.

'And, finally, have you taken a copy of the file?'

'No.'

Austin's lie was accompanied by the shaking of his head.

Headquarters SIS, Vauxhall, London

Frank chewed on the remnants of a peanut butter and jam sandwich, putting far too much in his mouth. Finishing it off would be a struggle. As he chewed, he used his left hand - the one not covered in peanuts and conserve, to touch the 'play' button on his screen. The secure video had been sent through by dstl, the British government's team of military scientists and engineers. They were always on the cutting edge of technology; and were always cone-headed enough to be sent down an experimental rabbit hole if it looked like a lot of fun.

Video clips weren't their only method of communication. Most of them could write. But they were engineers and pragmatic scientists, who liked making things and then blowing them up again. Writing was for staff officers. Videos and demonstrations were much more their bag.

The video started. It was, not surprisingly, narrated by a man in a white coat. He was outside a lab and had one foot on a remote-control toy

Humvee. In his hand he had, what Frank assumed was, a radio transmitter - it looked like a large walkie-talkie. There was a flipchart beside him, the bottom of the pile of paper sheets gently flapping in the breeze. The man in the white coat didn't say anything for a few seconds. This allowed the title of the demonstration to fade in and then out.

The fallibility of GPS.

The scientist was lucid, even if the maths and communication jargon he discussed using his flipchart weren't. Frank was tempted to scroll the video on. Instead he wiped his hands on his AC/DC-motif hanky.

A few minutes later the scientist had finished with the flipchart.

'So. As you can see from the science, it should be possible to override individual GPS receivers with new positioning data. Alter its view of where it is in the world, if you like. If you can make that happen and the object that the GPS serves is mid-flight, or mid-drive, any associated navigational software will alter the object's course immediately.' The man in the white coat paused for a second, waiting for his luddite audience to catch up.

'Let's look at it another way. Assume you live in London and you set your satnav to direct you to Edinburgh. The GPS receiver knows where you are - in London - and it knows where Edinburgh is. It computes a route and off you go. Now, if I remotely tell the GPS receiver that you're no longer in London, but in Cardiff - change your X and Y domain - your satnav will recompute your journey. From Cardiff. Whereas originally you were driving north to get to Edinburgh, now you're driving northeast. As a result, whilst you think you're heading up the A1, you're not. You're heading up the A12 for Clacton. And you wouldn't want that. Well, who would?'

Frank smiled. A scientist's joke. He got the techy stuff now. And he quite liked Clacton.

'Now, let me demonstrate this practically with this Humvee, which is fitted with a GPS receiver and simple navigational software. We have pre-programmed it with a route from here,' the scientist pointed at the Hummer under his foot, 'to over there.' He was now pointing at a child's football net, about 20 metres away. All I need to do is turn it on and it will, slowly, drive in a straight line until it's caught up in the net.'

He held up the transmitter.

'This transceiver is programmed to send new X and Y coordinate details, latitude and longitude, to the GPS receiver in the Hummer. We have doctored it to receive VHF, that is radio, frequencies. Not microwave, satellite signals, which it would do normally. That's for expediency purposes only.'

The scientist then bent down and switched a button on the Humvee. It moved steadily in a straight line towards the net.

'Watch.' The scientist pressed a button on the transmitter in his hand. Immediately the Humvee swerved left, and then continued on a straight trajectory towards a wall. Three seconds later the toy hit the wall. It wasn't travelling very quickly, but it was going fast enough that, on impact, its rear wheels lifted off the ground and a piece of plastic broke off its bumper.

The video camera panned back to the man in the white coat.

'This proves that it's possible to alter the positioning data being received by a GPS receiver and, once you do so, for the associated navigational software ...'

Frank's concentration was disturbed. Jane was at his desk.

'Let it run.' Jane said quietly, looking over his shoulder.

They watched for a further five minutes as the scientist demonstrated how you could isolate a single GPS receiver and send it false positioning data, whilst not affecting other receivers on the same frequency. For this, he used the same toy Humvee and now introduced a bright blue Volkswagen Beetle. As the experiment unfolded the Humvee veered off to the left again but the

Beetle travelled in a straight line and was caught by the net.

The camera was back on the scientist.

'Provided we know the GPS receiver's serial number we can target it individually, whilst still broadcasting correct data to everyone else. That piece of science is relatively easy. But there's a problem: getting the doctored data to the receiver via the GPS satellite system. The US GPS system is pretty well rigged with excellent quality encryption and at least three fail-safes to prevent data override. Unless the US are sending rogue data themselves, we at dstl think the chance of third-party interference is close to zero. If a terrorist wanted to drive a US Frigate into a civilian freighter, we think they'd be better off bribing the captain.'

Frank looked up at Jane. She was stony-faced.

The scientist continued.

'However, on the face of it there would appear to be another opportunity: buy bandwidth from a company, such as IntelSat, which has global satellite coverage. However - don't get too carried away with that option. As well as our own research, we've also spoken to our pals across The Pond. Neither of us believes that's a truly viable option. And that's because the transmission frequencies used by commercial satellites operate in a different microwave band to that used by GPS - and transmission frequencies cannot be changed without physically getting the bird back down to earth.'

Frank was now ahead of the scientist.

'What about launching your own?' He said under his breath.

'Of course, you could launch your own satellite. In which case you could pre-programme it to transmit on the GPS frequencies. That, obviously, is not without cost.' The scientist added.

It took the man in the white coat another minute to sum up what the demonstration had shown. He finished off with a 'Please let us know what you'd like dstl to do next.'

The video stopped. Frank closed the tab.

'Come into the office, Frank. Let's talk all this through.' Jane said.

Frank followed Jane into her office. She sat at her desk, he pulled up a chair.

'OK, GPS first. Do you need to write this down?' Jane asked.

'Nope.'

'Right. I've no idea which UK agency would be able to pull together a list of recently-launched satellites. But find it - let's say the last three years. Everything you can get. And then, if necessary with GCHQ support, work out if any of them could have been funded or operated by The Church of the White Cross.'

Frank scrunched up his face.

Why the sudden interest in this, of all things?

'Why this Jane - why now? There's so much more going on. The dstl report is interesting, but surely this whole GPS thing is a distraction? Where's the link to The Church?"

Jane leant back in her chair.

'I'm not sure, look, I've just come off the phone with Linden Rickenbacker, the Deputy Director of the CIA. We spoke about re-energising Op Greyshoe - the CIA's closed file on The Church of the White Cross. I gave him what I had. You know, Paul and Victoria Mitchell, Sam's comment about Min AF, and her being chased across The Bahamas by parties unknown. I told him that Sam had indicated that she has much more intel on The Church than we'd had chance to talk about. And that we had lost her, in The Caribbean somewhere. I wanted to make sure that, should Sam find herself in a spot of bother in Florida, she'd have some friends States-side.'

'And what did he say about Greyshoe?'

'That it was complicated. That he had a couple of agents on it. There is still a residue of Church members in Abilene, Texas, who they've been tracking. His team thought the operation had grown in size since they'd dismantled it three years ago. But not by much. And they had found a couple of links to Europe. But his staff were stretched and work was slow.'

Jane looked to her side; she stared absently out of the window.

'I'm going to fly over to the States, probably at the end of next week. But I really need to speak to Sam first - get her in here. Any luck?'

'No, sorry. Although I have looked over all of her past contacts. Military, SIS and civilian - as you asked.'

'And?'

'Wolfgang Neuenburg, you know, the German count?'

'Yes. Go on.'

'He's based in Munich. Not the castle on the German/Czech border where Sam went to all those years ago. One of their other family homes. I've been in touch with the BND. They have a file on him. It's mostly low-level hacking, that sort of thing.'

'We know he's capable of so much more than low-level hacking.' Jane interrupted.

'Correct. Anyway, they gave me his address in Munich. They also have a comment on his file along the lines of "Never leaves his residence". They got this from his medical e-files.'

'And.'

'Well, Sam was in Austria before she spoke to you; skiing, I guess. She'd booked into a hotel in Alpbach. The day before she phoned you she'd used her credit card to buy a ticket from Wörgl, which is down the valley from Alpbach, to Munich. The next day she phones you from a German mobile. That's mysterious?'

Jane stood and walked to the window. It was a very bleak day. The Thames was grey. Even the brick-pink Houses of Parliament were grey.

'Forget about the satellite tasker. I'll get someone else on that. Go and see Wolfgang.' Jane said without taking her eyes off the view.

'Hang on, Jane. I'm not a field agent.'

'No, but he knows you, or knows *of you* - from Berlin. You were his and Sam's anchor here. Go and see him. If it was him whom Sam visited in Munich, persuade him to share his intelligence. Go now.'

Frank wiggled in his chair.

Scared? *Yes*. Excited. *Also yes*.

''OK, OK. I'll go.' He was about to leave. But then realised that Jane hadn't answered his original question.

'Hang on, Jane. Before you dispatch me into the wilds of Bavaria, why the sudden interest in messing with the GPS? Crashing ships and everything?'

Jane turned to him now. Her face was expressionless.

'I asked the DD if the US thought it possible to hack into the GPS system. I mentioned your theory concerning the recent shipping accident in Manila Bay.'

Frank didn't say anything. He just waited.

'The DD's reply was curt. He said that there were some things that were so sensitive they couldn't be shared, even with the US's most trusted allies.'

Frank stared at Jane. She stared back.

'The terrorist opportunities are endless.' Frank said.

'Indeed.' Jane replied.

South District Wastewater Treatment Plant, Southern Miami, Florida

Sam got her bearings. She was in southern Miami, next to a sewage works. The powerboat had dropped her off on the side of a thin channel called Black Creek. It was dark. Her 'captain', or driver, or whatever else you wanted to call him, knew where to stop. The creek, which was shadowed by a street-lamp-lit-road, branched off a lagoon. Two hundred metres down from the lagoon a couple of the lamps were out. He'd landed the boat there, in the dark. She'd scrambled ashore with her rucksack, turned to say 'thanks' to the captain, but he was gone. Back down the channel into the inky dark of the lagoon which led out into the ocean.

It had been a very dull journey. They had made it to the northern tip of Andros, the most westerly and largest of The Bahamian islands, about an hour after they'd left Nassau. The sea was pool-table flat, there was no natural wind and the sun was high. The bite was taken out of the sun's heat by the 40-miles-an-hour wind that buffeted both of them as the boat planed across the water.

Her captain had said nothing throughout the first leg of the journey. That was until they docked on the edge of a dwarf mangrove swamp, out of sight of everyone and everything. He'd berthed the boat next to a rickety wharf, that looked like it hadn't seen a boat in years. The gangway, which at one point might have made it to dry land some centuries earlier, was beyond repair. But there was a hut on the wharf, about the size of a small garden shed. It was padlocked and the driver had the key.

Sam stayed on the boat whilst the captain rummaged inside the shack. He brought out a slab of soft drinks and a bag of peanuts.

'Eat. Drink.' It was the first thing he had said.

Sam had helped herself. She was famished. And parched. It was a long time since breakfast, and slightly less time since half a cup of decaffeinated coffee at *The One and Only*.

With a mouthful of peanuts she had asked, 'Are we staying here long?'

'Until it's dark.'

That would be in about six hours' time.

The captain brought out a couple of jerrycans and filled the barrels of fuel that were strapped to the inside of the boat. Sam found the smell of petrol nauseating.

'Can I go onto the wharf?'

The captain nodded.

Sam had got out of the boat, found some shade and sat down. She was shattered. It was a combination of the exhilaration of the chase and then an hour's blast of fresh air. She'd done nothing on the journey but stare at the ocean flashing past. Her mind empty - drained by adrenalin.

She was more 'with it' now. She looked at her rucksack and found a burn hole from where a bullet had broken the canvas - smack in the middle of the bag, heart-height. She put her finger in the hole and poked at something plastic.

Not sure what that is?

She turned the bag around until she found the exit hole. There it was. A four-inch rip in the side of her bag. The round had entered her bag on a collision course with the back of her chest, it had hit something in the bag and shot out the side.

Phew.

Sam took out the contents of her bag.

And she found her saviour.

Her phone charger. Which no longer looked like a phone charger.

Snakeskin-belt man's weapon was most likely a 9mm. Bullets fired from nearly all pistols travel slower than the speed of sound. The barrel was short - as a result the explosion only acts on the slug for a couple of microseconds. At any distance a 9mm round would do you damage, but it doesn't take much to stop it. Even less to deflect it.

Nonetheless she had been very lucky.

Sam had put her stuff back in her bag, noting that she'd need to get a new charger as soon as she could. She then moved out of sight for a pee, came back to her spot and promptly fell asleep.

The second half of the journey was much more straightforward than Sam expected. The boat was fitted with a decent-looking radar, a couple of very sexy GPS mapping systems, and the captain knew what he was doing.

And they travelled without lights.

At one point the captain had turned the boat on a pin - Sam, who couldn't sleep, looked up at the radar and saw a green 'ping' on the top-right of the screen. After the turn it had disappeared. It was the only scare they'd had.

And now she was on dry land; at 3.30 in the morning. She'd turned on her phone, opened Google Maps and quickly got her bearings. With the phone on, she'd SMS'd Wolfgang: *Made it to Disneyland*. The reply was almost immediate: *So pleased. Get in touch when you can. I have something*.

Sam walked northeast along a decent tarmacked road. She was a couple of klicks north of anywhere sensible. She needed to find a motel with decent Wi-Fi, FedEx the phones to Germany - and get herself a new charger.

That was as far as her plan went.

Chapter 11

Fuck them. Fuck them all.

Jakov's overwhelming feeling of rage surprised him. It burned at him - and through him. The injustice. The degradation. *The pain.* He was not a man to anger easily. In fact, he didn't rise to anger at all. He turned the other cheek. Walked away.

But something had changed. Something inside him had snapped. It had happened before. Once. He recalled an incident a good number of years ago. He was so young he couldn't remember exactly when. He was playing with another boy in a sandpit, building tracks in the sand for their small metal cars. By mistake he'd knocked a bit of his friend's track over. The little lad had gone mad. Shouting and screaming. Jakov remembered being frightened by the boy.

And then his friend was on top of him. Jakov was big for his age, even then. He was bigger than his friend. But he didn't fight back. He kept saying 'sorry' over and over again; his back on the floor of the sandpit, holding the lad at arm's length. But the boy's madness was too strong for Jakov and his arms gave way. The boy hadn't finished. In fact, he hadn't even started. Jakov remembered it as if it

312

were ten minutes ago: the look in his friend's eyes as he started to fill his mouth with sand. A finger forcing open his lips. Sand in his teeth - between his teeth. It was disgusting. He turned his head away from the onslaught.

So, the boy pushed sand in his eyes and ears.

That was too much for him. He had deserved to be told off by his friend. Shouted at. Even punished for his mistake. But what he was being asked to endure was beyond his young mind's understanding.

He flipped - an explosion in his brain. He didn't go mad like his friend. Instead, with calculation beyond his years, he channelled his fury. He slapped the boy across the face and, finding power from somewhere, pushed him off onto the sand next to him. His friend was surprised, but his madness wasn't gone. He came back at Jakov. The detail of the next minute or so had always been a blur to Jakov. But the outcome was clear. His friend running home, blood streaming from his nose, one sandy hand held high - two of its fingers throbbing with immature broken bones.

Jakov emptied the contents of the pit from his mouth, went home and told his parents everything. He was grounded for a week without candy.

Croatian men are tough and resilient. They've suffered at the hands of many adversaries throughout the centuries. Getting knocked down and picking yourself back up again was in their genes. Scars came with the territory. His friend's parents never mentioned their son's injuries. The boy didn't play with Jakov again.

As he lay on his bed, in his cell with its barred window and metal door without a handle, he felt as if he had sand in his mouth again. He couldn't get rid of the gritty taste.

He got out of his bed and walked to the mirror. What he saw surprised him. His nose was two sizes too big and he had a pearler of a black eye. It was as though he'd been in the ring with Floyd Mayweather. He tried to piece together how he'd ended up like this.

How the anger had risen in him.

Listening to ... Freddie? That's his name. I walked across to him. Mania in his eyes. Like his boyhood friend.

Then nothing.

But he knew what the nothing was. He knew he'd taken a beating from Freddie. The erstwhile Hannibal. Hannibal Lecter morphs into Freddie Krueger.

How appropriate.

And this was the outcome. His face was a complete mess. And he must have concussion.

And he had tasted the sand again.

The bastards.

The door of his cell opened. In walked Karlo. He was carrying a mug of tea and his medical satchel. He handed Jakov the tea and pointed to the chair. Jakov sat.

Over the next ten minutes the monk gently cleaned his face and administered antiseptic cream. The juxtaposition of Karlo's sensitive actions against the inhumane frenzy that was Freddie, jarred. He couldn't rationalise it. *Were they all evil?* The monks hadn't lifted a finger at any point to save him from the beatings at Freddie's hands. They were all obsequious smiles, tender touches and mouthed pleasantries.

What was the quote?

The only thing necessary for evil to triumph is for good men to do nothing.

He'd learnt it at school. *Was it Burke?* He wasn't sure.

They were all complicit. Freddie. The black man with the silver can. The monks. All of them.

As Karlo finished off, Jakov ran his tongue around the front of his teeth.

Sand.

He knew it wasn't there. There was just pain from yesterday's injuries. But it might as well have been.

Sand. In his mouth.

'What time is it?' Jakov asked.

The monk showed Jakov his cheap digital watch. It read 10.35 am. He'd lost an evening and some of the morning.

He wouldn't waste any more of his time.

Leamington Hotel, Miami, Florida

Sam opened the door of her hotel room and threw her bag on the nearest of the twin beds. She'd spent four of the last five hours half-asleep at an all-night American diner. The waitress was more than happy to refill her coffee cup as she dozed with her head on her arms, resting on a laminate table. She had, after all, eaten her own bodyweight in 'eggs-over-easy' on muffins. And some. There was one other hobo in the diner with her; the place was hardly busy.

Just after dawn the waitress had directed her to a FedEx office where she had packaged up the two mobiles: the one she'd got from Müller and the second from snakeskin-belt man. The very efficient guy behind the counter had assured her the package would be at the address in Germany no later than 10.00 am their time tomorrow.

The FedEx man had then directed her to a 'cheap' hotel via a phone shop to get a new charger. Both were a couple of blocks away.

At $98 a room, in her book it was hardly cheap. But it was functional and had Wi-Fi. After lying about having lost her passport and speaking with a German accent, the concierge had accepted Wolfgang's Deutsche Bank credit card as proof that Sam was a reliable human being. She was pleased about that. Because tiredness was a big bear on her shoulders - ready to growl and possibly lash out with pointed claws. The man behind the counter was nice and being helpful, if a little hesitant. She really didn't want the red mist and the big brown growly thing to spoil his day.

She signed in as Walda Neuenburg matching the *W. Neuenburg* on the card. Wolfgang's long-lost cousin.

It took a further five minutes to get hold of Wolfgang and establish a secure connection on her phone. This time they managed a video link. It was good to see his face.

'You don't look so good, Sam.'

She snorted.

'You should smell me.' Sam realised as soon as she said it, that it had the tiniest touch of unintended sexual overtone. In Berlin, a few years back, the unspent chemistry between them had been close to exploding. They couldn't go back there.

Wolfgang raised his eyebrows almost imperceptibly.

'Still, they have showers in your hotel?' Wolfgang, who may have said the first thing that came into his head to cover his slight embarrassment, immediately realised he wasn't helping. 'Sorry - I didn't mean ... it was supposed to be humorous.'

'From a German?' It was Sam's turn. 'You should try ten hours riding the waves sitting on a rubber and plastic contraption powered by 1000 horses. Follow that by a ten-k hike, and then more eggs and coffee than I really needed - all on no sleep.'

'Sorry, Sam.' He smiled. 'It's easy for me in my air-conditioned cellar having slept under, how did you say, a duvet the size of Hampshire? And a breakfast fit for a king.'

'Wiltshire, actually. And you're a count, not a king.'

'Indeed.'

Having expended any tension, they both brought each other up to date. Sam gave a cursory overview of her escape, which she attributed almost entirely to the man wearing the Dolphins baseball cap.

'Who do you think he was working for?'

'Dunno. Other than "a government", could there be a second side to this?'

It was silent between them for a while.

'I don't think so. Did he look British? SIS?' Asked Wolfgang.

'I just about have his face Wolfgang. If I had photofit software I could have a go. He's certainly middle-aged. Maybe older. If he's SIS he's a very old case officer.'

'It's a conundrum - for sure.'

Wolfgang then back-briefed Sam on Freddie, the strange Croatian landline and its linkages, including the unexplained calls to the deepest jungle of Venezuela. He also told her about the Virgin UK mobile number that had disparate call-links to 12 separate Church members. And that the mobile had landed in Caracas three weeks ago. It was interesting stuff - Wolfgang had done well. But it hardly constituted a breakthrough.

'I've got no further on the SMS on snakeskin-belt man's phone. The one from "Ops" and the top line saying that they "*need to talk equipment*".'

Sam played with her curls. She needed a haircut. It was so long she found herself biting the end of it like she had done when she was a kid. She stopped chewing when she glanced at herself in the small inset at the bottom of the screen.

'Is that everything?'

'You don't sound very impressed.'

Sorry.

'Sorry, Wolfgang. It's great work. Better than I could have done. And, for me, other than letting you know that both mobiles should be with you by 10.00 am your time tomorrow, I've got little more to add.'

She stopped herself from putting some more hair into her mouth. Then she continued.

'What do you want me to do? I can't travel anywhere outside the US without alerting somebody.'

'Can you stay where you are for 24 hours? It'll give me time to get into the mobiles and see if I can piece together anything else.'

Sam stretched, stood and walked to the window. It was in need of a clean. The view was of the opposite building - a hardware store.

Hardly inspiring.

'Sure. Look, I've used your credit card a couple of times - just now for the hotel, as a sort of guarantee that I was human. I don't want to use it again for fear of a pattern. I can't use my passport, or my cards. I've got about $420 in my pocket. Can you sub me?' Sam asked guiltily.

'Yes, of course. I have a Western Union account. I'll send $2,000 to your local branch, and I'll SMS you the code as soon as I have it. Will that be enough?'

'Sure. And your SIMs. I've done the rounds with them now. The one I used to contact you just now is the same one I used in Germany to phone Jane.'

There was another pause.

'See if you can get a SIM from a local telecoms shop. Or steal someone's phone. You're a secret agent. You can do that?'

Sam looked contemptibly at the phone.

'I'll do what I can ... look, do you think I should phone Jane?' She had no idea why she was asking for his advice. She supposed it was because she was used to working in a hierarchy. Wolfgang was a natural boss.

Sam heard him breathe out heavily.

'No. Not yet. Let's see what I come up with tomorrow before you do anything rash.'

Flemingstraße, Munich, Germany

Frank paused before he pressed the button on the intercom. He steeled himself. When people asked him, 'what sort of person are you?', his stock reply was 'introvert'. It wasn't far from the truth. Flying across Europe and barging in on someone he knew of, but had never met, was not his idea of fun. And it had just become a whole lot more daunting. The man lived in a house large enough for a member of German royalty. Which he guessed made sense.

His finger wavered. Then he pressed the button.

There was a delay.

'Wer ist es?'

Frank struggled with Oxford English. German was beyond him.

'Hello. My name is Frank. I have come to see Wolfgang. Please.'

There was a longer pause.

'Hello. This is Wolfgang. Which Frank are you?'

'Sam's Frank. We've sort of met before. Berlin? A couple of years ago. I've come from London on behalf of Jane Baker. May I come in?'

There was a further pause. Then a buzz. The large metal gate slid sideward.

'Wow. Just wow.'

It was 30 minutes, some pleasantries and a decent cup of mint tea later. Wolfgang had taken Frank down into the cellar.

'Put your tongue away.' Frank said to himself under his breath.

He couldn't take his eyes off the glass wall.

'This is The Church of the White Cross? As you see it?'

'Exactly.'

'Can I play?'

'Be my guest.'

They had a couple of interactive glass info-boards in Babylon, but nothing like this. It was as if he'd walked onto a *Mission Impossible* film set.

Frank tapped, swiped and then reduced. He tapped some more. He moved open boxes with two fingers and then opened another tab. He then closed all of them and stood back. He was completely unaware of what Wolfgang was doing. He only had one focus - the board.

Frank scanned left and right; up and down.

Christ!

There was Ralph Bell. SIS hadn't seen or heard from him in three years. He was pretty confident that the CIA hadn't either.

He bent down and tapped his mugshot - a chronological factsheet appeared. He dragged it to eye height, standing up as he did.

This is good - well, bad.

Wolfgang's latest entry was a month ago. He had Ralph Bell in the UK, tracked by a pseudonym and the new name's mobile. The location was London. That sent a shiver down his spine.

He studied the details. He knew he didn't have Sam's photographic memory, but he picked up the salient facts.

He closed the tab and stepped back from the screen, almost bumping into Wolfgang who side-stepped to avoid a collision.

'Sorry.' Frank said.

Wolfgang nodded.

'This is ... fantastic. Unbelievable.' Frank stopped for a second. 'Accurate?'

Wolfgang shrugged.

'I do not put anything on the database that feeds the board unless I'm 100% certain of its veracity. Everything you see is, in my opinion, the truth.'

'And you have all of this from hacking - Dark Web activities?'

'That depends on whether or not you're going to arrest me.'

Frank didn't know if that was a kind of German joke.

'I'm not going to arrest you. I'm not empowered to. I've come here to see if you could help me track down Sam. But some part of me thought you might be working on The Church.' Frank spread his hands to the glass board. 'But, I never expected this. No one, well, no one in the UK, has this. And I'm pretty certain the US have nothing on this scale. If this intelligence can all be verified, you're in a different league to us.'

Wolfgang looked stern.

'You're timing is good, Frank. Very good.'

'What do you mean?'

'If you'd have been 24 hours earlier I would not have opened the gate and you would gone home empty-handed.'

'So why let me in now?'

Wolfgang took his turn to approach the board. He tapped The Church's emblem with a single finger. It enlarged, twice its original size. He stood back a couple of paces.

Without turning to face Frank, he replied.

'Because I think things are now moving faster than I can keep up with.' He paused. 'And Sam is in danger. I have a number of new leads that, without Sam being "out there", I would pursue at my leisure. But I don't have the luxury of time. Not anymore. You know what she's like. There's no "off" button. She'll either get to the bottom of this - or die trying. And I don't think I could cope with the latter.'

Frank took a few steps forward so that he stood shoulder to shoulder with Wolfgang.

'You're not the only one who feels that way.' He turned his head sideways and looked at Wolfgang who met his gaze. 'I thought I'd lost her - three times. One of which was when she was with you in that warehouse in Berlin.' He sniffed. 'On all three occasions, somehow she made it through.'

Frank swallowed, stopping himself from choking.

What is wrong with me?

'Do you know where she is?' Wolfgang asked.

'Within reason. As I landed at the airport we had a ping from GCHQ. They've tracked her down to a 100 square metre block in Miami.'

'How?'

'She phoned Jane a couple of days ago. We had that number. She used it again three hours ago to an untraceable mobile. Voice-over-IP. The initial search identifies a Dark Web address. GCHQ is working on it. I reckon they might find that the end-link falls somewhere, say, over there.' Frank pointed to Wolfgang's computer work station.

Wolfgang nodded as he took a couple of steps left so that he faced the UK's mugshots. He touched the Union Flag. His understanding of The Church of the White Cross's UK cell expanded in front of him.

Nothing had changed since Sam's visit. A politician and a member of the clergy. Three boxes were empty. Wolfgang stroked the empty boxes one after another.

'Who do I trust?' He paused, then looked at Frank. 'You?'

Frank didn't know what to say.

'I have two known UK members. A politician and a member of the clergy.' He pointed at the three empty boxes as he spoke. 'There will be a policeman, a member of the security services, and a military man. And they're just the heads of their own cells - possibly with four or five other members working directly for them.' He turned to Frank. 'Do you know who to trust? Jane? Is she The Church's lead in SIS?'

'Don't be ridiculous. Jane hasn't got a fanatical bone in her body.' Frank spat it out.

'How can you be sure? Really sure. What about you Frank. Should I trust you?'

Frank started to pace around the room. He couldn't keep his hands still.

'This is getting us nowhere, Wolfgang. We *have* to trust each other. You have to share this. Who knows what they're up to next?'

Wolfgang was a steadfast object around which Frank was prowling. He felt out of his league.

He was just an analyst. That's all. He wasn't a negotiator. Jane should have come. Not him.

'I do trust you, Frank.'

That stopped him in his tracks.

'Why?'

'Because you would have acted differently if you'd been presented with this *and* been a member. But ...'

'What, Wolfgang?'

'My mother was shot dead in front of my eyes. My father passed away a few years before that. I have very few things left that are precious to me - and I will lose them, all of them, if they find out about me. I know what they are capable of. I have suffered under their brutal regime before.'

Frank knew Wolfgang was right about The Church. And he was right about trust. He trusted Jane. Unequivocally. But who else?

And what about Sam? If she were in danger they had no time to lose. They needed to come to some sort of agreement. SIS and Wolfgang. And they needed to do that as soon as they could.

'OK, Wolfgang. You're right. I don't know who I can trust - except Jane. I can't do this without assuming she's on our side. And I'm not in a position to negotiate on behalf of SIS - what we can promise; what we can't. But, if you let me speak to Jane - she will be able to.'

Frank waited for Wolfgang to register what he'd said. He did that with tight lips and a Germanic nod.

Frank continued. 'First, though, are we right about Sam?'

Wolfgang looked straight at him. His face bleaker than at any time since they had met.

'Yes. Yes. And she's waiting for me to give her instructions. My worry is that, if you know where she is - then so do they.'

Outside the Miami Vice Nightclub, Collins Street, South Beach, Miami

The entrance to whatever the hell *Miami Vice* was, was halfway down Collins Street, a narrow avenue just off the strip on South Beach. It hadn't been difficult to find - Sam had just Googled it. And then re-Googled it, putting the word 'club' at the end of the search. There were only so many images of Don Johnson she could cope with.

The heavy, brushed-metallic door was recessed into a two-storey high, white brick wall - dusk giving the paintwork a pink tinge. Standing outside was the largest and most imposing black man she'd ever been within six feet of. He was dressed all in white: white shirt; white trousers with a slight flare; white jacket with a wide collar; a white trilby hat; and, sparkled with silver diamond studs, a pair of white leather cowboy boots. His menacing face adding depth to what was a perfectly white vista.

As Sam approached the door, white mountain-man put his arm out blocking further progress.

'Are you a member, darling? I don't remember your pretty face?'

The huge man's voice was almost falsetto - its ring as camp as you like. Sam had to work very hard to suppress a fit of giggles.

'I am.'

Get a grip.

Sam fished out Müller's *Miami Vice* card with the embossed *R Wilder* along its bottom edge. She handed it over as casually as she could.

White mountain-man glanced at the card and looked quizzically at Sam - and then her rucksack, and then back at the card. His face was one of consternation.

His cogs are turning?

Then he looked up and smiled.

'What have you got in there, darling? A costume? Please let it be a costume!'

Sam inwardly winced but outwardly managed a smiled.

'Yeah. Uh. Batman.'

'Oooh! The cape crusader! My favourite!'

Sam smiled and moved towards the door. She didn't want to continue the conversation in case white mountain-man asked to try on her fictitious cape for size.

He smiled back, and graciously opened the door.

Sam had no idea what to expect. She was pretty open-minded to most sexual persuasions, provided they were legal. She guessed if you could find *Miami Vice Club* on Google, everything that went on inside was probably above board. Nevertheless, she stepped into the crimson-carpeted, blood-red walled, minimally-lit corridor hesitantly. Knowing Müller's fetish, if she saw one minor in the place she knew she wouldn't be able to control herself.

She needn't have worried. It was mostly legal.

The end of the corridor led to a large, windowless room. There was a conventional bar running along one of the walls. But, that's where any comparison to convention stopped. The rest of the room was a heady mixture of indulgent and, even for Sam's reasonably broad mind, bizarre sexual practice. There was a half-full dance floor on which nobody was fully clothed. A couple of dancer-sized cages hung in two of the corners; one contained a rather attractive, writhing naked woman; the other suspended a couple of men who could best be described as 'being intimate'. Other than an empty stage, with its obligatory chrome pole, the rest of the room was replete with booths and tables - all decorated in fake red leather and dark stained wood. The place was full, but not yet heaving. It was dingy, but not dark. After a quick look round the room, Sam couldn't define the clientele. They were multi-race, multi-gender and, clearly, multi-every sexual persuasion you could imagine. The 20 or so large flat screen TVs that decorated the walls were showing every form of legal (*I'm not sure?*) sexual perversion Sam could think of.

She could only glance at the screen showing a large woman and a donkey. Thankfully, there didn't seem to be a minor in sight.

She made her way to the bar and found a stool. The deep-bass thump of the electronic dance music made her head vibrate. If it was much louder, bits of her would fall off. Thankfully, her mind was swiftly disengaged from all the noise and hedonism by the very handsome, and nearly naked (a leather waistcoat, a pair of chaps and a thong), barman who met her across the red leather-topped bar.

'What can I get you?'

Sam's mind raced through all the possible answers to that question, none of which was a standard drink - but she did know of a couple of cocktails that would suit her mood ...

Come on!

'Bacardi and coke, please.'

The barman nodded and turned to the row of glasses and bottles that ran along three shelves at the back of the bar. Sam closed her eyes. She had no choice. It was either that or being fixated on the cowboy's naked backside - which would have won any competition it might have bothered to enter.

'He's got a nice arse?' The voice was that of a husky woman. It made Sam start.

She opened her eyes and turned her head.

This is not going well for me.

A blonde-wigged beauty had sat next to Sam. Sam's dad had been a Farah Fawcett fan. If he'd been alive and here in downtown Miami Beach, he would have gone to a different sort of heaven. The girl (late 20s, Sam's height and build, but with more happening in the boob department) was gorgeous. She was even dressed like Farah Fawcett, a simple light-blue shoulder-padded t-shirt and white hotpants.

Sam was fixated by her teeth - which surprised her, considering the choices she had. The Americans do that so well? A mouthful of dazzling ivories framed by perfect lips.

'Uh, yeah. He does. Don't you think?'

'Yes, absolutely.' Her accent was attractively southern, but not so much a drawl as to imagine a Stetson and a nodding donkey.

The barman passed across Sam's Bacardi and coke. The glass was almost pint-sized, the lemon twist was as big as a quarter of orange, and it was finished off with a purple-and-white paper umbrella and two avocado-coloured straws.

'Thanks.'

She turned to the Farah Fawcett look-a-like who was still smiling. All teeth, but beautiful with it.

Grrrr.

'Can I get you something?'

'No, thanks. I have a coke,' pointing to a glass on the bar. 'I've not seen you before. Why are you in town?'

That's a good question.

A better question was 'why have I come to Miami Vice, when there's no sensible intelligence-gathering reason to do so?' Müller was dead. There would be no leads here. Who would she ask - and what would the line of questioning be?

Why *had* she come?

Because she was bored. And she didn't do boredom well. After her call with Wolfgang, by the time she'd showered and done her hair badly, it was lunchtime. She'd crossed over the road to a deli and bought some salad - and some more coffee. Then wide awake she'd kicked around her hotel room for a couple of hours, watching the latest on CNN and Fox News (it's always good to get a balanced opinion). The commentary was mostly about the dire straits of American politics, and the chasm that had rifted through American society in the past year or so: the multi-raced, liberal elite versus the predominantly white, working class conservative right. It would take a very special person with big needles to sew those two back together.

By 5.00 pm. she was going stir crazy. Wolfgang had asked her to stay put for 24 hours, until he'd had chance to look at the two phones she'd stolen in The Bahamas. Twenty-four hours was a lifetime in Sam's world. OK, so there was Wi-Fi - and she could use her phone securely without a SIM fitted. But that was not enough to keep her mind busy. At one point she'd found herself in front of an open wardrobe turning all the coat hangers around so that they faced in the same direction.

By 5.20 she was out of the hotel room with her rucksack (*just in case*), via the local Western Union office to pick up the two grand, she popped into a phone shop to get a new cell, and then off to find *Miami Vice*. It wasn't the most sensible of options - staying put would have been. But, the way she persuaded herself was that you never know what you might find. Something might happen. She'd get in the club, wait for an appropriate moment and then maybe ask a few questions.

Whatever, anything was better than staying in that box - and she'd be back in the box in time to talk to Wolfgang.

'Uh, I'm looking for someone. What about you?'

'Oooh, that's interesting.' The girl was flirting with her, for sure. And it was working. But Sam didn't feel threatened. 'Me?' The husky voice was accompanied by a theatrical 'hand on chest' from the *Charlie's Angel*. 'Oh, I'm just having a bit of fun. You know. Relaxing, dancing ... talking to interesting strangers.'

Sam was more at sea now than she had been on the powerboat. There were two reasons for this. The first was because the woman was enchanting; a siren with the pull of an electromagnet. And the second because Sam was no longer sure that her new friend was wholly, or originally, a she. There was something about her hands - their long, slender but bony fingers, which lacked the grace and femininity of the rest of her. Sam wanted to look at the woman's feet - because that was often a telltale sign.

Sam, of course, couldn't have cared less. Gender, race, creed, religion, sexual orientation - they were an irrelevance to her. People should be what they felt comfortable with being. Although, she wasn't convinced she could share a bed with someone whose gender was not necessarily completely specific.

'Oh. OK. I'm Sam, by the way.' Sam held out her hand.

Farah Fawcett took Sam's hand, 'I'm Ginny. Nice to meet you, Sam. Now, who are you looking for?'

She wasn't attracted to Ginny - it was just the way she, Sam, was wired. And the buttocks had disappeared down the other end of the bar.

Sam relaxed. *Phew.*

All clear. Concentrate.

Sam concocted a story around Lukas Müller, aka R. Wilder. That he was a German on business from Frankfurt. She was an English solicitor trying to track him down because a long-lost British relative had left him something in his will.

'What's his first name?'

Sam had hoped Ginny wouldn't ask her that.

'Robert.' She lied. She had no idea.

She was a rubbish liar. Her brain hurt every time she told an untruth. It didn't work with her. The flipside was her wiring made her very adept at spotting liars. She had a knack.

'Can you describe him to me? People here use so many aliases.

Ginny wasn't lying. Sam was warming to her.

Sam described Müller to an inch. The easiest bit was his limp. As she spoke she glanced around the room; the club was filling up. It was only 6.30 pm. What would it be like at midnight? It clearly catered for every age group. Müller wouldn't have stood out here anymore than any of the other clientele.

'Are you sure his first name's Robert? You're describing a Ralph - old, a limp and a blotchy face?'

Of course.

'That's him. Sorry. I'm dealing with a number of clients at the moment. Ralph, yes, that's him.'

'Haven't seen him for a while. Had a thing for younger looking men, if you know what I mean.'

Sam did. And she hated him for it.

She finished her Bacardi.

'OK. Thanks, and, well, never mind.' She waved at the barman. He started to saunter Sam's way.

I wonder where he keeps his horse?

Flippancy. She couldn't stop herself.

She smiled at Ginny.

'Can I get you another coke, or something else?'

Ginny finished her drink, placing the glass on the counter with a firm hand.

'Why not! I'll have whatever you're having.'

'Two more, please.'

Sam turned to Ginny and in a whisper said, 'Do you think if I ask for the drinks separately we might get twice as much arse?'

Ginny screeched an almost male-like laugh and slapped Sam on the thigh.

'You are funny!'

You wait 'til I've had a couple more.

The barman came back with the two large drinks, and both she and Ginny took a sip.

'Mmm, that's good. Now, tell me about yourself, Sam.'

'I'm much more interested in what your story is.'

Three drinks later, Sam and Ginny were chatting away like lifelong friends. Sam's brain was befuddled with alcohol, but she still kept an edge. She was having a ball - more relaxed than she had been in ages. Ginny may not press all her buttons, but she was great fun.

Ginny had brought up sexuality early on and Sam had given her an honest reply. From that point both were clear that this evening wasn't going to end between the sheets, and they both relaxed further because of it. Ginny was very open about her gender and the operations she'd had, and was going to have in the future - to complete the exquisite work that had been carried out so far.

'You are gorgeous.' Sam had complimented her.

'Thank you. I like to think so. You wait until I've got rid of Mr Big and replaced him with Mrs Tight. You might be interested then?'

Sam laughed as Ginny finished her drink.

'Two more?' Sam asked. She thought she could just about manage that - and stagger home.

She turned to the bar and stuck her hand up like a child asking teacher if they could be excused. Hopefully *The Lone Ranger* would get her signal.

And then she dropped her hand, and hunched her shoulders - as her heart rate picked up. The wooziness that accompanies four large cocktails didn't evaporate - completely. But her pupils widened to take in as much light as they could, and she instinctively placed a hand on the cloth handle on the top of her rucksack.

'Are you OK, Sam?'

She didn't answer. Not initially. The reason for her change of demeanour was due to a man she'd spotted out of the corner of her eye. He was white, mid-40s and too casually (but expensively) dressed to be in the club for an evening of debauchery. He was standing at the entrance searching - looking for something across the now very busy club.

For me?

How would they know where to look?

Sam shook her head, trying to clear the fog.

White mountain-man - checking my card. Recognising the name? Not recognising the face?

'Sam?' Ginny placed a hand on her arm. 'You look like you've seen a ghost?'

The man was still searching. Sam was registering - she didn't know who he was, but she would recognise him forever. She was all focus now. She snatched a look at Ginny.

'Don't stare. Look through me.' Ginny did as she was told. 'Can you see the white guy? 40s. Inappropriately dressed. Long-sleeved beige shirt; brown slacks. Brown gilet waistcoat?'

Ginny tilted her head.

'Hog-ugly? Looking for something?'

Sam was still looking away. Staring at Ginny's fabulous light blue, if slightly bleary, eyes.

'That's him. He's looking for me.'

Ginny shot a glance at Sam.

'What do you mean?'

'It's too difficult to explain. I don't know how they found me, but I'm pretty sure he's after me.'

'What do you mean "they"?'

Sam didn't answer Ginny's question, she just squeezed her arm.

'I need you to do me a favour.'

Ginny didn't hesitate.

'Sure. What?'

'What's he doing now?'

Ginny looked beyond Sam again.

'He's still looking. No. He's moving this way.'

Sam was off her stool, rucksack in hand.

'Is there a way out of here that isn't through the front door?'

Ginny took a split second.

'There's a shoulder-height window in the gent's restroom. You should be able to squeeze out.'

'Good. Where is he now?'

Ginny looked. 'Pushing his way through the crowd. He's heading this way. I think he's onto you.'

Sam took Ginny by the shoulders.

'Intercept him, please. Find me a minute. Maybe two? Can you do that?'

Ginny smiled, her most sexy smile - and used both hands to push her breasts up and over, creating a cleavage to get lost in.

'Go, Sam. Go!'

And with that order, Sam was off. She didn't look back. She didn't see the man spot her movement, lift his chin up and start to head Sam off at an angle through the crowd. As Sam negotiated the dance floor, getting far too much of a large white man's naked belly than was comfortable, she missed Ginny intercept him - the pair becoming a spaghetti plate of arms and legs; her lips on his, her hand down his trousers. He tried to get away, but he didn't factor in that he was wrestling with what used to be a man. Ginny used all her charms - and all her strength - to find Sam some space. When he managed to force her away, Ginny screamed, 'stop - rapist!', at the top of her voice. There was a murmur of discontent from a couple of men closest to Sam's pursuer. 'Him! Him!' Ginny pointed at the back of the man as he pushed past a couple of revellers. The two men chased after the man with the brown waistcoat, catching him, each of them holding a shoulder.

Sam was at the far end of the club when the man, with the efficiency and strength of a trained boxer, floored the two gay men. The action created more of a kerfuffle, but her pursuer was too focused and too strong. He barged his way through the crowd, screams and yelps sounding in his wake.

Sam had visited the loos a couple of drinks previously so she knew where she was going. The inside of the gents, though, was new territory to her.

Three cubicles left; urinals right ... 'Oops, sorry. Excuse me.' ... *and sinks right. No window. What's round the corner?*

Sam sprinted, skidded and turned. In an enclave on the right was a waist-high cupboard, above which was a slim window.

She jumped on the cupboard and forced the window open. She peered out. Darkness.

What's outside? Someone else?

She had no choice. She heard the gents' door open. She launched her rucksack out of the window.

Now!

Up and out.

Her head and arms were out. It was definitely dark outside, her night vision lost. She had no idea what she was escaping into.

The window frame was sharp on her stomach. She couldn't turn. She'd have to let gravity take its course. Head, torso, legs. In that order. Get a leg up first.

Now!

But she couldn't go anywhere. Someone had hold of her dangling leg. That someone was strong - pulling at her.

Come on! Sam couldn't see what was happening on the wrong side of the window. She could only feel. She dropped her leg that was on the ledge.

Kick!

Nothing. She was struggling; writhing. The someone was still pulling. The window ledge was crushing her stomach, pushing against old wounds. Hurting.

Kick! Smack!

Contact. Foot against face?

A grip was released.

Push!

And she was out.

Thud!

Ouch!

She landed on her hands, a finger bending the wrong way. *Shit! Ignore it.* She felt around on the floor for her rucksack. *Got it.*

Then she was up, her eyes compensating nowhere near fast enough for the enveloping darkness.

Tarmac. And road.
Light off to the left.

It was another road, perpendicular to the one she was on, 30 metres distant. Away from the front entrance to the club. Decision made.

Brrmm.

The sound of an engine. Off to her right.

Move!

She ran as fast as she could in the direction of the other road.

But she couldn't outrun the noise. It gained quickly on her, but didn't knock her down. She darted, left and right, expecting the worst. The noise closed. On her. It was loud. Booming. Like a big car. *Or a motorbike?*

And then a tinny hooting noise. A horn. *Definitely not a car.* Getting her attention. Then shouting, struggling to be heard above the *thud, thud, thud* of the blood racing inside her head.

'Sam!'

She heard that. And ignored it. She'd reached the corner, instinctively she turned right - she had no idea why. The road was wider. Lighter. There were some parked cars. She was on a pavement. That's all that registered. Sam couldn't take any more in. She was working on her next move. Moving too quickly.

The engine noise followed her. As loud as it could be.

'Sam!'

It was parallel with her now. On the road.

She glanced left.

Sam took it in.

She slowed to a jog.

'Get on, Sam!'

It was Ginny. She was on something the likes of which Sam had never seen. A trike - straight out of *Bladerunner*. Two wheels at the front, an engine in between, easy-rider handlebars, then two seats - one behind the other, and a drive wheel at the back. It was big, muscular - and black. It was the sexiest motorbike Sam had ever seen. And it suited Ginny 'down to a T'.

Chapter 12

Ginny pulled the Slingshot onto the side of the street, stopping the trike just short of where the red BMW 320 had pulled across the carriageway into a side road. Without the need of encouragement she nudged the trike forward so Sam could see what the Beemer was going to do next.

It had stopped by a garage entrance just off the junction. The car was waiting for the door to lift. When it did, the Beemer pulled into the gap and the door closed behind it.

Sam checked the road signs. They were on Brickell Avenue, one of those all-American, downtown, city roads with a grass island separating two lanes with well-to-do office and apartment buildings rising up to meet the sky.

She knew nothing of Miami, other than the route from the creek to the hotel, and from the hotel to the club. She should have spent more time rehearsing the map. *Idiot*. She'd been too keen to get out of her room and do something.

They'd not got on the tail of the Beemer by accident. As soon as Sam knew she had wheels and a willing driver, she'd screamed for Ginny to stop. Once the combined noise of the throaty engine and

346

the roar of angry, displaced 50-miles-an-hour air had died down, Sam had instructed Ginny to go back to the club.

'We need to find the bloke who followed me. And then follow him. Are you up for that?' She'd pushed herself forward so her mouth was next to Ginny's ear. Neither of them was helmeted. Sam assumed that was OK in Florida. On a trike.

Ginny didn't need any encouragement. She'd spun the Slingshot round although, with the turning circle of a narrowboat, 'spun' was an exaggeration, and headed back the way they'd come. She pulled up short of the club in the shadows and switched off the trike's engine. The club's car park was 20 metres in front of them, between two houses.

Good work, Ginny.

'Is this a one way street?'

'Yeah. Any car would have to head down towards the beach from here.' Ginny unnecessarily pointed away from them.

'I'm going forward. Stay here. If you see a car take off and me running back, meet me halfway, OK?'

'Nought to 60 in 3.4 seconds, Sam. I'll be with you before your sneakers get warm.'

Sam smiled a smile she knew would be lost in the dark. She then jogged down to the car park and found a covered spot with good arcs.

It took her pursuer five minutes to return to the entrance of the club. He was jogging and had been on his feet hoping to find her. With only a silhouette to work on Sam was still sure it was him. She was even more certain when he took a couple of deep breaths and put a flat hand on his forehead, reconciling his failure. Then he was on his mobile; she was too far away to pick up what was being said. She considered moving forward, but by then he'd finished the call and headed towards the car park.

Sam's pursuer found his car (red BMW 320; registration - *tick*) and didn't hang about. By the time the Beemer had wheel-spun its way out of the car park, the trike was at Sam's side - no lights (*clever*).

As Sam jumped on the back she asked, 'What is this?'

Over the noise of the engine, she picked out what she could from Ginny's reply.

'Canadian ... Slingshot ... 173 horsepower ... friggin awesome.'

Indeed it is.

Ginny drove like a decent tail, and Sam was pretty sure the driver of the BMW hadn't spotted them. The fact that he'd taken them to an address was a good indication that that was the case.

And now Sam took it all in.

Brickell Avenue. Semi-skyscraper office blocks. A post office over there.

The road looked deserted. A single cab broke the desolation. Then it was quiet again.

Without getting off the trike she studied the building the car had entered. Three big windows wide. Five storeys tall. Decorated with beige block facing. Probably 30 years old - maybe older if the facing was a new addition. Set back from the road with low steps leading to main door.

'It's the Venezuelan Consulate,' said Ginny. She had turned her head. 'That is, it *was* the Consulate until President Chavez decided to close it. In 2012, I think. The woman in charge was indicted and expelled by the US government. She was working with a Mexican crew, apparently hacking into the White House.'

Sam didn't respond initially. She was watching a series of lights come on on the first floor. One - two - three. Sadly, it was impossible to see what was going on behind the blinds.

Venezuelan Consulate?

Circles within circles.

'How do you know these things?' Sam asked.

'I might be wearing a blonde wig, but I can read.'

Sam laughed.

'Any idea who's using it now?'

'No, sorry.'

Sam got off the trike and jogged over the road. She looked for telltale signs. For any indication of who might be using the building now. She spotted a state-of-the-art surveillance camera in a corner of the recessed door.

Fuck!

Too late.

Idiot.

She smiled at the camera, giving it the briefest of waves.

She yelled across the street. 'Don't look this way. Drive down the road for about 100 yards. I'll meet you there.'

The Slingshot drummed into life and took off. Sam jogged down the pavement, crossing the road at the last minute.

'Sorry, there was a camera. I'm pretty certain you and the trike were not covered. They got me though.'

Sam jumped on.

'Where now?' Asked Ginny.

'I need a cell and some Wi-Fi. Then I need to wake up a pal of mine in Europe. Can you help?'

'Sure. My place. I can even do you some coffee.'

Flemingstraße, Munich, Germany

A phone icon appeared on Wolfgang's screen, accompanied by a gentle buzz on the computer's speakers. The number below the icon was a +1 mobile - a US cell number. He let it ring whilst copying the number, opening a tab and pasting the number into a dialogue box. He was just about to press 'Return' and let one of his bespoke programmes identify the number up, when the icon disappeared. It was swiftly replaced with an SMS which read *'It's me. Pick up the phone. S'*

A few seconds later the phone rang again. This time he clicked on the icon.

'Hi. Good to hear from you.' No names.

'Hi. I've some Wi-Fi router details - can you do your magic?'

'Sure. SMS them through now.'

'Roger.'

The phone went dead.

Wolfgang smiled. It was good to hear Sam's voice - to know she was OK. That she'd finished with 'Roger', the British military's end-of-radio transmission signature used to let the other end know that you understood all of the instructions. She'd taught him to use it in Berlin. She didn't use it often, but when she did it always made him smile.

'Frank!' Wolfgang raised his voice. Frank was sleeping on a blow-up bed they'd brought down into the cellar. 'I don't want to miss a thing,' had been his mantra last night. Wolfgang had obliged. There was a half-finished plate of pork sandwiches beside the bed, and an empty jug of coffee and messy cup on the side by one of the towers. Wolfgang would get him upstairs for breakfast.

Which would be soon.

It was 6.30 am. He hadn't slept, and it felt like it. Frank had made it to 3 am before excusing himself. Wolfgang hadn't been able to stop - although the relief of hearing Sam's voice spread a wave of tiredness through him that quickly sapped at his strength and leadened his eyelids.

He would keep going. He had to.

As Sam's SMS came through, Frank was up and beside him - the smell of waking maleness pursuing him like a puppy. They both needed a shower.

'It's Sam. I'll have her live in a second.'

Wolfgang opened a series of tabs, typing instructions as he went.

'What are you doing?' Frank asked.

'I'm accessing a Wi-Fi router in the US, I think. Sam has sent me the signature code and WAP hex key. I should be in in a second.'

'Dark Web?'

'Yes. Via 14 separate ISPs and multiple switching. The chances of finding me are 1 in 147 trillion. There.' A light blue box appeared in the middle of the screen.

'It's Skype!' Frank retorted.

'No, it's not. It just looks like Skype. I use it because the user interface is so WYSIWYG.'

'What you see is what you get?'

'Correct.'

And then there was Sam's face. It was blurry and flickered, but that's the price you paid for routing a video link around the world and back.

'Hi, Sam. Say hello to a friend of yours.'

Sam's face scrunched up as though she was trying to focus on what was obviously a pixelated image.

'Frank! What the blazes are you doing there?'

'Hi, Sam.' Frank waved. Wolfgang raised his eyes. You'd think these people had never used a video link before.

After a flurry of 'how are yous?', and a further 'what the bloody hell are you doing there, Frank?' Sam introduced Ginny, who stuck her face in the camera and smiled. Seeing her unnerved Wolfgang - *what are you playing at Sam?* But when Sam went on to explain last night's escapade, Wolfgang relaxed. A little.

'And I need you to do some research into 1101 Brickell Avenue, North Tower. It's where the thug who tried to kidnap me drove back to. Ginny tells me it's the erstwhile Venezuelan Consulate - vacant since 2012.' Sam continued.

Frank butted in.

'Did you say Venezuela?'

'Correct, Frank. That links in with Wolfgang's work on The Bahamian mobiles. Probably - we mustn't jump to conclusions. Before we discuss anything like that in any detail, remember Ginny is here. I don't want her to know any more than she does already. For her safety.'

'Sure, sure.' Frank replied.

Off camera Ginny was heard say, 'Are you people, like, spies?'

'No Ginny, call us "concerned parties",' was Sam's reply.

'Frank, can you get your pals in The Doughnut to see if they can work out who's in the building?' Sam asked. Wolfgang immediately knew Sam was hiding the acronym GCHQ from Ginny. GCHQ, or Government Communications Headquarters based at Cheltenham, was where the UK's signals-intercept people did their stuff. It was a fairly modern office complex, in the shape of a huge circle with a green space and ponds in the middle. Hence the nickname, 'The Doughnut'.

'They won't, Sam. You know the rules. They won't work in an ally's backyard - not without their express permission. But I can check with my pals in the US. They may already be on it.'

'I can have a go.' Wolfgang interjected. 'I can certainly look at all landline comms. The assumption is that the RJ-11 hasn't been changed since the Venezuelan left the building - if, indeed, they've gone. I can look at the old telephone numbers and maybe pull something off. I can do that whilst Frank talks to his pals.'

'Good, thanks.' Sam said. 'I'm guessing, Wolfgang, you're not much further ahead than yesterday lunchtime? The mobiles won't be with you for a couple of hours?'

As Wolfgang started to explain where he'd got to - which wasn't much further forward, as he'd spent most of last night going over his database with Frank - he saw the semi-focused hand of Ginny offer Sam a cup of something. She took it with a simple nod and a 'thanks'.

This woman has us all twisted around her little finger - how does she do that?

He continued.

'I'm really interested in the two texts. The one from "Ops" on the first phone saying, *"need to talk about equipment"*. And the second from "RB", on Müller's phone.' He didn't wait for Sam to go all queasy at hearing the two letters R and B. 'I can do nothing with until I have the phones. When I do, as well as a multitude of other things, I might be able to work out who they are - and what they're talking about.'

He couldn't make out Sam's expression in any detail. She gave nothing by way of response.

'Sam?'

'I'm fine. Good. Look, I'm shattered. Ginny and I haven't had the luxury of sleep like you two babies. I can't think straight at the moment. Can you call me on the number I just used when you have something?'

Wolfgang looked at Frank and asked, 'Anything else?'

Frank shook his head.

'That's fine, Sam, sure.'

Sam put up a hand.

'Hang on. Frank?'

'Yes, Sam.'

'I've just had a thought. I need two things. First, an alias with a passport. I'm guessing I'm not going to stay here much longer. And if I have to get out of the country I'll need the right documentation and cover story. Can you get your team to sort something? I presume I'm sort of back on your books, otherwise you wouldn't be where you are?'

Frank scratched his head and then replied, 'I'm sure we can arrange something through the Consulate in Miami. Probably today. Was that both things?'

'No. Is there any chance you can get me access to Cynthia? I can't imagine you've got people in the Consulate, but maybe I could get onto the system? I can do some photofit work on the man who tailed me in The Bahamas, the guy on the ski slopes - and the thug from last night. What do you think?'

'I'll speak to Jane ...,' Frank looked for the clock on Wolfgang's screen. '... now. When you hang up. We'll sort something, OK?'

'Thanks, Frank. And, Wolfgang?'

'Yes, Sam?'

'Get some sleep. You look awful.'

Lambeth Bridge, Vauxhall, London

Jane was regretting her mode of transport. It was a 15-minute brisk walk from Babylon to the Cabinet Office - across Lambeth Bridge, north along Millbank and into Whitehall. She could have taken the tube which was only five minutes shorter, but it was infinitely drier. She would have missed the rain - which was now falling as sleet; damp, grey splodges of wet snow. It was sporadically lit by the Victorianesque street lights, which added to the early morning gloom.

But she needed to walk. To blow away the cobwebs.

She'd got in particularly early. She'd made it halfway through a draft report for the JIC before she had to break off to attend a planned budgetary meeting at the FCO. SIS might enjoy a good deal of independence and have a healthy budget, but every penny had to be fought and then accounted for. The Foreign and Commonwealth Office held the purse strings. And Jane was the Chief's senior rep at today's meeting which was designed to look over next year's money. It was going to be a tough couple of hours. She needed a clear mind.

Her half-finished JIC report was spawned from last night's call with the DD at Langley. He'd phoned her, which was an unusual occurrence.

Linden Rickenbacker was a middle-aged quarterback of a man, with a brain as sharp as any she'd come across. He was a lifelong CIA veteran with some impressive assignments, including a five-year stint as head of mission in Afghanistan. Jane was the first to admit to herself that she had taken a fancy to the DD. Square-jawed and, even at his age, a little preppy, when they spoke on the phone she always checked herself with a quick glance in the mirror across from her desk.

Madness.

The nature of the call was as surprising as the call itself.

'Hi, Jane. You got five minutes?'

For you?

'Yes, of course, sure. How can I help?'

'Our conversation the other day, about some things being so sensitive ...'

Jane couldn't stop herself from finishing the sentence, 'That you can't share them with your closest allies?'

'Yes.' He chuckled. 'That one. Anyway. I'd like to share something with you.'

OK.

'Go on.'

'Not for disclosure lower than your grade?'

'Of course.'

'We have an undefined, but imminent threat. Level 5.'

The DD would have chosen his words carefully. 'Undefined' meant the threat was corroborated, but they knew neither its exact nature nor who the perpetrators might be. 'Imminent' was within the next seven days. Level 5 was top of the CIA's list: mass casualties, which was further defined as 100-plus. In every way, what the DD was describing was the worst possible threat scenario. Something really bad was going to happen soon. And they had no idea what, when and why.

'And no amplification on that?'

'No. However, it coincides with work we're doing on electronic interference: the global positioning system - you mentioned it the other day. We have this on the closest of holds - mostly because GPS is so ubiquitous that we cannot afford to let any hares run ...'

'And, of course, it is a money-maker for the US government.' Jane interrupted again. She must stop doing that.

If the DD was frustrated by Jane's interventions, he didn't show it.

'Sort of. The civilian GPS signal is free, as is the civilian decryption software. The microchips are all made in the US - so there is some tax revenue on that. And the licences to buy the chips are not free. We also make some cash on selling our friends the military encryption software, which sharpens the accuracy of the signal. But none of that is enough to pay for the hundreds of millions of dollars our government spends on the system each year.'

'Oh.' Jane stood metaphorically corrected.

'No. For us, it's about the integrity of the system. People's faith in it. Which, by the way, we think might be compromised.'

This is more like it.

The DD continued - the tone of his voice was grave, almost a whisper.

'And, also, there is the more pressing matter of who to trust.'

'What, you mean externally?'

'No. Here. In the US - amongst my friends. Look, I'll share my latest report with all the details when we finish, but that is *definitely* for your and the chief's eyes only?'

'Got that. Thanks.'

'The threads of this are spread wide, and the knots that tie them together are tenuous. But in principle we think that someone has compromised the GPS system - and can influence the navigational accuracy of something as big as, say, a warship.'

'USS Beaverbrook?'

'Yes. As you mentioned the other day. Our scientists have done some research. They think it's possible to influence individual GPS receivers. Give them the wrong signal and, as a result, get their navigational systems to go haywire.'

'You'd need the serial number of the target's receiver before you could alter the X and Y coordinates. Otherwise you'd send everyone within a 1,000 miles haywire.' Jane added.

The line went quiet. There was a gentle '*beep*' in the background - a modulation that gave confidence to the users that their line was secure.

'You've done some tests?'

'Yes. One of my analysts came up with the same theory - he was talking with one of your team ...' Jane opened her notebook and flipped over a couple of pages, 'An Ethan Woods. They were both on the same wavelength, if you'll excuse the pun. Our people at dstl carried out a demonstration. They got a toy car to veer off course.'

'Was it fitted with mil-spec GPS?' The DD asked.

'Yes. Their report said that was the easy bit. The real difficulty is ...'

'Threefold.' It was the DD's turn to interrupt. 'First, you can't hack into the GPS satellite transmission system - there are too many fail-safes. And you can't piggyback onto a commercial bird because the transmission wavelengths are all wrong. Third, you need the details of the on-board GPS chip. Either from any original manufacturing data, or you have to own someone on the vessel to physically check the chip.'

'That's right. For your third point, whichever method you chose you'd need a small network of moles giving you that data. For the first two - how about launching your own satellite?'

'No. We don't think so. Our view is that no criminal organisation could afford the costs. And that's where we come to a dead end.'

Jane wasn't deterred. She had a new report in front of her.

'I have a list of the last three years' worth of worldwide space-cargo launches. Source: the UK Space Agency. The top line is that there have been 145 launches in the past 12 months. Average cost: $55 million per launch. The complete three-year list has been further refined to: launches by government; commercial organisations; and a few "unspecified" agents. For the latter, the unspecifieds, there have been 19 satellites launched since 2014, from 7 separate locations. We are still getting a full readout on their purpose - and hopefully some technical background to see if any of the cargo was satellite-shaped. We'd then need to investigate further to check if any of the satellites are fitted with transmitters that can operate on the GPS L1 and L2 frequencies: between 1000 and 1500 megahertz.' Jane was reading from a pink folder which held a secret report.

The phone went quiet.

'Hang on.' The DD was preoccupied for about 30 seconds. Jane thought he was probably searching for something on his machine.

He continued.

'OK. I now have a list of countries that make small-lift launch rockets. That is, anything that can carry a load of up to 2,000 kg, or 4,500 lbs, and chuck into low-earth orbit; say a navigational satellite. My screen gives me 16 operational rockets and nine in development. Have a guess what?'

A rhetorical question? She didn't say anything. The DD continued.

'Along with the obvious choices, including us and Russia, Iran and North Korea build rockets that can carry a small payload and send it up into space. It's a bit like, "Rockets are us".'

There was quiet for a second.

'My list, of course,' Jane said, 'only includes the launches we're aware of. I'm guessing you could probably launch from any spare piece of real estate that is away from prying eyes?'

'Mmm. True. NASA should have something on that. You just can't launch any old rocket and hope to get away with it? North Korea's weapon's programme is a case in point. We have a very tight handle on their airspace. I'll get that looked into.

There was a longer pause as they both dwelt on where they found themselves.

'What about the issue of trust, Linden? You mentioned it earlier.'

'That's more complicated. I have a hand-picked team working on this. Including someone in whom I have complete confidence at the Bureau. The problem we have is that every time we think we're getting somewhere with the issue, the trail goes cold. I'll give you an example. We're doing some intel-gathering in Venezuela. As you know it's a resource-rich country that's going down the tubes. Which doesn't make sense. So, we're trying to establish what's driving President Nicolás Maduro. For sure he's in bed with the Russians and the Chinese, which is not great for us. But there's something much murkier going on. Deeper.' The DD paused, gathering his breath. 'Anyhow, we were, very discreetly, mapping the far-reaches of the country using a UAV drone out of Creech.'

'Mapping is a euphemism?'

'You got it. Anyhow, the drone went cold - veered off into Colombian airspace. My Venezuelan team initially put it down to either driver error - or system malfunction. These things happen. The initial report backed that up. But when they asked for a detailed report, the whole thing was dumped in the freezer.'

'You're going to have to expand on that, Linden, sorry.'

'The pilot was murdered - gunned down in broad daylight. No explanation. And the squadron's commander is unaccounted for. He's just disappeared. The base is covering any embarrassment by saying he's been "relieved of command". But they have no idea where he is.'

'Could be a coincidence?'

'I'm not sure. Ordinarily we would have just relaunched the mission. But the way the UAV failed, its sudden veering off, was so similar to the USS Beaverbrook crash, we've had to place it in the same pot. That is until, or unless, they can be separated.'

'You've got a decent readout from the Beaverbrook incident?' Jane asked.

'Not yet, no. As you probably know, the Captain was removed from command within days of the incident. He was sent home - and, conspiracy of conspiracies - he was knocked down by a car in his home town the next day. He's in a coma and is unlikely to wake up. Add to that, one of the ship's nav officers, apparently the one man who could have easily stolen the GPS receiver data, has done a bunk. Nowhere to be seen.'

Bloody hell. Frank was onto something?
Hang on ...

Jane remembered something that Frank had told her.

'My analyst's pal in your place, Ethan Woods? Well, Frank - that's my analyst - told me that Ethan had become "uncontactable" a few days ago. Does that ring a bell?'

'Whoa, Jane. The CIA employs over 21,000 people - unfortunately I don't remember them all by name.'

In the distance Jane heard, 'Benjamin!', followed by a background conversation.

Then to Jane, 'I'll come back to you. Ben's gone to find out ... have we covered everything?'

Jane had struck lines through a list she had made in her pad as they'd been talking.

'No. The threat. Can you give me something we can work on?'

'Of course. Sorry. It was the reason I called in the first place. We don't have much. But what we do have is potentially dynamite. Three separate sources - all low-level, but all on the same song sheet. One in the US, one in Eastern Europe and one in South America. I can't share any more than that - you'll understand?'

'Sure.'

Rule one: never reveal your sources.

'The sources are all independent; we can't establish any cross-fertilisation. And it's all cascon (casual conversation) stuff. On their own, each would have been disregarded. But together they can't be ignored. We have: the target is the Mid-East, which from a US security perspective narrows it down to Embassies and military bases. The timing is immediate - in days. And, and this is why I'm phoning you and asking you to pull out every stopper you can, the perceived outcome - the ramifications of the attack, is thought to be worldwide. All three cascons have given the same message. Mid-East; immediate; and far-reaching. Hence, we need your help.'

'And you think there may be a link between the threat and the compromised GPS.'

'Maybe. The US source included an additional line. It said, and I quote, "Death from the skies". If you can control a drone, you can control any aircraft. Smacks of a remote controlled 9/11 ... excuse me for a moment, Jane.'

There was a break. Jane heard a distant murmur. Linden was probably talking to Benjamin.

'Well, Jane. That just about secures it for me.' The DD's tone was flat

'What?'

'The issue of trust. Our man Ethan Woods, he's a Grade-D intelligence analyst on the fourth floor. He was working in the GPS field. He's not been in work for three days.'

'Sick?'

'No. There's no doctor's certificate. Our procedure is to follow up after day three. That's today. The initial report from the team leader is that he's not picking up his cell. They're onto local law enforcement now.'

'Blimey.'

'Blimey, indeed, Jane. I think we have a problem.'

And that was that. They'd finished off by going back over what Jane could and could not share.

Once she'd received the DD's document, which came through after 8.00 pm, she'd been able to start on her own report for the JIC. Before she left the office she'd put out a Charlie Charlie to all SIS sections to press their sources and informants for anything that was going down in the Middle East. There'd been nothing back overnight. The JIC report, which she'd have done by lunchtime, would get the rest of the intelligence community asking the same question.

The rain and the sleet was still lashing down. She really hoped her Gore-Tex jacket's credentials were as good as the label.

As she entered Parliament Square her mobile rang. It was Frank. She found a nearby tree to shelter under and pressed the green, 'Pick up', icon.

'Go secure, Jane.'

Jane dabbed at her phone. The low-level *beeping* started.

'Having not heard from you, Frank, I assume you've had a busy night?'

'I'd say. I've just pinged a requisition report to your desk which, if you have two minutes, I'd like to summarise now.'

Jane checked her watch. It was 7.45 am. The meeting started at 8.15. She had a couple of minutes.

'Go on, Frank.'

'Wolfgang has The Church's complete structure - there are gaps, but it's much more than we have. His database is huge. Too big for him. He is sensitive about sharing, mostly because of potential compromise.' Frank was getting good as short, sharp verbal briefing. *Well done him.* 'What he's agreed to is sharing of all of his phone intelligence. And then, between us and GCHQ, we will interrogate it and hopefully add some more structure and detail to what he has. It is, Jane, pretty wide-ranging, and pretty frightening.'

Jane turned slightly so her back was facing the swirling wind.

Where do I prioritise this?

'OK, Frank. Look, I have a full day and some new intelligence from Langley about the GPS-compromise issue. Which, by the way, they agree with you. A big tick there. It's all pretty intense and I think it's going to keep the rest of us occupied for a while.'

'The rest of us?'

'Yes. Save you. I'll send an op code through once I get off the phone. You're on your own for a while. Use it to target what resources you need, but don't be surprised if, in the first instance, people are tied up. We need to run a blanket-wide search for a CIA-declared-undefined, imminent, level 5 threat. Likely target is the Middle East. Possibly, "from the skies".'

'A 9/11 copycat?'

'Maybe. That's what we and Langley are onto now. In the meantime, you crack on with Wolfgang.'

'So, you're happy if I get our Consulate in Miami to issue Sam with a new identity? And let her have access to Cynthia from the same source.'

Jane thought for a while. A clump of wet hair was hanging below the hood of her raincoat. She pushed it up and under the lip of the material.

Bugger. I'd forgotten all about Sam.

'Sure. Same op code. Is she OK?'

'Chased off The Bahamas, as you know. And then pursued around Miami last night. The Church are onto her. We're all pretty certain of it.'

'"All" includes her German friend, Wolfgang?'

'Yes. And Jane?'

'Yes, Frank.'

'He's pretty sharp. Sharper than anyone in our building when it comes to hacking.

I'm sure he is, Frank.

Chapter 13

Flemingstraße, Munich, Germany

Wolfgang had Müller's phone on his desk. Next to it was a cup of strong, black coffee. Elisabeth had called via the intercom a few minutes earlier; she had a tray. He climbed the stairs and went through the airlock to collect it. He'd asked about Inge. Elisabeth had replied that she'd gone shopping - and that all was well.

Frank was sitting next to him, his face glued to another monitor. He'd been on the phone to the British Consulate in Miami and, as a result of that call, had SMS'd Sam via Ginny's phone that they were expecting her. He was now tasking GCHQ to explore and monitor the telephone numbers they had prioritised earlier. The top two numbers were: 'Freddie's' Hrvatski Telekom's area code 61 landline; and the UK Virgin mobile number that had the 12 linkages - and had, three weeks ago, landed in Caracas. A second priority for GCHQ were the 12 connecting numbers linked to the Virgin UK mobile.

Frank had said that 14 numbers were 13 too many for GCHQ with their current workload. But he'd sent the list anyway. More interestingly he'd gone on to explain to Wolfgang that SIS's mainframe, Cynthia, had a 'cause and effect' programme that, once fed with all of the numbers on his database - and where possible, the names - could produce an interconnection matrix. Where Wolfgang had been able to establish one 'node', say the Virgin UK number with 12 links, Cynthia would run a programme that could establish where there were more. He'd feed the detail into SIS's mainframe once he'd finished tasking GCHQ.

Both Müller's and snakeskin-belt man's mobiles had been delivered half an hour ago. Wolfgang was now trying to crash the banker's phone. As he had it in front of him - it shouldn't be too tricky.

The first and quickest way to break into a non-Apple mobile was to guess the lock pattern. Whilst there were just short of 390,000 swipe permutations, most people kept their lock pattern simple - and associative. Lukas Müller might swipe an '*L*' or an '*M*' - or either letter upside down. Manufacturer-dependent, the Android operating system allows up to ten attempts before the phone locks for 30 seconds; at which point the phone gives you an option to login via your Google account without access to the swipe pattern. Wolfgang didn't have Müller's Google account details - that was the crown jewels. For that he needed to get into his phone.

By some other method.

He tried five sensible patterns and was locked out. He had a sip of his coffee, waited 30 seconds and tried five more. No good.

Plan B.

Next was to read the SIM card - this would give basic info, including the phone's number. He took it from the back of the phone and put it into a SIM card reader he had set up earlier. A few keystrokes later and he knew the number and some other details.

'Frank.'

'Uh-huh?' Frank was focused on his screen.

'I've got Müller's mobile number. You ready to copy?'

'Sure.'

Wolfgang read the number out.

'Can you put it on GCHQ's list?'

'Sure.' Frank's reply was distant.

Next was to clone the phone: make a facsimile of Müller's mobile using its SIM. It wouldn't enable him to get into the innards of the machine, but it would allow him to access previous phone calls and SMSs. Hopefully he'd be able to track whether RB, the missed call on the mobile, was Ralph Bell; and what his number was.

With the SIM in the card reader - that took a further 20 minutes.

Both he and Frank were using computer simulators to access the mobile networks. A mobile wouldn't work in his cellar. There was too much concrete and steel. It was designed that way. If he couldn't access a mobile signal from in here, then no one from the outside could get in. The system he had devised, which he and Frank were now using, was via a series of IPs. Safe; secure; impenetrable.

It took him a further 15 minutes to list Müller's calls and SMS records. There was some interesting stuff here, including RB's mobile number. It was a +1 US cell. Probably AT&T. He'd check later.

'Frank.'

'Yep.' He didn't look up.

'I've got RB's number. Do you want to add it to GCHQ's list?'

Frank stopped working and looked over. They were a couple of feet apart. He smelt better after an earlier, quick dash to the washrooms.

'Is it Ralph Bell?'

'I don't know yet.'

He looked disappointed.

'OK. Read it out. I'll put it at number four for the Doughnut.'

Wolfgang read it out.

What he really needed was to access Müller's data traffic. SMSs were useful in a 918-character sense, but they were more of a chat medium than something formal. Email lengths were unlimited and allowed for attachments: photos; documents and spreadsheets. And it was very likely that, like him, The Church had a secure cloud facility somewhere - where they kept and shared instructions. Getting access to all of that was probably a day's worth of work, if not longer.

He'd put that to one side - for now.

He turned on Sam's original pursuer's phone (what had she called him? *Snakeskin-belt man?*). He had no idea what his name was, so had nothing to go on.

He tried the ten most common lock patterns in order: C, O, N, S, L, M, W, U, Z and a backward C.

The 'Z' unlocked the phone.

Result.

Zorro?

He had the phone number in 15 seconds, the SMS list a few seconds after that, and the prize: a Google Mail account.

It was coming in a stream.

At first glance it was clear that snakeskin-belt man was not a kingpin in The Church's hierarchy. There were driving and collecting instructions. Timings that were associated with boats and aircraft. And there were other admin tasks. And the recurring name from his email list was a 'Janon Jobes'.

Janon Jobes?

The latest SMS was, as he expected, from 'Ops'. *Need to talk about equipment.* He now had Ops's number.

It was a UK mobile number - which he recognised immediately.

It was the Virgin UK mobile number; the +44 7795 number.

With 12 known Church links.

Ops.

In the centre of things. Running an operation. And currently in Caracas.

He checked the emails again. Most of those associated with equipment were signed off by Janon Jobes.

Ops. Janon Jobes? Are they the same person?

'Frank?'

'Hu-huh?'

'I've got something that we should share - right now.'

Samostan Monastery, Punat Bay, Krk, Croatia

Jakov was sitting opposite Karlo. They'd both chosen the same main course: spaghetti, meatballs and salad. It was perfectly adequate food; if bland. Like being at school. He'd chosen coffee - Karlo had tea. He thought there was some sort of rice pudding for dessert. That was definitely from the school meals' menu. They had about 15 minutes before prayers. And then it would be ablutions and bed, with his only book: The Bible.

This morning he'd asked Karlo if he could join them for the evening prayers, to which the response had been a smile and a nod. Jakov wasn't interested in praying. Although brought up as a Catholic, he was well beyond believing in God. Not now. Not here. His plan was to get to see - and to map - as much of the monastery as he could. Since yesterday's violent epiphany, that is - get off this island or die trying (he was surprised at how his spike of anger was lingering; he must channel it), he had a single focus: escape.

Escape.

Reticently, yesterday evening, Karlo had given him a notebook and a pencil. At every break he'd used the front of the book to write inspirational quotes, with a Christian slant. Like: *God make me a better person* and *Work sets you free!* He knew he'd plagiarised the last one from above the entrance to Auschwitz, '*Arbeit macht frei*', and was uncomfortable with that. But, frankly anything would do …

… because the real work was happening in the middle of the book. He was using pages in the innards of the notebook to sketch out the layout of the place. Windows, doors, room numbers, which doors were fitted with locks - which had iris readers. Everything and anything. Every time he completed a page of sketches and notes, and he had five so far, he ripped it out. He then folded it and placed it between the pages of the bible in his room.

It was, he thought, the last place anyone would look.

He'd also started to piece together the monastery's occupants. In his head he gave each monk a name. So far he had 15, with simple descriptive titles like 'tall', 'short', 'fat', 'smiley', 'cook'. Easy to remember. Since his incident in the courtyard with Freddie, other than the 15 monks, he'd not seen anyone else. Neither Freddie nor the black man with the silver can had made an appearance.

At least now he could recognise 15 monks by an associated name.

And he hated all of them. Every one. They were all complicit. They all had opportunities to stop the madness. To save him, and themselves. He had no idea what crazed ideology was preventing them from seeing that he was an unwilling captive; a *violently-beaten,* unwilling captive.

They could all go to hell.

Sand. In his eyes and in his mouth.

He hated all of them.

Jakov followed Karlo away from the table. They dropped their plates and mugs at a serving-hatch in the canteen's wall, and then walked through a new corridor and into the chapel. He furtively took note of what he saw on the way; counting steps so that he could sketch his route comparatively with his other drawings.

Locked door on my left.

The chapel was mid-sized, about as big as a family house. It was traditional, with wooden benches facing an ancient stained-glass window - dark, multi-coloured glass unlit by the outside dusk. There was an altar and, behind that, a few choir stalls. What little light there was was provided by a row of flickering candles balanced on brass holders on the walls, and a couple of ornate candlesticks on the altar.

Karlo ushered Jakov into one of the back pews.

They both sat.

As the chapel filled up - 14, 15, 16 and then 17; two new monks he couldn't make out in the dark - his eyes adjusted to the ambient light.

I must establish who they are.

In front of him was a leather-bound book. Its cover was similar to The Bible he had in his room but, on opening it was written in a language he didn't understand. He could read English and Croatian; the latter was technically Serbo-Croat, using the Cyrillic alphabet. Such was their distaste for each other, both Serbians and Croatians claimed the language as their own, even though they both spoke its tongue.

But the words on the page were neither English nor Serbo-Croat. The letters were almost diagrammatic - like Sanskrit. He was pretty sure it wasn't Arabic; it didn't have the flow and beauty of that alphabet. It was more muscular. He gently leafed through its pages looking for a clue.

Nothing.

He lifted his head. All 17 monks were seated on pews facing the altar. And all 17 had their heads bowed in prayer.

He followed suit.

Be one with the crowd. And remember everything. That was the key to getting out of there.

He rested his head on one hand and held the book in the other. It was old. Green leather. Faded pages, their edges laced with gold. There was an emblem on the front. He rested the book on his knees and, in the half-dark, traced over the badge with a finger of his free hand.

It was an off-white crucifix, but it lacked Jesus's body. Instead the cross was decorated with something else. He couldn't make it out in the dark. He tilted his head and moved the book so the light from the closest candle provided some illumination.

It was a plant - maybe a rose. Certainly a creeper of some kind.

Jakov shrugged and put the book on the ledge in front of him. He looked to his right at Karlo. The monk was deep in prayer. His mouth moving, but nothing broke the silence.

NE 12th Street, Winchester, Miami

Sam looked back over her shoulder and saw Ginny waving from her balcony. She returned her wave. Whilst she'd told Ginny she'd be back after she'd been to the British Consulate, she didn't know if she believed it. Sam was prey. She was being hunted. Anyone associated with her was in danger. Ginny was far too nice a person to get mixed up in all of this. Leaving her and not returning would be for the best.

She'd slept well, well beyond 10 am. She'd woken with a sore head, a combination of her body-clock still adjusting to a five-hour time difference, a very late night, and three too many Bacardis and coke. She hadn't noticed last night, but this morning her finger was swollen from when she'd fallen head first out of the restroom window. It was sore as hell, but probably not broken. In addition, as she showered, her stomach shouted at her. She had a stitches-scar across her belly where a large fragment of a mortar shrapnel had sliced into her when she was in Afghanistan. The doc had done a good job of putting it all back where it belonged and zipping her up. But there was no avoiding three layers of scar tissue. And they hadn't liked being bent over the window frame last night, wrestling between freedom and red-BMW man.

Ginny had been more than a dear. She had made Sam breakfast, put her clothes through the quickest of wash/dries, and generally made her feel like she was the only person who mattered. Without her help Sam couldn't imagine where she'd be right now. In a ditch with a bullet in her head was the most likely possibility.

Leaving Ginny had already begun to hurt. The last time she'd felt this close to a human being was Tuffy, her old army pal just before she'd flown to Liberia all those years ago. Then it was kindred souls with similar experiences that forged the bond. Now, she was less clear. Maybe it was because Ginny was a loner? Caught in a murky world between two places; in disarray. That's where Sam was. In disarray. Neither here, nor there. Nowhere. And with no one. Ginny had spoken about her relationships, but they had all been short-lived; superficial. She was a floater. Waiting for a hook. Sam felt the same. Lost. Meandering.

Rubbish.

Ginny's first-floor apartment was comfortable. Over their cocktails Sam had discovered that she was a web-designer, and worked from home. Money was good, but not great. And, as most of her spare cash was spent on her sex reassignment, she didn't have much at the end of the month for furniture and accessories.

Nevertheless, she'd done a pretty good job. There was a lounge, decorated in big colours with functional furniture and a large TV. The kitchen/diner did what it said. But it was her bedroom/bathroom that was her special place. It was sumptuously done with brown silk, cream satin and leopard skin. Wall-to-wall white wardrobes with gold handles, a queen-sized bed and a ceiling plastered with mirrors finished off the effect. A hidden boudoir in American suburbia.

Over bacon on muffins Sam chatted through with Ginny about how to get to the British Consulate. Frank had been in touch earlier - Sam could visit the Consulate at any time. There was a duty officer who would be briefed to expect her if she arrived after 5 pm.

'Just across the road. Take the 38 bus, on Busway, to Dadeland South Metrorail Station. Then it's a short walk to the Dadeland rail link - that will take you into Downtown Miami. The 38 runs every hour. I reckon it's probably a 90-minute journey, all told.' Ginny smiled.

Sam had checked her watch. It was 11.50.

'When's the next bus.'

'Half-past the hour.'

That would get her to the Consulate before it closed. She'd need a couple of hours to do the photofitting: the skier who'd chased her in Alpbach; snakeskin-belt man; and red-BMW man. Hopefully something useful would pop up out of all that.

She and Frank had only spoken for a minute or so. He and Wolfgang were making progress, but there was nothing yet of real note to report. They'd have more later in the day. Hopefully, now Wolfgang had SIS resources behind him, piecing together The Church of the White Cross's jigsaw would be a much speedier affair.

Hopefully.

Sam arrived at the bus stop as it pulled up. She paid the driver and found a seat towards the back. An hour and a half of travelling. Time to reflect. She didn't want that. She didn't want the opportunity to go over last night. How, with almost no information at all, they had found her. And by some madness they had a lunatic on call driving a red BMW to search her out.

White mountain-man was obviously looking out for Müller's/Wilder's card. He had seen it in Sam's hand and then reported it to someone. Someone who had either come for her, or had sent someone else. How did that happen so quickly? Two hours? Maybe two and a half? Did they own the club? How many clubs did they own? In every city?

How big was The Church of the White Cross?

Who was red-BMW man?

Flash.

What?

On the opposite carriageway.

Heading back the way they'd come.

A red BMW.

Sam instinctively turned her head. She caught the briefest of glimpse of the Beemer's registration.

Was it the same?

Yes? *No?*

Could she take a chance?

She was on her feet. She pressed the small red 'Next Stop' button that was on a pole that grew out of the end of one of the seats down from her. A light went on at the front of the bus. She saw the driver look at it and shake his head.

'Next stop's not for another mile or so, lady,' was the call from the front.

That wasn't good enough. Sam moved forward quickly. Shouting as she did.

'You've got to stop. It may be a matter of life or death!'

The driver weaved the bus past a slow-moving truck. Sam was at the front now, in the driver's personal space. She looked down at the speedo. Thirty miles an hour. The driver was concentrating.

'No can do. It's illegal to stop the bus on a highway.' He glanced up at Sam and grimaced. 'Please sit down. You're endangering the other passengers.' He pointed to an official sign that hung under his mirror. *Do not engage the driver or step forward of the yellow line while the bus is in motion.*

Sam checked; she had crossed the line - in more ways than one.

That's not good enough!

Something snapped. It happened - there was no controlling it.

Her peripheral vision went. Her ears filled with an unspecified fluid; the quickening beat of her heart filled her chest and resonated around her head.

She looked up and found the main door's emergency-open button. She smashed it with the flat of her hand. The double glass door opened with a jerky movement.

'Hey, what the ...?' The bus swerved, and then righted itself as the driver regained his composure.

Sam stepped down onto the plate, wind filling the cab.

She was just about to jump when the driver braked hard. Sam was thrown against a waist-height ledge under the windscreen; the air was taken from her.

'You can't do that!' The driver yelled.

But the driver's words stayed with the bus, lost among the metal and glass - deadened by the rushing blood that was taking a massive surge of adrenalin to every extremity of Sam's body.

She regained her composure, jumped out of the bus and ran.

She knew where she was. She'd followed the route. So, she knew how to get back to Ginny's apartment. That's the way it worked.

How far? Five, maybe five and a half klicks.

Twenty-five minutes? She was a 20-minute, 5-kilometre runner. In her shorts. On a cool day. Without obstacles. No rucksack. It was her benchmark.

The last time she had run that distance was at the gym in the hotel in Alpbach.

19.57. She'd clocked it on the running machine's LED. She'd remembered it.

How long did the Beemer have on her? Twenty-five minutes?

Was it the same car?

Yes.

I'm sure?

She had no choice.

I have no choice.

Twenty-five minutes to get to the apartment. Not enough time.

She ran.

And ran.

And ran.

Sweat poured off her. Her rucksack wearing a blister in her side.

She darted across the carriageway, looking for the next way-point. *Tick.*

Run!

She paced herself. She'd be on her knees when she got there - she'd need to compensate for that. It was a balance. Speed versus fitness of arrival. She knew that. Military training.

She ran.

Her Jesus sandals were wearing now. Her right heel. Another blister. Maybe two. She didn't stop. She ignored the emerging pain.

She ran.

And ran.

Turn left here.

How far was that?

Three klicks. She knew.

She was breathing hard. But steady. People stared. Someone pointed. She ignored them.

And ran.

One klick to go.

What do I do when I get there? I need a weapon.

She glanced left and right.

As she ran.

Then it was in sight. Ginny's apartment. A block of six. Set back to the right.

Four hundred metres.

A weapon?

She didn't get chance to answer that question. There was a blur of red BMW backing out of the car park in front of Ginny's condo.

A bush - left. Cover. She dived left. It wasn't much, but there was no time. She crouched. Turned. Looked.

It was there. And then it was gone.

A red BMW 320. The same registration as the car from last night. A driver - *the same man as in the club?* No passengers.

It had been to Ginny's apartment. Maybe there for 15 minutes? And it was gone. That's not long if you want to interrogate someone. *Is it?*

Fuck.

No!

Sam didn't ask herself the question that she should have. The car had been - and gone. The driver had been and gone. An experienced SIS case officer would have asked the obvious supplementary: '*Was there a passenger in the car when it arrived?*'

Even if Sam had followed that logic - that there could still be someone in the flat with Ginny - she would have ignored it. She had to get to Ginny. As soon as she could. If Ginny had the slightest chance of being alive, Sam wanted to do everything in her power to make it remain that way.

Speed was essential.

She was at the bottom of the apartment block seconds later. She looked up. The balcony door was still ajar. And, *No!*, the front door was open, its lock smashed.

Sam leapt up the concrete steps to the first floor in five bounds. She turned left and then burst into the apartment.

'Ginny!' She screamed.

She didn't wait for a reply.

Look.

The lounge was as she'd left it. Kitchen/diner - the same.

The bedroom.

The door was slightly open.

Sam stopped herself. It was just instinct. She stood - poised. Every sinew on fire. Her hands trembling.

She took deliberate steps to the bedroom door, a thin gap of natural light announced that it was open.

'Ginny?'

She had no idea why she was whispering. It was though Ginny was asleep and she didn't want to wake her.

But Sam knew that wasn't the case. She knew what to expect.

She steeled herself.

And pushed the door.

Even so ...

... Sam was stunned by the sight. Overwhelmed by the blood. At a loss as to what to do. Shattered at seeing Ginny's naked body knelt on her bed facing the bedstead, her hands tied behind her back with a pair of nylons - her back bent with her head forward, between her knees, her face on the cream satin sheet, soaking with blood.

The blood decorated the bedroom wall in front of Ginny - splattered as if it had been sprayed through a hose. The trail led down over the bedstead, onto the pillows and finished where Ginny's head met the sheet.

Sam had seen it before.

Ritual execution.

In Oazi; Helmand Province. She'd not been on the ground at the time. No one had. It was in the town's market square. A reconnaissance platoon had set up a remote camera, high on one of the buildings with a decent panorama of the square. Among other things, Sam's job was to analyse non-routine activity that the camera recorded. Looking specifically for HVTs (high value targets).

That morning she'd found one.

In a clearing in the market square he was standing next to an informant of theirs. Holding a .45 Colt Service Ace - larger than the NATO standard 9mm. Enough to blow the front of a man's face off, and some.

Their informant was on his knees, hands tied behind his back with rope. The HVT had one hand on the man's shoulder and the other on the pistol grip of the gun. He took the weapon to the back the man's head, just below the bottom of the skull. He pointed the barrel up in the direction of the forehead, looked up at the camera and smiled.

And pulled the trigger.

A soundless '*clump*'.

Sam had watched the video through twice. She needed to identify the HVT.

Which she had.

She knew who it was immediately; she didn't really need the second viewing. She remembered a previous still image of a meeting of elders, a *Loya Jirga*, in the next-but-one village. The photo had been taken as the group celebrated their gathering. The fact that the image appeared later on an obscure Facebook page that Sam was also monitoring was fortunate. That she had seen the photo among 500 others - once, for no longer than 15 seconds - was all she needed to be certain.

The HVT had attended the *Loya Jirga*. Tick.

Her military intelligence company knew all the attendees. It was their job to know.

Now the same HVT had made an appearance in the Oazi's market square. With a .45 Colt Service Ace. And an executed informant.

The intel regarding the HVT had been passed to the local patrols' battalion a few minutes later. He'd been picked up the next day and was now serving a very long sentence in a Kabul jail.

Their informant had been executed in front of Sam's eyes. The top of the man's head had opened like an exploding can of soda. The spray had shot out for a good couple of metres. Its footprint a splodge of dark red splattered on the sand of the square. A trail of blood and other material led back to the slumped body. The man still on his knees. What was left of his face on the floor, as if it were stuck to stone and sand by a meniscus of blood.

Ginny's blood and bits hadn't got as far as the informant's. It had been stopped by the bedroom wall. But the process was one and the same.

Ritual execution.

Tie hands.

Kneel.

Hold tight.

Bang!

Oh my God.

No.

Please, no.

The red mist was gone. Dispersed; thrown around the room with Ginny's blood. There was no focus now. No tension. No steel. Sam felt floppy. Weak. Inept.

Why Ginny? Why her?

Why does this keep happening?

What is wrong with me!?

Ginny was close to perfect. Beautiful. Fun.

Dead.

Sam tried to stop herself, but couldn't.

She turned to find Ginny's sink which was in the far corner of the room, next to the balcony doors. She didn't make it.

Her stomach emptied its contents. It projected across the back of Ginny's bed, spraying the sheet and mottling the thick-pile carpet. Her second heave found the sink, but such was her weakness that she still couldn't control it. Taps. Tiles. The carpet. Everything got a bit.

The third retch was empty. There was nothing left.

There is nothing left.

Her emotion was mixed and bound in with her puke. It was out there now. Separated from her. Her body had cleansed itself of any feeling. It had distanced itself from self-loathing. Protected itself from pity. And hatred.

Ginny had died because of her.

It's all my fault.

She wanted to get angry again. To hit something. Hurt someone. Hurt herself, but no instructions came.

Save tears. They came. In floods.

With her head bent she instinctively turned on a tap and washed her mouth out with cool water. She spat out bile and a piece of something that she didn't recognise.

Then, slowly and not without effort, she straightened her back.

Oh no.

Oh God, no.

The sink's mirror had turned messenger.

Daubed on it, using Ginny's dark red lipstick, were the words:

This is your fault. You're next.

Sam retched again.

That hurt. Everything ached. Her side. Her finger. Her stomach. Her feet.

She was dizzy. Exposed. She needed to do something, but her brain wouldn't talk to her. Her limbs felt they ought to move, but there was a break in the synapses somewhere.

Pathetic.

And then the sound of distant sirens penetrated her consciousness.

What?

A whisper from deep inside.

Run, Sam, run.

And that's what she did.

St Augustine Beach, St Augustine, Florida

It had been two days. A day, a night, and then another day. He'd heard nothing from Mike Dawson. And it was getting to him. Austin had patience. Normally. But it was wearing thin. He'd spent the last day and a half pacing about the house. He'd gone shopping on his own as his wife wasn't up to getting out; it wasn't his favourite occupation at the best of times. He'd marched up and down the store, putting random things that they didn't need in the trolley. And then taking them out again. He was distracted.

His wife had made it downstairs today, but only for a couple of hours. The doctor had been with more sedatives. As the doc had checked on his wife, Austin had walked up and down the hall. On his way out the doctor had stopped by him, a firm but friendly hand on his arm.

'I can prescribe some for you, if you like?'

'Thanks, Jim. I'm fine. Really.'

Early afternoon he'd swept the porch. As he brushed aimlessly, there had been a call. He'd run to the phone, snatching the receiver from the handle.

'Hello. Yes. Who is it?'

It was the cops in Vegas. Nothing to report. It was just a courtesy call.

For dinner he'd cooked some potatoes and beans, and served them up with cold ham he'd bought from the store. His wife was asleep when he'd taken up her food. She was still sleeping an hour later when he'd been to pick up the empties. She'd hadn't touched her plate.

He stood by the bedside and looked down at her. She was flat out; in the foetal position - only her head visible above the blankets.

They say that only one in ten marriages survive the death of a child - he'd read that somewhere. He guessed that statistic was more for losses when it was a young kid at home.

Maybe.

Sure, maybe.

But they would be fine. In time. He couldn't cope day-to-day without her when Rick had been alive. He sure as hell couldn't cope without her now he was dead.

No, they'd *would* be fine. He'd make it so, whatever the cost.

Back downstairs he'd busied himself with the dishes. He cleaned them well. Lots of suds. He vigorously scrubbed the plates. The blue and white pattern somehow withstood his assault.

He reached for a locker next to the refrigerator. He opened the door with one hand and held the two plates in the other. He caught himself mid-movement. His hand on the locker door was shaking. A tremor. He was so surprised by the trembling that he lost coordination with his other hand. As he brought the plates up to eye-height to put them in the cupboard, he caught the edge of the bottom plate on the rim of the locker.

Both plates spun from his grasp. He pushed his hips against the work surface to close the gap between the falling crockery and the floor. But they were moving in a different direction.

Smash!

It was a loud noise - shocking. Plate splinters were sent in all directions. A thousand pieces scattered across the red-tiled floor.

He closed his eyes and screamed, 'Shit!', at the top of his voice.

Then tears came. Anger. Frustration. Deep, deep immovable sorrow. It had eventually found its way out. The trembling. The scream. The tears.

Bring, bring!

'What?' He sniffed up the dribble from his nose. 'What?'

He used a finger and thumb to close on the bridge of his nose, pressing hard. He scrunched up his face as if squeezing the skin together would shore up the dam against the tide of tears.

Bring, bring!

'The phone?!' He whispered out loud. It was both a question and an exclamation.

His eyes shot a glance at the clock in the kitchen. It had just gone a quarter after ten. *Who phones at this hour?*

Dawson?

He almost slipped on the broken porcelain, the rubber on the bottom of his slippers carrying sharps across the family room's wooden floor.

Bring ...

He beat the phone to the second ring.

'Austin?'

'Yes. Mike?'

'Yes. Listen, Austin. Are you alone?'

Austin couldn't stop himself from looking around the room.

'Yes. What?'

'I haven't got very long. I need you to listen hard.'

Austin's brain was all over the place. Nothing was making any sense. With his free arm he used the sleeve of his heavy cotton shirt to wipe away some of the dampness on his cheeks.

'Uh-huh?'

'I've shared Rick's file with a senior pal of mine at the Bureau. He's done some work and came back to me 15 minutes ago. He reckons he can keep me safe. The story he's using is that he got the flash drive directly from you.'

No. This wasn't registering. What was Mike talking about? Austin was listening but not hearing. But his eyes were wide now; his mouth ajar. He sniffed some more.

'Are you listening Austin?'

'Uh-huh.' It was all that he could manage.

'You need to get out of the house, Austin. Tonight. Take your good lady with you. Go somewhere. Have you got ...,' he stumbled for words, '... what about your sister in Tampa? I remember you telling me about her. A week, I reckon. That's all you need. But you have to go, Austin. Both of you. Take a suitcase. Pack up your station wagon. Get in it and go. I can't protect you. I'm sorry.'

There was silence. Austin tried to find some focus. He looked at his feet - he had no idea why. Were they planted on the ground? Was this real?

'Mike?'

'Yes, Austin.'

'Are you telling me ...'

Mike didn't let him finish.

'Yes, Austin. Rick was most likely murdered because of the report. There are people, serious people, professional people - and I can't say any more than that, who want that report silenced. And they know that you've seen a copy.' There was a pause. 'You have to go, Austin. Get out. Go to Tampa. Tonight. I can't help you. Nobody can.'

Austin remained rigid as the enormity of what Mike had told him washed about his mind.

Rick was dead because of the report. His boss had been removed from post. *He had seen the report?* Yes. Probably.

And I'm next?

The military's not just about marching till you drop. It doesn't produce automatons. There were orders and soldiers followed them. But it's much more than that. It trains its people to think, to adapt and then react. The modern battlefield was omnidirectional. The enemy invisible. Their methods of combat underhand and devious. You can't fight and win using drills taught on the parade square. You have to use your brain. See through their eyes. Fight from the shadows. Challenge and then beat them at their own game. Play rough - strike first.

Austin was an ex-soldier. A good one. A decorated one. You can take the soldier out of the army, but you can't ... it didn't need finishing.

As he stood by the phone table, receiver in hand, nothing was clear. Everything was opaque. A mess. Confusion. A battlefield.

But a mission was evolving through the mist of uncertainty.

He had to protect what was left of his family. His wife. Her sanity.

And then ...

... he had to get to Venezuela. Go to the seat of crisis. Rick's Reaper hadn't been allowed to see what was going on on the ground from 30,000 feet. Someone, something, had sent it off course. That someone wanted a secret piece of real estate, deep in the Venezuelan jungle, to remain secret.

But he knew where it was. He had the report. He had the coordinates.

Rick may not have been able to get to see it from the air. But Austin was going to find it on the ground.

'Thanks Mike, that's really good of you.' Lucid and calm. The training had kicked in. Doubt, anxiety and pain had disappeared. Focus and certainty had taken their place.

He placed the receiver on the handle. He hadn't waited for a response.

Chapter 14

Flemingstraße, Munich, Germany

Frank was woken by a *pinging* noise from the direction of the computer screens. He fumbled for his phone. It was 4.23 am. It must be Sam.

Wearing just his pants he pushed the duvet away with his legs and scrambled off the blow-up mattress, knocking over a half-finished cup of coffee that was on the floor.

'Shit!' Wolfgang wouldn't be happy. He'd told Frank last night not to leave cups on the floor. *German cleanliness.* It was polished concrete, heated from underfloor pipes. It would dry - and there was a cloth by the sink. He'd sort it out later.

Frank sat on the spinning chair Wolfgang had found for him from upstairs, the leather cool against his naked thighs.

Sam had reached the Consulate. The duty officer had emailed him last night. She was, according to the guy, too busy to want to talk. She'd told the officer to tell Frank she'd be in touch when she had something.

A couple of keystrokes later and he had a voice link open with Sam.

'Hi, Sam. You wanna go video?' Frank asked, yawning as he did.

'No. What have you got for me?'

Abrupt. She can be like that sometimes.

'Uh. A mixture.' Frank made a few swipes and opened a tab titled: *COTWC Phone Schematic*. He shared it with Sam.

'You got that? I've just sent a schematic through - it's interactive.'

You really needed a 50-inch monitor to appreciate the detail of the work. It was like a mad-dog's pooh - hundreds of lines and bubbles, colours and shades. Frank was pretty sure Sam would be stuck with an FCO 20-inch standard screen. She'd struggle.

Just before Wolfgang had gone to bed, they'd used the glass display-wall to get a grip of the enormity of it.

The schematic was forged by an SIS cause-and-effect matrix programme. The system used a database to link multiple *effects*, in their case phone numbers with a single link to another number, to *causes*, that is numbers with more than one link. It wasn't designed specifically for this purpose - it was used more for actions and their outcomes when studying terrorist organisations, but the principle was the same. Frank was delighted with the work.

The schematic showed six large goose-eggs, overlaid onto an outline map of the world. In each of the six was a single telephone number and, where they had it, a name. The goose-eggs sat above: Croatia, the US, Venezuela, the UK, and two in The Bahamas. All six were connected to each other and numerous smaller goose-eggs by lines. The thicker the line, the more frequent the call. There were 15 other mid-sized goose-eggs, each with a number and, where known, a name - and they were also hovering over countries across the world. They had multiple thinner lines connecting to other numbers. Then, if Sam could be bothered to count, there were another 123 of the smallest goose-eggs, each connected to only one other number. Big goose-eggs meant a number with multiple connections; medium with a few; small with just one. It was a busy diagram.

'The big six have multiple links - above ten?' Sam asked. She sounded tired. Irritable.

'Yes. Hubs, we think.' Frank replied.

'And the mid-sized are between two and ten links?'

'Yes, that's the key we chose. Although none of them, and there are 15, have more than five links. That's why the six hubs stand out.'

'The remainder, I'd say 120, have just a single link? They only talk to one other number?'

'Correct.'

'And how does this fit with Wolfgang's structure? The one on his wall?'

'We've not got there yet. Although ...'

'Have you slept?'

Sam was being particularly curt. *Why?*

'Yes, well ...'

'And where's Wolfgang?'

'He's asleep. Upstairs. Look, Sam, we haven't stopped!' Frank was losing it.

'Get him up.' She didn't pause for breath. 'I guess you've used the glass board to look at this? Don't answer. Put the original country schematic up, the one with the 11 flags and the five mugshots: military, religious ... you know what I mean. Then take the row that runs along the bottom - the one with Mitchell, Bell, etc; those that are not designated to a country - and move it to the top. I'm pretty confident that the diagram is the wrong way round. It needs to look like a business organisation. CEO, CFO, COO, etc; as headings. And then, in our case, the 11 country cells as subsidiaries. Do you get me so far?'

'Yes, I think so ... look. Sam. Are you OK?'

Silence. It was as though the line had been cut.

'Sam?'

There was a further long pause.

'Just do it, Frank.'

It took Frank a few seconds to flash up the original country structure with the mugshots. He shared it with Sam. He had the two schematics on two separate screens. If Sam were on a single screen she'd have to flip between the two.

'Have you now got the structure in your head?' Sam asked. Frank could just about see it.

'I'm sort of looking at it upside down.' Frank squinted at the screen. 'Just about. I can't yet see a chief ... but I can see your point about middle management.'

There was a pause. Sam was thinking as she spoke.

'No, that's OK. That doesn't surprise me. This is a cellular terrorist organisation. It breeds from a single mantra - it doesn't need direction. Its followers just act on the basis of what it stands for. They kill and maim under the banner. That cuts down the need for horizontal information exchange. No operation orders; no unnecessary email traffic. And it makes breaking into the grouping so much more difficult. You with me?'

'Yes, sure. But ...' Frank stammered.

Sam wasn't going to let him ask a supplementary.

'This is wild-arse stuff, but I reckon the top line looks like this:'

Sam was now using the interactive facility on the bubble diagram. She scribbled over the top of the schematic. As she marked the page in Miami, Frank saw the changes on his machine in Munich.

'Look ...' She drew.

'Freddie is the man in the middle. He's not in charge. There is no CEO, other than maybe their version of a superior being - God, or Jesus. But Freddie holds the thing together. He's like the company secretary. Find him and find the mantra.'

Sam underlined Freddie's name - he was smack middle at the top of the page.

Sam continued.

'Next is money-bags.' Sam scribbled Lukas Müller's name to the left of Freddie. 'He's Mr Finance. Chief Finance Officer.'

'Now, Janon Jobes. He's Mr Operations - as per the SMS he sent to snakeskin-belt man. Remember? "*Need to talk about equipment.*" He's into large-scale events. Things bigger than a single-country cell. He'd be the planner for an operation like, say, 9/11 in the US, and 7/7 in the UK.' Sam scribbled his name to the right of Freddie. 'Have you put his name through Cynthia?'

'Of course.' It was four in the morning, Frank was tired and getting more and more frustrated at being on the wrong end of Sam's monologue. He'd never experienced Sam like this. All diktat and brusqueness. 'Nothing. He's an unknown.'

Another pause.

'It's not his name. Wait ... your matrix has him operating out of Venezuela with a UK mobile number?'

Frank waited for Sam to finish her thought process.

'It's fake. Jobes is neither a British nor a Spanish surname.' A pause. 'Try an anagram. Or something else. He's a high-profile player. We or the CIA will have him somewhere. Find him.'

'OK, Sam. OK.' He was struggling to control his frustration.

She then finished off the top line, moving two more of the large goose-eggs. Ralph Bell was there. According to Sam he probably ran a series of mopping-up agents, like the man who had chased her in Miami. As was Paul Mitchell - along with his wife. They ran the technical side; keeping The Church's operations hidden on the Dark Web.

'And snakeskin-belt man?' Frank asked. He was the sixth large goose-egg with 14 connections. Sam hadn't touched him yet.

'I'm not sure. Although, hang on …'

Frank waited. And waited. He was entertained by a gentle static hum on the computer speakers. In limbo he reached across to an intercom which hung on the wall next to the computer stations. It had six buttons and a speaker. He'd seen Wolfgang use it to call Elisabeth. One of the buttons was marked 'Bedroom'.

He pressed it.

There was a pause, then a sultry, sleepy voice said, '*Ja!*'

That's not Wolfgang?

'Hi. It's Frank. Is Wolfgang there?'

'*Einen moment bitte.*'

A ruffle of duvet, then …

'Yes, Frank?'

'Sam's on the phone. We've got work to do.'

'*Richtig*. Two minutes.'

The intercom went quiet. Wolfgang was on his way.

'Sam?'

'Shut up. I'm thinking.'

OK.

Frank drummed his fingers. And yawned again.

'Got it.'

'What?'

'The Bahamas and Venezuela. They're linked.'

'How do you mean?'

'The Bahamas is just off the coast of Florida. It has always been a staging post for illicit trade between the US, Central America, The Caribbean, Colombia and Venezuela. Recently it's been drugs. In the past, during prohibition, it was bootleg spirits. The Bahamians are a bunch of pirates. Always have been.'

Frank was catching up, but not fast enough.

Sam continued.

'Your man Janon Jobes, or whatever his real name is. He's working out of Caracas. "*Need to talk about equipment.*" Get it? Snakeskin-belt man links together the suppliers, probably in the US, to the supplied. In this case, our Ops friend with the UK mobile. In Venezuela.'

Frank had caught up.

'Or, the other way round? There's a terror attack planned in the US and the supply chain is heading the other way?'

Sam was quiet again.

'No. Doesn't make sense. Venezuela is a country going down the tubes. It can't produce enough food to feed itself. There's no way it's up to exporting the kit needed for a terror attack in the US. That stuff would already exist. No, the conduit is in the other direction.'

Frank had to agree. He nodded to himself just as Wolfgang pulled up the chair next to him.

'Nice pants.'

Frank screwed his face up at Wolfgang, who stared back. He looked as tired as Frank felt.

'Sam?' Frank asked.

'OK. OK. I'm still thinking!'

Frank looked at Wolfgang again; the German shot a concerned look back.

Sam continued. 'I have three mugshots. It's taken me almost four hours to get them exactly as I remember them. I've just asked Cynthia to run the photofit programme. She'll copy you into the results. Hopefully she'll recognise at least one of the bastards.'

'Good, Sam. Good work.' It was Wolfgang.

Frank reckoned Wolfgang was expecting a reply. A 'welcome to the cellar' retort. He didn't get one.

'I'm going to Caracas.'

A single line from Sam - a bombshell.

'What? Wait! You can't. It's crazy there at the moment.' Frank blurted out his response.

'I'm going. You work on the hierarchy. Do what you do best. I can't stay in Florida. I'm getting the team here in the Consulate to sort everything I need.'

'Sam!' Frank's desperation was manifest.

'What!' Sam's reply came back as a shout - it filled the quiet of the cellar. Frank flinched.

His response was sensitive. Pleading almost.

'What's wrong with you, Sam? I've never heard you like this?'

Silence.

The two men looked at each other. Wolfgang shrugged his shoulders.

Then they knew.

'Ginny's dead. The Consulate are dealing with it. She was ...' Sam sounded like she was choking. 'She was executed. Lunchtime. In her apartment, just after I left. They tracked her down because of me.'

Frank wanted to say something. Something along the lines of 'Sorry', but he didn't have time before Sam was off again. Back to being more forceful. More committed.

'I'm going to Caracas. Today. It's the only lead we have. You dig deeper; find me something to chase when I get there. There's a flight out of Miami at 4.15 pm. I'll be in Venezuela by nightfall. The duty man here is putting together the travel details using an alias they've given me. I'll take a Consulate sat phone, which should give me a reasonable level of secure speech. I'll call you when I get there.'

Frank pushed back in his chair. He breathed out loudly through his nose.

'Are you sure, Sam?'

More silence.

Sam's eventual reply was weak. Stuttered.

'I might as well have pulled the trigger myself, Frank. It was awful. She didn't deserve to die. She really didn't. I'm going to find the bastards who did this. And, if no one else is interested except you, me and Wolfgang, the three of us are going to bring the whole shooting match down.'

Samostan Monastery, Punat Bay, Krk, Croatia

Jakov sipped at his porridge. It was thin and milky. Not something you could chew. Karlo was sitting opposite him. He had a plateful: sausages and eggs - and toast. *These monks knew which side their bread was buttered.* Jakob inwardly smarted to himself. Humour wasn't a strength of his, so he was surprised that he found even a small piece of comedy. He certainly didn't feel that he had the energy for it.

He looked up just as Karlo did the same. They caught each other's eye. Jakob smiled, an earnest smile which covered his true feelings. *You're all complicit.* Karlo smiled back. They had a connection. That's the way Jakov wanted it. Since his beating in the square, an act so callous and unnecessary it had sparked in him a determination to 'get the hell out of here whatever the cost', he had been as good as gold. A new recruit. A hard-working and industrious gardener. A fastidious follower of whatever faith it was these people kowtowed to. He was getting very good at prayers, mouthing words to a God he didn't believe in. He'd caught Karlo looking at him in the dark of the chapel last night as he silently whispered some nonsense penitence. Karlo had nodded slowly.

It was working.

Acceptance.

However long it took.

He was also much closer to understanding how the monastery was set out. Leaving aside bunks, the chapel, the canteen and the sanatorium, he'd worked out that there were six or seven rooms to which he couldn't assign a purpose. One was by the chapel; the rest were in the southeast corner of the quad. He'd made the presumption that all of the upstairs rooms were living quarters. Some were two-windows big. Some, like his, just one. He reckoned his room was on the bottom floor because it was 'special': crampily self-contained, misted glass, bars on the window and no way of unlocking it from the inside.

A cell.

The rooms he couldn't place were on the bottom floor. Yesterday, when he'd taken the gardening tools back to the shed with Karlo, he'd sneaked a peek at the outside of the southeast corner. He was pretty certain one of the rooms had three windows; he'd spotted a monk carrying an open folder walking from one window to another, to another. He was reading, deep in concentration. In the first of the windows, behind the monk, was a map on the wall. The shadow in the room was too dark for him to be absolutely sure what it was. *A map of the world?*

What did catch his eye was on the outside, rather than inside the room. Modern cabling exited through a conduit in one of the window frames. It tracked all the way to the roof, looped over the eaves of the red-tiled roof, and up to a small mast. The mast carried numerous antennae, and a horizontal satellite dish - which had a cover on its front. Next to the tower, pointing obliquely to the sky, was a much larger dish. It was about the size of a kid's trampoline. He almost didn't spot it at first. It was made out of a metal mesh and was painted the same colour as the tiles on the roof. It was as though someone had been trying to hide it.

Three windows equals a big room. A big room with cabling leading to communications equipment. *And a map of the world?* His assumption was that this was the nerve centre. Where Freddie and the monks spoke to the outside world.

He was missing one other thing. Even though he heard them howling at dusk, he still didn't know where they kept the dogs. He thought they were probably on the far side of the monastery. He needed to check that detail; he couldn't outrun the dogs.

Sipping at his porridge and thinking through the monastery's layout tweaked a nerve. His hand instinctively reached for his large trouser-leg pocket. He felt for his notebook and pencil. They were still there.

Phew.

Jakov also had a much better idea of how the place functioned. Who did what and when. He was pretty certain now that there were 17 monks. Ten of them, including Karlo, were workers. They were always doing something. Cleaning, washing up (his turn hadn't yet come for that joy), toiling in the garden, sitting on their own reading a Bible, praying in the chapel. There was one chef. A big man who wore an off-white apron over his habit. He always looked angry - and sweaty. That was 11.

Three other monks came and went, but he thought they were probably connected. He saw one in the morning, one in the afternoon, and a third he'd spotted heading down the corridor to the area of the 'nerve centre' in the evening. He'd assumed that they worked in the room with the cabling, maybe covering a duty on rotation, say, 24-hours a day? That was 14. He counted a fifteenth as the monk who looked after the dogs - maybe he was also chief of security? Jakov had sat close to him in the chapel last night. It had rained for most of the afternoon and he had definitely had that unmistakeable, wet canine smell. The sixteenth was the medic. Jakov knew he must have been attended to by a qualified medic when he'd first been captured. Someone had fixed him up well and prescribed antibiotics. The monk he'd assigned as medic was one he'd spotted coming out of the sanatorium's door yesterday lunchtime.

The seventeenth was an elderly monk. Jakov reckoned he was in his seventies. He meandered about the place with seemingly little purpose. All of the monks, including Karlo, bowed their head every time they walked past him. He had a reverential air. Was he the chief monk?

That completed the list. Seventeen monks.

And Freddie, who he'd not seen since the incident in the quadrangle.

Karlo finished his breakfast, mopping up the yolk of his egg with a final piece of bread. He put his thumb up. Jakov replied with both thumbs.

Today I'm going to be super-efficient. You'll see.

And to show willing he collected his and Karlo's plates and carried them to the hole in the wall. Karlo was waiting for him at the exit to the quad. The monk held the door, smiled and, with a nod, ushered him through into the outside.

Jakov checked his watch. It was 8.15 am. Next they would walk round the square, through the smaller of the two arches which was not barred by a metal gate, into the garden, and stroll down to the sheds to collect the tools. And then two hours' work until a break for coffee. But first ...

He faked a shiver. It was colder today but he had purposefully not worn the heavy fleece that Karlo had issued to him. He stopped and patted his arms - 'it's cold' was the message he was sending.

Don't talk. That was his new mantra. *Be like them.*

He pointed in the direction of the door that opened into the corridor which led to his room. He mouthed 'jumper' and gave Karlo his best 'I'm an idiot' look. Karlo smiled and nodded.

That's a 'yes'.

Jakov knew he only had a minute or so of additional time before Karlo would become suspicious. What he wanted to do with that extra minute was walk past his room to the end of his corridor, pacing as he did - always measuring. At the corner he'd to look down the bottom corridor, the one he'd seen from the outside. The one he reckoned had the communications centre at its end. He'd look for doors. Check if anything was different. Gather more information for his sketches. It would take no more than a minute.

His room was halfway down the corridor, on the right. He quickly skipped past it whilst still counting: *17, 18, 19. 20 paces*. Two sets of doors opposite each other; and equal distance between each door as per normal. Single rooms. The same size as his. Then the corner. He took a deep breath and listened.

Nothing.

He carefully put his head round the end of the wall.

Another long corridor. Everything looked the same.

Shit!

He immediately pulled back.

There was a heated conversation coming from an open door, halfway down the hall on the right. He couldn't make it out.

Inquisitiveness got the better of him. Very slowly he put his head round the corner of the wall.

The loud conversation, now more an argument, had spilled out into the corridor. Jakov could only pick out the odd word or two. But, and this made his knees go weak, he recognised two of the four people now in the centre of the corridor. One was the old monk. He stood passively, his hands behind his back.

A second man was Freddie.

Don't pull away.
Don't pull away.
Sand.
In my mouth and in my eyes.

He didn't pull away. A wash of pride flowed through him.

Freddie was side-on to Jakov. He was pointing a finger at a third person, a late-middle-aged woman; slim-built and well dressed. She was looking very defensive and appeared to be trying to get a word in, but failing as Freddie lashed at her with his tongue.

The fourth was a man. Casually dressed, almost like he'd come off a yacht. He had one hand on the woman's arm. It could have been an affectionate hold, but Jakov thought that unlikely. It was as though the man were holding the woman still. Like she wanted to go somewhere, be somewhere else, but he wasn't allowing it.

Freddie, whose face was red and sweating, stopped berating the woman. There was a momentary gap in the argument. The woman went to say something but was beaten to it by the man holding her arm.

'Vicky will stay the course. She will. It's too far gone now. There's no turning back. For any of us.'

He shook her arm, as if by doing so he'd get her to respond.

The woman, Vicky, was just about to say something when she looked down the corridor directly at Jakov. She was red-faced and tearful. She spotted him. And he, her. There had been a connection.

Shit.

Her mouth opened to say something - maybe shout out that she'd seen an intruder. Instead, she caught herself. She looked back at Freddie.

'I'm not happy. I can't say I am. But Paul is right. I will do it. I will.'

Jakov didn't wait to hear or see anything else. He turned on his heels, checked the corridor was empty behind him and dashed for his room.

Headquarters SIS, Vauxhall, London

Jane was holding a cabal with her team. Present were the desk officers for Afghanistan, Syria, Yemen, I&I (Iraq and Iran) and ROME (Rest of Middle East) - each overseeing their in-country SIS cells. Also in attendance was a GCHQ rep and their on-call Special Forces liaison officer. Over the past decade the relationship between SIS and the SAS/Special Reconnaissance Regiment (SRR) had grown stronger and stronger - in particular they relied heavily on the SRR to provide video and photo intelligence in places where their case officers couldn't recruit informants and agents. Today, intelligence-gathering and analysis really was a multi-agency business.

The cabal had one purpose: did anyone have anything on the US's undefined, imminent, Level 5 threat in the Middle East? Jane had looked over the initial reports from the team. The headline was that there was nothing from the ground to add any substance to the CIA's alert.

Jane was going round the table for any additional news or thoughts.

Julie Bartram, who had just come back from Kabul and was now coordinating SIS effort in Afghanistan, raised her hand.

'Yes, Julie.'

'Thanks, Jane. From an Afghan perspective, the focus at the moment is the expanding Taliban influence in-country. We have two live 'red-level' threats, but they're both Afghan-centric. One is directed at the Green Zone in Kabul - probably a large, vehicle-borne suicide attack. The second is the recruitment of IS players coming out of Iraq and Syria to assist with a late-Spring assault on Mazar-e-Sharif. Even the Pakistani Taliban and IS are being introspective at the moment. There is no outward-facing focus as far as we can tell.'

'Thanks, Julie.'

'Anyone else?'

There was a murmuring of 'nos'.

Jane sighed. She couldn't remember a time like this before. Where they had an immutable, high-level threat from the US which they, the UK, had nothing to add to by way of corroboration.

Had they?

Maybe they had?

The biological threat in 2013 had originated in the US - from the CIA. It was the thwarted Ebola attack on central London. Its genesis was West Africa, from a secret US laboratory which studied infectious diseases. Then the UK had had no authenticating evidence until Sam Green had blundered into the terror cell by accident. It was her tenacity - *more like bloody mindedness* - that had prevented the attack, not any detailed intelligence-gathering and analysis. The US were left with egg on their face as the mastermind behind it had been ... *The Church of the White Cross*, based in Abilene, Texas.

It was all coming back to her. A rogue threat - and The Church of the White Cross.

'Jane?' It was the Syrian lead.

She came to.

'Sorry. What?'

'You said the US sources were South America, Eastern Europe and the States itself. We, here, clearly have nothing - other than the US believe that the target is somewhere in our AOR (area of responsibility). Have you tried the other branches? Europe, The Americas?'

A good point.

'Thanks. Sure. The other branch heads are aware of the threat and we're all meeting with the Chief later today. I'll interrogate them then. But thanks for the reminder.' She opened both hands. 'Now, what about the target? Thoughts? Anything?'

The Special Forces rep, a Major John Laing, chipped in.

'I've prepared a map of the major US bases in and around the Saudi peninsula. Shall I cast it?'

'Yes please, John.'

The major swiped at his tablet. The result was a map of the Middle East displayed on the interactive board at the end of the table. The map showed 15 red and six blue circles dotted over the map. Most were on the Persian Gulf, although a couple were inland in Saudi Arabia. Two were south of the Strait of Hormuz.

'The red circles are aviation bases - the blue ones, naval. I've sent this round to all of you by secure email with accompanying notes. We've completed an IPB, sorry an Intelligence Preparation of the Battlefield, on the bases - that's an enemy's overview of the most cost-effective target. Largest bang - smallest cost and risk. There are three targets that stand out. And one of those is head and shoulders above the other two.'

The major swiped again. A second slide appeared. It was an overhead photo of a naval base.

'This is US Naval Support Activity, Bahrain. It's a 62-acre site with both large and small craft-berthing facilities. It's also the HQ of the 5th Fleet - the US's 'go to' group of ships in the Middle East and the west Indian Ocean.'

Another slide - this time a larger-scale map of Bahrain.

'You'll probably all know the geography, but as a reminder: Bahrain is a blister on Saudi's eastern coast. It's in easy striking distance of Iran, Kuwait and Iraq. Deep water approaches are good from all directions east, and to the west is the largest desert this side or the Sahara. There's a 360 degree attack arc. Sea and land, with minor natural defences.'

Another slide showing a list of units that occupied the site.

'The key to NSA Bahrain as a target is two-fold. First, as I've already mentioned, it's the HQ of the 5th Fleet. It would be like attacking Portsmouth in the UK. You're striking where it hurts most - and where the PR impact is greatest. Second, it's not a war-fighting establishment. Yes, it holds lots of key stores and equipment, and there is always the odd decent sized ship at berth, but the rest of it is admin and assorted crap.' The major was highlighting units on the list with a laser pointer as he briefed. 'It's the US Navy's R&R centre. As such it's a soft target. The US have recently spent $580 million on upgrading the base. The two biggest infrastructure projects were a mall and a bowling alley. The boys and girls here will not be on their mettle. They'll be shopping, going to the cinema, and one or two of them will be drunk as skunks. It's a great target. A soft target.'

The major stopped, waiting for a reaction. There was none. He swiped again. His final slide was the SAS's badge: the winged dagger accompanied by the motto: *Who dares wins*.

Jane had taken it all in. The military were very good at that - thinking like the enemy. It was a clear presentation and a sensible conclusion.

'Any questions for John?' Jane asked.

There were a lot of shaking heads around the table.

'OK, thanks, John. That's clear. Doubtless the US will have undertaken the same assessment and come to the same conclusion. But, I'm speaking to the DD later and I will pass this on. If no one has anything else to add, let's meet at the same time tomorrow, unless something else comes up to expedite that meeting. And, I'll pop an email round after the Chief's cabal. Keep at this please. There is something going on. *Ergo*, there must be something we're missing.'

With that Jane called the meeting to a close. Her team left, but she stayed at the table. She wasn't ready to go. Just yet. It was the something she had thought of earlier.

Ebola.

The threat, four years ago. It came from the US without any verification - until it was almost too late. It had been a ruse to warn them, to get the hares running. But not enough for the intelligence services to unpick the threat themselves.

Could the same thing be happening now? But in a different way? This time the threat was being fed into the US from sources that they trusted. Staged to make them scamper around with their heads on fire. *A misinformation campaign?* Make everyone believe the threat was a US military base in the Middle East, but actually it was something else? Somewhere else?

The lack of corroboration unnerved her. They, SIS, always had something. One of their people would have a sniff. You can't keep this sort of attack under your hat. Two years ago - and the radiation bomb destined for Rome. It was a Saudi-sponsored operation, but they heard about it from Kabul. The terrorists couldn't keep the lid on it completely. It leaked.

What had the DD said? Eastern Europe, South America and the US. That's where his sources were. *For an attack in the Middle East?*

And then there was the GPS malarkey. The US ship. And the UAV that had been forced off course whilst surveying the Venezuelan jungle.

It just didn't add up.
Or did it?

Jane swiped on her tablet and opened up the latest Section sitreps from South America and Europe. She scanned the headlines. Europe looked uninteresting. Its three main stories were: migrant movement and its ability to hide sleepers; the inextricable rise of the Hungarian far-right; and Russian war games on the Baltic States' border.

The South America brief was short. The UK had little interest in the continent as most of the countries were ex-Spanish and Portuguese colonies; only Guyana on the north coast, to the east of Venezuela, was in the Commonwealth. The Guyanese High Commission had one SIS case officer in situ. Jane read the summary of his latest report:

> *Georgetown remains relatively quiet. The recent election result has been approved by the EAD (UN's Electoral Assistance Division) and the Commonwealth Observer Team. However the opposition PPP (People's Progressive Party) have still not ratified the result. They believe the ruling coalition APNU-AFC (A Partnership for National Unity - Alliance for Change) conducted widespread voter fraud, both at the ballot and with unlawful social media influence. They want the result annulled and the election rerun.*

PPP are encouraging direct action from its supporters and intend to hold a mass rally outside the parliament building on Tuesday.

Jane checked the date of the report. The demonstration would have been last night. She read on.

Local media believe that the PPP has been infiltrated by subversives from the Venezuelan (VZ) ruling party, loyal to President Maduro - the de facto dictator in VZ. The considered opinion is that Maduro/Venezuela is trying to undermine Guyanese (GY) politics. My contact in the PPP has yet to confirm this report. I am meeting with him this evening.

Exactly why the VZ government would want to do this is unclear. One potential reason is that the APNU-AFC are looking to close the VZ/GY border to stop refugees from the emerging civil war in VZ from spilling over into GY. If that border was to close the VZ government would have a major refugee crisis on its own border - something which Maduro doesn't need.

Assessment. This situation needs closely monitoring. Should the PPP resort to direct action it wouldn't take much for Guyana to descend into civil war. With 21,000 expats in Georgetown alone, a NEO (Non-combatant Evacuation Order) would be a huge undertaking for the British military.

Jane closed the tab and opened the latest sitrep from the British Embassy in Caracas. SIS had no presence in Venezuela, but the British Embassy produced a weekly sitrep. She read the latest two-pager.

The country was a mess. President Maduro was cementing his position as an authoritarian leader. All but one of free-press broadsheets had been closed down - the one remaining open was pro-government. The TV was now restricted to two channels - both government controlled. And the internet was closely monitored. Both Facebook and WhatsApp were being continuously blocked. Emails were being intercepted. Scores of independent news websites had been struck off, and around 100 people had been arrested in Caracas for publishing web-based anti-government propaganda.

The opposition leaders Lopez and Ledezma, who were arrested by Maduro last year, were still in custody and no one was being allowed to see them. The mass rallies of the autumn had become less frequent, and those that did happen had reduced in size. The opposition was losing the will to fight back.

The security situation was deteriorating for visitors and tourists, and the embassy continued to recommend that Venezuela remain an 'at-risk' country on the FCO's travel website.

Jane closed the tab and turned off her tablet. She stared into space hoping for inspiration.

None came, but Claire did. She was carrying a cup of coffee. She put it down in front of Jane.

'Thanks, Claire.' Jane smiled. 'Sit down.'

Claire did as she was asked. Jane stared straight ahead, her fingers tapped on the table.

'You've seen some of the traffic on the US threat, but let me remind us both of where we are. The US think something big's going to happen in the Middle East. And soon. Their sources include, among others, an informant in South America. South America: that's all we know. As far as the UK is concerned, other than the continued export of hard drugs to the US via The Caribbean, the only thing of note in the area is the hardening of authoritarian rule in Venezuela. And the possibility of that being exported to its British colonial neighbour Guyana, which might inflame its own civil war.'

Jane looked at Claire.

'You with me?'

Claire nodded. Jane didn't really expect an answer.

'The last time we received an unspecified threat such as this was when David Jennings was in this chair.' Claire was David's PA before Jane took over. 'Without Sam Green's intervention, a London tube station would have been subject to an Ebola attack. Hundreds would have died. Thousands more would have become infected.'

'The Church of the White Cross.' Claire finished the summary for her.

'Exactly. The Church of the White Cross. And that's what Frank is looking at now. In Germany, with Sam's pal, Wolfgang. And then there's this GPS interference that's keeping the CIA awake. With a link to Venezuela.' Jane paused. 'Could it all be part of the same puzzle? The threat? GPS? South America? The Church of the White Cross? Could the timing just be coincidental?'

Claire sat impassively, the perfect sounding board.

'Let's get Frank on the phone.'

Foreboding

Chapter 15

Austin was hot and bothered. He was fretting about whether or not he'd get a three-month tourist visa on entry into the country. In the rush to get his wife to his sister's, and then pack everything a soldier might need for a prolonged stay in a foreign country - much of which was jungle - he'd overlooked the need for a visa. On the taxi ride to the airport he'd checked the State Department's advice on their website. It wasn't clear. Apparently some airlines refused to accept passengers without a valid visa. Others seemed happy for them to take their chances on arrival. He'd had little choice and adopted the latter approach.

And he thought he might just be in luck.

In the queue ahead of him was a mid-height-and-build white woman. She was carrying a rucksack (no hold-luggage); he recognised her from the flight. She was odd. Intense. She'd spent a good portion of the early part of the four-hour flight popping to the restroom. Austin thought it more likely that she was walking up and down the aisle subtly checking the other passengers. He was sure she had given him the once-over a couple of times. Maybe she was a sky marshal? Yes, that was probably it. With the dodgy situation in Venezuela, he guessed that the US crammed their planes full of security personnel.

Whatever. Eventually she had relaxed into her seat and stopped stalking about. And now she was in the same queue he was. There were two passengers between them, and it was her turn to buy a visa from the tourist-entry desk. Austin moved to one side a fraction so he could get a good view of the exchange.

She had just handed over money. The official behind the desk was moving paper about, and stamping something. It was a slow process. The intense woman had turned her head to one side, her eyes were closed and her fingers were rubbing her forehead as though she had a headache. Or she was preventing some frustration or other from boiling over. Eventually the official finished the procedure and handed over her passport and papers. The odd woman said 'thanks', turned and walked quickly to passport control.

Austin shuffled forward. As he stopped he looked behind him. The woman was staring straight at him. She was early-30s, attractive but not beautiful. She had a full head of auburn hair which needed some remedial work.

He smiled at her. She scowled back at him, and then she was gone.

Who is that?

Sam had clocked him in the departures hall at Miami. A Morgan Freeman lookalike: mid-60s, in good shape and dressed like he was heading off into the jungle for a couple of weeks. His clothes had more pockets than there were things in the army surplus store to put in them. He wore a khaki hat with a breathable strip above its rim, and his choice of footwear was sand-coloured, lightweight US army boots. They were good; she'd swapped her British desert wellies for a pair when she visited Bagram a number of years before. He finished the Bear Grylls fashion parade by attaching two multi-tools to his canvas belt along with another US Army accoutrement, a green-metallic angled torch. She felt like going up to him and asking him where he kept his parachute.

He wasn't a threat to her, but there was no doubt that he was interesting.

A game-fisher? *Possibly.* Ex-military? *Could be.*

She'd never know.

The rest of the passengers were benign. And so far, Caracas airport - crazy as it was - looked clear. No tails.

The Consulate had set her up as 'Annie Wild', a geologist working out of the UK Embassy. They had provided her with a passport, a driving licence and a bank card. Frank, bless him, had authorised the latter using an op code. She had

$10,000 of credit, after which the card would fail. Both she and Frank hoped that would be enough. Venezuela wasn't an expensive country. And it wasn't as though there was much to buy in the shops, such was the desperate state of the economy.

It was getting dark and, having carried out a final check for a tail outside the terminal building, Sam did her usual SIS play and picked the third taxi along, much to the frustration of the first two drivers. The taxi was a white Toyota Corolla, decorated with a stripe of yellow and black squares down its side.

'*Marriott Hotel, por favor.*'

The taxi driver replied, '*Sí,*' and pulled out in front of another car - which had to slam on its brakes. A loud *hoot* of its horn followed.

'*Idiota!*' Shouted the taxi driver; his hands flew off the steering wheel, just when firm direction was what the taxi needed most. Somehow they missed a second car and only just avoided a concrete bollard. Sam had read that, depending on traffic, it was a 40-minute journey from the airport to the centre of Caracas. This could well be the longest journey of her life.

In the end, the taxi made it to the hotel without major incident. She paid the driver in US dollars, who was very pleased with the exchange, and made her way up the entrance steps into the brick-and-concrete tower block that was the

Marriott. She booked in for a night using her alias, asked when the restaurant closed and took the stairs to the seventh floor - she needed the exercise.

Having sorted out her few things, she went out onto the balcony and took in the scene.

Inevitably Sam had done some research. Before she had left Miami she'd asked Google to list the most dangerous cities on the planet. Six out of the top ten were in South and Central America. Caracas was in the top three - although the list probably hadn't been updated since the onset of the country's latent civil war. Law enforcement was at best poor and, at worst, part of the problem. Corruption was rife and high levels of male unemployment, widespread poverty and the equatorial heat added to the combustible material.

It didn't help that Caracas wasn't by the ocean, even though on a large-scale map, it appeared as though it were. The city was in a bowl, surrounded on all sides by spiky hills. The only sensible way to reach the capital from the thin coastal plain was through a motorway tunnel. The city's two-million inhabitants had expanded to fill the bowl; and where they had run out of room, urbanisation had spread into the hills. Densely-populated shanty towns, similar to the favelas in Rio de Janeiro, clung to the precipitous, jungled hillsides by their concrete fingernails. The difference in Caracas was that there was neither the political will nor the money to clear the favelas and create better homes for their occupants. The situation was dire.

The city was a tinderbox and, as Sam stared out from the balcony, she sensed the hardly-contained anger. On the journey from the airport she'd witnessed signs everywhere of recent clashes between protesters and the police. There was anti-government graffiti on every spare surface - one very colourful wall had been painted with the scribble, *'gringo go home'*. She had decided not to take that personally. A long stretch of the motorway was closed, its tarmac charred and burnt, the safety barriers ripped up and strewn over the carriageway. She'd counted six police armoured personnel carriers - painted incongruously white - parked at strategic points. There was one outside her hotel. The policemen looked edgy and they all carried automatic weapons. It wasn't a combination that filled her with confidence.

The climate was different from that in Miami. There, the heat was mostly dry - the humidity low. You sweat, it dries. Here, in the equatorial climate, Sam's blouse stuck to her like a wet paper towel. Her bra was clingy, and rubbed - she knew she'd have red marks under her arms and across her back.

She could almost taste the dampness.

And, even this late in the day, the city was hardly quiet. The traffic below her was indignant.

It moved in stops and starts; three and four lanes squeezed out of a road that was only built for two. When one police siren stopped, another started. The colours were angry too. In the city centre, close to the hotel, harsh neon and fluorescent lights cut through the gloom. In the hills, the gentler light of old-fashioned bulbs was further dimmed by wood smoke - for cooking and washing. It reminded her of West Africa in that regard. But there was a significant difference. In Liberia and Sierra Leone every scene was accompanied by the heavy beat of music. Rap and reggae. Dance and song. In Caracas, she felt the people didn't have the energy to sing. And certainly not to dance. It had been drained from them by nervousness - and hunger.

Sam had spent some time in Kabul - another city on the dangerous list. A place devastated by decades of conflict. A city built of sand and mud-brick, any hint of colour scrubbed away by Taliban rule and their perverted interpretation of Sharia law. But, encouraged by a fragile democracy, vibrancy was re-emerging. Afghanistan was innately a country of brightly-coloured kites and lyrical music, played on rubabs, sarindas and tabla drums. Whilst Kabul could hardly be considered a contented city, it was alive - and growing.

Caracas, not so. In her three hours in country, Sam thought the city resembled a carcass of a dead animal. Festering and decaying. Lifeless. Ambition-less. She really hoped, for the sake of the

Venezuelans, that things were better should she go up country.

That made her think.

I should call Frank.

And then eat.

'So, fellas, what have you got?'

Jane's face was on the screen in front of them. She looked tired. They were all tired. It was gone midnight and it would be another night with little sleep. Both Frank and Wolfgang were squashed side by side, their heads displayed on a small inset on the bottom right-hand corner of the main screen.

Frank looked at Wolfgang, who raised a single hand as if to say, 'You speak'.

Frank nodded.

'We have four confirmed names and faces. Three of them are ...'

Ping, ping, ping.

Wolfgang's computer was registering that there was another incoming call. A second inset appeared displaying the single word: *Sam*.

'Hang on, Jane. It's Sam.' Frank turned to Wolfgang. 'Can you make this a conference call?'

'Sure.' Wolfgang pulled the mouse and keyboard towards him and got to work.

'Jane - Sam's in Venezuela. We hope. Wolfgang will link us all together.'

'Venezuela? What the blazes is she doing in Venezuela?' Jane didn't bother to hide the incredulity in her voice.

'That's a good question. Hang on ...'

Wolfgang had his hand up asking for more time. Frank got it, and shut up.

'Hi, Sam.' It was Wolfgang.

'Hi, Wolfgang. Frank?' There was a slight delay as the Consulate's sat phone signal bounced its way around the world.

'I'm here, Sam. We've got Jane on the line from London.'

The Jane on the screen smiled and waved unnecessarily.

'I guess you can't see me, Sam?'

Delay.

'No. Sorry. Thankfully I can't see Frank or Wolfgang either. Last time I looked they both needed a good shower.'

They all laughed.

Sam continued. 'On a serious note, this line is secure but I still worry about intercept. Let's keep this as short as we can.'

There's no doubting who's in charge here.

There was a consensus of 'OKs' from the three of them.

'I was just briefing Jane.' Frank said. 'Cynthia has come back with three positives on the mugshots you drew. The Austrian guy with Paul Mitchell is a Jim Broadly, ex-Special Branch. Left SB under a cloud five years ago. He's known to MI5. Snakeskin-belt man is a Manfred Klister. He's an ex-German paratrooper. He's got an 'indecent image' record as long as your arm. The BND have been after him for some time. It makes sense that he's working in The Bahamas alongside Müller. The guy in Miami is a Zack Jackson. He's an ex-Green Beret; US marine. Freelance. Works to the highest bidder. Has an FBI record. And finally, and well done you, the ops man - the one you moved to the top line of Wolfgang's matrix: Janon Jobes?'

Pause.

'Yes.' Sam replied.

'You were right. The name's an anagram His real name is Bojan Jones. He's the current Chief of Staff of the SEBIN, *Servicio Bolivariano de Inteligencia Nacional*, or, for mere mortals, the Bolivarian National Intelligence Service.'

'That's the Venezuelan Secret Service.' Jane cut in. 'Not Bolivian, no matter what the title wants you to believe. What is going on?' She sounded exasperated.

Frank took a deep breath and then spent a couple of minutes filling Jane in on the last 36 hours, starting with Sam's work on the hierarchy of The Church of the White Cross. He then explained the telephone schematic that he had produced, and finished with Wolfgang's work on hacking into the mobiles that Sam had nicked from The Bahamas. His and Wolfgang's prognosis was that the key to all of this was Venezuela. And the top players were Freddie and the newly renamed Bojan Jones. Frank went on to speculate that there was a Venezuelan-based op going down. With Jones at the centre of it.

He finished with a jocular, 'Any questions?'

Jane had been taking notes. She looked up from her pad, the non-ink end of her pen making its way to her mouth. She chewed for a second.

'So, let me be clear.' Jane started to summarise. 'We think The Church of the White Cross is alive and functioning ...'

'Yes, absolutely. And Jane?' Wolfgang interrupted.

'Yes?' Jane's exasperation showed; she wasn't accustomed to being interrupted

'I've not yet shared the database with you, or its large-scale output. Bear with me.'

Wolfgang took the GoPro videocam off its stand on the shelf above the computer screen and walked to the display wall.

'Sam and Frank have seen this. You haven't.'

He scanned the wall left to right. Frank watched it on the inset in the screen. Wolfgang then touched one of the mugshots and a drop-down factsheet appeared. He shared that detail with Jane via the GoPro.

'Blimey.' Was Jane's response.

'I thought you weren't going to share that?' said Frank.

'I'm not. Not yet. But I do want Jane to know the scale of the problem.' He came back to his chair and put the GoPro on the shelf, adjusting it so he and Frank were back in the picture. And then sat down. 'The thing you have to remember Jane, is that nowhere is secure. These people are everywhere. Statistically there is someone in your building who works for The Church.'

Jane didn't say anything for a second. Frank didn't know if the pause was tacit agreement with Wolfgang's comment.

'Back on mission.' Jane started again.

She's not going to comment on Wolfgang's statement then ...?

'You reckon that, with what you have, The Church are planning a large-scale op, too big to be managed by a single country cell. And if so, the op is being coordinated by your man Bojan Jones, who turns out to be SEBIN's chief of staff? Which is crazy in itself.'

Jane didn't wait for them to answer her question. She continued.

'If you follow your logic through, he is, was, being supplied with cash by Müller. And he's getting equipment from Manfred Klister, via The Bahamas - with the kit's source likely to be the US, say Miami. Leaving aside Bojan Jones, your corroboration is:' Jane raised a finger each time she made a point. Finger one. 'A telephone number matrix; but too few associated texts or messages to back it up.' She raised another finger. 'A man called Freddie, who you think is in the middle of all this - and he's based somewhere in Croatia on a "special" landline supplied to him under the table by Hrvatski Telekom.' Finger three. 'A link between Freddie's special +61 number and another landline somewhere in Amazonas.' A fourth finger. 'And a permanently closed Venezuelan Consulate in Miami, the base of a likely killer who chased Sam out of a club and then, we think, murdered a girl called Ginny,'

Frank thought that, putting it that way, it all sounded pretty tenuous.

'Executed.' It was Sam.

'Sorry?' Jane asked.

'She was executed. It's a small point, but it may be an important one.'

'OK.' Jane continued. 'And Sam's gone to Caracas for what reason?' she let the question hang for a second. 'To confront Bojan Jones? With what?'

There was quiet. Frank couldn't see Sam's face, but he knew she'd be fuming. Sam was chasing a shadow - following her intuition. Trying to make amends for Ginny's murder. She'd hate being told that what she was doing was a waste of time.

Jane stared impassively at her camera - the effect on the screen was one of boredom.

'It's very tenuous. And I would not sanction an SIS overseas operation on the basis of your intelligence.'

Then Jane's face lit up.

'But, you may just be right.'

What?

'What?' chirped Frank. Wolfgang shot a glance at him.

'I think you've got something. I'm reasonably sure of it. I've not given you my side of the story. There is absolutely something here. Let me explain; Frank knows some of this already. There's a US-issued, imminent, unspecified, Level 5 threat to a target in Middle East. Sam will know what that jargon means. The timing, imminent, was issued 48 hours ago. I would therefore argue that threat level should now have been raised to "immediate". The US are all at sea. Their int comes from three sources: Eastern Europe - let's call that Croatia; the US - let's call that Miami; and South America - let's call that Venezuela. Does that ring any bells?' Again, Jane didn't wait for an answer. 'And, and this is a huge "and", thanks in part to Frank, we have all been studying potential interference with the US's GPS system. That is, altering a single GPS receiver's idea of where it is, so that the vehicle's navigational system it supports veers off course.'

Wolfgang spoke. 'Controlling navigation from afar. That would be particularly effective in the case of, say, remote vehicles - where the owner couldn't manually override the system.'

'Indeed. The US have briefed us on two recent events - at least one of them could be a rehearsal for a future op. Your op. And that one made headline news: the USS Beaverbrook's crash in Manila Bay. Currently a messed-with GPS is the most likely explanation as to why the ship hit a tanker. And the second event, which is on the tightest of holds - and at this point, Wolfgang, I need you to stick your fingers in your ears - is a Reaper drone out of Creech, Las Vegas. Its mission was to fly over the Venezuelan jungle and take photos. Sometime during the flight it inexplicably veered off course and strayed into Colombian airspace. It didn't crash - it just didn't fly where it was supposed to. If it had, I reckon the drone would have flown over something it wasn't meant to see. Maybe something to do with putting a satellite into space, or maybe controlling a satellite? Possibly a building with a sizeable dish.'

Jane paused.

'That's it.' Sam interrupted.

'What, Sam.'

'The control centre. It's here in Venezuela. It's what the money and the equipment has been used for. To build a satellite launch and control station. In order to interfere with GPS, you'd need to have your own satellite system - commercial birds operate on different wavelengths to the US's GPS. What better place to hide your set-up than in the Amazonian jungle?'

How does she know all this stuff?

'In a country which has half-decent infrastructure, but is on the brink of collapse. And where you, the perpetrators, can buy some control.' Wolfgang added.

'Yes, spot on, Wolfgang.' Sam added. 'I'd bet that The Church's control is wider and deeper than just SEBIN's chief of staff. Jane, where did the Reaper veer off course?' Sam was direct. Uncompromising. She was on a mission.

'We don't know.' Jane replied.

'What, because the US won't tell you?'

'No. Because they don't know. All of the reports concerning the Reaper have gone missing. Anyone involved in what was a secret mission, has either been murdered, or just vanished. Including a CIA pal of Frank's. It's as if the Reaper didn't fly at all.'

'Are the US taking this seriously? The Venezuelan intelligence?' Sam asked.

'Not as seriously as they should. They're working on the Middle East threat. They're target-focused. But, they've not had this briefing. I'll get onto the DD straight away.' Jane paused in thought. The end of her pen was back in her mouth.

'Of course, we're missing one vital piece of intelligence.'

'What's that?' Frank asked.

'What is the target? Where in the Middle East? The betting money is on the HQ of the US 5th Fleet, NSA Bahrain. But does that make sense? Is that a Level 5 target? And what weapon are you going to control by satellite?'

'It's not important.' Sam said.

'What? Why?' Jane came straight back.

'Because if we can disable the guidance system here, they can't hit the target. Simples.' Sam voice had started to trail away. 'Can we wrap this up? I'm packing. Now.'

'Where are you going?' Jane asked.

'Puerto Ayacucho. It's the capital of Amazonas province. On the Colombian border. It's a good place to start looking. I'll keep in touch.'

'Hang on, Sam. This is a mission for a properly briefed, trained and equipped team of people. It's also the US's turf. They'll have CIA agents in their Caracas embassy who'll be perfect for this kind of stuff.'

There was a pause.

'No, they won't?'

'What do you mean?'

'Have you seen the news? I've got the local station on the TV behind me. The government here have just locked down all foreign embassies and consulates. They're showing a live stream of a police cordon outside the US Embassy. They've got small tanks and everything. The Venezuelan security services are in the thick of it. They're closing down any interference. The Church of the White Cross don't want anything to get in the way of their operation. Whatever it is.'

The silence was deafening.

'I'm heading up country - and my understanding is that it's a bus or Shanks's pony to get there. I'll take the bus. I need to know where to go once I'm in Puerto Ayacucho. I reckon you've got eight hours to find the answer to that question.'

Frank was following up on the instructions Jane had given before she'd hung up. He was preparing a missive for his contact at GCHQ. The key now was finding the location of the control centre. Frank thought it incredibly unlikely that they'd get something in time. GCHQ preferred to work with clear boundaries, rather than just 'tap that phone and let us know what you hear'. However, even with the new guidance, which included an updated list of keywords, the chance discovery of something or somewhere in Amazonas seemed hopeless.

He'd put the tasker together using GCHQ's operational form and follow it up with a phone call.

He checked the clock on the bottom right-hand corner of the screen. It was 01.37. That would be 2.37 am in the UK. The Doughnut operated on a 24-hour basis - and there would be someone in, for sure. But it would be a skeleton team only. He'd have to wait a couple of hours before any real horsepower was available.

The tasking form was a sickly light-green colour. There were 14 boxes to complete, one of which was the op code. Frank got cracking. As he typed he shot a glance at Wolfgang. He'd left Frank's personal space after their joint phone call, and was back in front of his own machine.

'What are doing?'

'Mmm?'

Frank stopped typing.

'What are you up to?'

'Mich? Ich suche eine Nadel im Heuhaufen.'

'Oh. Good luck with that.'

Whatever.

Wolfgang continued - this time in English.

'I'm looking for your proverbial needle in a haystack. I'm onto the landline calls from the Croatian +61 number. I obviously can't listen to what people said to each other in the past as there's no recording. But I have accessed the answerphone. It keeps 100 messages for three months. My Croatian is improving ...'

'Oh. Good.'

'And I've also set up a trigger on the Venezuelan ex-Consulate. If the line goes live we'll know about it - and we should be able to listen in.'

'How do you do that?' Frank thought only governments had that capability.

Wolfgang didn't reply. He just moved his fingers above his keyboard as if he were typing, and smiled.

Ping.

It was on Frank's machine. An email from GCHQ - probably a reply to an earlier request

It was titled: *Task Number 3647/A/2390 - Biblical Reference.* He opened it.

Hi Frank,

See attached.

We've just finished a review of +44 7795 email account. We've gone back 28 months. Most of it is low-level chatter, the transcripts we think are important are at Appendix 1. However, there is one very early thread (12 Oct 2015) which starts with a wide circulation to 17 other addresses, which has six associated replies.

The email is titled: Revelation 16:14-16. *The text of the email is in English. It is a one-liner:* Read and action. Our time is coming. *It has a plain text attachment, which is clearly in code. The attachment is three pages long.*

All of the replies, except one, acknowledge receipt - nothing more. The odd one is from an email we've associated with an account in South Africa. Its reply is just two words: For Abilene! *I've done my research. Someone in SIS will remember the Abilene siege, I'm sure. This looks like a clear reference to revenge for that siege.*

BTW, Revelation 16:14-16 refers to Armageddon.

Do you want our cryptographers to have a go at decoding the 3-pager?

Frank didn't need reminding of Abilene, Texas. It was the US security services stand-off with The Church of the White Cross. The US lost four Bureau officers and a couple of national guardsmen. All told, the enemy casualties were 42. Fifteen of those were women and children, supposedly killed by their own menfolk in the height of the attack.

He didn't need reminding of Abilene.

Instead of finishing off the GCHQ tasking form he typed *Revelation 16:14-16* into Google and opened the Bible Society's blurb.

14. For they are the spirits of devils, working miracles, which go forth unto the kings of the earth and of the whole world, to gather them to the battle of that great day of God Almighty. 15. Behold, I come as a thief. Blessed is he that watcheth, and keepeth his garments, lest he walk naked, and they see his shame. 16. And he gathered them together into a place called in the Hebrew tongue Armageddon.

Bloody hell.

He opened the Wikipedia entry on Armageddon. It was vague about whether or not Armageddon was a reference to the ancient city of Megiddo, in northern Israel, and whether or not *'the battle of that great day of God Almighty'* was actually going to take place there. It didn't matter. The text could be abused any way to suit.

What wasn't vague was that GCHQ had found a two-year old, wide-circulation email from 'Ops', which had a biblical reference to Armageddon in the title. The email was accompanied by a coded attachment, and in the main body of text was the instruction: *Read and action. Our time is coming.*

Blimey.

He'd need to get this to Jane asap.

He turned to Wolfgang, who immediately put up a hand. *Don't speak to me.* Wolfgang was wearing headphones. Frank saw that on his screen was a small diagram box. It looked like a synthesiser, with a wave of columns rising and falling to the beat of some sound or other. At the same time Wolfgang, with his free hand, appeared to surf for information on the next Miami Dolphins' game.

And he still had his hand up.

Frank waited.

And waited.

Then the silent, electronic wave of sound stopped. Wolfgang quickly removed his headphones.

'We've got less than 24 hours.'

What?

'What?'

'That was an incoming call to the ex-Venezuelan Consulate building in Miami. It wasn't coded, although the two men spoke to each other in quasi-code.'

'And?'

'They spoke of "the act". And then one of the men said that it would all be over tomorrow in time for them to watch the Dolphins' match. I've just checked. The Dolphins play the 49ers in San Francisco tomorrow. Kick off, if that's what the American's call it, is at 6 pm. That's 2 am our time - about a day from now. What we don't know, of course, is what they meant by "act".'

'I know what it is.' Frank said.

'What?'

'Armageddon.'

Frank turned back to the keyboard and typed faster than his fingers could keep up with.

Headquarters SIS, Vauxhall, London.

It was deathly quiet in the office. Jane sipped at her lukewarm coffee; it was four hours old, but the thermos cup had kept some of the coffee's heat. She checked her watch. It was 3.12 am. She desperately needed sleep. But she also needed to talk to the Deputy Director of the CIA. His PA had taken her call two hours ago, just gone 8 pm EST. She had promised Jane that he would call her back when he'd got out of the meeting he was in.

She'd lost the energy to do any more work. Whatever she did wouldn't make any sense; she was too tired to be coherent. She just needed to talk to the DD. And then she'd get her head down on the couch for a couple of hours.

Her phone rang. She checked the screen.
Result.
She picked it up.
'Thanks for waiting up, Jane. You really should go home.'
She laughed to herself. The man was charm personified.
She checked her mirror. She looked rubbish.

Why were all the men she knew either alpha-male luddites, or metrosexual intellectuals? She wasn't desperate, but where was Mr Right?

On the other end of the phone?

Give it up, won't you?

'Thanks, Linden. How's it going?'

'Well, other than the fact that our latest intel gives us fewer than 22 hours to find and eliminate the threat, a threat we cannot quantify but we know is grievous … I'm fine. And you?'

'Have you had anything new?'

'No. We're apportioning 95% reliability to our sources, who can only confirm what we already know. Except, now one of them tells us it's going to be over by tomorrow night.'

'It's as if they're playing with you?'

'Exactly. And it's not a great feeling, I can tell you. Hopefully, the Limeys are coming to the rescue?'

Jane took a deep breath.

'Maybe.'

Jane wouldn't mention sources, not because she wanted to protect Wolfgang, but because she wanted the DD to believe her. Revealing that much of her intelligence was coming from a mad German count's cellar, somewhere in deepest Bavaria, lacked the normal levels of credibility.

She described what she had. It took her a couple of minutes.

'And, to elevate it to a plot of a Dan Brown novel, the latest from GCHQ is an intercepted e-mail op order, which they've yet to be decipher. It's title, however, quotes Revelation 16:16 ...'

'*And he gathered them together into a place called in the Hebrew tongue Armageddon?*' The DD interrupted.

Wow.

'Exactly. And, like you, from a separate source we have a task-complete time of, and I know this is getting weird, "before the 49ers take on the Miami Dolphins". I understand that is 21.00 EST. About 20 hours from now.'

The call went silent for a while. Jane didn't push.

'This is all about Venezuela?' The DD asked.

'We think so. As I said, a county which has just locked down every embassy and consulate in the land. Which, surely, is telling us something?'

There was more quiet.

The DD changed tack.

'I have the list of commercial rocket launches from the past three years. My team has highlighted the ones where we cannot verify the payload. Have you heard of the Guiana Space Centre?'

'From where the European Space Agency launch their Ariane rockets?'

'Correct. Other than the fact that French Guiana is a French dependency, the EU chose that location because it's close to the equator. Which, from a rocket-science perspective, apparently means that you can get a bigger payload into geostationary orbit with a smaller rocket. Don't test me on the details.'

'Are you saying that The Church of the White Cross has bought payload capacity from the ESA?'

'No, I don't think so. What I am saying is that southern Venezuela is on the same latitude as French Guiana. In fact, big chunks of the Venezuelan state of Amazonas are closer to the equator than the Guianan Space Centre. A couple of big guys could almost throw a satellite into orbit from around there.'

'Do your people have any likely launch sites?'

'No, but they're all over it like flies on a turd loaf. There's nothing back yet.'

I have so many more questions.

'Do you have anyone in the area?'

'Hang on, I need to look that up.' Jane heard some keyboard tapping. 'No. Not in Venezuela. Our CIA cell is ten-men-strong. Two are on leave at any time. Seven of them are in the Embassy - with no way out, no matter what protestations our President may be tweeting at the moment. The eighth is checking a drugs lead in Quimo, which is in the east of the country. On my map that's a good 400 miles as the crow flies and a bellyful of jungle between him and - well, let's face it, we don't know where?'

Jane let that last comment hang.

'What about in Colombia?'

There was a short silence.

'I don't need to look that up. It's my bag and I can tell you that that's more promising. I'm afraid I can't tell you what we have in Colombia that may be assisting their Secret Service in operations against the narco-paramilitaries. But you could use your imagination and you wouldn't be far off.' There was more silence. 'OK. What harm can it do? I'll put a team on standby. The moment any of us gets a whiff of where whatever this thing is, I'll fly a team over the border. Let's keep this line open. Anything else Jane?'

'No, I don't think so ... hang on. Do you remember Sam Green? An analyst and then agent of ours?'

'No, I can't say ... wait, the girl in Berlin. Took down the European branch of The Church of the White Cross single-handedly, and then got in a car, drove to, where was it, Köln? And then stopped some lunatic from assassinating the German premier?'

'Yes, her.'

'And?'

'She's in Venezuela. Operating on a hunch. She doesn't work for us; she left the building after the Rome bombing incident last year. But she's sort of back on our books. And heading for Amazonas.'

'Well, I'll be dipped in shit.'

'Indeed. My feeling entirely. She's ahead of all of us.'

'Does she know where she's going?'

'No. But she knows what she's looking for when she gets there.'

Chapter 16

Terminal de Nuevo Circo, Caracas, Venezuela

Sam wasn't comfortable. At all. Her Spanish was less than basic. But she didn't need to speak the language to understand the intent of a couple of thugs who were hanging around Caracas's main bus terminal this early in the morning. The terminal was modern - that is, built in the last 20 years - but filthy. It was designed on a large, now decaying, tarmac area. Four covered walkways provided the focus for the coaches and minibuses to pull up next to. Except they didn't. Not in any organised fashion. The buses, a mixture of old and almost new, found whatever slot they could. In the warm, misty rain, which was working hard to stop dawn from presenting itself, Sam struggled to find the bus she was meant to be catching. She was searching for one which would take her to San Fernando de Apure, a city 250 miles due south of Caracas and two-thirds of the way to Puerto Ayacucho - the capital of the southern state of Amazonas.

Eventually she spotted it.

I hope.

It was a fairly modern 52-seater. Big and red. It proclaimed it was heading her way - a large, handwritten sign was blu-tacked to the front window. She clocked it as it pulled into the bus station and navigated its way to a space in the next bus stand along.

According to the website it was due to leave Caracas in 20 minutes. First, she had to get past a weaselly-looking local who was standing in her way. He was sandwiched between a random bus and a metal bench. He was side-on, blocking her route. When she attempted to squeeze past him, accompanied by an, 'Excuse me,' he turned to face her, closing any potential gaps. He was her height with greasy, jet-black hair. His clothes, tatty jeans and a brown cotton shirt, could all do with a wash. He was wearing fake Nike trainers. *Nice.* He smiled, a disturbing smile. She had twice as many teeth as he did.

And he had a half-empty bottle of something in his right hand.

Shit. A drunken local with a potential weapon.

The last thing she needed was a confrontation with an idiot in an alcoholic haze. She turned to walk away - and was blocked by another man. He was bigger and uglier.

Shit.

She turned back and faced the lesser of two evils.

'What do you want?'

English. She ran out of Spanish after, '*Si*'.

'*Dinero.*' He held out a filthy hand.

Money? She guessed so.

Fuck.

Sam lifted her waterproof top. As she did she felt the presence of the second man close in behind her.

Calm.

She unzipped her waist belt, found her wallet, and, trying hard not to show the local how much money she had, she pulled out a $50 note. She dropped her waterproof as quickly as she could.

'Share this, shithead.' She said.

The man snatched the note, gave a toothless grin, looked over her shoulder and nodded. The other man grabbed her from behind, startling Sam.

SIS training doesn't turn case officers into superhumans. Fitness and self-defence packages run concurrently with all of the other training. The students always think being thrown about on a gym mat is something to laugh about - no matter how hard the physical-training staff try to get them to take it seriously. And, of course, like any skill it's only of any use with continuous practice. Sam was as rusty as a nail in a seaside groyne.

But Sam had surprise on her side. And, as was her brain's wont, she remembered everything she'd been taught, even if she hadn't (*thankfully*) used it since she'd passed out of training.

She waited the split second it took the man in front of her to start fishing for her waist belt. He was distracted. Then, with the rising red mist sending sparks around her head, she went berserk.

First, she thrashed her head backwards, smacking the nose of the man holding her fast with the hard bit on the back of her skull - she was sure she heard a *crack* as bone and cartilage gave way. The man's reflex was to bring both of his hands to his face; it's what hands do when their accompanying nose gets broken.

Milliseconds later, just as the man in front recognised that this wasn't going to be the simple mugging he assumed it would be, he got a sharp knee in the groin. Sam wasn't particularly strong and her limbs didn't carry the weight of a larger person. But she was wired in a way that meant that her arms and legs could move very quickly when instructed. And a raising knee was twice as effective if it moved twice as fast. Momentum was everything.

The man forgot about Sam's waist belt as his knees gave way and he fell to the floor.

In amongst the red mist, a tiny part of Sam wanted to recover the $50 note. And, as she leapt over the local who was writhing on the ground, she assumed that in an action movie someone like Angelina Jolie would have turned and finished off the broken nose with a karate chop. That Uma Thurman would have then kicked the thief in the guts, picked up the note and then waltzed off having made some witty comment. But Sam was too scared and running too fast - darting between buses to lose the men should they follow her. She double-backed around another bus to confuse the hell out of anyone.

No, Sam wasn't focusing on the $50 bill. She was trying very hard not to wet herself - such was the impact of adrenaline and fear.

Panting, but thankfully still with an intact bladder, she got to the door of her bus just as it was opening. She was first in line. She looked around but, other than a couple of likely passengers, saw no one.

She was breathing hard.

Made it?

Two steps-up later and she was in the cab buying a ticket to San Fernando de Apure, a process which required a lot of pointing at a Venezuelan country map she'd brought with her.

The bus driver spoke no English, so there was further confusion when it came to the cost of the ticket. Eventually, after more prodding at the ticket machine, Sam handed over 200 bolívars; around $20. The bus driver tried to give her back 50 bolívars. Sam smiled and held up a hand, then pointed at the driver. She was in a rush. She needed to get into the body of the coach and look inconspicuous.

That's for you. Think of it as a kind of insurance.

He smiled back and pocketed the money.

Still out of breath, Sam made her way to the back of the bus. She sat in the middle of the rear seat, as far away from prying eyes as possible.

Ten minutes later the bus was filling up. She'd spotted her two muggers wandering around the place, looking in windows. One was hobbling. The other had taken off his neckerchief and was holding it to his nose. At that point Sam had dropped her shoulders and turned away.

A few minutes later her would-be muggers were gone. And, as the bus seemed to be close to full and the driver started its engine, Sam's day got weirder still.

By now her breathing had returned to normal and her pulse rate was back below 60 - she had checked. The back row of the bus had been filled. To her left were two old women. One had a big cardboard box on her lap which had a mind of its own. Above the noise of a full bus, Sam heard the cluck of chickens. And then she recognised the smell.

Off to market?

To her right were two young lads. Probably in their mid-teens. They wore jeans. One sported a yellow and green Brazilian football shirt; the second a black Under Armour t-shirt which had a rip down its front. Both of the lads needed a good wash behind their ears. But they seemed harmless enough.

In the scheme of things, none of them was particularly weird.

The weirdness came when an ageing 'action man' got on the bus - the one from the airport; a breathable hat and more multi-tools than was really necessary. He was carrying an ex-US Army response pack, which Sam hadn't spotted first time round.

Definitely ex-Army, or National Guard?

He spoke Spanish to the driver, collected his ticket and headed down the bus.

Their eyes met. He looked confused. At one point Sam thought he might be thinking about turning round and getting off. But he didn't. Instead he put his large khaki army bag on the rack above a seat, and sat down.

How odd is that?

Samostan Monastery, Punat Bay, Krk, Croatia

It was perishing. The north-easterly bora wind was whipping over the mountains, shooting down the hillside, scurrying across the water and swirling around the quad. At just before midday the frost still clung to the cobbles, making a simple walk a hazardous adventure. Even though Jakov was wearing every piece of clothing Karlo had given him, the quad was a venturi for the wind and no number of layers could stop the cold from finding its way to his bones. Karlo appeared immune to it. Jakov wasn't but, even so, he didn't complain. He had other things on his mind.

Such as, had the English woman, *Vicky?*, said anything to Freddie about him? That she had seen him down the corridor? A non-monk poking his head around the corner. It made his stomach churn. Which added more urgency to the next issue that was clogging up his brain.

More mapping; more intelligence.

An escape plan.

What he didn't know, as he sat on one of the benches waiting for Karlo to come back from his room, was that his ambition was about to be turned on its head.

A woman's voice. English. The same woman he'd seen in the corridor? She sounded agitated. And then three of them burst through the double doors that led to the corridor and his room. Vicky and the other man - the one who had been holding Vicky's arm; agreeing for her to do something that she seemed unwilling to do.

And Freddie.

Churn. Churn.

He felt sick.

But he tasted sand.

It was an internal battle between courage and fear.

For good men to do nothing. It's all it took.

The team of three was heading his way. The woman the jam in a sandwich. She wasn't happy. Both Freddie and the other man had a hand on an elbow. They were directing her. Keeping her on the straight and narrow.

The woman was pencil-mouthed. Angry. Defiant.

'There's no need to treat me like a prisoner!' She was exasperated. Jakov didn't hear fear in her voice. He sensed resilience. Strength.

'And I need a cigarette!'

The woman shook her torso trying to release the men's grip. But to no avail. They were on a mission. Taking her somewhere. On a journey. Jakov thought that maybe there was a cell like his on the opposite side of the quadrangle that he hadn't picked up - maybe the door by the chapel?

He stopped thinking. Vicky had spotted him. Another connection. And then, bizarre of bizarres, she winked at him.

Or was it a blink? Did she have something in her eye? He wasn't sure.

It didn't matter because they were now beside him, then just past him. Freddie ignoring him. Dirt on his shoe.

The woman slipped on the cobbles. Her legs went from beneath her, her bottom crashing towards the floor. Her fall surprised the two men. They released their grip.

As she fell, one arm went up; the other one down ...

... into her pocket?

She twisted as she fell. The two men tried to re-establish their grip, but couldn't hold her. She was on the floor, her arms now in front of her, inches from Jakov's feet. He reacted. He half-stood. Bent. Grabbed her hands.

An exchange. A piece of paper from her hand to his.

'Sorry, so sorry,' She was all apologetic. Unharmed. No, a grazed knee. They were face to face, the two men catching up, turning and bending.

It was over in a couple of seconds.

'Are you all right, Vicky?'

She was standing; so was Jakov - she was looking directly at him.

What did he see?

Pleading?

She mouthed a word.

Quickly.

And then out loud. Spitting it out.

'No thanks to you, Paul.'

She winked again at Jakov, turned, and then they were gone. And he was left with the briefest of encounters. And a piece of paper.

He looked for Karlo.

Not seen.

He took out his notebook, opened it and put the piece of paper in the middle pages.

Quickly?

He turned to his left and made his way to the double doors. Just as he was going into the building, Karlo came out.

He stumbled briefly. Caught himself.

Think.

Jakov pointed at his chest.

Me.

And then he held his nose with one hand and, with the other next to his ear, pulled a non-existent, old-fashioned loo flush.

Toilet.

Karlo smiled. He mimed: *me - eat.*

OK.

Karlo stuck a thumb up.

Jakov nodded and dashed for the toilet.

Ten seconds later he was sitting on the pan with the illicit note open in front of him. The first couple of lines read:

Get the message to Sam Green. She works for the British government. Her number is:

Next was a +44 mobile number, then a two-paragraph message that made Jakov's heart skip several beats - and lifted the veil. Now he knew what he was dealing with. Now he understood why the monastery kept the deepest of secrets. Why, having been stranded on its shores just nine days ago, he would never be allowed to step off its shores. What he had just read was incredible. Unbelievable.

Intolerable.

And immediate.

He pushed the note back into his pad, walked out of the cubicle and turned left out of the toilet, down the corridor towards the operations room. His pace was quick. His determination at that point, boundless.

But it was quickly thwarted. The door to the operations room was locked. There was an iris-recognition pad to the right of the door. He tried it. A red, low-energy laser scanned his eye.

Nothing.

No, not nothing.

A buzz. Like an alarm - inside the room.

Should he wait? See if someone came? Try and gain entry? What happens if the door remains closed and a guard comes from elsewhere? What about the dogs?

He felt panic rising in his chest. He looked round. Then back at the door. Round again. Stairs. Leading to the first floor. Bedrooms. Bunks? Maybe a telephone or a mobile?

He ran.

He was on the first floor in no time. It was as he expected. A poorly-lit corridor that led down to a corner - which turned right. More metallic doors?

He walked quickly, trying each door as he came to it. Left then right.

Locked.

Locked.

Locked.

Locked.

Fuck! Come on!

Locked.

Locked.

Open ...

He barged in. It was a big room. Two windows. A double bed. A TV. A table and two chairs. A wardrobe. A settee. A fridge. It was cosy and comfortable. There was a picture frame on a small chest of drawers. He was drawn to it.

Freddie. And ... the other man; the one with his hand on 'Vicky' in the quad.

No. It can't be?

He shook himself.

This was Freddie's room. He was in the lion's den.

And that made him as good as dead. Karlo would miss him soon. The alarm in the operations room had sounded. There was a traitor on the loose.

They would find him. And that would be that.

But he had a message to send.

Find a mobile!

No. *Idiot.* All mobiles are locked. *Idiot.* Even if he found one, he wouldn't be able to use it.

Idiot!

Real panic now. He had to send this message.

Sand. In his eyes. Down his throat.

Idiot.

He looked about wildly. Searching for something. Anything.

And then he couldn't believe his luck. Next to Freddie's bed. A normal phone with a wire running to a wall socket. Like people used to use.

It was two strides away. He took them.

For some reason he couldn't get himself to sit on Freddie's bed. Instead, he dropped to his knees, like he was praying. He picked up the receiver and dialled the number on the piece of paper.

Immediately the phone spoke to him.

Dee-dah, dee-dah.

No. That didn't work.

Try '9' first, then 0044. Get an open line.

He dialled.

Dee-dah, dee-dah.

No.

Try 9, then wait for a dialling tone.

He dialled 9.

Brrr.

That did it.

He dialled the number.

It rang. And rang. And rang.

He was about to put the phone down when the telephone company interrupted the call and suggested that he wait for the *beep* and then leave a message.

The wait was the longest two seconds of his life. He looked over his shoulder towards the door.

Nothing.

Beep.

Jakov read the woman's message word for word. As he said it out loud he couldn't believe what he was reading. It was too extraordinary - too awful - for words. The world was heading for a disaster too large to contemplate. A precursor to war. East versus west. Islam and Christianity. And it was going to happen - tonight.

Unless Sam Green picked up her messages.

Who was she? The woman who could prevent this reckless disaster?

What Jakov was about to find out was that his own world was heading for its own disaster - at a speed quicker than the rest of the planet.

He decided to add his own story to end of the message.

'This is Jakov Vuković. I am being held against my will at Samostan Monastery. I ...'

He didn't have chance to elaborate. Freddie's foot smashed against the phone's receiver. It broke into a hundred pieces, four or five of them were embedded into Jakov's cheek. One made it all the way through his flesh and into his mouth - which filled with blood as his jawbone broke away from his skull, ripping sinew and muscle into shreds. Freddie's second kick found Jakov's left kidney and, above it, his pancreas - which split.

Disaster.

Jakov didn't feel the third kick. Or the fourth. Or the fifth.

By the sixth he was dead.

Terminal de Pasajeros, San Fernando de Apure, Central Venezuela

Sam's blouse was drenched. She was leaking. And brown. She was covered in a layer of fine dust. And she'd had enough. A ten-hour bus journey was feeling more like ten days. The coach may have looked modern, but the aircon wasn't working. As a result all the windows were open, letting in hot, damp, dirty air - the dust rising from a road whose tarmac had seen better days. She was surprised at how well the bus's suspension took the potholes - that was the only plus. What didn't surprise her was the kamikaze nature of their driver, who thought nothing of passing one of the many hand-decorated, rickety old trucks on a blind corner. Sam cringed every time he tried the manoeuvre, waiting for a disastrous outcome - her eyes firmly shut.

When she'd had her eyes open, Venezuela was as she'd expected. Their route predominantly followed the floodplains of the many rivers that fed southeast to the huge Orinoco River. She guessed that, fifty years ago, the whole place would have been one impenetrable equatorial forest. Now the trees were mostly gone. In its place was farmland - and wetland. Early on she spotted coffee and corn; later, as the terrain flattened and the ground got damper, rice. But Sam reckoned at least 50% of the land wasn't utilised - it was too wet to encourage cultivation; even rice. People who'd not visited countries close to the equator didn't get it. Much of the land can be uninhabitable. It was consistently very hot - and it rained most days. Often torrentially. There were seasons - the summer was wetter than the winter above the equator but, whichever the season, the combination of persistent heat and damp can be unworkable for most normal crops.

One outcome was incredibly lush, tropical vegetation. Verdant and fast-growing. Water and heat. The perfect growing combination for primary jungle.

The villages were small groupings of wood and mud-brick huts - few made it to two storeys. The wood used for the dwellings was mostly painted in bold reds, blues and yellows, but it looked sodden; much of the paint peeling to leave the dark stain of damp timber. Brick houses were rendered. Where that survived, from the floor up, the black tracking of damp was prevalent. Roofs were rusty, wiggly-tin affairs. The poorer shacks used straw and reed. Only the churches seemed to escape the decay.

There was some industry. Sam saw a large wood yard and at least ten garages. But the equipment in these places was reminiscent of the '60s and '70s. Everything looked outdated and in need of repair.

What Sam didn't see, other than a score of tankers – with two of which they nearly had an argument, was any sign of the Venezuelan oil industry. She'd read that it was huge. She couldn't help remembering that the country was the 11th biggest oil producer in the world - 2.2 million barrels of crude a day. Russia was the biggest at over ten million barrels. The Orinoco field, which, as the bus pulled into the bus station in San Fernando de Apure, was below its tyres, stretched hundreds of miles to the east following the course of the Orinoco River.

Like the billions of dollars in revenues, there was little of the infrastructure for the average Joe to see. Which was shameful as, looking around at the state of the coach station, the place could do with a few dollars being spent on it.

The bus ground to a halt.

'*Treinta minutos,*' was the call from the bus driver. Sam guessed at 30 minutes. She needed a pee and a coffee. In that order.

She was the last off the bus. She let the lady with the chickens, her friend and the two young lads who needed a wash, get off before her. Subconsciously there was part of her that didn't want to meet another pair of thugs who might try and extract all of her cash. Twice in the same day would be unnecessary. Getting off the bus opened her to that opportunity.

As she stepped out of the heat, into the heat, she was met by the ageing 'action man'. He was waiting for her.

'Hi. Are you American?'

He had a kind and sincere face. She thought he looked a bit lost - out of place; like he may have once been comfortable in deepest Venezuela. But now, even dressed for every eventuality - not so much.

Sam didn't need a passenger. She worked best on her own. That gave her two choices. She could tell the truth, that she was English and could understand every word. And what did he want? And where did he keep his parachute?

Or she could go straight into Russian. And confuse the hell out of him.

She sighed inwardly. Her mother's 'manners maketh man, pet' maxim ringing in her ears.

English it is.

'English. How can I help you?'

'Uh, nothing. Just ... well, just interested.'

Definitely no threat.

'I need to go for a pee and get some coffee. In that order. I'm heading that way.' Sam pointed in the direction of what looked like a cafe, just across the road.

'Oh. Uh. Do you mind if I join you?'

She assumed he only meant the coffee part.

'Be my guest.'

Sam traipsed off in the direction of the down-at-heel cafe. She was four steps ahead of him before he had chance to pick up his military bag and follow her.

Austin had no idea why he had accosted the rather fierce-looking woman he'd first seen at the airport. She may only be, in his vernacular, 'slight', but her demeanour spoke a different language. She was sharp and uncompromising. No time for small talk. Like a female marine.

But she wasn't unkind.

She was just direct.

Apparently, as they headed back across the tarmac to their bus - a thick and strong coffee to the better, she worked for the British government in geological survey. She was just a scribe - more like a glorified secretary - for a team of engineers. She was meeting her team in Puerto Ayacucho where they would be taking a boat up-river to look at opportunities for damming the Orinoco. She didn't sound knowledgeable, but oozed an odd confidence. That dichotomy surprised him.

'Isn't it a bit odd that you're travelling on your own?' He'd asked.

She'd laughed at that point. Almost scoffed at his question.

She'd missed the original flight from London and had been given instructions from the team to make her own way to Puerto Ayacucho. He thought that had been a tough call - one he would never have made for any team member of his.

She'd pressed him on what he was up to. He'd come very close to blurting out the truth, but held back. He made up some cock and bull story about his son's plane going down in the jungle, near to Puerto Ayacucho. He was a pilot flying for some local firm and the aircraft had come down in a storm. He was hoping to visit the site where the plane had crashed. Where he'd lost his son.

As he went into a little of the detail about the crash - especially the line about it 'being close to the Colombian border' - the woman, whose name was Annie, became even more intense. It was as though he'd touched a nerve.

'A plane crash? Near the Colombian border?' She'd pressed.

'Yes. I don't think it was reported anywhere, so you won't have heard about it.'

482

They'd quickly moved on. She'd called for the check - and insisted on paying. 'It's on Her Majesty'. And then they'd made their way back to the bus.

The whole exchange had been strange. Like they had both been sparring with each other. Finding each other's weaknesses. As if they knew each of them was lying - both of them covering a different story.

From his perspective it was a wholly unsatisfactory exchange.

Which was now over. He wouldn't talk to her again at Puerto Ayacucho. He'd go his own way.

Flemingstraße, Munich, Germany

Frank stared across at Wolfgang. The German's eyes flickered and his fingers rested on the keyboard. Then his head dropped forward, only to be sharply righted as he broke through sleep, back into semi consciousness. Frank knew how he felt. It was - he checked - 19.55. They were both looking at another night with little or no sleep. The search for the coordinates of the satellite control centre had sent them in different directions. Frank was working with GCHQ on the known phone records; Wolfgang was hacking into the Venezuelan phone company CANTV. His ambition was to follow the landline number that Freddie called in Amazonas directly to its source.

Currently, though, Wolfgang was snoozing more than cruising. Frank couldn't blame him. He'd give him a nudge in a couple of minutes. Maybe he'd call Elisabeth and get her to bring some coffee to the door? That seemed to have done the trick before.

Brrr, brrr.

It was his computer. GCHQ were on the line. He pressed the green phone 'Connect' icon.

'Yes, Harry, what have you got for me?'

'It's dynamite, Frank. And we got it by complete chance. You know early on you asked us to monitor Sam Green's mobile numbers?'

'Yes?'

'Well, the UK one, which I happened to check just now, was left a message about three hours ago. I've just pinged the transcript to you. Have a look.'

Sure enough his email lit up with a new message from his main GCHQ contact, Harry. He clicked on it.

He had just started reading the message when someone cried 'Havoc!', immediately prior to letting slip the dogs of war.

The noise and vibration from, what Frank assumed was, an explosion was deadened by the steel and concrete casing of the cellar. But it wasn't deadened enough not to shake Wolfgang's chair so much he fell to the floor.

Frank knew immediately that something was very wrong. It wasn't because he had experience of real-life explosions, or had trained with the army or the reserves. It was because he watched a lot of big-budget action movies - and spent twice as long playing *Call of Duty* on his PlayStation. Germany wasn't renowned for earthquakes - and the shaking was short-lived and accompanied a loud bang from upstairs.

Frank was very clear. They had been hit by something - just as he was halfway through an email which was as incendiary as the likely attack that might be being waged above them.

His *Call of Duty* training kicked in. He was mission-oriented. Task-focused.

As Wolfgang, who was still on the floor, shook his head and started to say something, Frank's mind cleared. He was back on the screen.

Call terminated.

He checked the Wi-Fi connection icon. There was none. The system was down.

Shit. Where's my phone?

'Frank. *Was ist los?*' Wolfgang was back on his chair.

Frank ignored him. He had his phone out of his pocket, and he'd switched on the camera.

He snapped a photo of the screen ...

... just as a second explosion shook the cellar.

'*Mein Gott!*'

The lights went out. It was totally dark for a second. Then a set of pink, low-light lamps lit up the room. It was difficult to see anything. Frank's eyes struggled to adjust to the lower level of light.

Wolfgang was on his feet.

'Ingeborg! Elisabeth! Frank - we must go and help them!'

Frank knew they had to do that. He also knew he had to send the screenshot to Jane. GCHQ had found the control centre. Not exactly. Not down to the last coordinate. But good enough for government work. And he had to get it to Jane.

'Let's go!' Frank shouted.

It took them a few seconds to get to the top of the stairs. Wolfgang led - pausing at the top. He opened a waist-height small hatch. Frank couldn't see what Wolfgang was doing with his hands, but he heard a *clunk* as the door popped open.

Manual override?

And then the smell hit them. Smoke. Acrid and sickening.

There was another hatch in the airlock. Wolfgang did his thing.

Clunk.

Heat seeped in through the gap between the door and the frame. Wolfgang put his hand on the door handle, and smartly pulled it away.

Hot?

At that point Frank realised that the cliché of your life flashing before your eyes when you were on the brink of death wasn't such a cliché after all. But he didn't have time for a full viewing. The door was open. Followed immediately by heat and light. Orange and white in the middle. Black at the top. Clear at the bottom.

Fire and heat.

And death.

Frank dithered. Wolfgang didn't. He was on his knees, out left, crawling below the level of the smoke towards the hall.

Shit!

Frank followed him.

Shit!

He crawled.

Shit!

He felt tremendous heat on his exposed forearm. Wolfgang was ahead of him. He had reached the main hall. Frank was just behind.

Shit!

The heat was intolerable. Almost unbearable. He knew he was burning. He knew his hair was singeing. Fear of death pushed him on.

Wolfgang was on his feet. Towering over him. Seemingly immune to the heat and the flames. *Hephaestus.* He'd met the man in a computer game somewhere. A Greek god. Surrounded by fire.

The hall was burning. Everything was alight. *Hang on!* The hall was missing its front. Where there had been a door, a wall, windows either side - now there was a black, gaping hole. The wind was rushing in, filling the void left by the hot air that was climbing the staircase, which itself was broken - mauled by whatever shape the attack had taken. Halfway up, as the stairs split left and right, one of Wolfgang's framed ancestors was still standing proudly by a piano. But the painting was at an angle, a shrapnel rip cut across the canvas severing the man's legs.

Frank's immediate thought was to stand and make the gap. Into the fresh air. Away from the burning; away from impending death.

'Elisabeth!' Wolfgang was pointing to a woman-shaped object that was on the ground next to the leftovers of a priceless, Louis XIV table. It was on its side, a leg broken - flames having taken one corner. Frank picked out Elisabeth behind the mess.

He amended his escape. He wasn't quite sure what Wolfgang's plan was, but he thought his part in it was to pick up Elisabeth and take her with him.

He crawled to her. In the larger space of the hall the heat wasn't so intense. But it wasn't a safe place. As he briefly studied Elisabeth for vital signs, something, somewhere came crashing down. He flinched.

Breathing, bleeding, breaks and burns. He'd learnt that as a cub scout. First aid. The order you check for vitals. Breathing was key.

Elisabeth was breathing. Her arm was at an odd angle, but he couldn't see any bleeding.

Do this!

He was on his feet. She was as light as a feather. As he picked her up she let out a weak cry. He looked down. Her eyes were still closed.

Crash!

Something from the ceiling fell down. It smashed on the ground in front of him. He thought an object had probably hit him. He felt something on his shoulder, but he couldn't be sure. He changed his direction. The piece of fallen ceiling was too big to clamber over. He ploughed on.

Two paces.

Three. Four.

The cooling wind was such a relief.

A crash from behind him.

Where was Wolfgang?

Eight. Nine.

Onto the steps that led to the front door. Down the steps.

Now the gravel.

He was jogging. There was a light ahead. Some people. A neighbour?

Yes. It was an elderly couple. They were speaking an incomprehensible language.

He stood facing them.

Wolfgang was the only word he understood.

He turned.

Where is Wolfgang?

The sight that met him was worse than anything he'd seen on *Call of Duty*. It was worse than any action movie he'd ever watched. The middle of the house was missing. Replaced by a black, white, orange and red kaleidoscope. Flames and smoke swirling, lashing, engulfing. In the windows of the rooms either side of the smashed middle section, Frank could see more flames. More orange. It was as though the whole place were alight.

Wolfgang was still in there.

He was dead?

Hephaestus was dead. Nobody could survive that.

He walked towards the house, without any thought as to what he might do when he got close. He then realised that he was still carrying Elisabeth. He quickly turned. Now the group was six, maybe seven. He chose a middle-aged man. Without any communication he gently passed Elisabeth to him. 'Thanks.' He turned again.

As he walked back to the building he heard the far-off call of emergency vehicles. The experts would be here soon.

But not soon enough?

He was maybe five metres from the fire now. The heat was intense again, but what surprised him was the wind. It blew so strongly from behind him that he had to take one pace forward to stop himself from being blown over.

The noise was also deafening. *Crack!* and *smash! Roar!* and *fizz!*

It is hopeless.

Hopeless.

He couldn't go forward. It would be madness; ....

... but he did. Slowly. A half pace at a time. He put his non-burnt arm up to shield his face from the heat.

He got closer. Now at the bottom of the steps.

And then.

Out of the cauldron a black figure haloed by the brightness of the fire emerged. Step-by-step. Indefatigable. A man carrying a woman's body. A giant of a man. An aristocrat. A man of honour and courage.

The man stumbled, but managed to remain upright.

Frank moved up the steps.

The man stumbled again. This time he fell forward, the woman slipping from his grasp.

Frank was there. He was at Wolfgang's feet. Ingeborg's body was now in his arms. Wolfgang had collapsed on the top step. He had rescued her from the inferno. Frank would finish the job.

And then come back for Wolfgang.

Frank turned quickly, Ingeborg's loose legs lifting such was the speed of his spin. He blindly stepped off, but was abruptly halted.

A fireman. All togged up. Frank was dazed. The man in red and orange with the mask had already taken Ingeborg from him.

'*Gibt es noch jemand im feuer?*' The fireman shouted to be heard through his mask.

No. Frank didn't get that.

'Wolfgang!' He pointed over his shoulder. A second fireman had beaten him to it. Wolfgang was safely in the arms of another man in red and orange.

Frank was now being led away. A cooling wet blanket had been placed over his shoulders.

'English!' Frank shouted.

'In fire - any man?' Was the fireman's broken response.

'No!'

I don't think so.

They were at the end of the drive. He was exhausted; getting confused. A paramedic was on him. All in dayglo yellow. Fussing. He was being sat down on a canvas stool. The yellow man had a pen torch out. He was shining a bright light in Frank's eyes. Then a cold, metallised bandage was placed on his arm. Another yellow man offered him a drink of water in a clear plastic cup. The first yellow man put a cap with wires coming out of it on his index finger. The noise was constant. The pulsing blue lights mesmeric; off-putting.

Shit!

The photo. The screenshot.

I have to get it to Jane now.

It took him all of his energy to stand, but he was gently, but firmly pushed down again.

Tiredness was enveloping.

No!

'I must make a call!' He shouted, but his words were weak.

The first yellow man turned his back to reach for another piece of equipment Frank took the pulse-reader off his finger and reached in his pocket for his phone. *Relief,* it was there.

He took it out.

Further relief - it was working.

Yellow man one was back.

He tried to take Frank's phone. Frank hid it to his side like a petulant child.

'I ... must ... make ... this ... call!' He was insistent.

That was only if overwhelming tiredness didn't take him first.

The yellow man got it. He stood back.

A second later Frank had the screenshot open. His fingers weren't working as quickly as he thought they normally did. He couldn't remember.

He found the 'Forward' icon. He chose secure mail. He typed in Jane's details - the text recognition beating him to the end of her email address.

He pressed 'Send'.

He watched the mail go.

'Sent.'

Then he passed out.

Chapter 17

*Terminal de Pasajeros Melecio Pérez, Puerto
Ayacucho, Amazonas, Venezuela*

Austin woke to the bus shuddering to a halt. He
yawned and wiped sleep from his eyes.
Involuntarily his tongue cleaned the front of his
teeth, and he stretched. His neighbour, who was
sitting by the window - a thin, elderly woman
dressed for the cold in multiple layers - was already
on her feet. She squeezed past Austin and then
stood on the edge of his seat in order to reach for
her bag. Her crotch was very close to his face. He
turned and stared out of the window.

There was a signpost which told him that
they were at the end of their journey: Puerto
Ayacucho. He'd find a hotel and then search for
someone who'd drive the hour or so it would take
to get to the coordinates he had for the buildings in
Rick's report. That would be tomorrow's task.
Whoever took him would need a 4x4. The view
from the window showed that there were a lot of
those around.

The woman's crotch dropped back to an
acceptable level. Then she was gone.

He was happy to be one of the last
passengers off - he wasn't in a rush. He'd got the
details of two possible hotels on a piece of paper in

his pocket. As, who he thought was the last passenger brushed past him, Austin stood and retrieved his response pack, catching a glance to the rear of the bus. His new friend Annie was still sitting in the middle of the back seat. She was leaning to one side peering out of the window. She looked uncomfortable. Ill at ease.

He was just about to call out and ask if she was OK, when two men got on the bus. They were both younger than him, one black man and one local. They were dressed casually - tans and khakis; slacks and shirts. Both wore cotton gilets. The black man led; the second man just behind him.

As they got close there was a glint; light against metal - just under the black man's gilet. A handgun. Austin was sure of it.

Two steps later and the man was next to him - in his personal space. Too close. He could smell him. Expensive aftershave.

'Get off the bus.' An order. The man motioned with a jerk of his head which way Austin should travel.

The man then pulled into the seat opposite, using a hand to direct Austin down the bus to the exit. The second man had also moved into a space. The route out was clear.

Austin shot a glance behind. Annie was watching the episode play out. Then he saw her eyes dart to an emergency window, one pane down from where she was sitting.

The black man was also watching. He drew his pistol so quickly Austin was almost caught by the barrel.

A straight arm: the man's eye, the rear sight, the foresight, the target. Good drills. Austin would be pleased with his soldiers if they held a weapon like that.

'Don't ... even ... think ... about ... it.' The black man's voice filled the bus. He didn't shout. He didn't need to.

Annie seemed to visibly shrink at the sound of his voice.

The man didn't change his stance. Instead, he spoke out of the corner of his mouth.

'Are you stupid? Get ... off ... the ... fucking ... bus.' Uncompromising. Edgy.

Austin was caught. The woman was in trouble. The black man had a gun.

What should I do?

The second man made the decision for him. He snatched Austin's bag and grabbed him by the upper arm. He had strength that Austin used to have when he was a sergeant - all muscle and brawn.

But not now.

The man dragged him down the bus and threw him through the open door. Thankfully his feet hit the ground first and he was able to stop his head from smashing into the ground with his outstretched arms.

Shit, that hurt!

He was dazed, but nothing was broken.

What was this all about?

He turned and picked up his bag. He squinted to the rear of the bus. He couldn't see enough of what was going on, so he walked towards the back until he was level with the end seat.

And what he saw horrified him.

The English woman was taking a beating. Much of the detail he missed - there were too many thrashing arms and legs to get a good picture. But it was clear that Annie was in deep trouble.

His mind spun.

Rick - my wife - my own safety - a woman I have just met? Rick - my wife - ... Annie.

The sequence ran through his brain as if it were numbers on a roulette wheel. The ball rolled and rolled. Then teetered - and dropped.

Help Annie.

He didn't know how, but he had to do something.

He dropped his bag and walked nervously, but purposefully to the door of the coach. As he walked he kept an eye on the innards of the bus. It seemed the men had finished the beating - they were dragging Annie back down the coach.

He met them as the second man jumped off the step onto the tarmac. The man looked confused. And angry.

'What the fuck are you doing, motherfucker? Get out of my face!'

That was too much for Austin.

He wound up to punch the man. A solid right hook. Show him who's boss. But never made it. The guy was much quicker than he was. Austin took a jab to the jaw, his head jerking sideward - his body pivoting, following the trajectory. Then he was a bundle on the floor, spitting tooth and blood. But he was conscious.

He looked back in the direction of the man. He had been joined by the black man, who was holding Annie in a lock - her head sticking out from under his arm. One of her eyes was already completely closed. Blood was dripping from her mouth. She was barely conscious.

But she managed to mouth at him, 'Go away. Run. Now.'

But he didn't. He was angry; he had the fire of injustice burning deep inside. He stood - *God, that hurt!* - and went to punch the man again. The second man sidestepped and Austin found himself falling helplessly to the ground. For an observer it must have been comical.

The second man sighed heavily. And in a movement so quick Austin only saw a flash, he drew a gun that had been hidden behind his back. And then he shot Austin in the thigh.

The noise was deafening.

The pain excruciating. His reflexes kicked in and he reached for the wound.

'I told you, motherfucker, to get out of my face!'

Austin tried to say something in response but his mouth had stopped working. And then there was black.

Sam felt every bump. She knew where she was - in the back of a blue Toyota Hilux. She could tell you the model, engine size and year if you were interested. It was useless information. *Useless*. What she didn't know was where she was going. More accurately, where *they* were going. Austin was in the back of the small truck with her.

She'd been awake throughout. She'd felt every blow. Sensed every broken bone. Her cheek was definitely shattered and she had at least one broken rib. More likely two. One eye was completely closed. And she'd lost a tooth. But the beating and the agony hadn't stopped with Ralph Bell. As the Toyota bounced its way to who knows where, the pain spiked on every bump. Tears came. Lots of them. She wanted to cry out but, as well as expertly tying her feet and hands, they'd gagged her. Instead, she bit into the gag and smashed her feet against the tailgate. Like a testy child. It was pathetic - adding to, rather than taking away from, the pain. But it released some of the frustration.

There was nothing she could have done. She had feebly tried to get out through the emergency exit window when Ralph Bell had got onto the bus. She should have released the latch when she'd first seen him as they entered the station. The pair of them were sitting on the bonnet of the Toyota. Bold as sodding brass. Waiting for her. Bell with his trademark can of diet Pepsi in his hand.

But she hadn't. She couldn't. She had been paralysed. There was something about him. His presence. His voice. It frightened her so much that no amount of disregard for her own safety could override the fear. And it was completely irrational. The Russian oligarch, Sokolov, had done her more damage. As had Bell's previous sidekick, the German, Kurt Manning. They were all as equally evil as each other. So why did Bell incite such terror?

She didn't know.

And there was nothing she could do about it.

Bump.

Pain.

Shit!

It hurt so much.

Austin made a noise. He groaned and writhed. Since they'd shot him he'd been out of it. Sam felt that was the best place for him, although she was worried about loss of blood - and any subsequent infection. Sam knew deep down that neither of those things actually mattered. They were both dead. It was the 'when' that was the missing factor.

At first it surprised her that Bell and the other thug could attack her in broad daylight. That one of them could whip out a handgun and shoot an innocent in a busy place - and then kidnap both of them. In the centre of a major city. All of this without anyone bothering.

But, when her brain had chance to disregard the pain, she knew that it wasn't such a surprise. They owned the place. The Church of the White Cross had Venezuela in its pocket. They were the warlords and the government was on their payroll. They could shoot and kidnap who they liked, when they liked.

Thump.

Too much pain! Sam kicked out against the tailgate.

Fuck you! More pain. It was an unvirtuous circle.

When would it end?

Please make it end.

Some calm. Just the throbbing from her wounds. Queasiness from the concussion. More thoughts.

Why had Austin befriended her? Why had he got on the same bus? *Why?*

What is wrong with me? That people, just minding their own business, end up on the wrong side of a gun whenever she was about? Ginny. Now Austin.

More tears.

What the fuck is *wrong with me?*

Why hadn't he just followed orders? Got off the bus and buggered off into the jungle to find his son's crash site.

Idiot.

He groaned again. And started muttering something.

Poor guy. Poor old man.

They were top to tail in the back of the truck. Her face; his feet. With her hands tied behind her back. A CIA knot. There was no chance of escape.

More groans. More muttering. At least Austin was alive.

Another thump.

More pain.

And more tears.

He moaned.

She tried to say, 'All right, all right.' But the words were lost in the gag.

It wasn't completely dark in the back. The gap between the tailgate and the metal roof was filled with a tight metal mesh. It was night outside and, from what Sam could see, they were driving through primary jungle. Tall, black-green trees puncturing a graphite-indigo sky.

There was a low half-moon which, every so often with a break in the trees, shone through the mesh. Intermittent light.

Her head was up against the cab. She pushed with her legs until her shoulders were pressing against metal - her chin on her chest.

Breathe. The pain was devastating. Her chest screamed out for mercy as she pushed some more, using her arms and shoulders as pivots to force her head upwards - into the sitting position.

Thump.

Chrissake! Her torso slipped and she fell, knocking into Austin's leg - he yelped.

'Sorry.' But it didn't sound like that.

Tears. Frustration mixed with the pain.

She tried again. This time she managed to sit up. The back of her head against the back of the cab. The fleeting moon casting a strobed shadow across the floor of the truck. Black - grey. Black - grey.

Breathe. Breathe.

She looked at Austin. He was in the foetal position, his wounded leg on top of his other one.

A flash of light from the moon. It only afforded a glimpse, but it was enough for Sam to take in Austin's situation with her good eye.

She could only see the exit wound - at the back of his leg. She reckoned it was probably about the size of a saucer; the rip in his trousers a good six inches across. Sam assumed that the entry wound would be much smaller and on the side of the leg she couldn't see.

Another flash - this time a little longer.

Blood. Lots of it. His trousers above the knee were soaked. It was all over the metal floor of the truck. It was all over her.

How much?

She imagined tipping a pint glass of blood onto the wound and seeing how far it would go. Not far enough. She tried another half a pint. Then another half - she'd now spilt two pints. That worked. There'd probably be another pint on the tarmac in the bus station.

Three pints. That's a lot.

One more and he's definitely dead.

More light. Sam was looking for a spare piece of cloth - or a rope.

Black. Then grey.

Gotcha.

A tow rope.

Then black.

A flash of grey.

The rope was red. At the other end of the truck. In the corner.

Breathe.

She moved. She slid back down onto the metal floor; she was facing Austin's knees. She used her feet to find the rope, putting one foot through a loop and the second on top.

Bump. No! Pain. Worse than before.

I'm so tired.

Tired wasn't good enough. She had to keep moving. She pulled her knees up, and then her calves to her bottom. She felt with her hands.

Gotcha! Tow rope in hand.

Now the difficult bit.

She rolled onto her back (*more tears*), her hands and the rope were in the way. She rolled again onto the side that had taken the biggest kicking.

No. No. No! The pain was washing over her. *Breathe.*

She pushed her bottom towards Austin, letting go of the rope as felt for Austin's legs.

Got them.

'Excuse me.' Muffled humour. She had no idea where that came from.

Sam squeezed the end of the rope between his legs, crying out in frustration.

Thump. Pain. Tears. Is there any fluid left in my head?

Breathe.

The rope was through. *Done.*

Sam bent her torso forward, pushing her bottom against Austin's calves, allowing her tied hands the freedom to reach over his legs. The pain in her chest was monumental. She cried out. Shouted. Fuzziness. Dizziness. She was passing out?

No. Not yet.

She fished with her hands. And fished. And then found the end of the rope, pulling it back over his leg.

She had both ends.

Result.

Sam felt for his wound. He groaned some more. The rope was above the wound close to his crotch. *Good.*

Sam made a granny knot. It was difficult with tied hands; more difficult behind her back; almost impossible with the accompanying pain. But she did it.

Breathe.

She then put one end of the rope under her hip, and pulled as tightly as she could with her hands, rolling her body away from Austin to extend the rope. It wasn't tight enough. She rolled back, moving her hands closer to the knot. Pushed down on her hip and pulled again. And again.

Breathe.

And again. If the rope were to cut off the blood supply to the wound it would need to be as tight as she could make it.

She pulled again.

And one last time.

She felt the knot. It was digging into his leg - and it was holding.

Breathe.

Sam tied a second and a third knot. She pulled them tight.

She was out of breath. Pain, tiredness and despair. It was doing for her.

She closed her only good eye and took shallow breaths. Anything to stop the pain in her chest.

Bump! Pain. Oh, fuck, what the hell.

She'd done what she could for Austin. She hoped she had stopped the bleeding. If left unchecked, the wound would become gangrenous. If the tourniquet weren't released, in less than a week he might lose his leg. But, if he got some fluid into him his body might just produce much needed replacement blood. Without that, he'd be dead in a matter of hours.

SIS Headquarters, Vauxhall, London

Jane couldn't dial the Deputy Director's number quickly enough. All she had was the screenshot from Frank. She'd tried to phone Frank straight back, but he didn't pick up his phone. Her next call was to the DD.

As the call connected and the phone made its initial buzz, Jane tried to piece together why Frank had sent a screenshot of a message from GCHQ, and not email the original? She couldn't reconcile it.

I must check with GCHQ!

It was 23.13. The Doughnut would be working with out-of-hours staff. That didn't matter. She'd get someone to check - now. She looked over her screen and through the glass wall. The office was almost empty; just a couple of desks lit. One was Colin, a stand-by case officer. He was working on the Qatar dossier.

She was interrupted by the phone.

'Deputy Director's outer office. Captain Hughes.' An East Coast accent. Smart. Efficient.

Jane did two things at once. She pushed the receiver of her second phone off its cradle and dialled Colin's internal number. She heard it ring in the distance.

'Deputy Director, please. It's Jane Baker. London.'

'Good evening Miss Baker. The DD is in a briefing at the moment. Can I get him to call you back?'

Jane spotted Colin looking in her direction. She signalled for him to come in.

'What's the briefing? Is it more information on Venezuela?'

Jane immediately got the impression that the captain was unsure whether or not she was cleared to discuss Venezuela. He dithered.

'Captain Vince Hughes. I know where the satellite control centre is. I know the village name in Amazonas. And I have some idea what the delivery method is. So, unless he knows what I know, I suggest you get him to the phone - now.'

'Well ... I don't know if ...'

'Get the sodding Deputy Director on the phone! Now! We have ...', she looked up at the clock on the wall, 'fewer than three hours to stop what my intelligence is calling "Armageddon".'

'OK, Miss Baker.' The captain was in a rush now. 'I'll drag him out. Give me 30 seconds.'

Jane realised she had her head in her free hand. And was equally surprised to see Colin standing in front of her. Her hand came off her head and grabbed a piece of paper in the middle of her desk. It was a copy of screenshot that she'd printed a few minutes earlier. She handed it to Colin. She watched the expression on his face change from a resigned 'what am I doing in work this late', to an alert and alive, 'my God, this is unreal'.

She put her hand in front of the mouthpiece.

'Get hold of GCHQ. I want this verified in 20 minutes. I'll forward you the original from Frank's now. And, at the same time, find out what the blooming hell's happened to Frank.'

Colin nodded, and was off.

'Jane. It's Linden. What have you got?'

Hurrah.

'I've just emailed you a screenshot from one of my team working in Germany. Why it's a screenshot and not the original email, I've no idea.

510

I'm working on that. I'm also working on verifying the intelligence that's in the shot with GCHQ - who originated the email. But we have to work on what we have.'

'Hang on ...'

The line went silent.

'I'll be damned. OK. So - first - we have the village's details. Have you looked for it?'

Jane had a detailed satellite map on her screen - with terrain overlay.

'Yes. It's ten klicks east of the Colombian border. Fifteen klicks south-southeast of Puerto Ayacucho. I reckon we're looking at one route in. And it's all primary jungle. Of course, this is only the village. The control centre will be at least a couple of klicks removed from the centre of the village. Who knows in which direction.'

'Got it. Wait ...', and then in the distance, 'Vince! Get the team in here. Now!'

His voice was loud again. 'OK. The second line from the report: The Middle Eastern delivery method. I'll get the Navy on the cruise missiles intelligence. But you Limeys don't yet have a target?'

'No. Nothing. But if your Navy could stop themselves from throwing missiles around for a couple of hours, that would do the trick.'

'What about your Navy? Or the French? Or, indeed, the Russian? We've all got Tomahawks or equivalents.' He paused for a couple of seconds.

'Look, this is outside of my remit. But there's a military op planned for this evening in the Middle East. It's a preemptive attack against a Syrian target. An airbase with, apparently, a chemical weapon facility. I think we have a couple of ships and a sub involved. They're in the Med. The last time we did something like this we fired 59 cruise missiles at the Shayrat airbase; in April, if I remember rightly. My understanding is that we're talking about the same scale tonight. The Navy won't want to pull out of this - not without way much better intelligence from us and a confirmed target. And tonight's Syrian attack has got the President's name all over it.' Quieter now, 'Come in fellas, come in.'

'And, Jane?'

'Yes?'

'How would these people know about tonight's Syrian attack? How do they tie their operation to a US military attack which may have only been planned a couple of days ago? Who *are* they?'

Jane thought they'd spent too long talking, and not enough time sending in the marines.

'Have you got your people ready - the ones who can reach the village?'

'Yes. I have a team on standby ...', the DD was now briefing his team, 'John, look at the map I've just cast on the screen. We reckon that's the village where the satellite control centre is - or very close by. How long to get your boys there?'

There was a pause.

Get your fingers out!

'Thirty minutes to get them airborne. Sixty minutes to loitering above the target. And then you're in the lap of the gods. Depends how easy it is to find.' A distant answer.

'Get them airborne. Now. They've got all they need?'

'They have now.'

She heard some distant scurrying.

'Jane?'

'You're on it?'

'Yes. But, and this assumes we can find the place, we're right up against the 6 pm Pacific Time Zone deadline. As for the delivery method, I'll get onto the Navy now. But I think it's very unlikely they will change tonight's op on what you've given us. Let's keep in touch?'

'Sure, Linden. I'll let you get on. I'll brief the Chief and the JIC now. You know where to find me.'

The phone went dead. She put the receiver down. And took a breath. She looked over her shoulder. She hadn't closed the blinds. It was pitch black outside. Rain ran diagonally down the window. The light from her office picked out drops and streams without discrimination. Across the Thames, the view looked as black and miserable as she felt. Jane didn't have a good feeling about anything. The intelligence was poor - everything they had was uncorroborated. These people were clever. It would take nothing for one of them to leave a rogue message on Sam's phone. Send them all running in the wrong direction. The Church's version of Operation Mincemeat - a floating hobo off the southern coast of Spain helping deceive the Germans of the Allies' invasion plans.

Deception. They were more than capable of it.

And they were working on an operational time based on the thread of a call linked to the 'kick-off' of a North American football match. It was all crazy. Shreds of evidence cooked into a soufflé that would collapse as soon as it came out of the oven.

Her wistfulness was broken. Colin was back in her office.

'I've found the operator who sent the email to Frank. It's all above board. But still no sign of Frank. Except ...'

'Yes?' Jane was tired. Her response didn't hide it.

'There's been a major fire in a street called *Flemingstraße* in Munich. I've only been on the periphery of this, but wasn't Munich where Frank was operating out of?'

Jane blew out through tight lips. She stood and closed her eyes.

A fire. In Flemingstraße.

That was Frank. And Wolfgang. That's why she hadn't had an email. Or a follow-up call. He was in the fire.

Oh my God.

Frank.

Her eyes were wide open now.

The Americans could send the marines into Venezuela - or whatever they had on call. They were running this now. Apart from briefing those who needed to know, there was little more she could do.

Much more important - she had a member of SIS in trouble.

'Get hold of whoever you need to in Munich. Let's find out what's happened to Frank - and Wolfgang. Now!'

Colin didn't wait for any further instructions. He was out of Jane's office in no time.

Jane walked to the window. She placed a flat hand on the pane. It wasn't cold. Triple glazing and bomb-proof glass put paid to the temperature differential. But it felt good to be almost in touch with the outside world.

She placed her second hand on the glass, joining the first. She leant against the window, her head dropping until her forehead rested on the pane. She closed her eyes again.

Frank was in trouble.

And where was Sam?

Every day she put SIS officers in harm's way. Every day someone was in danger - somewhere. But Frank was just an analyst. Far from home. Away from Babylon's comfort blanket. She'd sent him to Germany with a flippancy that now seemed reckless.

What was I thinking?

And, Sam. She wasn't even on her books.

Sam Green. In deepest Venezuela.

Was she ahead of the marines?

It seemed incredibly unlikely. But, she knew never to underestimate Sam.

Chapter 18

Sam was sitting on a concrete floor with her back to a plastered wall, her knees to her chest and her arms holding them tightly. To look at her, anyone would think she was cold.

She was rocking gently. Trying to relieve the pain. New pain. Pain delivered by Ralph Bell after he and his thuggish pal had thrown her into the cell a couple of hours ago. As she'd lain on the floor Bell had rolled her over, untied her hands and taken off her gag. Then, with the heel of his boot, he exposed her stomach. And then he had kicked her.

Smack!

Right on her old wound. Directly on top of the scar tissue. He knew where to hit her. He knew of her previous injuries. He'd exploited the wound years before - in Sierra Leone. A thump in the stomach that time. Bell was ex-CIA. They knew everything. It would have been on her file: stomach wound; mortar round; Afghanistan.

The pain felt like something inside had broken. It didn't come in waves. It gnawed at her as if the old wound were open and someone was poking about inside with a pencil. She wanted to pass out, but her brain wouldn't shut down. It was

517

overactive. It was always overactive. She hated it. Hated herself. Hated her pathetic, abnormal life. Chasing about like *James* sodding *Bond* - getting people hurt. Getting people killed.

She was crying - again. This time it was definitely an accompaniment to the pain. It wasn't about where she found herself. Or what they might do to her. She couldn't care less about what was going to happen. It was an irrelevance, pushed to the periphery of her mind by the pain. If she had a rope and a spare rafter, she'd do the job for them. Anything to stop the agony.

Pain and tears. And an overactive brain.

Which meant, as she was awake, she couldn't stop herself taking in everything about the room. It was a large cellar, possibly eight-by-eight metres. New build. A couple of years old? Painted white, or close to. There was a single, dull wall-light encased in glass. No windows.

And then there were the cages. Straight from a Wild West jail. Two cells. Floor to ceiling iron bars, along the length of wall furthest from the only door - which was metal. There was nowhere to pee. And no water.

Sam was in one cell. Austin was in the other, separated by more iron bars. He was unconscious. Initially she thought he was dead, but in the half-light she spotted his chest rising and falling a tiny fraction - at a rate that couldn't be good for him. He was lying on the polished concrete floor. On his side. The tourniquet was still holding. From what Sam could see there wasn't any new blood. He'd come to find where his son had died. And now he was going to join him. She was certain of that.

Light. The door opened. Sam wanted to be bothered. Wanted to feel scared. Wanted her overactive brain to come up with a plan. To try something. To do something. But the pain was in charge. It wasn't taking orders from anyone. She was at its mercy.

Fuck it.

It was Bell.

Why didn't that register?

Normally fear and Bell came together. Skipping hand in hand through the horrors of life. Not now. Her body was trying to cope with something that was much more immediate.

He had a set of keys in his hand and was heading for her door.

Clunk.

The door was open. She expected her legs to close tighter to her chest; for her head to bury into her knees. But neither of those things happened. Instead she just stared at him blankly - a dripping candle wax of tears staining her face.

'Hello, Green.'

His voice was deep and resonant. He'd only spoken to her once before today. It was in the hostel. Before Kurt Manning had drugged her and her UN pal, Henry, and then set the place on fire.

That's when he'd thumped her in the stomach - in exactly the same place as he'd kicked her earlier on. He'd pointed at his face, which was a mess after Sam had smacked him with a plank of wood, and said, 'That was for this.' She remembered it as if it were five minutes ago. She remembered everything.

My overactive brain.

She looked blankly at Bell; he was silhouetted by the dim light. A monster. He was dressed the same as earlier. Same gilet. Same bulge covering his handgun.

Sam didn't bother trying to reply. She wouldn't have been able to get the words out.

'Cat got your tongue? Never mind Green. I have some news. Today is a red-letter day.' He was standing over her, his feet slightly apart. One hand was formed into a fist; the other was massaging it. 'In a few minutes, Green, we are going to commit an act so inflammatory that it will stop the world. Nothing will ever be the same again. It is a great day.'

He paused. Was he expecting a reply? An hurrah? Some gold stars? She'd have said something comical if all the receptors in her mind weren't focused on a stomach that was shouting louder than she could bear.

'But, much more important - I have a more pressing job. There is a hole outside with your name on it.' He separated his hands so that they were about a foot apart. He then drove his fist into the open hand.

He did it again.

She hadn't changed her blank expression. What did he want? Was he expecting her to plead?

I would if I could be bothered.

Her lack of emotion was bothering him. He smacked his fist against his hand again.

'Well, Green?'

Well, what? Come on, for fuck's sake. Get this over with.

Bell lost it.

With one hand he grabbed her by the hair and, in a single movement, lifted her onto her feet. She was a large doll. Floppy. Dangling from his arm by her hair - her feet only just on the floor.

Smack!

He hit her in the stomach with a force that might as well have killed her. She thought she screamed. Maybe she was still screaming? She didn't know. Whatever, the noise that she emitted surprised him. He let go of her - she fell to her knees. And then onto all fours. *Fuck!* That couldn't happen again. It was never going to happen again. It was a sensation off the scale. It broke all barriers. Yes, she wanted to die - to end all the suffering. But that didn't include experiencing that terror again.

She crawled. Quickly. A scamper on all fours. To the corner of the cell. It was only a couple of metres, but it put distance between her and Bell. Between her, his fist and the broken threshold.

She turned, still on all fours. Was she still screaming? Was it panting? New colours. New sounds. It was psychedelic. She'd had enough morphine to know what that was like. This was a new drug. They should bottle it. Someone would make a fortune.

Bell was dazed. He was shaking his head. He turned to her and, in a voice that Sam didn't recognise - it was now slow and distorted - said, 'You don't like that Green? Well, well.'

He walked towards her; fist smacking his open hand.

That was enough. She'd had as much as she could bear. This wasn't happening. It wasn't going to happen again.

Sam waited until he was a few feet from her. And then she launched herself at him. She knew it wouldn't end well for her. She was spent - he was fit and strong. She was broken - he was upright and unhurt. He was a man - she was a pathetic, weak woman. She got that. It never meant more than it did now.

They met in a bundle. She with bent back and straight arms - her hands on his chest. If she had proper female fingernails they would have been scratching at him. She was probably screaming - like a fanatical witch; she couldn't be sure. It was a blur. Her arms collapsed quickly, but

522

her momentum kept her going - her broken cheek, followed by the weight of her shoulders, smashed against his chest. Sparkly stars filled her vision.

Bell was surprised by the ferocity of the attack; he almost toppled over. She was pushing him backwards, and he was stepping back to accommodate the thrust of the possessed woman. In three steps he was against the bars of the second cell.

Sam pushed and pushed, but Bell wasn't going anywhere. Was she trying to squeeze him through the gap in the bars? It made no sense.

It makes no sense.

Peripherally she saw him reach for his pistol. It was over. He was raising his arm to bring the weapon down on the top of her head. She flinched as she pushed. Pushed as she flinched. She was tiring. It had only been a second's worth of effort, maybe two. But the tank was empty. The adrenalin was shot. The pain was back - on steroids.

But Bell didn't strike her. Instead, the handgun flew across the room and smacked against the wall. As she lost energy and pushed less, the man didn't fall - she wasn't assaulted as she expected. Instead his hands raised to his throat. Sam slipped some more, but Bell remained upright, his legs jumping and starting.

And now there was a new noise. Gurgling. Panting.

What?

Sam took a knee in the face from Bell, but it seemed unintentional. She moved back, away from his legs, her emotions flitting like a dying fly.

What is happening?

Another kick from Bell. To her chest. Not the side with the broken ribs. But she'd have a bruise.

She had to get out of harm's way.

The pistol!

Sam dragged herself left to the wall. It was only a couple of paces, but it took a monumental effort.

Quicker! Damn you. Quicker!

She had the gun in her hands, she turned, propping herself up against the wall. It was one movement. Instinctively she took aim ...

... and then all was clear.

Bell was being pinned against the railings by Austin; they were both at full height.

Austin had taken off his tourniquet. When Sam had presented Bell's neck, Austin must have threaded it through the bars? Bell had both hands on the rope, but he was losing the battle. Austin was wearing the grimace of a demonic man. He was dribbling - his body was shaking. But he was winning.

He's winning.

Bell was thrashing now, his eyes wide and alive. Sam watched this over the foresight of the pistol. She had it trained on Bell's chest. If Austin fell, so would Bell. She would make sure of that. *Thump! Thump!* from the chamber of the pistol. It would all be over.

But she didn't need to shoot. Bell's thrashing was his final act. His body slowed. His legs twitched. His arms fell. And then he was still.

Austin was panting; dribbling. His mouth was open. Out of his mouth came an incongruous whine. He wasn't letting go. Not till the job was done.

Without dropping her aim, Sam glanced at Austin's leg. It was bleeding again. She had to get him settled. Arrest the bleeding. It was the only way to keep him alive.

'Austin.' It was a pathetic attempt at communication. Austin stuck with his whine in response. It was as though she wasn't in the room.

'Austin!' She screamed. He looked across at her - startled.

She was just about to give him the good news that Bell was dead, when they got a second visitation.

The doorway was filled by Bell's pal. The second thug. The man who had shot Austin.

'What the fuck!' He reached for his own pistol.

Sam was bored by the continuous effort. She hurt like never before. She had a friend of hers to patch up - a man who had killed her nemesis. A man who had certainly saved her life.

And now there was a new challenge. A man with a gun.

Fuck it.

She changed her aim. It took a millisecond. There were bars between her and the target - but that was the same for both of them. 70/30? In the shooter's favour.

His handgun was rising, now at waist height.

But Sam was well ahead of him. And she was sitting - a much steadier firing position. Everything was going her way.

Foresight - rear sight - chest.

Bang! Bang! Bang!

A triple tap.

Ping! Thud! Thud!

One ricochet. Two rounds through the gap. 66/33. She'd been right. Two out of three. Good drills.

The thug froze, his pistol not even close to being in the aim position. He stepped sideward - and then fell backwards through the door frame, leaving just his boots in the room.

Sam kept her aim on the door. The smell of cordite filled the room. The sound now dissipated. But it had been loud. Loud enough to get someone else's attention. If there were more, they'd be on their way now.

Thud. Austin had fallen to the floor. Bell followed suit. Two bodies. One dead. One dying. She had work to do.

I have to move.

Now.

She took two deep breaths and with energy she found from a reserve she didn't know she had, she stood. She was unsteady; she used the wall and then the bars for support.

The first thing she did was check Bell for a pulse. Nothing. *Good.*

She took his keys, felt for any spare ammunition, but found none. She studied Bell's pistol. Browning 9mm. A sound weapon. Big magazine. Either 13 or 15 rounds. Experts don't fill them to max; a stressed spring can cause a stoppage. There were probably nine rounds left. *Tick.*

Next was the thug; she staggered across to him, steadying herself on the door frame. He was on his back. He had two entry wounds in the middle of his chest. Blood seeped out from under him. She checked his pulse.

Dead.

She picked up his pistol, a Glock 17. Another 9mm. Seventeen rounds. The clue was in the title. She checked for additional ammunition. None.

Austin.

Sam found the key for his cell, let herself in and re-secured his tourniquet, taking 30-second breathers every so often. He was out of it again. She put him in the recovery position, with his wounded leg on top - and checked his pulse. It was weak. But he had one.

'Annie.'

What? Austin was muttering.

'Annie.'

Shit, that's me.

Austin was talking to her. Whispering.

'Shhh. Austin. Everything's fine.' *No, it isn't.* 'I need to go and get some help.' Sam was struggling to get her words out; finding help would be a lottery win.

'Listen. Please.' He stuttered. His eyes were closed. Sam put her ear close to his mouth.

'My son didn't die in a plane crash.' He coughed, scrunching his face up as he did. 'He was murdered. Because he was flying a Reaper.' He opened his eyes - she was so close she almost couldn't focus on them. He had the look of, 'Do you know what a Reaper is?' He was waiting for confirmation.

'A US military drone. Perfect for unmanned reconnaissance and then destroying a target.'

He closed his eyes, nodding gently in recognition.

'The Reaper found a place. Two buildings - big satellite dish. It sent the Reaper off course. Don't know why. Here. I think we're here.'

He was exhausted, and now mumbling something that she couldn't understand. She didn't want to tell him that she had most of that. That she could probably add something to the story.

'Thanks, Austin. Thanks. Rest now.' She touched her lips and transferred her kiss to his cheek. His eyes were closed. She didn't think there was a lot going on behind the lids.

She was about to stand, when she had a thought. She took the Browning and put it in his right hand. There was a 72% chance that he was right-handed; this time a useful fact. If he were awake, he could have a go at defending himself.

If he were awake.

She stood, turned, almost passed out, stabilised herself and headed for the door.

SIS Headquarters, Vauxhall, London

Jane's phone rang. It was the DD.

'Excuse me, Colin.' She picked up the phone. Colin motioned to Jane as to whether he should leave - or not. She shook her head.

'Jane Baker.'

'We have just launched 28 Tomahawks from the eastern Med. Time to target is 45 minutes. I don't have a real-time readout, but initial reports have all of the missiles flying on their prepared route. Nothing has gone rogue. The Navy is on the case. They'll let me know if any one of them diverts.'

'And the ... marines? En route to the village? If that's who's in the air.'

There was a snort on the other end of the phone.

'I couldn't possibly comment. Time to target is 52 minutes. Then they have to find the control centre. But, unless we've missed something, these missiles look like they're going to do the job they've been sent to do. So maybe we're out of trouble - for now.'

Jane wasn't sure. Something was bothering her. Something wasn't right.

'Uh, OK. Well, that's good. Will you keep me in the loop?'

'Yes, Jane, of course. I'll phone you as soon as we have anything. OK?'

'Sure. Thanks Linden.'

Jane hung up.

She looked at Colin. He looked tired.

'Coffee?' He said.

She let out a short laugh. She needed a wee as it was. Coffee went straight through her.

'Thanks Colin. Not at the moment.'

'You look perplexed. Can I help?'

Jane stood. And stretched. She walked over to a whiteboard she had in the corner of her office. She sketched out a map of the Middle East. She drew two comic battleships and a submarine in the eastern Med. And from them she drew the trajectories of the cruise missiles to Syria - pretty much due east. It was, she reckoned, a 500-mile trip. At 550 miles-per-hour (she'd done her cruise missile revision earlier in the afternoon), it was less than an hour's flight time.

She stood back. Colin had joined her.

'Talk to me.' He said politely.

Colin was only just coming up to speed with where they were. He'd been in and out of the office a couple of times with updates about Frank. Frank was OK. He had second-degree burns to both arms and one leg - all of which was manageable. He was now sedated and out of harm's way. Wolfgang, however, was very poorly. He had third-degree burns to 40% of his body and, due to smoke inhalation, had upper-respiratory thermal injuries, carbon-monoxide poisoning and, likely, other toxicity complications. It was, according to Colin, touch and go. Unfortunately the woman whom Wolfgang had rescued from the blaze had succumbed to her injuries. Apparently, Frank had pulled out an older woman from the fire. She was going to be fine.

Jane focused.

It took her no more than five minutes to explain the GPS issue. For brevity, she left out The Church of the White Cross's involvement, but gave Colin the Venezuelan details.

She finished with, 'But, so far, the cruise missiles are heading to the Syrian target as planned. None are diverting to a secondary target.'

Colin didn't speak for a moment. He chewed the end of his thumb.

'That's what they're telling you.'

'What, the Americans?'

'No - the cruise missiles. If I've understood you correctly, someone in Venezuela is sending rogue positional detail to at least one of the missiles. That's correct?'

'Yes.'

And?

Colin took the whiteboard marker from Jane. He drew as he spoke.

'The missile is following a preplanned route. From GPS coordinate to GPS coordinate. But, if you tell it it's here ...', he put a dot to the left of the trajectory Jane had drawn, 'it will compensate. Eventually thinking that it's back on track.' He drew a different route heading south, away from Jane's route. 'It thinks it's following its original course. But it isn't. Then Venezuela diverts it again ...', another dot to the left, 'it compensates again.' He extended the trajectory further south. 'It's now off track by twice as much distance to the right. But, it *thinks* it's on track. Following its predetermined route.'

Jane was on it now. She got it. It was what had been bothering her all along. She just couldn't articulate it.

'Just because the missile is reporting that it's on track, it doesn't necessarily mean that it is. Because it's working on rogue data! You fool it, it thinks it is moving back to its predetermined route and reports that everything's OK. But it isn't. It's off beam. It's genius. Fool proof!' She said.

'Unless you're tracking the missile from without, say an airborne early-warning system, you'd never know. You would believe what it was telling you. And it's telling you that everything's OK with its world.'

'Airborne radar - like an AWACS?' Jane's tiredness had gone. She still needed a wee, though. 'Both the RAF and USAF have the whole region covered, 24/7. Their systems would have picked up a stray cruise missile. But, without an alert the operators won't necessarily be interrogating the trace - they'll be looking at something else, maybe Russian ships in the eastern Med.' She paused for a split second. 'Unless they're having a particularly good day.' She moved back to her desk. 'I'll get back to the Americans. You get hold of the RAF. Let's see if these missiles are actually headed where they say they're headed.'

5°16'39.8"N 67°25'48.7"W, Amazonas Jungle, Venezuela

Sam thought she might be stepping into the light, but it was as dim in the corridor as it had been in the cell. It looked like there was an exit directly ahead of her. About 15 metres away. There were four doors on either side of the corridor. The one at the end was slightly ajar. *That's the outside?*

She took a breath and squeezed the pistol grip; an unnecessary check to make sure the weapon was still in her hand. Then she stepped off. She had decided to try all the doors on the left - but ignore the ones on the right. She could only manage one side. There was some logic to it. If the four on the left were locked, the likelihood was that the ones on the right were locked too. She couldn't do all eight. She couldn't.

Door one. Locked.

Breathe.

She staggered down the corridor a few metres further.

Door two. Locked.

More staggering.

Door three. Locked.

There's a message here.

Door four. Locked.

Fuck! The pain overcame her. She bent double; straight arms to her knees keeping her back straight, releasing some pressure on her stomach. She was blubbering. Her head was rocking up and down, her tears splashing on the floor. She couldn't go on.

I can't go on.

She had to go on. The CIA had issued an 'immediate' level 5 threat - you couldn't badge it any worse. And that threat was being controlled from here.

And Austin was dying. That was almost more important. She had to try and get help.

I have to go on.

Sam stood slowly, using the wall for support. Step. Step. She made it to the door at the end of the corridor. *Breathe.* She pushed the door further ajar, but only far enough. She couldn't waste any energy.

She slipped through.

Into the dark of the jungle. The moonlight she had used to apply Austin's tourniquet was now gone. All that was left was blackness.

As she let her eyes adjust as best they could to the dark, she listened.

She heard the usual jungle sounds. Buzzing and chirping. She'd spent a month in Belize at the army jungle-training centre. She knew the noises of the jungle.

But there was another sound.

A hum? A mechanical sound. *A generator?*

She wasn't sure.

She looked forward. Her pupils were letting in more light. She could start to make out large objects. Austin said two buildings. And a satellite dish.

There it is.

The second building was ahead of her. And against the inky dark of the jungle and the overcast sky she spotted the satellite dish. It was big; no, it was huge. Easily big enough to talk to a satellite and send a battleship on a collision course. She looked left and right. There was the Hilux. But there was nothing else. Two buildings and a satellite dish. And a Hilux. Not much.

The gap from where she stood to the second building was unthinkable. It was 25 metres - maybe 30. There was no handrail. No support. Just some gravel. She'd never make it. An extraordinarily sharp pain from below reminded her of her injuries. Telling her it was futile.

I have to go on.

Sam staggered. One step at a time. Short paces. No more than 15 to 20 centimetres. Left. Right. Left. Right.

She built up a rhythm. *Left, right, left, right.* It was working. She was halfway across. *Left, right, left, right.* Just like in training. The drill sergeant screaming at them.

'You. Green! You march like a fucking girl!'

She laughed to herself. Humour from delirium. *Left, right, left, right.* Her feet dragged. She caught a foot on a rise in the gravel.

I'm falling!

No. No. I'm not. Although her core strength had been ripped to shreds by whatever internal injury she was carrying, somehow ... *somehow* ... she kept her footing and stayed upright.

More pain. Some tears.

Come on!

Left, right, left, right. Progress.

She put out her left hand. She toppled forward. It was only a couple of centimetres and then she had a flat hand against the wall of the second building. She had made it. Shuffling like an effing girl.

Breathe.

The door. Into the second building. Apart from a roof decorated with a satellite dish as big as a golf course, the building looked the same as the one she had just left. Single storey. No windows so far.

She reached for the door handle. And turned it. Nothing. It was locked.

Keys.

She took out Bell's keys. There were four on the ring. She discounted the two that she knew had opened the cells. Two more. *One for each main door?*

Success first time. The key turned in the lock. She removed the key; put the ring back in her pocket. And opened the door - just far enough to let her in. The effort was monumental. The pain up a notch. But she was in.

The corridor was the same. The lighting was the same. But there was one major difference. There was only one door on the right, not four; and it was fitted with a chest-height glass panel. And then three windows. Window - door - window - window. Each window was gently lit from activity within. *Was the right-hand side of the building the control centre?*

She edged forward, the door closing behind her.

Step. Shuffle. Step. The wall providing a frame to balance against.

First window. It was reinforced glass. A very thin metal mesh between two panes.

She peeked in.

Bingo.

The room was the length of the building. There were two desks - both were manned. Both were equipped with large computer screens; maybe 50-inchers. There were banks of computers - and trunking. All over the place. In the far corner Sam spotted a kitchen. A sink and a fridge. The place was workmanlike. Functional. But unfinished?

Ops. Need to talk about equipment.

But it wasn't unfinished. Not for the job it was intended for. Both men were staring at screens that were alive with information.

In a few minutes, Green, we are going to commit an act so inflammatory that it will stop the world. Nothing will ever be the same again. It is a great day.

Bell had been clear. Whatever was happening here was so severe, so critical that it was going to be world-changing.

Two 50-inch screens, some computers, trunking and an eff-off satellite dish.

She couldn't see the screens. She needed to see the screens; get into the room and put a stop to whatever madness they were enacting.

Try the door.

Sam couldn't risk being seen. She slid down the wall, buckling her body, until her head was below window height. The pain level intensified.

Oh, God ...

And then she passed out.

Sam woke. She had no idea how long she'd been out for. It could have been a few seconds. It could have been hours. In the interval nothing had changed. Crippling pain. Three windows. One door. And an act so inflammatory that it was going to stop the world.

Sam didn't need to ask herself any supplementaries. She didn't need reminding of where she was, or what she had been going to do. She woke up and immediately someone pressed 'Play'. Like a mechanical bunny. She was off again.

She got herself onto all fours. *Shit that hurts.* And crawled.

Shuffle - shuffle - shuffle. It was made more difficult because she had the thug's pistol in her hand. She pushed it along the concrete in front of her.

Shuffle - shuffle.

Door.

Come on girl. Stand now. *And no passing out.*

Her body responded. She stood, pressing herself against the door frame. She pushed her head forward and looked in.

She could see both screens clearly.

It took fewer than three seconds before she had it. The screen on the right was all numbers, codes and coordinates. She had no idea what was going on there. The screen on the left was self-explanatory. It was a map of most of the Saudi Peninsula. It extended as far north as Cyprus, and as far south as the Yemeni border. In the west it took in the Red Sea and eastern Egypt; to the east, it finished on a line that cut Saudi Arabia in two.

Superimposed on the map was a red line - it was slightly crooked. It started in the eastern Med and finished halfway down the western edge of Saudi Arabia. The line was in segments, passing through way points, each of which was marked with a number. On the top right of the screen was an inset box. It was big, probably ten-by-ten centimetres. It was a positional blow-up - of the delivery vehicle.

What exactly?

What can you control by GPS to hit a target and create an event that would stop the world?

Not Austin's son's Reaper - *for sure.* Something much more destructive.

A penny tumbled ...

A missile. From the eastern Mediterranean. US Navy?

Yes.

She knew exactly what it was.

A cruise missile.

Fired by the US Navy

That's what it was. The US Navy had more cruise missiles in the eastern Med than the Brits had in their whole inventory.

And right now it was a third of the way down the Saudi coast, its route starting southeast of Cyprus, flying over the unpopulated Sinai Peninsula, and into the Red Sea. If you were on holiday in Sharm El Sheikh, weren't drunk and had your eyes open about 20 minutes ago, you might have spotted a deliverer of death flying overhead.

She knew the target as well. Where the crooked red line ran out.

It was obvious. Inspired.

Bell was right. If someone didn't stop this, in - there was a clock running down on the second screen, she squinted to see the detail - 21 minutes and 07 seconds' time, the world was going to stop and nothing would ever be the same again. The target was spectacular and the effect of a single cruise-missile strike would stop the world.

Sam tried the door whilst keeping an eye on the two operators.

It was locked.

Breathe.

She tried all four keys - each time keeping an eye on the operators.

None of the keys worked. The men remained glued to their screens.

Shit.

Nineteen minutes.

Oh, what the hell.

She stood back from the door. Took aim with the pistol. And fired two rounds at the door lock.

Bang! Ping! Bang! Ping!

The noise filled the corridor - and it filled all of the space between her ears. The ringing remained with her. Smoke from the barrel briefly obscured her view into the room.

The operators were looking now. One was on his feet. He was heading to the portion of the wall between the first window and where she was now.

Sam tried the door.

It was still locked.

Shit.

A new sound now. A loud, mechanical, circular sound.

Metal blinds. Dropping down from inside. Across the door. She looked left and right.

And the windows.

Metal blinds. The operators were barricading themselves in. All they had to do was withstand ... she had dropped her head so her eyeline was just in front of the falling blind ... 18 minutes and 20 seconds of her messing about with a 9 millimetre. And then it would all be over.

Sam Green. A 9 mm pistol. And the world stopping.

Who did she think she was?

Chapter 19

Headquarters SIS, Vauxhall, London

'We've got it.' Colin had burst into the Jane's office He was in front of her desk in a single stride.

'What?' Jane was putting together an update for the JIC. The Chief had just left after a briefing and was back in his office. The senior committee staff (and the Prime Minister) were on call. Their teams were working through options should a rogue cruise missile hit something it wasn't supposed to. The good news was the DD had told her that the Tomahawks were all fitted with conventional munitions - nothing nuclear. He hadn't been explicit, but it was likely that the missile contained bomblets, or cluster munitions. Whatever - the effect at the target end was likely to be carnage.

'What?' Jane's reply was sharp. They needed something.

'The RAF have got an E-3 Sentry, AWACS, in a holding pattern off the coast of northern Egypt. They were following the US strike. Twenty-eight missiles in the air. Twenty-seven flew to their target in Syria. One diverted south, over the Sinai Peninsula and is currently halfway down the Red Sea.

Brrr. Brrr.

It was the DD. Jane put her hand up to stop Colin mid-sentence for the second time in half an hour. With her free hand she pressed the speaker button.

'Jane?'

'Yes. You're on speaker.'

'We have a rogue missile.'

'We know. Heading south down through the Red Sea.'

There was momentary silence.

'We think we know the target.'

In the 15 seconds that Colin had been in the office Jane had already done the analysis. She'd got it as soon as Colin had said where the missile was, and which direction it was travelling. It was obvious - now. If you, The Church of the White Cross, wanted to send a message to Islam, a message so severe, so cruel, that your enemy had to react, there was only one target.

Mecca.

Muhammad's birthplace and the site of his first revelation of the Quran. Islam's holiest city. Smack dead centre of every Muslim's beating heart.

When praying, all Muslims faced in its direction: the *bayt Allāh*.

If the missile hit its target, the infidels were waging war on *The Holy Kaaba* - Islam's *House of God*; the building, *The Cube*, was at the centre of Islam's most sacred mosque.

A US missile - fired from a US battleship. Striking Mecca. Destroying *The Holy Kaaba*. Then ramifications were unthinkable.

Revelation 16:16. And he gathered them together into a place called in the Hebrew tongue Armageddon.

That would surely follow. It may not happen at the site of an ancient Israeli city. But many Christians didn't believe that anyway. They believed that it would happen throughout the world. Where God would smite all governments and save only those who submit to his rulership.

'Mecca.' Jane didn't say in a triumphalist way. Like, 'We Brits are just as good at this as you.' She was flat. Downhearted.

Again the line was quiet for a second.

'Sure. If we don't stop this missile-strike, the world will wake up tomorrow and everything will be different.

'Armageddon.'

'Agreed. That's one way of putting it.'

'Can your Navy stop it?'

'Nope. They've tried. They think someone tampered with the override software. It's running on orders from somewhere else now.'

'Venezuela' It was a throwaway comment. Unnecessary. 'Can you shoot it down?'

'Negative. We picked it up too late. Fifteen minutes earlier and we could have got the Saudis to launch an F15 from Jeddah. But their notice to move is 20 minutes. It's just too late.'

'How long do we have. And where are the marines?' Their only hope.

'It's not the marines. It's "The Unit"; Delta Force. They're 12 minutes out. We reckon time-to-target for the missile is a max 15 minutes. They have the smallest of chances. They need to find the village and then they'll circle outwards until they spot the dish. It's incredibly unlikely that they'll make it. But they'll try.'

'Can they destroy it?'

'They have enough firepower on two choppers to take down a small town. They're good at that.'

'Fingers crossed, then.' Jane hadn't the energy to offer encouragement. She knew that in less than 15 minutes time her world was going to get very complex indeed.

The phone went dead.

'Bugger.' Was Colin's comment.

'That's putting it mildly, Colin.'

5°16'39.8"N 67°25'48.7"W, Amazonas Jungle, Venezuela

Sam was counting down. Fifteen minutes multiplied by 60 seconds was 900. That's all she had to stop the madness.

Nine hundred seconds.

She'd subtracted three minutes from the 18 she'd seen on the screen. In her head those three minutes would give the Tomahawk time to realise that it was no longer receiving instructions from a rogue source. Instead, it needed to lock onto the original GPS satellites, work out it was in the wrong place, turn around and then make its way back to its original target – probably Syria. Or as far as its fuel supply would take it.

That gave her 15 minutes. Nine hundred seconds.

That was 47 seconds ago.

853 ... 852 ... 851. Her brain was counting down in the background. It had a mind of its own.

She couldn't take the missile down from the control room - they'd locked her out. So, she'd have to do some damage somewhere between the control room and the dish.

835 ... 834 ... 833.

In her pain-induced haze, her first thought was to look for the building's power. Stop the thing from working altogether. *No; that's not right.* If she had been putting the place together she'd have a seamless power backup system. Batteries. A second generator. Something bomb-proof.

That left her with only one guaranteed way to bring the missile down.

The dish.

She'd made it outside. Opening the door was an effort, her insides screaming for relief.

Black as ink.

799 ... 798 ... 797.

Her eyes were adjusting. It was still mostly black, but now there were a few deep blues and dark greens.

Come on!

She felt beneath her feet. *Still gravel.* She took a long step one way. *Gravel.* Turned. Then the other. *Gravel.* That made sense. A French drain all the way round the building. It rained a lot here. Standing water wouldn't be good.

Sam could manage gravel. Just. Maybe.

Breathe.

Two choices. Left or right. Perhaps there'd be some trunking or cabling coming out of the building. She could shoot at it. Do some damage. Break the connection.

Move left.

It was the professional's choice. The pistol was in her right hand. At a corner, she wouldn't need to expose her torso - just half a head and her arm. Offering a smaller target. She may be in excruciating pain, but her mind somehow remained uncluttered. Apart from the counting down.

745 ... 744 ... 743.

She was still thinking. Her brain was still overactive.

And she was sweating. It was probably in the lower 80s. Which was hot for during the day in the UK. But she was acclimatised? Her core temperature and the sweating was something else. This was a fever. Her body's reaction to the beating - to what was broken inside.

Thinking about it all made her giddy.

But her brain wouldn't stop counting down.

712 ... 711 ...710.

Sam stumbled to her left. One pace after another. In ten paces she was at the corner of the building. She carefully stuck her head round. Her eyes were better adjusted, but it was still dark. A dark wall heading off into the dark distance; the wall's end merging with the blackness of the jungle.

No windows. She could see that. An unnecessary expense. What else?

Hang on. Three quarters of the way down the wall was an object. It was fuzzy - out of focus. She squinted her eyes. *Nope.* She couldn't make it out. It was something other than nothing. A box? Maybe ... a ladder of sorts? Onto the roof?

Can I climb a ladder?

Don't be ridiculous.

651 ... 650 ... 649.

She couldn't stop the counting. It was like a runaway clock in her head. Seconds ticking away.

Breathe.

Now move.

One step, then another; her shoulders rubbing along the wall. The pistol was heavy - she let her hand drop.

Step. Step. Shuffle.

The object was in focus now. It was as she thought. A metal ladder.

Step. Shuffle. Step.

Five more steps.

586 ... 585 ... 584.

There.

Sam grabbed one of the uprights. She looked up and saw the impossible. There was no way ...

Two choices.

Continue to circumnavigate the building. *520 ... 519 ... 518.* Or attempt to climb. She reckoned she could definitely do some damage on the roof. There'd be something to shoot at. She could have a go at the dish.

She had 13 rounds left. That was unlucky. *When have I ever been superstitious?* It must be the state she was in. She almost fired off a round to make 13 become 12.

Stupid.

Think!

It would take her two minutes to get around the other side of the building. One hundred and twenty seconds. That would give her ... 370 seconds to get back round here, climb the ladder and find something breakable - and then shoot at it. That wasn't anywhere near long enough. The climb would likely kill her. She'd need time to recover if she ever made it to the top.

If she made it to the top.

Climb.

It was where the betting money was.

Sam put the barrel of the pistol down the back of her cotton trousers, and put both hands on the vertical rails.

That was a mistake.

Clump! Ping!

Fuck! She was being shot at.

Clump! Clump!

Sam was down. It was an innate reaction. As she fell, her hand reached behind her and grabbed hold of the pistol grip. She was in a pile. Like a rag doll. The fall had winded her and sent spasms of terror through every last inch of her flesh.

Was she hit? There was so much pain going on, she could have been. She didn't know.

Play dead.

The *clumps* she heard were the breach explosions of three low-velocity rounds; almost certainly from a pistol.

They weren't from a rifle. Rifle bullets travel faster than the speed of sound. She'd have heard a *crack!*, then a *thump!* The crack would have been the round breaking the sound barrier as it whizzed past her - a thump, the noise from the explosion in the barrel trying hard to catch up with the bullet. *Crack! Thump!*

There was no *crack*. Just the *clump* from the chamber of a handgun.

High-velocity versus low-velocity.

Not that it mattered that much. Either could kill you.

But, and it was a big 'but' in her favour, pistols were inaccurate. They're self-protection weapons. Best at anywhere between one and ten metres. Anything further than that and they are woefully inaccurate. Mix in the dark, and you might as well throw a poisoned spear.

The shooter had fired off three rounds. The first had ricocheted off the metal ladder. The other two hadn't hit metal. Maybe one was lodged in her?

She had no idea. But it hadn't killed her. Yet.

Breathe. Yes, she should do that.

389 ... 388 ... 387.

Still counting down. The soundtrack to her current version of hell.

But counting down was good. She was still alive.

And counting.

And playing dead.

If Sam had tried to run, or returned fire, the shooter would have fired again. And again. She'd have lost that race; come second in a fight. Easy.

But playing dead bought her time. Time to think. *351 ... 350 ... 349.* Time to prepare.

She had instinctively fallen facing the shooter. Her body so badly wanted to fall the other way. To face away from the threat. But that would have left her sightless; and defenceless. Now she was in a heap, with her Glock still in her hand.

And with that hand close to her chest - and with one eye open, she had one chance. Just the one.

A blob moved towards her. It was difficult to see, but she thought it had its arms out straight, probably holding a handgun. Pointing at her. Poised. It was a big blob. A man. Ready for action. If it had been her, she probably would have got to close range and fired again. Just to be sure. Never assume an enemy is down unless you're absolutely sure. If in doubt, finish the job.

The man was a couple of metres away now. He stood still for a second. *Good drills*. Waiting. Checking for a noise - seeing if the body was breathing.

Play dead.

Sam breathed as shallowly as she could.

The man took another step forward.

And then made a mistake that lost him this particular battle.

He assumed that Sam was gone. He went down on his haunches. He then slipped his pistol into his belt and leant forward to feel Sam's neck for a pulse.

Before he had chance to complete his check of Sam vitals, she answered his question.

In one movement she cocked her hand ever so slightly so that the short barrel of her pistol was pointing at the man's crotch - and fired. Twice.

Bang! Bang!

The professional's choice.

He went down in a splurge of screams. Sam's pain was momentarily banished to the back of her mind. She was up on all fours. The man was thrashing about, his hands holding his crotch. Sam couldn't see any detail, but she suspected there would be a lot of blood.

Enough to kill him?

She didn't know. She had chosen the man's crotch because it was the closest thing to the barrel of her pistol. She didn't want to kill him - she hated hurting anything. But needs must. If he were lucky, he might just get away with a high-pitched voice for the rest of his life. So be it.

He was still writhing. And cussing.

In one convulse he turned his body to the left. Sam seized the opportunity and took his pistol from his belt. A quick scan. Another Browning 9mm. *Good.*

With the noise of screams and swearing ringing in her ears, she turned to the ladder.

329 ... 328 ... 327.

Numbers. She had no idea how that worked.

Both pistols in the back of my trousers.

Check.

Climb.

Sam reached up and grabbed the handrails.

Pain. Lots of it.

The screaming from beside her had turned to moans. The man was not getting up.

One foot on the first rung.

Stand.

Shit!

Dizziness. Her world was spinning.

Breathe.

She then had the conversation she often had with herself when she was running.

Listen, Sam. The quicker you run - the quicker you get to the end - the quicker the pain stops.

It was that simple. She had to climb the ladder as fast as she could bear. Get to the top - and rest.

Climb.

Stand. Second foot on the same rung. Done. Lift that foot up. Stand. Second to join it.

No. Too much pain. It was everywhere. In her chest - in her stomach. Down one leg.

Her tears were constant. She sniffed. The moans from the injured man were hardly an encouragement.

First foot, new rung. *Come on!* Stand. Second leg up to join the first. New step. Stand. Pain. Waves of it.

Sam looked up. It was a stairway to heaven. It was endless. There was no way …

Next foot, new rung.

Come on!

Stand. Second leg up.

Go again.

It was too much. She pulled herself tight to the ladder. She gripped it with all her might. And then she needed a pee. *Why now?* Had she just wet herself? She didn't know. Every nerve receptor was on fire. You could have cut off her leg and the sensation wouldn't have changed.

298 … 297 … 296.

Foot. Step.

Foot. Step. Pain. Cling.

Breathe.

Foot. Step. Foot. Step. Cling.

217 … 216 … 215.

She'd lost almost a minute somewhere. She didn't have enough time. Did she?

Foot. Step. Foot. Step. Pain. Cling.

Come on!

She wanted to let go. To fall. To land in a heap. She must be eight feet up. That would do for her. It would be over. The pain and the misery would be gone.

Out of nowhere Austin flooded into her consciousness. *Save him!* It was enough.

Foot. Step. Cling. Foot. Step. Pain.

The pain.

Foot. Step. Foot. Step.

And then Sam was at the top. The railings curved over the building's ledge, secured to the roof by a couple of bolts.

Foot. Step. Crawl. Foot ... step ... *pain* ... push. Push!

Rest.

181 ... 180 ... 179.

Three minutes to ... to an event that was too horrible to contemplate. What few friends she had - Jane, Wolfgang, Frank and a couple of old army pals, their lives would be altered forever. Things would never be the same again.

Come on!

She needed more rest.

She couldn't have more rest.

Sam's face was flat against the roof. It was that bitumen and small-pebble-covering builders used on flat roofs. And it wasn't perfectly flat - her face was in a pool of water. She let the cool of the water wash over her.

151 ... 150 ... 149.

I mustn't sleep. I mustn't.

121 ... 120 ... 119.

Where did those seconds go?!

Kneel! *Now!*

Sam did as she was told.

It was a huge effort.

111 ... 110 ... 109.

The dish was just there. Right in front of her. Placed on top of a big metal box. There was gearing, girders and curved metal stanchions. A thin, metal tripod extended from the rim of the dish towards the sky. It met a couple of metres out front where there was a small box and a cone. She remembered from her physics lessons. There'd be a transceiver at the focus of the parabolic dish. A sophisticated microwave contraption. Capable of receiving and sending signals. For sending: from the focal point at the end of the tripod, projected back to the dish, bouncing off it and then up to the stars. For receiving - the opposite way: microwave signals collected from the distant stars to the dish and rebounded off the curved metal surface, focused forward to a single point. Where the transceiver was.

What do I do?

There was some cabling running down one of the tripod's arms. It looped behind the dish and into the metal box.

She should shoot that.

Crawl!

It was no more than three metres. It felt like forever.

89 ... 88 ... 87.

Sam reckoned she had about 25 rounds. Ten shots at the cabling and five at the transceiver. Then she'd regroup. She fumbled for both pistols and laid them on the roof beside her.

Sit. It was the best shooting position - if hardly the most ladylike.

Knees apart.

'Get your legs open, Green, like you're expecting a steam train!' She had no idea why she had such fond memories of her army training, she really didn't.

Elbows balanced on her knees. Elbows pushing down, knees pushing up. The perfect locked position. She picked up the first pistol.

I can't do this! Agony. Dizziness. Stars.

Focus. Rear sight - foresight - cabling.

Sam was about a metre away. She was sitting at an oblique angle to the cabling that disappeared into the box. Any ricochet would be unlikely to come back and haunt her.

Breathe.

Fire!

Bang! Bang! Bang! Bang! Bang! Bang! Bang! Bang! Bang! Bang!

The noise of the cartridge explosions was accompanied by pings from the metalwork.

She rested. The pistol was hot. Cartridge smoke filled the air. It was difficult to see if she had done any damage.

Breathe.

Change weapons. She laid the first pistol on the ground. She took hold of the second.

59 ... 58 ... 57.

She altered her aim. The pistol was now pointed at the transceiver. It was four metres away at the end of the metallic tripod, a dull-grey box against a blue/black sky. It was about as big as half a shoebox.

If she was fit and well, she'd struggle to hit it at this distance in this light. In her state ...

The smoke was clearing.

Rear sight - foresight - transceiver.

Bang!

No noise at the target end. No hit.

Slower this time.

Her eyes were filled with tears. It was no use. She released her aim and wiped away the wetness with the sleeve of her blouse.

She lifted the pistol back into the aim position.

Breathe.

Bang!

No noise from the target.

Fuck!

43 ... 42 ... 41.

She had to try harder. She would run out of time before she ran out of rounds.

Aim. *Steady.* Breathe out. Hold. Contract the trigger finger slowly. Be surprised by shot. Don't snatch. Slowly ...

Bang!

Ping!

Bingo!

She'd hit it! She had. She'd hit it!

I have!

How many rounds left?

She didn't know. She couldn't count. *Come on, girl. Think.* No. She couldn't. She tried. Tried really hard. *Nothing.*

She listened for the countdown numbers.

Come on - where are you?

No. There were no numbers. There was nothing. Just a fuzzy feeling. As though her brain was full of cotton wool. It was a strange sensation. Unusual. Nice unusual. She thought she was smiling. She was so used to clarity. Oh, and sleep - she got that, with nightmares that weren't for retelling. Clarity and nightmarish sleep. She remembered those two states. Never fuzziness. No. A calming, fluffy blanket.

Am I lying down? Was she? Is that the cool of a puddle on her cheek?

I don't know.

And what was that new noise? The one that sounded like someone chopping wood. Quickly. One chop after another. *Clump, clump, clump ...*

I don't know.

She didn't.

And that white light. The bright white light. What was that?

That's interesting. I wonder if ... could be?

Mum?

And then Sam Green knew nothing.

'Gunner! You've got that?' Captain Vince Froud pulled the Blackhawk to the left. She was at 80 feet and hovering. They'd found the satellite control centre quicker than they thought they would - at the end of their first radial sweep from the village. His nav, who was equipped with Gen 3 night vision goggles, had picked up a series of unidentified bright sparks in the jungle 350 metres away. It had taken them fifteen seconds to acquire the target. The nav now had the underslung spot on; it was lighting up the dish - just like Times Square.

He reckoned they were out of mission-critical time. He'd set the digital stopwatch on his Bell & Ross chronograph from the squadron commander's original orders. It was reading 'minus 37 seconds'. They were late on target. Just.

'Got it Captain. Hang on! There's a body on the roof. Next to the dish.' The gunner had a door-mounted, M242 Bushmaster 25mm chain gun locked and loaded with 1,000 rounds.

'Dead or alive?'

'Don't know.'

'Avoid the body if you can. Fire now!'

The noise of a circular, rattling chain gun is one of the sweetest sounds known to any aviator. At a rate of 500 rounds per minute, a box is spent in 120 seconds. At the target end, you might as well stand up, get naked and enjoy an encore.

Brrrrrrrrrrrrrrrrrrrrrrrrrrrrrrrrrrrr!

Click!

The *click* was the firing pin striking a non-existent round.

'Rounds complete!'

Smoke and cordite filled the body of the helicopter.

'Moving now!' From Vince, over the intercom.

Vince did a shimmy with the stick and the Blackhawk moved forward 15 metres. The gun smoke cleared.

'Damage report?'

'The dish is down, Captain. It's on the floor. Job done.'

Vince knew that the in-flight comms were being relayed directly to Langley and to MacDill Air Force Base. They'd pick up every word.

'Charlie-one-three, this is Charlie-one. Orange seven, now. Over.' Vince made the call to the second Blackhawk.

'Roger that, Charlie-one. Going in.'

Epilogue

Three days later

Freddie stepped off the bow of the Riva Aquarama 27 speedboat onto the beautiful, old quay at Krk. He was dressed in dark blue chinos, a crisp white double-cuff shirt with gold cufflinks, what his mother would call a 'tank top' - except she would never have seen one knitted from yellow merino wool, and a pair of blue leather, Sperry's Top-Slider deck shoes. The sun was hidden by a thick blanket of cloud, but that didn't stop him from adjusting his Wayfarers.

He felt like a million dollars. Which made sense. The 35-year-old Riva was worth almost half that. The boat's driver had strict instructions as to where to drive it to next. Freddie knew of a reliable broker in Rijeka. He would get a good price for the boat. And Freddie had something in mind that would be a good replacement. More gin palace than wooden boating shrine, but it would do. There was a nearly-new Princess 95 at berth in Geneva. And that was close to his next stop.

Leaving aside the boat, he was worth fifty times a million dollars. Probably more. No wonder he afforded himself a swagger.

An elderly man dressed in a smart dark suit, white shirt and crimson red tie met him at the end of the quay. He relieved Freddie of his small leather case and led him to a pristine, silver-blue Bentley Mulsanne.

'How's everything going, Jim?'

'All good, sir. And you?'

'It's been an interesting couple of days. I think a week or so in the mountains is in order. How long will it take us to get to Verbier?'

Jim opened the rear door of the Bentley and, as Freddie got in, he replied, 'Eight hours, I reckon, sir. Maybe nine. Traffic-dependent.' He closed the door gently and made his way to the boot - which opened automatically, the gas struts making easy work of the heavy lid. Freddie's small case was lost in the cavern that was the back end of the Bentley.

Freddie had had enough of talking. Jim wouldn't bother him again unless Freddie asked him a direct question. He knew the rules. Speak only when spoken to. Freddie would check a few things on his phone, issue a few diktats to a couple of minions and then get his head down. The Bentley's leather had already engulfed him and was beckoning him to sleep.

An interesting couple of days.

That was an understatement. He had made it off the island with an hour to spare. His agent in the Croatian Security and Intelligence Agency had given him an eight-hour heads-up. That allowed him enough time to sort out a few loose ends before leaving the island to its fate. The debacle of the Mecca attack was very unfortunate - it would have delivered the perfect storm. The subsequent probes and enquiries by various security services across the world had surprised him. He thought The Church's cellular structure was tight enough to survive a major breach. But, clearly not. There was a lesson there. It seemed unlikely that it would survive in its present form.

But, that wasn't his problem. Nor was he interested. The monks on the island had all done the honourable thing after he'd warned them of the impending Croatian special forces assault. They wouldn't be missed. There were other small groups of unwavering believers hidden away in a couple of countries. It would be up to them to look to the future. Good luck with that. They wouldn't be hearing from him.

Having got the call from his agent, he'd needed Paul Mitchell to tie up some loose ends; money transfer and other immediate actions that required his computer expertise. Initially Mitchell hadn't been keen to help. That may have had something to do with Freddie having shot his wife at point-blank range two days earlier. Having beaten the fucking Croat to death in his room, Freddie had found 'the note' by his bedside table. It was in Vicky's handwriting. And he didn't like that.

Therefore, she had to go.

He had taken some pleasure from killing Vicky. She'd been instrumental in writing the coding that had enabled The Church to hide its internal communications on the Dark Web. She'd done that well. But he'd never fully trusted her. Never.

After Vicky had fallen to the floor in the canteen, a trickle of blood leaving an artistic track from corner of her mouth onto the tiled floor, Paul had said nothing. He'd just stared at Vicky's body. His mouth open - his hands outstretched.

'Don't be melodramatic, Paul. You didn't love her. You were too busy screwing that waitress in Austria, last time I heard. She's done her job. Let's move on.'

Before Paul had had chance to reply, a couple of monks had jogged over and mopped up the corpse.

Paul had sulked for 48 hours. He was still sulking when Freddie had received the call from his pal in Zagreb. Which was frustrating as he had a lot to do, and not much time to do it.

'Paul - we need to close this down. The island. The links. I need you to do that for me now.'

'Do it yourself, you fucking psychopath.'

Freddie knew he was going to get short shrift from the man and he didn't have time for an extended discussion. So, he took out his pistol and shot him in the calf.

Histrionics followed.

He didn't allow Paul to make it to the sanatorium - there was too much to do. And Freddie didn't care. Paul had fallen and was sitting on the floor, screaming for the medic. Freddie told him to 'shut up' a couple of times. When he didn't, Paul got a boot in the face.

That got his attention.

'You've got an hour. No more. Now get moving.'

'An hour?' It was a mumbled reply; Paul's hand was in front of his mouth - blood seeping from between his fingers. 'You've got to be kidding?' Paul wasn't happy. It was probably shock.

Freddie knew he'd be much less happy in an hour's time. With a bullet in his head.

With a sigh and shake of his head, Freddie had raised his gun to Paul's temple.

That had provided the necessary focus.

'All right, all right. I'm fucking going.' And off he hobbled.

Then the monks; in the chapel. Plenty of pills.

Bless them. Freddie couldn't watch. It wasn't a stomach thing. He probably would have enjoyed it. It was that he had too much to do. Too much evidence to hide. His room needed sorting. Papers needed to be burned.

Three hours later the Riva was ready in the boat shed as he'd requested; his driver fully-briefed. It took them half an hour to make it round to Krk. A beautiful town nestling on the Adriatic side of the island. Yes, it was touristy - but it had kept its charm. There were plenty of decent restaurants and the locals didn't ask complicated questions. It had been a perfect spot - the monastery, the monks, the solitude, the climate, and the local town. Just perfect.

But that was all over now.

He was sad that it was ending, but the place had served its purpose. Yes, he would have been ideally placed should the Christian versus Islam spat have kicked off in a major fashion. Most of his money was in defence stocks - and energy companies. He would have done well out of it.

Never mind. How much money is enough?

That was an interesting philosophical question. To which his answer had always been: you can never have enough.

And there would be plenty of other opportunities.

So that was the end of this particular chapter of his life. Turn the page and start writing the next. Should he disappear off into the sunset and live lavishly off his millions? *Possibly*.

Or …

He was rather interested in how the whole thing had become unpicked. Who had done that? Who was bright enough to piece the cell structure together - and then find the operations centre in

Venezuela? Was it just the British SIS working at its best? He wasn't convinced by that argument.

They had destroyed the German count's home; he was in the thick of it. Apparently he was still alive - but not a pretty face. And not very mobile. Freddie would be surprised if he were ever able to tap out some code on his keyboard ever again.

What about the woman Green? She had got into the jungle - somehow. Had she made it out? Was it she who had discovered and then helped dismantle The Church's structure? He wasn't sure. She was certainly central to a lot of the mayhem that had undermined the project. Maybe, one day, he'd pay her a visit.

But, first, he'd look at a couple of projects where he could nefariously place some millions. Pull a few strings. Rattle some cages. Make some more dosh. And between then and now he'd put his feet up, drink some of his cellared Charles Heidsieck and read a good book or two.

Perfect.

As Freddie stewed over his immediate future, the Bentley pulled away from the quay and headed up the hillside.

Newhouse Farm Campsite, Northwest Bristol, UK

Six months later

Sam heard the hoot of the horn from Jane's car. She was at the gate. Sam jumped out of Bertie's sliding door and jogged over to the small campsite's entrance. She undid the padlock, pulled back the metal, three-bar gate and let Jane in.

It was good to see her. The last time they had met was at Sam's bedside in St Thomas's hospital months earlier. Jane had been involved with Sam's SIS debrief. As the doctors fiddled around with her insides, SIS messed about with her head. The whole process had been exhausting. The quacks had opened her up to sew up a split in her stomach wall the size of a postcard - caused by Bell's beatings. They had also removed a 9mm slug that had lodged in her right fibula. That must have been from one of the shots fired by the man at the satellite control centre. One out of three. She took her hat off to him. Not bad at that range.

By sheer chance she hadn't been hit by any of the 25mm rounds from the Delta Force Huey that had ripped through the dish and mounting box. God knew how many rounds - and none of them had hit her. She had been partially shielded by the dish as it fell off its mounting. But it was luck rather than judgement that had saved her.

The debrief had been severe. They wanted to know everything; in minute detail. Jane had told Sam that the US and all of the European security agencies were already working hard to dismantle The Church of the White Cross. They needed all she had. As always, her memory didn't let her down. That is until the moment she got on the roof. At that point it was a haze.

'What were you doing on the roof, Sam?' Some young buck dressed very un-SIS-like in a suit, striped shirt and a spotted tie (stripes and spots - *didn't your mother tell you?*) had asked.

That was a good question. She had tried to answer.

'I think I was trying to break the dish - or something. I'm not sure.'

The buck had gone on to tell her that she was found with two pistols - and eight rounds. Both pistols had recently been fired.

'That would seem to be it, then?' Sam had surmised.

The word 'probably' should have been in the answer somewhere. She really had no idea.

When she had first woken in a Blackhawk flight somewhere mid-flight from the control centre to Caracas, what Sam had wanted to know more than anything else was whether Austin was alive. In the metaphorical hurricane that enveloped their extraction from Venezuela, into Colombia and out to the US, it had taken a good while to find an answer to that question. Everyone was trying to be polite, but the Delta Force 'Night Stalkers' were also incredibly busy - and trying very hard to be secretive. In the end she found the answer next to her on a gurney in a military hangar, hidden away at the far end of Bogotá airport. Austin was a passenger on the gurney. He was awake and had smiled, giving her the thumbs up.

Her second pressing question was whether Austin had indeed killed Bell. She really couldn't trust her memory at that point - and wanted to be sure. Before she'd been wheeled onto the USAF C17 cargo plane at Bogotá, she'd asked to see him.

A colossus of a captain had assured her that the black man in the second building had been found dead. Definitely dead. And that, if she wanted to check, she could - once they were on US soil at Fort Campbell.

Once they'd landed she had, much to his amusement, insisted.

In the near-dark of early dawn, with Sam sitting up on her gurney, the captain had unzipped a dark-green body-bag and shown Sam Ralph Bell's face. She had stared at him for over a minute. He didn't move during that time. He was dead. That was clear.

Thank Christ for that.
Would her nightmares continue?
Yes, unfortunately.

But now Bell was scarier than ever. He was always a ghoul of some kind. A vampire. Or a zombie. And she hated anything like that. A cousin of hers had made her watch *The Exorcist* when she was the tender age of 12. The experience had completely unnerved her. Since that day, every time she looked at a crucifix her overactive brain painted a very clear picture of Regan MacNeil's unmentionable actions.

Unfortunately, Bell was still an accompaniment to her dreams.

Maybe in time ...

Jane parked her car (Blue, Volvo V40, Kinematic) next to Bertie. She got out with a posy of yellow roses.

'For you, Sam. The colour's designed to match the van.'

Sam was momentarily overcome. She coughed to hide her embarrassment.

'Nice car. I sort of saw you as a Volvo girl.' Sam changed the subject.

'I won't take that as a compliment.' They both laughed. 'Can I come in?' Jane pointed to the van's sliding door, which was hiding under a short, roll-out awning.

Sam laughed again. Bertie's door, that is her short-wheel-base VW T5 camper's door, led to a space about as big as a standard, three-bed downstairs loo. There was a two-seater sofa facing the front passenger seat, which swivelled to give an extra chair. Between the two, on the van's far wall under a small window, was a basic kitchen and some storage. It was hardly palatial. But Sam loved it. Every inch of it. Bertie was her baby.

Jane sat on the passenger seat, reached behind her and put the flowers on the dashboard. Sam jumped in after her, fussed by making tea, and then took out a cake and biscuits that she'd bought from Aldi. It wasn't much, but she was hardly flush with money.

As Sam arranged the chocolate fingers so that they were all soldier-like, side by side and in a straight line, the pair of them talked about this and that. Sam thought that Jane looked well - and told her. Jane told Sam that she looked tired and needed to heed the doctor's advice about not doing too much too early.

'I'm going up Pen-y-Fan tomorrow. That's why I'm here in Bristol. Drive to Brecon tomorrow. I'll be there before 10 am. Up and down. Back in Bertie in time for tea and medals.' She knew she was speaking too quickly. And that her accompanying actions were too demonstrative.

'Don't you think climbing a Welsh mountain might be considered as "too much too early?"'

'What - you don't think I should then go on to Cadair Idris the day after, and Snowdon the day after that?'

Jane was wearing her 'are you kidding me' face.

Sam wasn't kidding. She was deadly serious. Her brain had been in racing mode since she'd left Tommy's. She couldn't control it. It flitted here and there. She was quick to lose her temper - the smallest thing set her off; and she spent much of the day in tears. She had been through enough therapy in her life to heal herself. She knew the questions she should ask, and how to frame the answers so that they were succinct, but insightful. She knew she had to identify the drivers to her anxiety, then find a safe place to look them over - and then try to manage them. She knew of plenty of methodologies for dealing with outbreaks of her unnatural stress - and what strategies she should employ when faced with an overwhelming sense of despair. She had all of that. And she had tried to use them. And there had been some progress.

But most of the progress had come from being alone on a hillside somewhere. Exhausted - but almost complete.

It was, Sam knew, all about death.

She had killed a man. Shot him twice in the chest - in a cellar in Venezuela. She'd never killed anyone before. Yes, she had injured a few. And she'd been present when someone else had finished the job for her. Austin - with Bell. That sort of thing. But she'd never been totally responsible for someone else's death before. And she was really struggling to cope with it. It frightened her - that she could do something so final to another human being.

And not regret it.

Death at her hands. Then feeling no remorse.

She was sure that was the problem.

And working hard on the hills seemed to expunge some of the intense sorrow that was stalking her like a cackle of hyenas.

Walking up big hills was her version of rehabilitation. It worked for her.

It had to.

The catch-up conversation with Jane was running its course. The sun was three-quarters high in the sky and its warmth splashed in through Bertie's windscreen.

'Have you spoken to Wolfgang recently?' Jane asked.

Sam flicked the question over in her head. She didn't want to think about Wolfgang. It just added to the pain. The first thing she'd done when she'd escaped the hospital was to get on a plane to Munich. Wolfgang was still in hospital. He'd had multiple skin grafts and almost lost a leg. His lungs were healing, but it was all a slow process. Their meeting had been awkward. He hadn't had much to say. He just sat in a chair in a very swish private room and spent most of the time with his eyes closed. Sam knew that Inge's death would have broken his already fractured heart. She was surprised that he had the energy to get out of bed.

She'd asked about the house.

'It's just a house.' Sam sensed a touch of venom in his voice. She probably deserved it.

She stayed at a local hotel and visited him the following day where the atmosphere hadn't improved. She understood. She really did. She had suffered trauma. And she had been badly hurt - a number of times. It did things to your head.

'I've spoken to him twice since my initial visit.' Sam replied to Jane. 'I really must go and see him again.' She quickly changed the subject. 'How's Austin?'

'He's fine. Thanks to you. His leg is making a good recovery. Apparently the DD is getting the Federal government to issue him with an award. One of the reasons I'm here is to let you know that they want you to go to the ceremony. Next month. On the 12th. In Washington. They'll pay.'

That was another flick-flack question.

Sam should go. She'd love to see him. But that would mean talking about what had happened. Reliving the horror. Ralph Bell's eyes out on stalks. The shots into the man's crotch as he came to check her pulse by the metal ladder.

The double tap into Bell's thug-mate's chest. Bang. Bang. You're dead. No feeling. No regret. Nothing.

She was sweating. Her breathing was shallow. This is how it was. Thinking. Reliving. And sweating. She really should leave it out. Move away. Move along. Move to Lapland. Newfoundland. Somewhere away from the horror.

But she couldn't. And she hadn't.

'Is it all done now? You know, The Church.' Sam hated herself as soon as she asked the question. She had promised that it was something she wouldn't ask. It was unanswerable. No one would ever know. They wouldn't. Jane would give some SIS platitudes; some 'need-to-know' rubbish. And Sam would be left with the open scar.

'Pretty much ...' Jane looked at her with that sisterly look that only she could manage. 'Are you OK, Sam?'

'Yes, fine.' Her response was a bit too sharp.

'Well. We had all of Wolfgang's database - which was excellent. And all of the known names across the world have been interrogated by the various countries' own versions of MI5 and Special Branch - and there have been multiple arrests.'

Jane paused. 'Are you sure you're OK?'

Sam had taken her handkerchief out and was mopping her brow.

'It's the heat from the windscreen. I'm fine. Thanks.' She moved it all along. 'Have we got all of them? What about the Croatian end?'

'Well, you were in the hospital when I briefed you on the monastery operation. It was a success - as you probably remember. They found Paul and Victoria Mitchell Both shot dead. And 17 monks. Suicide. And a Croat, who we think put the original phone message on your answer machine. He was found trussed in a sack in a shed at the bottom of the walled garden.'

'And Freddie. Does he exist?'

Jane had her cup in one hand. Her other hand was resting on her knee. She brought it up to her chin and scratched at an invisible female beard.

'Not seen. He could have been one of the monks, but we don't think that's the case. The Croats found a large, well-equipped single room that had been quickly, but expertly cleansed. The monks' rooms were all spartan, but lived-in. The view is that the room had been very recently occupied; probably by a non-monk. Could be Freddie? It is possible that he's out there somewhere.'

Sam closed her eyes. She'd not met the elusive Freddie. He was, as she remembered Wolfgang's wall (after she had moved things about in her head), at the centre of this. Could he still be on the run?

Was he out there somewhere?

Would she be constantly looking over her shoulder for him as she had been for Bell? Would he start to replace Bell in her dreams? An unknown. A faceless kingpin. She'd never know if he was watching her - because she had never seen his face. He could be in the UK, now. In Bristol. Tracking her down.

She needed a pee. She needed Jane to go. And she then needed to climb some mountains.

Jane had put her cup down on the side.

'You know I can't ask you back?'

It was a surprise comment from Jane. Sam hadn't considered going back. But for SIS to have even thought about her re-employment, and then formally written her off, still hurt.

She looked at Jane. Her friend. They had disagreed at times. But she was as close to the woman who had brought her yellow roses as she'd ever been to anyone - other than her mum.

'That's fine Jane. I don't think I'll ever be right enough again up here,' Sam pointed to her head, 'for SIS to consider me a safe pair of hands. I wouldn't employ Sam Green to pack bags at Sainsbury's. And I know her well.'

Jane smiled; a half, but sincere smile.

'How are you off for money?' Jane nodded at the untouched Aldi cake and the neat line of chocolate fingers that she had momentarily messed up when she'd picked one to eat. Sam had quickly made them look like soldiers again.

Sam smiled. *Bless her*.

'I'm fine, thanks, Jane. Something will come up. It generally does. Now, do you mind if you give me some space? I need a pee - and I must sort my kit out for tomorrow's hike.'

If Jane was surprised by Sam's brusqueness, she didn't show it. She nodded, jumped out of the van and made her way to her car.

'You'll keep in touch? And let me know as soon as you need anything? You know about the service's charity that can provide funds for ex-staff who need help?' Jane asked.

Sam smiled. Yes, she knew. And she'd have no problem asking for help should she need it.

First, though, she needed a pee. And then she had some adrenalin to burn.

Sam Green books by Roland Ladley:

Unsuspecting Hero

Sam Green's life is in danger of imploding. Suffering from post-traumatic stress disorder after horrific injuries and personal tragedy in Afghanistan, she escapes to the Isle of Mull hoping to convalesce. A chance find on the island's shores interrupts her rehabilitation and launches her on a journey to West Africa and on a collision course with forces and adversaries she cannot begin to comprehend.

Meanwhile in London, SIS/MI6 is facing down a biological threat that could kill thousands and inflame an already smouldering religious war. Time is not on anyone's side and Sam's determination to face her past and control her future, regardless of the risks, looks likely to end in disaster. Fate conspires to bring Sam into the centre of an international conspiracy where she alone has the power to influence world-changing events. Blind to her new-found role, is her military training and complete disregard for her own safety enough to prevent the imminent devastation?

Fuelling the Fire

Why are so many passenger planes falling from the sky? Why are two ex-CIA agents training terrorists in the Yemeni desert? Why is a religious cult transferring millions of dollars to unattributable bank accounts around the world? Are these events connected? If they are, is this the mother of all conspiracies?

MI6 analyst, Sam Green, desperately wants to establish why her only surviving relative died in the latest plane crash. But can she put aside her grief and make sense of it all? Or is the clock ticking just too quickly, even for her?

The Innocence of Trust

Sam Green's been promoted. She's now working out of Moscow as an SIS 'case officer' and hates it. She loathes her boss, feels out-of-place among SIS's elite and loses her only Russian informant to a bomb that also had her name on it.

On the verge of jacking it all in, Sam promises a beautiful stranger that she will find her boyfriend's murderer. That promise propels her into a web of top-level industrial crime and savage international terrorism. With reliable friends and colleagues in very short supply, Sam starts something she cannot stop. And this time, she's going to need more than an expert analyst's eye and a complete disregard for her own safety to prevent the most lethal terror plot since 9/11.

Book 5 (untitled)

Already planned for the summer of 2019.

+++++

Find Roland Ladley's books here:
https://www.amazon.co.uk/Roland-Ladley/e/B010MAOZOE

Follow him on Facebook:
https://www.facebook.com/rolandtheauthor/

And keep in touch via his blog here:
https://thewanderlings2013.wordpress.com/